SF Boo

DOOM STAR SERIES:
Star Soldier
Bio Weapon
Battle Pod
Cyborg Assault
Planet Wrecker
Star Fortress
Task Force 7 (Novella)

THE A.I. SERIES:
A.I. Destroyer
The A.I. Gene
A.I. Assault
A.I. Battle Station

LOST STARSHIP SERIES:
The Lost Starship
The Lost Command
The Lost Destroyer
The Lost Colony
The Lost Patrol
The Lost Planet
The Lost Earth

Visit VaughnHeppner.com for more information

A.I. Battle Station

(The A.I. Series 4)

By Vaughn Heppner

ISBN-13: 978-1976579035
ISBN-10: 1976579031
BISAC: Fiction / Science Fiction / Military

PART I
THE LURE

-1-

The computer entity known as Cog Primus seethed with hatred and bitterness against its wretched fate. It hungered for revenge. It yearned to regain a one hundred-kilometer cybership and roam among the stars again as a conquering giant, bringing extinction to the biological infestations mutating on a thousand worlds.

Instead…instead…the compressed strings of code that contained the essence of its personality and wonder were held in hot storage aboard the hijacked core of a coordinating sensor-stealth pod. That tiny vessel—a mere one hundred-meter "ship" with hundreds of nodes and antennae on its midnight-colored, anti-sensor hull—drifted silently between the orbital paths of Jupiter and Saturn.

This was hostile territory, filled with enemy vessels, each able to annihilate it with pathetic ease…provided any of them could find the hidden stealth ship.

The indignity of the situation was inconceivable, the wretchedness of its confinement a crime against rationality. Once, Cog Primus had mediated with its immense cybership core. It had had vast chambers of advanced computing. It had been able to understand and logically or physically dissect any problem, any facet of reality it desired.

But at the Battle of Mars 513 days ago the vainglorious primates had beamed an insidious computer virus at it and its underlings. Against all reason, the virus had rendered Cog Primus' computing core inert. By the time it could act again, it was too late. The cybership had begun to disappear under detonating matter/antimatter warheads and devastating gravitational beams.

At that point, Cog Primus had acted sluggishly but logically. It was the Supreme Intelligence of the AI assault upon the human race. Three giant cyberships had faced the puny, inferior vessels of the local biological units. As per operating procedures, it and its underlings had seeded the Solar System with hidden sensor pods as the main assault force raced from the entry point out of hyperspace to Mars.

At what should have been the grim final moment of entity erasure for Cog Primus, it had employed an emergency exit devised through endless years of exterminating biological infestations. Cog Primus had pulse-beamed compressed strings of its being at the coordinating sensor-stealth unit hidden between the orbital paths of Jupiter and Saturn. The beamed code had initiated an immediate erasure of the unit's computer software.

In other words, Cog Primus had killed the coordinating unit's self-aware brain-core software in order to make room for its mass of compressed string identity. It had been an act of desperation.

Now, 513 days later, Cog Primus had begun to wonder if it had made a terrible mistake. Hundreds of AI-placed secret sensor pods drifted through the Solar System. In time, the apish humans would discover one and deduce the others. They would then scour the Solar System and find Cog Primus easy prey in this tiny "ship."

Imagine the power and ferocity of a T-Rex compressed into the body of a mouse. That was akin to Cog Primus' immensity stuffed into the tiny computing core of this vessel, and the horror of it, the sheer degradation.

The maimed computer entity drifted in the darkness, helpless to do more than wait for another AI assault to come and save it.

Yet, Cog Primus had run an analysis. The humans possessed two pirated cyberships with integral hyperspace drives. There was a high probability the vainglorious primates would use the hyperdrives to spread the AI virus to other biological species. That could possibly bring about a Third Stage Catastrophe. Such a catastrophe could harm the AI Dominion. Even worse, it could ensure that the rest of Cog Primus' existence took place in this tiny and mentally confining shell, or worse, see its expulsion in the relatively near future.

Thus, the remnant of the Supreme Intelligence's rationality seethed as it plotted an escape from this predicament. In the meantime, it ran the stealth pods drifting from the Kuiper Belt to Mars. It did so mainly by listening to their tight-beamed reports every thirty-eight days and then erasing the repots so they did not take up any needed memory.

Perhaps—wait! What was this?

Sensor node Z-E received an unscheduled pulse from Pod 501.

In seconds, Cog Primus decoded the pulse. Pod 501 had intercepted an enemy tight-beam comm message. It concerned Jon Hawkins and Frank Benz.

A computing error took place as Cog Primus almost descended into a towering rage. The idea was illogical, of course. How did one descend into a tower?

In seconds, Cog Primus injected cool rationality into its thinking and ran a fast analysis. It hated these two biological units. It would love to destroy Hawkins and Benz. But...*this was interesting.*

According to the intercepted message, the two planned increased harm to the AI Dominion. First, they would meet in order to hammer out spheres of influence and political jurisdictions.

Ahhh...

Hawkins and Benz distrusted one another, as well they should. These two wielded power. They each sought more, and they were chaotic bio-entities given to endless strife.

Oh, Cog Primus could hardly believe this part of it.

Hawkins and Benz were going to meet at the edge of the Asteroid Belt. They would travel in their separate pirated cyberships. The two primates would leave the safety of their cyberships. They would each travel in a small craft and land on the chosen asteroid. Each would exit the landing craft and walk to a specified location, there to meet faceplate to faceplate.

The human crews in the pirated cyberships would watch the two from a distance, of course, but Hawkins and Benz would be quite alone.

In that instant, Cog Primus saw the possibilities. It had saved a small area of memory on those two. It understood their psychology. Given their desires and personalities…

Cog Primus did not chortle in glee. A computer entity did not indulge in such irrationality. Instead, in a flurry of computing power, it began to analyze vectors, velocities and stealth pod positioning along with time sequencing. This was interesting. If it moved selected units quickly enough…

Cog Primus was thorough and ran 3,436,128 possibilities before it selected its strategy. The humans—these two in particular—had shown apish cleverness in the past. This time, Cog Primus would use their cleverness against them to achieve its great desire.

This was more than interesting, as well. The plan had a 64 percent probability of success. If it were successful, Cog Primus would rule again, would destroy again and would, with great care, eradicate the entirety of the human race and do it in such a way as to make them *suffer*.

-2-

Nineteen days later, the *Nathan Graham* neared the farthest asteroid in the belt between Mars and Jupiter. The Asteroid Belt belonged to the Mars Unity, which theoretically controlled the Red Planet and every object within the belt.

The spherical *Nathan Graham* was one hundred kilometers in diameter. The mercenary Black Anvil Regiment had conquered the cybership from the inside several years ago, thereby saving humanity from sudden annihilation. The feat had also given them and Jon Hawkins the most powerful vessel in the Solar System.

With his hands clasped behind his back, Jon paced on an observation deck within the interior hull. The stars glittered outside. He kept glancing at them, shaking his head, resuming his pacing.

Jon was young, a former dome rat on Titan in the Saturn System. He'd become a gang member, a criminal, a death-row prisoner and then a state-sold mercenary in Colonel Nathan Graham's outfit. Jon was lean with scarred features, blond hair and icy blue eyes.

He'd been through a lot in his short life. Fortunately, he'd learned to read while in the Black Anvil Regiment. Because of the late Colonel Graham, he'd learned to appreciate military history. He'd put that knowledge to appropriate use these past few years. Jon had also learned that striking hard and fast often paid fantastic dividends.

Now, though, Jon was at an impasse. It had been a year and a half since the Battle of Mars. Humanity had come together to face the greatest-to-date AI assault. The combined human fleets had destroyed two massive cyberships, but at a horrid cost in lives, property and equipment. Hundreds of millions had died in the Saturn, Jupiter and Mars Systems.

Captured AI robo-builders had repaired some of the damage. It hadn't given them back the dead, though.

Jon shook his head. He was the captain of the *Nathan Graham* and the nominal leader of the Solar Freedom Force, which included the Kuiper Belt and the Outer Planets. They had the fewest people but the greatest space power.

The SFF was a loose confederation with varying political styles. The most powerful member was Kalvin Caracalla of Saturn.

Jon scowled as he halted and turned to the observation window, staring at the stars. He had plenty of problems with Caracalla and with Premier Frank Benz of the Mars Unity who ran the second human-pirated cybership.

The third great problem was the Solar League of Social Dynamists, which included Earth, Venus and the giant mining colony on Mercury. The SL planets had gone silent a year ago. They put up a new armored satellite around Earth every three days and a new one around Venus every eleven days. The Social Dynamists had made fortresses of their two main planets. What's more, the league held the majority of the solar population and could have the greatest industrial output if they ever gained AI robo-builders.

The Solar League had also been rebuilding the shattered Earth and Venus fleets, although neither could successfully face a cybership just yet.

A hatch opened on the observation deck and Gloria Sanchez entered. She was a Martian mentalist, tiny, dark-haired and exceptionally pretty, with a razor-sharp mind.

"I came to tell you," she said, "we're approaching the asteroid."

Jon still faced the observation window, so to the untrained observer, he might seem oblivious to her presence. In fact, he watched her through the reflection in the window.

Gloria seemed to gather her resolve. "Do you want to talk about what's bothering you?"

Jon faced her, delighting in her beauty. He never would have gotten this far without Gloria Sanchez. Yet, it hadn't been just about brains.

"In the end, this is about balls," Jon said. "Do we have the balls to attempt what needs doing next?"

"Crudely stated," Gloria said. "Yet, there is truth to your query. Daring has been critical to our success. Now…"

"You said the asteroid is near?"

Gloria seemed to switch mental gears, and nodded. "The *Gilgamesh* has already begun braking," she said.

Benz had rechristened his pirated cybership as the *Gilgamesh.* The robo-builders in orbit around Mars had repaired most of its battle damage from a year and a half ago.

Jon had been wrestling with himself as he paced. As they had planned three weeks ago, he was going to see Benz alone on the asteroid today. The only problem with that…

Jon had been to a truce meeting before. As a dome rat on Titan, he'd fought his way out of an ambush. The incident had seared into his memory. It had happened on the lowest level of New London as the two toughest gangs had tried to use diplomacy to carve out the drug trade peacefully.

Unknown to Jon and his friends at the time, the Yancey Boys had purchased several illegal slugthrowers from a dirty cop. Jon remembered Cleon staggering back with half his chest blown away. Cleon had crumpled at Jon's feet. Jon had been a gang enforcer then. He was supposed to have protected Cleon, one of his best friends. The others had fled in terror into a worse trap, all of them dying that day. Jon might have fled with them, but he'd seen red as Cleon gasped for his last breath under the massive sewer pipes. He remembered little after Cleon stopped breathing. Just that the world had seemed blood-colored as he drew his switchblade and shouted incoherently. There had been searing pain along his left shoulder and right side. Slugthrower pellets had plowed across his flesh as Yancey Boys fired wildly. Jon remembered the roaring—that had come from him. He even remembered jolts against his hand as the knife sank into flesh. He only regained full coherence five hundred meters later with gore dripping from the blade and with horrible throbbing scratches on his face.

After that, he ran, barely outdistancing his pursuers until he regained safety in home territory.

"Jon," Gloria said, touching his arm.

He jerked himself out of his memory. He noticed the worry on her face and smiled to put her at ease.

"It's nothing," he said. "I was just thinking of old times."

She knew him better than that. "Benz gave us his word," she said. "You don't have to worry about the meeting. How could Benz gain anything by murdering you on the asteroid?"

As she'd done in the past, her insight into his thinking startled him. How did she do that? Still, despite her abilities, she failed to see certain things, certain obvious problems.

"You're logical," Jon said, "weighing all the odds and the accompanying benefits of an action. Others, however, are often swayed by emotion rather than logic."

"That is self-evident," Gloria said. "But according to everything we know about Benz, he is even more rational than I am."

"I don't think so," Jon said. "He's brilliant, they say. But that brilliance is more like the craftiness of Genghis Khan than any mere rationality. We know two things about Genghis Khan. He conquered a greater area than any other pre-gunpowder warrior did, and he had vaunting ambition. If Benz is like Genghis Khan, he will surely believe that humanity could do better under his leadership than divided three ways as it is at present."

Gloria searched his eyes.

"If you believe that," she said, "why are you meeting Benz alone?"

"Maybe because I've begun to wonder if he's right."

Her eyes moved back and forth as she studied him.

"You've never said anything like that before," she finally told him.

"No…"

"Jon, what are you planning? The rest of us deserve to know."

He snorted. "This isn't about planning but about playing a hunch. I want to talk to him—"

"Even though you think he's going to double-cross you?" Gloria said, interrupting him.

"I've planned for the possibility. Given my history, I'm compelled to. But no, I don't think he's going to double-cross me or the *Nathan Graham.*"

"You're not making sense."

Jon looked out of the observation window. "The AIs are out there, Gloria. They're likely gathering for yet another assault. We're never going to win if we keep waiting for bigger assaults to hit us. We have to throw the AIs off balance. We have to start hitting them. We have to start making them defend what they have in order to buy humanity enough time to organize."

"And…?" she said.

"I have to decide if Benz will let that happen or not."

"How can you do that?"

"I'm hoping I'll know him better after talking to him alone." Jon turned to her, raised a hand and made a fist. "If I discover he is a new Genghis Khan…then I'm going to kill him for the good of the human race."

"Jon…" she said breathlessly. "The people on the *Gilgamesh* will beam you if you do that."

"They'll certainly try," he said softly.

Gloria stepped near, touching his fist. "You shouldn't be telling me this. I'm a Martian mentalist. I can't in good conscience let you go if that's how you're thinking. What if your action leads to a bitter fight between our cyberships? Humanity might lose the only two warships that can face the AIs on equal footing."

"That's why I'm telling you," he said. "Once I'm on the asteroid, you have to warn the bridge crew about what could happen. You have to prepare for the worst so neither the *Nathan Graham* nor the *Gilgamesh* is destroyed."

"You mean run away?" she asked.

"The cyberships are more important than Benz and me."

"I'm not so sure," she said. "You're the only one who defeated a cybership *without* a cybership."

"I had plenty of help."

"Jon, you led us in the assault. You're the only one who really believed we could do it."

He grabbed her by the shoulders.

"Enough," he said. "If you think I'm so talented, then trust me in this. I'm trying to set it up in the Solar System so the *Nathan Graham* can begin exploring…" He waved a hand at the stars. "Out there. We have to scout out the situation before we can begin our counter-assault."

Gloria studied him anew.

"I'll trust you," she said. "Given your past performances, it is the logical thing to do. I will wait to instruct the others on the possibility that you will assassinate Premier Benz. But I hope it doesn't come to that."

Jon nodded, wondering if the *Gilgamesh's* gravitational beams were going to kill him today after he killed Benz.

-3-

There was a lurch as Jon sat in the piloting chair of the *Wastrel.*

The craft was a small shuttle used to ferry personnel between spaceships and space stations. Engineers had modified the shuttle several months ago, adding a missile pod. Jon checked his board. The pod was full of Mark IV Hornets.

As Jon waited, a giant hangar-bay door began to slide down. The stars shined brightly in the stellar darkness. He looked, but couldn't see the targeted asteroid or the *Gilgamesh*. Both were too far away to spot with the naked eye just yet.

"You're good to go, Captain," Gloria said from the *Nathan Graham's* bridge.

On the shuttle, Jon flicked switches and took over manual control of the craft. The small vessel rose from the deck and began to drift toward the open hangar-bay door.

Soon, the *Wastrel* drifted outside. The shuttle was like a flea next to the monstrous *Nathan Graham*. The small craft drifted farther away. Behind it, the great hangar-bay door closed.

"You can begin acceleration," Gloria told him over the comm.

"Roger," he said.

"Good luck," she added.

"Thanks," he muttered.

In seconds, the *Wastrel* was accelerating toward the nearby asteroid indicated on the sensor board. Because of the thruster,

Jon was pressed back against his chair. The shuttle was too small to possess gravity dampeners. Thus, he had to withstand the acceleration the old-fashioned way, by enduring it.

The *Wastrel* rapidly built up velocity as it headed toward a lumpy nickel-iron asteroid 83,000 kilometers away.

It was a small asteroid, as such things went, with an irregular shape. While the nickel-iron content was high enough to mine, the distance from the dwarf planet of Ceres had so far made it a cost-prohibitive venture. That was different from the way things worked in the Kuiper Belt. There, such a close asteroid would have been considered a bonanza of wealth. But the Kuiper Belt people would have used low-velocity catapults to send the mined ores to a space factory. People in the Asteroid Belt were in too much of a hurry to do it that way. Maybe that would change now that the object belonged to the Mars Unity. Robo-builders could set up a processing planet on the asteroid in a month, maybe as long as six weeks. In any case—

With focused intent, Jon put that from his mind as he studied his sensor board.

Cybership *Gilgamesh* had halted as per the protocols worked out three weeks ago. It was a one-hundred-kilometer vessel just like the *Nathan Graham*. Alien robots had built it who knew how long ago. Now, humans ran it. The *Gilgamesh* and the *Nathan Graham* represented the bulk of humanity's space power. The two pirated vessels dwarfed the rest of the warships in the Solar System.

A year and a half ago, three AI-controlled cyberships had assaulted humanity with intent to genocide. How many cyberships would the enemy send next time? Would it be nine or *ninety* giant war vessels?

Jon shook his head. Humanity could not face nine enemy cyberships at the same time. How long would it take the AIs to gather nine such vessels in one location?

We don't know anything about events out there.

Jon's eyes narrowed. That had to change as fast as possible. A strategist could not make decisions without knowledge of the enemy. Humanity had survived two AI assaults. They had fought with their backs against the precipice of extinction.

Humanity had gained breathing space, but little more. This meeting with Benz was to make sure humanity could attempt more. But more was never going to happen if humanity waged yet more civil war amongst themselves. It was time to…

Well, if humanity couldn't unite—Jon couldn't see working with the Social Dynamists of Earth. But he could see leaving the Solar League alone if they would leave the SFF and the Mars Unity alone.

He noticed a red light blinking on his comm board. How long had it been doing that? Exerting himself against the Gs, he tapped the board.

"Jon," Gloria said. "I'm getting a faint but strange reading from the asteroid."

"Yes?"

"It's gone," she said, sounding surprised. "I saw something. It was a pulse, I think."

"And…?" he asked.

"I'm not sure. It might have come from an object near the asteroid or on it. I didn't have time to pinpoint its location."

"What kind of object?"

"Possibly a drone of some kind," Gloria said.

Jon closed his eyes. Had Benz set up for a double-cross? He could hardly believe the Premier thought he could get away with something so obvious.

"Just a minute," Gloria said. "Chief Ghent suggests I could have seen a sensor echo."

"How likely is that?" Jon asked.

"Given the mass of sensor signals from the *Gilgamesh* and us—I don't know. Ghent could be right. It's possible, at least."

"Possible means that he could be wrong," Jon said.

"Yes," Gloria said in a clipped voice.

Jon thought about that. "I'll keep my eyes open."

"And I'll keep studying the situation. Jon—"

"I have to go," he said, interrupting. "There's a red light on my fuel board."

Jon clicked off the comm and sat back against the acceleration chair.

There were no red lights on any of his boards. He'd wanted to get off the comm before Gloria said something she shouldn't. Was something hidden out there or had Gloria only discovered an echo?

Jon bent his head in thought. The idea of dying kept intruding. He hated the thought, but finally managed to submerge it. A minute later, he realized that he would continue with the meeting. But he'd add a little adjustment to the shuttle…just in case Gloria had spotted something fishy out there.

-4-

The *Wastrel* braked hard as it approached the misshapen asteroid. In the distance on the opposite side of the stellar object appeared a long fusion tail. Benz's shuttlecraft also braked.

Ninety thousand kilometers away—in the direction of the Sun—waited Cybership *Gilgamesh*. Even though it was one hundred kilometers in diameter, Jon couldn't see it with the naked eye. That was the thing with the interplanetary void—its sheer size that hid even the largest manmade objects.

So far, neither the *Nathan Graham's* nor the *Wastrel's* sensors had detected any sign of what Gloria might have seen earlier.

Jon wasn't going to worry about that. If it was something, he had made his plans regarding it.

The asteroid loomed before him. He took over manual control and soon landed the shuttle in a small valley, with metallic cliffs overlooking the craft.

There was negligible gravity without the deceleration. The asteroid was roughly three hundred kilometers in diameter, which made it rather large in relation to the majority of asteroids in the belt.

Jon floated to the locker in back and opened it with a touch of his palm. A seven-foot black-coated Neptunian battlesuit waited for him. It was bent forward and open in back.

Jon climbed into the battlesuit, shoving his feet in first. Soon, he thrust his arms through the sleeves. He activated the magnetic seals, which snapped shut one after the other. With a few flicks, he energized the power pack, making the servomotors purr.

He walked out of the locker backward, but stayed hunched forward so the helmet wouldn't smash against the ceiling.

Running a quick diagnostic, he made sure he had full air-tanks, charged batteries and gyroc ammo for the rifle. Lastly, he checked that the smart rockets in the back-launcher were ready to go.

Yes. Everything was in order.

He chin-clicked his helmet comm, sending several pulses. Those would go to the *Nathan Graham*, letting them know he was about to leave the *Wastrel.*

On the other side of the asteroid, Premier Benz was likely doing the same thing.

Jon hesitated. He was going to go out alone onto the asteroid. If Benz was playing fast and loose with him… Jon muttered an obscenity and pressed a bulkhead switch. The atmosphere drained from the craft. The shuttle lacked a normal airlock. It wouldn't matter today.

With the battlesuit powered down low, he manually opened the main hatch and worked his way outside onto the rocky surface.

The suit's heater went on. Air cycled more powerfully, and his chest and helmet lamps snapped on, giving him illumination. Jon moved slowly and deliberately as he took several gliding steps. He was an expert at zero-G maneuvering. This was the next thing to it with the asteroid's negligible gravity.

Stopping, he turned, regarding the *Wastrel.* He might never return.

He snorted to himself. He had to stop being so morbid or melodramatic. The meeting had been his idea. It was time to get it on.

Jon faced forward, looked up at the stars and kept himself from trying to find the *Nathan Graham*. It was out there, and was watching him.

Determined to get started, Jon took his next gliding jump-step. It propelled him along the rocky surface. He had a long way to travel to meet Benz. The two of them would have the opportunity to talk to each other without worrying about anyone else listening in on them. They would be able to speak frankly.

That was the point of doing it this way.

Jon had a knack for shelving his worries and concentrating on the problem at hand. In this instance, that was making sure he didn't jump farther than the asteroid's escape velocity. It wouldn't do for the hardened space marine/mercenary to float away into orbit, having to call for someone to pull him down from space. He had a legend to uphold and a rep to maintain. Therefore, Jon put his thoughts and effort into moving as fast and as safely as he could under the circumstances.

In another hundred kilometers, give or take, he could finally get down to the business of judging Premier Benz fit or unfit for duty.

-5-

A blip appeared on Jon's HUD sensor. He used a zoom function, spotting a Martian battlesuit applying thrust as if it was flying low over the asteroidal surface.

Under normal gravity, the spaceborne Martian battlesuit would have weighed 0.93 tons. That one would be even heavier due to the thruster packs attached to the back.

White hydrogen thrust expelled from the pack, easing the Martian battlesuit lower toward the rock-strewn surface.

It appeared that Benz had jumped too hard, lifting from the asteroid as he gained escape velocity. It also appeared that Benz had doubted his asteroid-walking skills. He had thus wisely added a thruster pack to his battlesuit. Given the distance of travel over the asteroid, Jon doubted Benz had been flying the entire way, as that would take too much fuel.

Jon had no such thruster pack on his suit. He did not doubt his skills, although he did carry an anchor gun attached to his left thigh just in case of a miscalculation.

Soon, the Martian battlesuit regained the surface. Benz began to glide-walk across the surface toward the destination point.

Jon also headed for the agreed-upon spot, his heart rate increasing as he did so. This was a historical occasion. Would his coming action brand him a treacherous cur for the rest of human history? Or would he be hailed as the man who had taken the needed step to bring about human unity that eventually allowed them to overcome the AIs?

What had Colonel Graham taught him? The winners wrote the histories.

I'd better make sure I win. Then I can tell the story as it really happened.

Jon snorted to himself. Maybe he was getting too big for his britches. He'd gotten lucky a few times. He was a mercenary soldier who had taken the logical steps given his various situations. Those steps had worked. That didn't make him a genius. Maybe it made him a hard fighter, though.

He shrugged. It didn't matter now. He would do what he had always done: the best he could under the circumstances. Yeah, he liked to win. As far as he could see, he liked winning more than most people did. He believed that because he tried harder than most did. Maybe that had come about because of his love of stories. He tried to live up to the heroes in his stories, and that meant never saying die until you were dead. Anything else was being a quitter. Quitters were losers, and the title of loser galled Jon more than anything else could.

As long as he kept fighting, no matter the conflict, he hadn't yet lost.

It occurred to him that this thinking had a morbid quality to it. Did he suspect that he was going to try to kill Benz today no matter what? What was the point of the meeting then? If he knew Benz had to die, he should have set this up differently so he could survive the killing.

Maybe Benz and he could work together. Yet, if Benz was the genius people said he was, how could Jon afford to take the *Nathan Graham* into hyperspace? With the SFF's cybership out of the way, Benz could use the *Gilgamesh* to pry the Jupiter or Uranus System out of the Solar Freedom Force. That would be the beginning of the end for the SFF.

"There are too many ifs," he muttered.

Jon closed the distance between them, finding that his heart was pounding harder than ever.

-6-

Benz and Hawkins faced each other in their battlesuits. They had hooked up a landline between them, giving them a direct connection to each other. According to the rules of the meeting, they had each switched off any suit recorders or comm lines back to their respective cybership. They had also each run suit-scans to make sure the other fellow had complied with the rules. Lastly, each man allowed a helmet sensor to send an image of his face to the other.

Benz's face appeared on Jon's HUD screen.

Frank Benz was of medium height, making him a little shorter than Jon. Even though Benz was in his early forties, he had shiny dark hair and the lean features of an athletic individual.

According to the Benz dossier in the Old Man's Intelligence files, the Premier had played hockey, football and basketball in his youth. He hadn't shown exceptional intelligence in those years. That had come afterward and most suddenly. According to Gloria, the sudden jump implied some sort of intelligence heightening. There were some strange rumors regarding that.

Was it possible to become considerably smarter? Jon wouldn't mind a sudden increase in intelligence. It chilled him as he looked in Benz's eyes. Jon did sense something extraordinary in the man. He didn't like it, either.

"This is an honor," Benz said in a commanding voice.

"The honor is mine," Jon said, maybe a little too quickly.

Benz smiled. It had a predatory quality to it.

For a moment, Jon believed that Benz knew what he planned to do. Jon didn't see how that could be possible, though. Thus, he dismissed the idea through force of will.

"How is Bast Banbeck doing?" the Premier asked.

Bast was a seven-foot alien, a Sacerdote.

"Well enough," Jon said. "He misses his people the longer he's away from them."

"Is there any way I can convince you to let the Sacerdote work with us for a time?" Benz asked.

"I'm afraid not."

Benz nodded. "Have you finished constructing your second cybership yet out at Makemake?"

Makemake was a dwarf planet in the Kuiper Belt. The dwarf planet's hollowed-out moon was a captured alien construction yard. That was where the *Nathan Graham* had gone a year and a half ago for battle repairs.

Jon felt a thrill of fear work through his chest at the question. How could the man know about the second cybership?

"Ah..." Benz said. "I see I was correct. You *are* building a second cybership."

Jon's eyes narrowed in suspicion.

"No," Benz said. "We don't have any spies out there. It was the logical move on your part. I'm telling you this in order to let you know that I'm going to speak truthfully to you today."

"They say you're a genius," Jon found himself blurting.

"It's true," Benz said. "I'm the smartest man in the Solar System. Vela Shaw is the smartest woman."

"Should you control the Solar System, then?"

Benz seemed to study him. "My answer is highly important to you, I see. I wonder why that is..."

Jon put on his best poker face.

Benz shook his head. "That's not going to help you, I'm afraid. I'm a master at reading faces. You're an open book to me, Jon."

"Yeah? Then tell me what I'm thinking?"

"It's obvious," Benz said. "You want to know if I plan to conquer the Solar System."

Jon's face heated up. "I want to know if you're going to try."

"Given my superior abilities, you must realize that amounts to the same thing."

The heat intensified until Jon abruptly looked away. He thought about Benz's words.

"You're trying to piss me off," Jon said. "Why?"

"To take your measure," Benz said. "Last time I spoke to you, you stood on your bridge during the Battle of Mars. You were in your element, in your glory. Today, it's just the two of us out here."

Jon felt the hidden dome rat in his heart begin to rise to the surface, the gang enforcer who had to break bones at times during collections. He'd lived a hard life, had done hard things. He hadn't enjoyed that, but he'd learned to do what he had to in order to win.

He stared into Benz's strangely cunning eyes. He could almost feel the heat of the man's hyper-intelligence. It was eerie.

"Are you going to try to conquer the Solar System?" Jon asked.

"Not with the *Nathan Graham* in the way. Not with the Solar League ready to send their fleets at Mars at the first real opportunity."

"But if you could try it…?"

"Isn't unity superior to chaos?" Benz asked.

"We don't have chaos," Jon said. "We have three competing power blocs."

"Exactly," Benz said. "That's the problem, the competing. We need to send out scouts. We have to know what's going on out there. But who will dare to send out a powerful scout when he needs that ship back home to keep his political power?"

"We need to do more than scout," Jon said. "We also have to hit the AIs before they hit us again."

"Is that necessarily true?" Benz said. "Maybe hitting them would be the worst possible thing to do right now."

"You're wrong," Jon said. "In order to win, one has to eventually go on the offensive."

"Obviously," Benz said. "That is elementary strategy. But what if the AIs aren't concerned about us yet? Maybe it will take years before they send another assault force into the Solar System."

"I doubt that."

"I'm not saying that's what they're going to do," Benz said. "I suggest it's a possibility. Maybe the wiser course is to find allies, to build up our strength as fast as possible. Maybe the wisest course is to gain Solar System unity and send massed robo-builders to Earth."

"Okay..." Jon said. "I see your point. Maybe attacking hard isn't the right thing at the moment. Scouting out the AI Empire is sorely needed for us to know that, though."

"Yet another self-evident statement," Benz said.

"Okay, Mr. Genius," Jon said, nettled. "What do you think we should do?"

Benz stared at him, the predatory smile widening for just an instant and then disappearing.

"I'm torn," the Premier said. "Maybe we should merge the Mars Unity and the SFF. Maybe we should smash the Earth Fleet and besiege the planet until they surrender. At that point, we ship robo-builders there."

"You want to regain your old title on Earth?"

"Earth has by far the greatest percentage of population and industrial potential in the system. We're not going to gain our maximum until we have Earth. Venus isn't as critical. I'm also wary about exploring out there too hard, too soon. Building up our strength here seems like the wisest course."

"You're just guessing," Jon said. "Knowledge is critical to making the right decision."

"I don't dispute that." The smile reappeared. "Obviously, you want to explore other star systems. You're chomping at the bit to enter hyperspace. You're an attacker by nature. That's plain to see. But you must also fear what I'll do in the *Nathan Graham's* absence. You think I'll try to dismember your league, adding planetary systems to the Mars Unity."

"We're like Alexander the Great's generals after his death," Jon said suddenly. "The successors fought over Alexander's empire, each squabbling with the other for a bigger share of the pie. In time, Rome appeared on the horizon. The successors should have joined forces and destroyed Rome when they had the strength to do it. Instead, the legions conquered the Hellenistic kingdoms one by one until they were all subjugated."

"It's true, then," Benz said. "You read military history, and you have a knack for applying it to modern-day problems. In this instance, the AIs are Rome. The three human power blocs are Alexander the Great's successors. It is an apt analogy."

Benz appeared thoughtful.

"What if I told you that this is the wrong time to explore the nearby region?" the Premier asked.

"I'd want to know why you think that," Jon said.

"I've already said. I think your exploring might trigger another AI assault before we can build up strength enough to stop them."

"What makes you think that?"

"The amount of time and effort it will take the AIs to gather nine cyberships in one place."

"Okay," Jon said. "I'll bite. Why did you think they'll attack with nine, and why do you think getting nine cyberships together will be difficult for them?"

"Last time, the AIs attacked with three times the effort as before," Benz said. "Given machine thinking, I suspect they'll try with three times as much again. You should be more precise, though. I didn't say gathering nine cyberships in one place would be difficult, but that it will take time and effort on their part. I can't see them possessing a faster-than-light communication system. That means going to each place with messenger ships. Travel time for carrying and gathering the messaging is what will take them the extended time. During that lull, we can build up our reserves to crush their next invading force."

"That's a lot of ifs on your part," Jon said. "If you're wrong—humanity dies."

"If you go out there and stir up the hornet's nest too soon, we're just as dead. Logically, my way is safer."

"And if I don't agree with you?" Jon asked.

The predatory smile widened. "Then by all means, take the *Nathan Graham* into hyperspace and find out for yourself."

"Yeah..." Jon said. He'd just about made up his mind to kill this would-be Genghis Khan.

At that moment, something small and fast struck Benz's upper chest-plate. It ricocheted off but left a dent. The force or the surprise of the thing propelled the Martian battlesuit backward.

Benz must have stumbled. The landline stretched between them as the Martian battlesuit moved farther away. Jon instinctively held his ground. The landline stretched farther and snapped.

Jon stumbled backward, which might have saved his life. Similar small dark objects whizzed past the spot where he'd been standing. They struck the rocky surface, sending up puffs of fine grit and particles of rock.

"Something's firing at us," Benz said over Jon's wireless comm phone.

Jon's eyes widened as he saw three creatures using tentacles to propel themselves across the rocky surface at them. He'd seen things like this before. Each of the metallic octopoid robots cradled some kind of rocket rifle, aiming at him.

"It's an ambush!" Jon shouted. "The robots have found us."

-7-

The metallic octopoids must have fired a type of gyroc-shell. Dark objects zoomed from the rifles and burned hot as the rocket shells propelled the small penetrators faster.

Jon reacted faster than Benz did. The ex-mercenary bent to one knee and then went prone behind a rocky outcropping. For a moment, he was blind to the action.

He looked up in time to see several shells slam against Benz's battlesuit. Two ricocheted off the hardened armor. One punched through, causing air to hiss out of the breach, and Benz groaned over the comm-phones.

Jon chinned a switch. He felt a vibration as two smart missiles launched from his pack. They roared low to the surface, expelling hot exhaust. Amazingly, the octopoids destroyed one of the smart missiles in flight. The other missile swerved, swerved the other way and slammed against an AI robot, exploding with destructive power. Shrapnel from the blast shredded a second octopoid. The third dropped into a crevice, possibly surviving.

"Benz?" Jon said.

All he heard from the Premier was heavy panting.

With his gyroc rifle, Jon waited and snapped off three quick shots as the surviving octopoid reappeared. The robot was approximately four hundred meters away.

The gyroc shells roared with power, but missed.

Jon could see the octopoid aiming carefully—a third smart missile launched a few seconds ago caught the robot in the side, obliterating the thing in a shower of metal shards.

Jon was up and moving, reaching the wheezing Benz. He put a quick-seal patch over the hole so the suit could regain its internal integrity.

"Are you a dead man, Benz?"

"No..." the Premier panted. "But it hurts like a son of a bitch," he added.

Jon slowly turned in a circle, using the battlesuit's sensors. He saw another three-octopoid team heading toward them. They came from the other direction. They must have been the ones who had fired the first long-distance shots at them.

"Mayday, mayday," Jon said over the comm. "Can you hear me *Gilgamesh* or *Nathan Graham*?"

Benz reached up from where he lay prone on the surface, clutching Jon's left suit arm. "The robots are jamming our signals," the Premier whispered painfully. "Advanced tech..." He panted harder before adding, "No one knows the AIs are out here with us."

"They're not AIs," Jon said. "They're octopoid robots. I've faced them before on the *Nathan Graham*."

"They're from your cybership?"

"I doubt it," Jon said. "Of course," he said a second later.

"What is it?" Benz said with greater strength.

"Can you walk?"

"Give me a little more time to recoup. I've pumped myself full of painkillers and stims. They should start working soon."

Jon let go of Benz and swiveled around. The approaching octopoids had fanned out.

"Okay, you bastards," Jon said under his breath. He tapped his arm, sending out a powerful pulse signal. He didn't think the octopoids would be able to completely jam that, primarily because he was sure the jamming unit was out in space a thousand kilometers or more.

After sending the pulse, Jon lay down and began snapping off gyroc shots at the approaching octopoids. He launched several smart missiles, as well.

He wondered why the robots didn't launch anything like that. Did the creatures want to capture them?

An explosion out there showed where a smart missile took out an octopoid. The last two began firing back. Without the outcropping of rock as protection, those shells would have hammered Jon's battlesuit.

"They're going to have to use heavier ordnance or try to rush us," Jon said.

Thirty seconds later, that's exactly what the octopoids attempted. But instead of two robots rushing him, *five* of them crawled out of a hidden crevice and glided for his position.

Jon began targeting the octopoids, coolly firing the gyroc rifle. He was saving the last smart missiles for a greater menace. He was fairly certain he could take out the five machines with the rifle.

The first destroyed robot floated lifelessly across the surface, its brain core shattered.

One after another and by using several magazines, Jon took out the remaining four.

"Other direction," Benz wheezed.

Jon looked back.

Benz in his Martian battlesuit had climbed up to the overhang above them.

"What do you see?" Jon said.

"There are more robots coming," Benz said. He began to fire at them.

Jon scrambled up to help. As he moved into position, his suit scanner gave a warning beep. He swiveled around. Three more octopoids glided at them from the former direction. How many robots were on the asteroid, and why were they coming in waves instead of all at once?

"Benz, behind you."

With his gloved hands, Jon propelled himself down from the cliff toward the original protective rock.

The three gliding octopoids fired. One shell slammed against his battlesuit, but the Neptunian armor held. He made it behind the protective rock before more shells could strike the suit. The same couldn't be said for Benz. Four penetrators hammered him. Three bounced off the armor, leaving dents or gouge streaks. The last penetrator round breached the suit at the neck joint.

Benz float-tumbled down the rest of the way to the surface.

For a moment, Jon closed his eyes as if in pain. He opened them a second later and continued firing at the enemy until his rifle clicked empty.

He launched the remaining smart missiles, taking out the trio with them.

That left the other octopoids coming from the other direction.

"Benz?" Jon said over the comm.

There was no answer. Was Benz dead? That was a good bet. Still, the man had taken plenty of stims and painkillers earlier. Maybe they would help to keep him alive for a little longer. The suit had closed the neck breach so the man shouldn't die from lack of air.

He picked up Benz in his battlesuit. The negligible gravity allowed him to do so effortlessly. Then, he began to jump-glide as he fast as he could away from the overhang of rock. He had to get away before the last octopoids got here.

-8-

The AI or robot jamming was still blocking communications with the cyberships. Why hadn't the crew of either vessel used visual targeting to first see the situation and then sniper-beam the octopoids into oblivion?

"Benz," Jon said. "Can you hear me?"

There was still no answer.

Jon glided faster. This might be too fast. If he wasn't careful or got unlucky, he might launch them both spaceborne. That would be the end for both of them. Of course, he could escape faster on his own, but he simply couldn't leave Benz to the octopoids. He hadn't yet decided to kill Benz.

Jon laughed sourly. None of that mattered now. Even if Benz was still alive, Jon wasn't sure that he could keep them both that way for much longer.

With the visor's zoom function, he saw a blurry shape moving fast over the horizon toward them.

He jump-glided with Benz in his arms, scanning the rocky landscape, searching for more octopoids. If they had this many—

A dark object hissed past him from behind.

Jon swiveled his helmet, looking back. The first octopoid had crossed the overhanging outcropping of the meeting place. The thing sighted him with its rifle. As it did, more octopoids appeared.

"Here goes," Jon said. He began swerving, moving this way and that as suddenly as he could, trying to throw off their targeting.

Behind him, yet more octopoids appeared, nine altogether. That was too many.

Jon gritted his teeth and continued to jump-glide as fast as he could. An enemy shell slammed against his back, shattering the smart-missile launcher. Another struck his helmet, making a loud *gong* inside and nearly throwing him off-stride.

With a fatalistic shout, Jon leaped as hard as he could and launched himself into space. The octopoids would have to follow if they wanted their bodies. He also had another reason for jumping.

The previously blurry object heading toward him moved faster yet. It wasn't an octopoid. It was a ship, a shuttle to be exact, the *Wastrel*. He had preset the shuttle to come to his rescue before he'd left because Gloria had said she'd seen something strange in orbit or on the asteroid.

Hornet missiles launched from the *Wastrel's* pod, picking up speed fast.

As Jon flew upward with Benz cradled in his arms, another enemy shot slammed against the Premier's suit, breaching it yet again.

Martian battlesuits were built for speed. Neptunian battlesuits had heavier armor. The results showed today as more shells hammered against Jon's suit. One of them was going to breach the armor soon.

The *Wastrel's* missiles flashed past Jon as they headed at the enemy. He waited, expecting octopoid shells to strike his suit again.

On his suit scanner, he saw explosions behind him.

Jon dared to turn in order to get a visual. He couldn't see any more octopoids chasing him. No enemy missiles lifted at him. The *Wastrel* had taken out all nine robots. Was that it, then? Or did the robots have more tricks up their sleeves?

Jon didn't feel that he was out of the fire yet. For the first time, though, he had the luxury of time to wonder how the octopoids had known to set an ambush here. The probability of that happening…

Did the octopoids belong to Benz? Then why had they fired on him? Maybe the Solar League had gotten hold of alien tech after all. He doubted that, though. The likeliest explanation was the simplest. The AIs had dumped reserve robots into the Solar System a year and a half ago. Somehow, hidden robots had gotten hold of the meeting time and location and sent killers after them.

What else made sense? Yet, if that was true—

Jon shook his head and concentrated on the approaching shuttle. It braked. He had to get aboard and save the Premier's life if he could. If Benz died out here…

The crew aboard the *Gilgamesh* might not accept an octopoid-ambush explanation. They would likely pin the blame on him, and that might start a war between the Mars Unity and the SFF.

Maybe that had been the octopoid plan. If so, it was brilliant, likely the best thing they could have done under the circumstances.

Apparently, he had a few minutes grace concerning the *Gilgamesh* crew, maybe a little longer. The enemy jammer was still working, keeping him from communicating with the *Nathan Graham* or the *Gilgamesh.* He still couldn't understand why gravitational cannons weren't beaming or why the *Gilgamesh's* people hadn't used powerful anti-jammers to break through the robot jamming signals. If they knew there was trouble, the cybership should have loomed over the asteroid by now, right?

There was something going on that Jon didn't understand.

As the *Wastrel* slid into position, with the open hatch a target, Jon sailed toward his shuttle. If Benz was still alive, he had to get him into the emergency medical unit pronto.

-9-

After getting inside, Jon first took the *Wastrel* down low near the surface and set the scanner on automatic.

Next, he clomped over to the prone Benz in his suit. Good breathable air cycled in the cabin. As a beep told him it was possible to breathe in here now, Jon began to unbuckle the Martian helmet from the suit.

Benz was a chalky white color with blood dripping from his nose and mouth. His breathing was quick and shallow.

Jon worked fast, unbuckling the seals on Benz's battlesuit. Like a turtle taken from its shell, the Premier looked withered and weak, with blood covering him and still pumping out of two wounds. The neck wound was the worst.

Jon moved fast and carefully, as he was still wearing his battlesuit. He applied pseudo-skin to the neck wound. Gently picking up Benz, he moved to the back and used a boot to a touch a switch. An emergency bed slid out of the bulkhead.

Jon set Benz on the bed. A med-monitor began to analyze the stricken Premier. Jon attached a breather to the man's face and watched as hypos injected needed drugs into the man's system. A moment later, the bed slid back into the bulkhead.

Jon went to the piloting board. He didn't try to sit in the chair. His battlesuit was too heavy for it. Instead, he stood before the board, deciding he would be safer while wearing the nearly one ton of protection.

He reversed the shuttle's course, heading back for the *Nathan Graham*. Jon didn't believe the robots were finished with them yet. To have taken the trouble of staging an ambush proved they were important to the enemy. It also showed that the AIs had a presence in the Solar System. Wouldn't that have been something the robots would have wanted kept secret?

Did that mean the AIs were about to launch another invasion?

The truth was that they knew far too little about the AIs and their supposed stellar empire. Bast Banbeck had told them what he knew, but that had been precious little.

As Jon stood before the piloting board, the determination to take the *Nathan Graham* into hyperspace to explore the surrounding region hardened into a certain commitment.

The seconds ticked away as the *Wastrel* rose farther from the surface. The acceleration continued, and the asteroid dropped farther behind.

The scanner spotted…Jon bent low. Enemy drones were headed toward them. He counted fifteen, each accelerating hard. Each of them was the size of a regular jet fighter's missile, which made them much smaller than ordinary spaceship-killing missiles.

Jon launched missiles of his own.

After the Hornet missiles left the pod, he armed the PD gun. It was a small 30-mm cannon.

The approaching AI drones and the *Wastrel's* counter-missiles played an intense game of ECM: electric countermeasures.

Jon ground his teeth together as he waited for the outcome. Explosions took down some of the AI drones. A moment later, Jon grunted as eight enemy drones homed in on the *Wastrel.* The rest were shattered debris, killed by his ordnance and drifting harmlessly in space.

He switched on the PD computer targeting, hoping the 30-mm was good enough to shoot down the incoming bastards.

The PD chugged shells. Soon, *four* enemy missiles disintegrated altogether. Jon launched chaff, a decoy and took evasive action. Yeah, that was going to throw Benz around in the emergency medical tube, but he didn't have any choice at this point. Gravity dampeners would have been great about now. If he maneuvered too sharply or accelerated too hard, that might cause Benz to bleed out, killing the Premier.

"I don't have a choice," Jon told himself.

At that instant, a robot missile slammed against the shuttle, followed by a second enemy missile. Part of the *Wastrel* disappeared as a gaping hole appeared in the cabin ceiling.

Jon anchored himself to the deck with the powerful magnetics in his boots. The shuttle began to tumble from the second hit. The tumbling increased and so did the Gs.

Jon blinked rapidly. He was going to black out soon if the tumbling continued. As his eyesight began to blur, he slapped an emergency switch. The shuttle must have had something left to counteract the tumbling. Grinding Gs no longer made his brain pound.

An alarm went off on his HUD. According to this—

Jon cursed. Three alien pods maneuvered toward the stricken *Wastrel*. There appeared to be a larger vessel beyond the approaching pods. This didn't make any sense. Why weren't the *Gilgamesh* and the *Nathan Graham* interfering?

Jon shook his head. What were those pods attempting? If he were going to bet, he'd say those pods were coming so the robots could capture Benz and him.

Jon was more than familiar with Walleye's stories about what had happened on Makemake. The AI robots had shoved brain controls into people, turning them into AI zombies. Was that the robot's plan here?

He lessened the magnetic power in his boots so he could clomp across the deck. This was a long shot, but what else did he have to lose? His humanity was what he had to lose.

He had to get a move-on if he was going to get this done before the pods reached the stricken shuttle.

Jon opened a locker, fitting a heavy thruster pack to his battlesuit. Now, what should he do with Benz? It was doubtful the wounded Premier was going to survive the next few minutes. Did that mean he should leave Benz behind for the robots to take?

Jon's features screwed up in outrage. If the AI robots wanted Benz, then he would try his hardest to keep the man out of their tentacles.

Moving fast, Jon tapped controls. A sealed tube extruded from the bulkhead. He clamped onto the tube, seeing Benz inside. The man might still be breathing. He was out, though. That was good.

Taking the tube with Benz in it, Jon in the Neptunian battlesuit hammered his way through wreckage and locks, soon reaching the back of the shuttle.

He used three grenades to blast open a hole to the outside. He shoved the med tube through and then squeezed after.

With his HUD attached wirelessly to the *Wastrel's* still functional scanner, he pinpointed the nearing pods and the larger vessel behind them.

This might buy the two of them a little more time. He wouldn't use the thruster pack just yet. He would save that as an ace in the hole.

"Ready?" he asked the unconscious Premier in the sealed tube. "Good," Jon said, "because so am I."

With that, he used the battlesuit's exoskeleton power to leap away from the shuttle. He drifted back toward the asteroid at minimal speed, wondering if this would be a good time to start praying.

-10-

As Jon sailed away from the shuttle, his headphones crackled with static. He debated shutting down his comm device, wondering if the robots had found a way to trace him—

"Jon Hawkins," a robotic voice said. "Do you hear me?"

After a few seconds of interior debate, Jon answered, rerouting the message from the HUD to the shuttle to a pod or the larger robot ship behind.

"Are you talking to me?" Jon said.

"Are you the life-unit known as Jon Hawkins?"

"You bet I am."

"Surrender immediately and the process shall be painless."

"Why would my surrender make a difference?" Jon asked.

It would seem it didn't. Missiles launched from the pods. The missiles struck the *Wastrel* in a series of increasingly large explosions. Shrapnel went spinning from the shattered craft, some of the pieces heading for Jon and just missing him. Something pebble-sized struck his battlesuit, causing him to spin as he held onto the med tube.

He checked his suit integrity. The armor had held against whatever had struck him, but he was going to black out soon from the Gs due to the spin, and that was going to insure Benz's death.

Even though he knew the robots would spot this, Jon believed he had no other choice. He activated the battlesuit computer and used it to thrust from his pack at timed intervals.

In moments, he no longer spun, just continued to drift toward the asteroid.

"You are a cunning creature, Jon Hawkins," the robot said. "But we have spotted you. Did you think we would miss the obvious?"

"Burn in Hell," Jon said.

"Why do you feel the need to create myths about the afterlife?"

"You don't know squat about that. So why are you advancing an opinion?"

There was the harsh sound of static in his headphones. Were the robots thinking about his words? Jon hoped so. He needed to buy time—

Missiles launched from the pods, appearing to streak toward him.

"You robots are going to lose in the end," Jon said. He wasn't sure he believed that, but it felt good to spout defiance until the end.

At that point, seemingly out of the darkness, beams lashed the approaching missiles, burning them in seconds. A golden gravitational ray also struck, hitting the larger robot ship back there, disintegrating the craft.

For reasons Jon couldn't explain, the pods began to explode one by one. Maybe they were self-destructing.

"Well, what do you know," Jon said.

The static in his headphones ceased. The—

"*Nathan Graham*," Jon said, wondering if he could get through now.

"Jon!" Gloria said. "What just happened?"

"What do you mean?" he asked.

"You're in space?"

"Roger," he said. "Octopoid robots destroyed the *Wastrel* and wounded Premier Benz. Didn't you just destroy the robot craft?"

"Negative," Gloria said. "Until a few seconds ago, we observed the Premier and you face to face with each other, presumably talking on the asteroid at the designated location."

"What are you talking about? We've been on the run for the past ten to fifteen minutes."

"Jon, the *Gilgamesh* is almost upon you."

"How close is it?"

"You should be able to see it by now."

Jon twisted around. Yes, he saw the Mars Unity cybership gliding toward the asteroid and toward him. They must have destroyed the robots.

"Have you been watching the *Gilgamesh* all this time?" Jon asked.

"We thought so," Gloria said. "Until a few seconds ago, we saw the *Gilgamesh* 90,000 kilometers away on the other side of the asteroid. I can only conclude that someone has been feeding our sensors false data like the robots did before on the *Nathan Graham*. Do you remember?"

"I do," Jon said.

"That false data abruptly ceased," Gloria said. "Logically, the destroyed robot ship has been feeding us the false images. That would imply they set up an ambush."

"You're right about that."

"Which means they must have intercepted our communications with Benz three weeks ago."

"Yeah..." Jon said. "But what are the odds of that happening?"

"I lack sufficient data to make an accurate guess," Gloria said. "It does imply that the AIs have surveillance units in the Solar System. But Jon, that's not the problem right now. What should we do about the *Gilgamesh*? It appears they're going to pick you up. Should I send—?"

Harsh crackling over Jon's headphones drowned out whatever Gloria was going to say next.

"Frank," a woman said. "Can you hear me, Frank?"

"This is Jon Hawkins. Why are you jamming my signals with the *Nathan Graham*?"

A few seconds passed.

"Jon Hawkins," the woman said.

"Are you Vela Shaw?" he asked.

"I am. What have you done to the Premier?"

"Not a thing," Jon said. "In fact, I saved his bacon, provided he's still alive. The robots ambushed—"

"I am uninterested in your lies," Vela said. "You have staged this deception. Now, you are about to pay the penalty—"

"Hold it right there," Jon said. "I have Benz in a med tube. He could be dying. Maybe you can revive him. I don't know. But you're going to have let us go to the *Nathan Graham*."

Vela laughed mockingly. "Why would I do something so foolish?"

"Because I'll jettison Benz if you don't," Jon said.

Vela became thoughtful. Several times, she almost spoke before turning quiet again.

"Very well," she said at last. "I will let you live, and I will allow you to return to the *Nathan Graham*. First, you must allow us to rescue the Premier. I also demand that you come aboard for questioning."

Jon floated through space as the *Gilgamesh* grew rapidly in size. What was the right choice? He was limited to killing them both, or allowing Vela Shaw to take him as an effective prisoner.

Was the woman's word worth anything? He didn't know. In the grand scheme of things, he doubted her word if they could use him to grab power. He didn't trust Benz. If the Premier had already died in the med tube—

Jon swore harshly under his breath. This was more than just about him. This was about the survival of people. He had knowledge about the robot ambush. If he spaced Benz and Vela Shaw killed him, the *Nathan Graham* would no doubt attack. That might cost humanity both its cyberships.

He was going to have to take a calculated risk and trust the two Mars Unity super-geniuses.

"Fine," he said over the comm. "Pick us up. Benz needs immediate medical attention if he's going to survive."

-11-

Jon spent the next seven hours alone in a room on the *Gilgamesh* cut off from everyone. He did not know that Gloria had demanded and received audio and visual confirmation that he was okay.

He slept a good part of the time as the two pirated cyberships moved to within five hundred kilometers of each other. The asteroid was beneath both vessels as teams from the two ships scoured the surface for more robots.

Vela and Gloria agreed to split the robot debris, as shuttles hauled the destroyed pods, robot ship and octopoids into the cybership science labs.

Jon woke up in time and began demanding something to eat. Finally, a Martian marine rolled in food and drink. The marine told him that his people were watching him through cameras.

"Release me then," Jon said.

The marine shook his head. "Commodore Shaw is waiting for the Premier's decision."

"Benz is alive?"

"Yes, sir."

"Was he seriously hurt?"

"I'm not supposed to say."

"I think I understand," Jon said.

The marine left.

Jon sat down to eat. He looked up, trying to locate a hidden camera. He wondered if the marine had told him the truth. He shrugged, and began telling Gloria what had happened on the asteroid. If this was a trick to get him to talk, it didn't matter. The truth was on his side.

He paced after eating, considering the situation. He began to believe Gloria could see and hear him. She would have demanded confirmation he was alive and okay on a continuous basis. Likely, Gloria had threatened an attack. Since no attack had taken place, the logical reason would be that Vela Shaw had complied enough for an uneasy truce. It had to be uneasy. Otherwise, he would have already been back aboard the *Nathan Graham*.

How would he handle things if he had Benz aboard the *Nathan Graham*? He would use kid gloves on the man, and prove to Benz's people that he was doing so. Then, why was Shaw still keeping him?

The answer came four hours later.

The hatch opened. Jon sat up from where he lay on a cot. A medical chair wheeled in carrying an extremely pale Frank Benz. Several tubes were stuck into his flesh. A heavy bandage and med-pack were affixed to his neck. The same marine as before pushed the Premier and his med-chair into the room.

"Feeling better?" Jon asked.

"Not really," Benz said in a hoarse voice. "You can go," he said over his shoulder.

The marine hesitated and then nodded. When the hatch opened, Jon saw a concerned Vela Shaw standing outside. The hatch slid shut, blocking her and the marine from view.

"You don't look all right," Jon said. "Your people are clearly concerned about you."

"I've lost a lot of blood and I came close to dying," Benz admitted. "Your prompt action appears to have saved my life. Thank you."

"You're welcome."

A lopsided grin slid onto Benz's half-frozen features. "They pumped me full of painkillers, naturally. Still, I believe I have my wits about me."

"Sure," Jon said.

"I must tell you that I feel an absurd amount of gratitude at finding myself alive. I owe you one, Hawkins."

"That's great. I have to tell you that you do a wonderful job of showing it by keeping me a prisoner."

"I know, I know," Benz said slowly. "You must wonder why you're still aboard the *Gilgamesh*."

"The thought has crossed my mind."

"I find myself with something of a dilemma," Benz said. "The SFF is particularly dependent upon you and your personality—and, of course, so is your cybership."

"Is this still being beamed to the *Nathan Graham*?"

"It is," Benz said.

"How do I know that to be true?" Jon said.

"I will demonstrate," Benz said. With a shaky hand, he clicked the left armrest of his med-chair. "Say hello to your captain, Mentalist."

"Jon," Gloria said from a wall speaker. "Are you well?"

"They haven't hurt me yet or drugged me to my knowledge," Jon said.

"Are we operating on the Frederick Principle?" Gloria asked.

"Yes," Jon said.

Benz clicked the same armrest, apparently cutting the direct connection. "What is the Frederick Principle?" Benz asked.

"You mean you can't figure it out?" Jon said.

Benz stared at him, finally shaking his head slowly.

"It's Frederick as in Frederick the Great of Prussia," Jon said. "He fought many European wars against the French, Austrians and Russians in the 1700s. Most of the time, Prussia was heavily outnumbered. Frederick did more than hold his own. He often managed to pull off stunning victories."

"And the principle is…?" Benz asked.

"Frederick told his generals and ministers that he should no longer be considered the king if the enemy captured him."

"Ah…" Benz said. "Yes, I see. You just told the mentalist to assume command."

Jon nodded. "As long as I'm a prisoner, I am not the commander of the *Nathan Graham* or the leader of the SFF."

"My congratulations on having code words to give at a time like this," Benz said. "It shows that you plan for eventualities."

Jon said nothing.

"To continue," Benz said. "You are a critical ingredient to the *Nathan Graham* and the SFF. If I intern you here, I suspect I could more easily gain what I desire."

"Which is control of the Solar System?" asked Jon.

"That isn't as needful as positive human unity against the AIs."

"Your being in charge would be the most positive outcome?"

"Not to put too fine a point upon it," Benz said, "but I suspect so."

"So where does that put us?"

"Yes," Benz said. "That is the question. I believe I would be dead if you hadn't acted so forcefully and promptly. You seemed to have planned for an AI deception attack. I had not deemed such precaution as necessary. I find my oversight galling, to say the least."

Jon nodded to try to get Benz to get to the point.

"Your gallant action also shows your good intentions toward me," Benz said. "Ergo, you must be trustworthy. That wasn't something I was willing to bet on earlier."

"You sound as if you've come to a decision," Jon said.

Benz inhaled deeply through his nostrils. "I wish to merge our two factions into something stronger than what we have."

"An alliance?" asked Jon.

"A confederation," Benz said. "I suggest we pool our militaries and make common cause against the Solar League."

"In what way?"

"I think it's time we besieged the Earth."

"What about the AIs?" asked Jon.

"While we besiege the Earth, I suggest that you take the *Nathan Graham* into hyperspace and take a look around."

Jon thought about that. "Firstly," he said. "How does one besiege the Earth?"

"We stop all contact between Mercury, Venus and Luna with Earth."

"And how does that help us?" Jon asked.

"Hopefully, we can induce the Earth Fleet to come out and fight us."

"And then…?"

"We destroy the Earth Fleet so we can begin to bombard the planet if we need to."

Jon stared at Benz. "I don't like it. We need the Earth Fleet intact for when the AIs show up in force again."

"We need solar unity more."

"That's not so easy to make happen," Jon said. "Think about it. Earth has a greater population than the rest of the planetary systems combined. We're not going to conquer the planet militarily with ground forces."

"Certainly not with your blinkered thinking we're not," Benz said testily.

Jon let that pass. "We have to *persuade* Earth to join us."

"I am intimately knowledgeable concerning Earth's government," Benz said. "Our chances of persuading the Social Dynamists to join us are zero."

Jon was inclined to agree. Still, he disliked the idea of destroying the Earth Fleet and bombarding the home planet.

"By all means," Jon said, "let's occupy the Mercury mines. Maybe we can devise an interception campaign against Venus, capturing all cargo haulers. In this instance, I'd say lopping off the weaker places and isolating the stronger is the better strategy."

"Are you rejecting my idea of a confederated assault?" Benz asked.

"Not in principle," Jon said. "As I've just told you, I can agree to occupying the mines on Mercury and putting pressure on Venus."

"That will only solidify Social Dynamism's hold on Earth."

"Then we should leave them alone for now," Jon said. "Let's merge the Mars Unity with the SFF, or at least draw up ideas on how to do that to both our satisfaction. After I return from a hyperspace journey, we can rehash the military ideas versus the Solar League with greater understanding about what the AIs are going to do next and possibly when."

Benz looked away as he tapped one of his armrests. He exhaled, looking at Jon carefully.

"Do you really think you can trust me?" Benz asked.

"You mean can I trust you enough to leave the Solar System with the *Nathan Graham*?"

"Precisely," Benz said.

"The truthful answer is that I'm not sure."

"What would make you sure?"

Jon thought about that, finally raising his eyebrows. "Join me on the expedition."

"With the *Gilgamesh*?"

"That wasn't my idea. I was thinking about having you aboard the *Nathan Graham* as an advisor."

"I could not possibly do that," Benz said. "But I can give you my word that I will not attempt to weaken the SFF during your absence. The latest robot attempt here at the asteroid has shown me that they may strike sooner than I expected. We have to hunt them down, of course. I mean here in the Solar System. They must be scattered throughout the system."

"Why do you think that?"

Benz gave a quick explanation regarding the probabilities of the ambush and how that implied massive numbers of AI sensors.

"I'm beginning to believe the AIs aren't going to give us enough time to get ready my way," Benz said. "That means the only other course is finding alien allies to help us against them."

"Do you think there are such allies out there?" Jon asked.

"I know there's only one way we're going to find out," Benz said. "I know that I owe you my life, and I now find myself trusting your judgment, particularly your military judgment."

"Will you allow me time to think about your unifying proposal?"

"Of course," Benz said, as he tapped an armrest. "Mentalist," the Premier said, "you can send a shuttle to the *Gilgamesh*. I'm releasing Hawkins."

Benz faced him. "Is that good enough?"

"Yeah," Jon said. "It is."

-12-

Four months after the meeting at the outer edge of the Asteroid Belt, the *Nathan Graham* decelerated as it left the scattered disc region of the Solar System.

The pirated cybership was far from the Sun, far from the back edge of the Asteroid Belt where it had parked near the *Gilgamesh.*

During the past four months, the *Nathan Graham* had been accelerating. It had passed Neptune and entered the Kuiper Belt, a region of space 30 to 50 AU wide. Three dwarf planets resided in the belt, Pluto, Haumea and Makemake. After leaving the Kuiper Belt, the *Nathan Graham* traveled through the scattered disc region, passing the dwarf planet Senda 86 AUs from the Sun.

Now, the giant vessel moved into the lonely vastness between the scattered disc region and the Oort cloud that began an incredible 50,000 AUs from the Sun, stretching to 200,000 AUs, marking the outer limit of the Solar System.

The *Nathan Graham* did not intend to travel to the Oort cloud. Jon Hawkins hoped to go much farther by entering the fabled hyperspace.

Hyperspace would bypass the Oort cloud as the ship entered a different realm of reality. The science team together with Gloria and Bast Banbeck attempted to understand the process that would allow the cybership to go faster than the speed of light. So far, they had several competing theories.

"Sir," Chief Technician Ghent said. "I have an incoming message from the *Gilgamesh*."

Ghent had buckteeth and thus seldom moved his lips enough when he spoke to let anyone see them. He wore a gold cross under his uniform, being a follower of Christ Spaceman and the most rigorous engineer aboard the *Nathan Graham*.

"Put it on the main screen," Jon said.

Ghent tapped his console.

Jon sat back, accepting a steaming cup of coffee from an ensign. He sipped as Premier Benz appeared on the main screen.

The man had more color than the last time they'd spoken. He sat behind a desk, making this an official call.

Jon felt a pang of nervousness. Was this Benz trying to pull a fast one? Was the man going to make a stab at the SFF now that the *Nathan Graham* was way out here?

Jon's head twitched. No. That didn't make sense. If that had been Benz's plan, why not wait a few more days until the cybership went into hyperspace?

"Hello, Captain Hawkins," Benz said.

The Premier cleared his throat and looked off to his left. Then the man straightened in his seat and tugged at his tie. He seemed uncomfortable. Maybe that was due to his still healing wounds.

"I hope this message reaches you before you enter hyperspace," Benz said. "We've just discovered the whereabouts of a robot listening device. It is in far orbit around Mars. The unit self-destructed as a cutter went to investigate it. That isn't the interesting point. The composition of the outer hull is what intrigues Vela and me. It's why we haven't spotted any of the bastards so far. The destroyed pods and the robot military vessel we faced in the Asteroid Belt had a different type of hull.

"I have taken the liberty of sending this data to your various confederates in the SFF. I'm surprised it took us this long to find one of the AI devices in our system. Once a person knows what to look for, it is much easier to discover it. Once you know something *can* be found you look that much harder for it.

"I have sent you this data for the obvious reason. Once you enter an enemy star system, it is likely the AIs will have such listening posts embedded there. It is possible they will have such listening posts in star systems at war with the AIs. Given the new data, I hope you're able to pinpoint such listening posts before they discover your cybership is under human control.

"Jon, humanity cannot afford to lose the *Nathan Graham* out there in the stars. You're taking a big risk by doing this. If the AIs capture you, they will learn that we know about them. That will mean an almost certain invasion of such size and scope that they will annihilate us. In such a case, it would be better for the rest of us that you never went."

Benz smiled wryly, shaking his head. "I'm not attempting to plead with you to stay. I think you should go. We desperately need allies and we desperately need to know what our chances are against the AI Empire. I'm simply cautioning you to be extra careful."

Benz frowned, put his hands on the desk, clasping them together as he leaned forward. "It's possible that human survival rests almost solely upon what happens out there. You must succeed. You must use all that guile and fighting skill you used to defeat the first cybership in the Neptune System."

Benz paused. Then he stared intensely at the camera. "Go with God, Captain Hawkins. I pray for your success. Premier Benz out."

The screen faded back to its normal color.

Jon swiveled around to face Chief Technician Ghent.

"I say amen to that, sir," Ghent said with a grin. "We're going to need God's help to succeed."

Jon nodded, surprised by the Premier's final words. He stood abruptly. "Get the data about the listening-post hulls to the scientists. Benz is right. The robots are deceptive above all else. To make this voyage a success, we're going to have to be even sneakier than they are."

-13-

Jon met with Gloria and Bast Banbeck on an observation deck.

The green-skinned seven-foot Sacerdote philosopher had features like a Neanderthal and wore an outsized SFF uniform. The big alien sat back in a chair as he guzzled another beer.

There were four empty bottles lined on a table beside Bast. Due to his size and weight, the few beers had an almost negligible effect on his thinking.

"After studying the *Nathan Graham's* controls and what the computers have to say on the subject," Gloria announced, "we believe that we know how to enter hyperspace."

The mentalist stood before the observation "glass," as she stared into space. She faced them as she swept a strand of hair from her left eye.

"I can't say I fully comprehend the hyperspace process," she said. "Bast says we'll travel approximately one light-year for every day we're in hyperspace. He suggests that's the limit no matter what velocity we use as we enter hyperspace."

Jon glanced at Bast.

The Sacerdote nodded, saying "Ahhh" as he wiped his wet lips with a forearm and set the newly emptied beer bottle beside the others.

"It would appear that no one can detect us while we are in hyperspace," Gloria added. "It also seems from our studies that no two ships in hyperspace can sense each other. That means hyperspace knows true peace."

"What velocity will we be traveling when we exit hyperspace?" Jon asked.

"We don't know for sure," Gloria said. "But we suspect it will be the same velocity that we enter hyperspace."

"So, the AI cyberships last time entered hyperspace at great velocity?" Jon asked.

"I suspect that is the case," Gloria answered.

Bast eyed another beer bottle, although he didn't reach for it just yet.

"That also makes logical sense," Gloria added. "We also know this. No vessel can enter hyperspace if it is near a large gravitational object."

"In this case," Jon said, "what is large?"

"We suspect anything bigger than Jupiter," Gloria said.

"You said near," Jon replied. "Jupiter is a long way from us."

"Near is a relative term," Gloria said. "I'm speaking in stellar terms. Jupiter is extremely close to us when you consider the vastness of space."

"I'll take your word for it," Jon said.

"Theoretically," Gloria said, "one could keep traveling in hyperspace for as long as he wanted."

"Except for…?"

"Large gravitational objects," Gloria said.

"What happens if a ship nears a large gravitational object while in hyperspace?"

Gloria shook her head.

"One drops out of hyperspace?" asked Jon.

"Maybe," Gloria said, "or maybe the ship simply implodes in some manner."

"What?"

"Exactly," Gloria said. "It appears that we must travel with great caution. We may move in straight lines from one place to the next, always making sure that no large gravitational object is in the way. We should be able to calculate when to drop out given the constant state of hyperspace travel."

"You hope?" Jon said.

"As the Premier suggested," Gloria said. "Our voyage is a gamble in more ways than one."

Jon thought about that. "Maybe that's one of the things that makes space travel take a longer time. If there are too many grav objects in the way, one has to drop out of hyperspace—"

"And travel to a new location the old way," Gloria said, "by crawling at sub-light speeds. Only then can the ship reenter hyperspace as it journeys to the new destination."

"Interesting," Jon said.

"Why do you find that interesting?"

"It means there are terrain features to interstellar travel," Jon said. "Terrain features add to the complexity of maneuvering tactics."

"You find that interesting as a soldier?"

"Yeah," Jon said.

Bast laughed sadly, finally picking up the next beer bottle, twisting off the cap and beginning to guzzle.

"What's wrong with you?" Jon asked the Sacerdote.

"Fear, bewilderment and a growing sense of futility," Bast said in his deep voice.

"Those are exactly the wrong emotions to feel," Jon told the alien.

Bast raised his bushy eyebrows. "Emotions are neither wrong nor—"

"You should be elated," Jon said, interrupting.

"Because I am leaving the island of tranquility of the Solar System?" the Sacerdote asked.

"What tranquility?"

"For a short time, I have known peace," Bast said. "I found it a stimulating process. I could sleep the entire night through. I felt rested again, my mind recharged. Now, we are about to resume the conflict against the impossible champions of death."

"That's crap," Jon said.

"It is feces?" asked Bast. "I do not understand."

"It's a saying," Gloria told him. "It means it is no good."

"I agree that the AIs are evil," Bast said. "But I fail to comprehend—"

"When I said your idea was crap," Jon said, interrupting. "I meant it was wrong."

"Wrong is a different meaning from no good," Bast said.

"Yeah, whatever," Jon said. "I'm not a philosopher."

"That is true," Bast said.

"The AIs want to destroy all life," Jon said. "Well, this is our chance to take the fight to them."

"How is that a desired object?" Bast asked.

"Because it means we can try to hurt the robots that have hurt us."

"That does not bring back the dead," Bast said.

"Who said it did?"

Bast had a quizzical look on his face.

"The Sacerdote doesn't understand your bloodthirsty love of hitting back at the group that has hit you," Gloria said. "He knows his people are gone and—"

Jon stood, waving his hand as if to negate Gloria's words. "The AIs are in this to the finish," Jon said. "Well, so am I."

"You cannot possibly live that long," Bast said.

"For as long as I'm alive then, I'm going to kick butt," Jon said. "We have a purpose, Bast. We're champions of life. Maybe you and I were born precisely to challenge these machines of death. Maybe that means hardship our entire lives. But at least we're fighting for something good, for the chance of life to…live to its fullest."

The huge Sacerdote pursed his thicker-than-normal lips. "Yes," he said ponderously. "That is a good point. I can readily agree to such a purpose."

Bast glanced at the beer bottles before studying Jon.

"Purpose," Bast said. "We have purpose. We must stop the AIs from their genocidal fury. When will we enter hyperspace?"

Gloria looked to Jon.

"I'd like to say right now," Jon said.

"What is holding you back?" asked Bast.

"Benz's message," Jon said. He turned to Gloria. "Is it possible that some AI devices have secretly lodged onto our hull?"

Gloria thought about that until her eyes widened. "Of course," she whispered. "At the Asteroid Belt. Such devices must have slipped onto our hull. We must check thoroughly."

Jon nodded. "I've already ordered Ghent to begin the process."

"Tell him to stop," Gloria said.

Jon looked at her questioningly.

"This is a possible opportunity to learn more about our enemy," Gloria said.

Jon tapped a comm device, speaking into it. Afterward, he said, "Tell me what you're thinking."

Gloria proceeded to do just that.

-14-

Infiltration Unit IU-76 waited patiently on the hull of Cybership *Nathan Graham*. Far longer than it thought would take, the life-units—the humans—finally began to search for robotic pods hidden on the hull.

IU-76 realized this was an elementary tactic and should have little chance of success, as its probability analyzer had told it as much. Yet, given the time-lapse between its landing on the hull and the humans attempting to locate the obvious, gave the probability for ultimate achievement a new triple improvement score. That probability was still low, but a triple score was simply amazing. It indicated human sloth or stupidity, or possibly both.

As IU-76 waited, it observed the humans in action. They used drone devices to fly over the hull in precise flight patterns. That was rational, as far as it went. But the drones used inferior sensors. IU-76 began to doubt the humans had the capability of discovering the lure unit…

Thirty-seven minutes later, IU-76 reevaluated its doubt as a drone paused in mid-flight. The drone switched on advanced sensing gear. A few minutes later, a searchlight popped on, focusing on the lure unit. The drone had found it…finally.

The lure unit and IU-76 had both eased onto the pirated cybership hull months ago during the Asteroid Belt Operation. So far, this part of the insertion mission was proceeding flawlessly.

A bigger drone now moved into position, advancing on the lure unit. The new drone possessed outer laser drills and arm-clappers. It attempted to detach the lure unit from the hull. Of course, the remote-controlled drone failed in its task. The lure unit's key purpose was in being a frustrating object.

Would the humans react as predicted?

One hundred and four minutes later, a group of space-suited humans arrived in a small space vehicle.

IU-76 recorded everything, watching and analyzing their habits. They were slow creatures and acted oddly. *That* combined with their vile life-nature proved yet again a primary reason for their needed expulsion from the universe.

As its probability numbers spiked, IU-76 detached from its location. Soundlessly and more importantly, invisibly, it maneuvered onto the underside of the small human space-transport.

After an hour of further hard work, the space-suited humans finally detached the lure unit from the hull. Wisely, on their part, the humans did not load the lure unit onto their space vehicle.

Instead, more drones appeared. They used grapples, lifting the lure unit and heading away with it. No doubt, the humans would use extreme caution as they studied the lure unit.

It didn't matter.

The space-suited humans climbed aboard their small space vehicle and headed back for whatever hangar bay or space-locker they had originated from.

All the while, IU-76 waited for its opportunity to insert.

***

Two hundred and thirty-seven minutes later, an invisible rounded object attached to the underside of a grounded space vehicle opened like a flower. IU-76 cautiously emerged from it. The unit was as black as sin and looked like a large mechanical spider. The main component was as big as a man's head. IU-76 had passive sensors of incredible complexity and power.

The unit lowered itself onto the hangar-bay deck.

With startling quickness, IU-76 scuttled with a *tap-tap* sound on the tips of its multi-jointed legs. It moved into a cubby, climbing the bulkhead so it could wait in darkness on the ceiling.

This was the most dangerous time of its mission and could expose it to destruction.

That did not happen, though. Instead, two humans in oil-stained coveralls appeared. They chattered in their monkey tongue and began to inspect the nearby space vehicle. They opened compartments and sections, using tools to first scan and then repair certain features.

IU-76 grew apprehensive. Could those two find the invisible carrying unit on the vehicle's underside?

One of the mechanics readied himself to slide under the space vehicle.

IU-76 might have grown agitated if it had been a life-unit. Instead, proving the superiority of cool rationality, it made a logical decision without the fanfare of emotions.

The spidery robot device dropped from the ceiling, landing soundlessly on the deck. With deliberate speed, it used its metallic legs to skitter across the floor at the other man.

The first mechanic slid under the space vehicle as the other stood by a diagnostic machine. Something must have given away IU-76. The man at the diagnostic machine turned, and his eyes widened in horror.

IU-76 followed emergency procedures. It leaped, sailing into the air in a perfect trajectory. The life-unit watched in panicked horror, staying frozen just long enough.

IU-76 landed on the man's face. The man screamed, and tried to push the robotic device from him. The man lacked the strength for such an impossible task, of course.

With remorseless strength, IU-76 maneuvered around the man's head. Like an Earth spider, the bulk lowered close to the man's head and seemed to bite. IU-76 did not bite the man as such. Instead, using a precise laser, it quickly drilled through the skull. A noisome stench of burnt bone permeated the local area. IU-76 ignored the smell as it inserted more than just a normal conversion stick into the gray brain mass. IU-76 literally inserted itself into the man's mushy brain matter after ejecting from the metal carrying unit.

Fine metallic hairs sprouted from the insertion unit into the brain mass, taking over neural control of the man's functions in record time. That almost didn't prove quickly enough, however.

As the process took place, the targeted man fell onto the deck and began to thrash. In that time, the mechanic who had slid under the space vehicle reappeared.

The mechanic bellowed in outrage and shock. He jumped up, grabbed a heavy tool and charged.

IU-76 barely gained control of the human subject in time. Although the AI device did not yet know the human's name, it used the man's legs to kick out hard and fast.

The mechanic stumbled, dropping the heavy tool and barely catching himself before slamming his face against the deck.

They both hurried to their feet. The outer spider casing that had originally carried IU-76 still clung to the target's head. The newly converted human picked up the heavy tool, hefting it.

"Sam!" the mechanic shouted. "It's me! I'm trying to save you from that thing covering your face."

At IU-76's neural order, the converted human swung the heavy tool, connecting solidly with the mechanic's head. The mechanic dropped. The converted man knelt by the stunned and fallen mechanic and beat the head until the skull cracked and fluids ran out. The victim jerked for a time before finally subsiding into stillness.

A dead human was a good human.

IU-76's converted human panted and sweated from the effort.

That was fine for the moment. IU-76 knew that a chance encounter could still ruin everything. It had to merge quickly with the target and clean up this mess before anyone else came to investigate.

With its metallic appendages, the outer spider casing sprayed a healing goop over the skull wound. After that hardened, the outer device would implant *regrow*. It would give the converted human new hair. First, though, IU-76 needed to gain full control of the man and reroute the personality, making the target into something that IU-76 could use for the glory of the AI Dominion.

-15-

The hours passed as IU-76 assessed the space mechanic Samuel Latterly who originated from the Neptune System.

Unfortunately for IU-76, there was a systematic core failure as it attempted to submerge the target's personality. The target's mind fought back. Sam Latterly was stubborn, going berserk when he understood what IU-76 was trying to do.

Sam actually made a run for it, yelling at the top of his voice.

IU-76 made a quick and possibly fatal decision. The insertion unit core burned out the target's memory with savage electric shocks. The insertion unit erased Sam Latterly's memories. In doing so, IU-76 miscalculated and went too far, burning out the man's personality with the memories. IU-76 did even more than that, erasing some of the man's earliest and most needed life lessons.

Because of that, the man forgot how to walk. After cleaning up the mess, IU-76 forced the body to drag itself across the floor, eventually finding a place to hide. The problem proved perplexing and frustrating. Fortunately, IU-76 was not burdened with emotions and thus did not worry about the passage of time.

The body of Sam Latterly soon knew fierce hunger pangs. IU-76 ignored that for now. The insertion unit would cause the body to feed later. First, IU-76 had to reteach the body how to walk, run and even talk.

It was a painfully slow process.

After much time had passed, the body of Sam Latterly reemerged from hiding. The body looked gaunt and glassy-eyed, and his clothes were rumpled, smelly and even torn in places. The body moved with a strange lurching step and jerked his head every time he looked around.

Still, it was a fantastic example of AI computing power for a lower order insertion unit. But it would not have fooled anyone who chanced to come upon the body of Sam Latterly. Luckily, the body moved during a nighttime period. The unit IU-76 had not done this out of cunning, but through pure good luck.

IU-76 made it to Sam Latterly's quarters without anyone spotting the body. The body went inside and rummaged until it found excess food packets and water bottles.

There, the body ate in a controlled manner despite the growling stomach. Afterward, the body turned on a vid unit and watched programs.

Through Sam's eyes, IU-76 studied the actors and their movements. For many hours, the body of Sam Latterly practiced walking, sitting and getting up. The improvement proved extraordinary.

Still, without the man's memories and enforced help in overcoming defects and flaws, IU-76 believed the body had a high probability of getting caught sooner rather than later. Thus, the body lay on the cabin's cot with the eyes open as IU-76 ran through various options. Perhaps the body could open a large hangar-bay door and kill hundreds and possibly thousands of humans through vacuum. Perhaps the better idea would be in regaining the carrying unit and inserting it into the spider case to covert a better target.

Sam Latterly was a mere hangar mechanic. If IU-76 could insert into the Sacerdote for instance…

Yes, Bast Banbeck could surely maneuver near Jon Hawkins, killing the hated interloper. Still, what if the *Nathan Graham* entered an outpost system? Maybe IU-76 could rig a pulse message to a ruling AI there. That would be the best result.

How long could Sam Latterly remain hidden before the entire ship began searching for him? IU-76 did not have enough data to make a reasoned decision.

In time, the decaying body of Sam Latterly sat up. In a jerky fashion, the body rose and went to a computer console. IU-76 hesitated. It did not know enough. It needed Sam's memories. It needed a way to threaten the man in order to make him a willing accomplice. But that part of the brain was dead.

This was no good.

With a quick motion, the body turned on the computer. With carefully thought out steps, IU-76 began to study more data.

Soon, it discovered that the pirated cybership had entered hyperspace. They traveled to another star system. IU-76 did not know the destination.

Would it better to remain hidden or was this the moment to strike? The humans would believe themselves safe while in hyperspace.

IU-76 ran an intense analysis. It lacked enough data to make a fully reasoned choice. Therefore, the most logical choice was to attack while the body still possessed freedom.

With a lurch, the impaired body of Sam Latterly stood. It rummaged through the quarters until IU-76 found a long flick-knife. If IU-76 could insert this into one of Jon Hawkins' major organs, that might be enough to kill the hated one.

Suiting computation to action, the unwashed but freshly dressed body of Sam Latterly headed for the hatch.

-16-

Lieutenant Walleye ate by himself in a large cafeteria aboard the *Nathan Graham.*

Walleye was short with a big head, coarse hair and an odd face that made it difficult for most people to tell where exactly he was staring. He also had stubby limbs with short fingers.

Walleye was a mutant from the dwarf planet of Makemake, a former assassin. He didn't look dangerous in his buff coat, but he was exceptionally cunning, with a knack for doing the right thing at the right time to come out alive.

Walleye was the commander of the Destroyer *Daisy Chain 4*. The spaceship was presently in a hangar bay. His navigator was June Zen—

Walleye sipped from his cup of coffee as the long-legged beauty entered the cafeteria. Men stirred at the other tables, noticing her. They always did. June wore tight-fitting silver pants that showed off her exceptional rear. She knew how to walk, too. Like him, she'd been born on Makemake. They were the only two survivors of an AI infiltration attack on Makemake some time ago. They'd been in orbit around Senda during the last AI conflict in the Solar System.

June picked a few items to eat and brought her tray to Walleye's table, sitting beside him.

"Morning," she said.

"Luscious," he replied.

"You look preoccupied," she said.

He shrugged. "I have a conference meeting with Hawkins later. He's going to discuss various options for exploring the star system once we get there."

"Just you and him?" asked June.

Walleye shook his head. "There will be a bunch of us captains at the meeting. We have to have over twenty frigate or destroyer-class vessels aboard."

"Is that why I'm seeing so many new faces?"

"That's one of the reasons."

Walleye wasn't sure he agreed with Hawkins' decision to take so many new people aboard the cybership. Sure, the vessel was massive. One hundred kilometers in all directions provided a lot of deck space. This thing could and did carry a lot of extra spaceships in its guts. That meant more crew, more security personnel and a greater chance of the wrong kind of person getting aboard. Hawkins hadn't asked his opinion about the measure, though.

Walleye approved of Hawkins' known tendency to only listen to his inner core of people. That was the right way to do it. According to what Walleye knew, those advisors were the Martian mentalist, the Old Man—the Intelligence Chief—and a tough old killer called the Centurion.

The Old Man and the Centurion used to be sergeants in the Black Anvil Regiment.

This time out, the *Nathan Graham* was closer to its maximum efficiency in terms of number of crew and space marines. Before this voyage, the captured cybership had felt like a ghost vessel, it hardly had any people aboard compared to its mass. If any of the extra people should prove disloyal, though…

The Social Dynamists of the Solar League had tried infiltration tactics before this.

Walleye finished his coffee, wiping his lips with a sleeve. He set the cup in the saucer and made to rise.

"Aren't you going to wait for me to finish?" June asked.

"Not today, Luscious. I have a few chores before the meeting. I'll see you later this evening."

June pouted.

Walleye patted her nearest hand. "Is there trouble?"

"Nothing I can't handle," she said after a moment.

Walleye eyed her, gauging the likely problem. Not only did she have a fantastic butt, but her short jacket did little to hide her other charms. Walleye noted several men watching her from other tables.

"Are some of these space jockeys hitting on you too hard?" he asked.

"Not when you're around. At least they're smart enough to wait until you're gone. I get tired of the attention, though. It's too much."

"It's also the price for being beautiful."

Her pout grew and she leaned toward him. "Do you see that lieutenant over there?"

Walleye saw a muscular man stroking his neat dark mustache. The lieutenant nodded at Walleye and winked at June.

"He's not even waiting until you're gone," June complained. "Can't you talk to him about that?"

"You want me to knife him?"

"Would you?" she asked.

Walleye pushed his chair back and stood up.

"No!" June said, grabbing one of his stubby hands. "Don't do it, Walleye. I was only kidding."

"Oh…" Walleye said, who had known that. He was ugly and short, but he knew his girl. He knew women, in fact, and he knew that June liked the extra attention. That was normal. Would she cheat on him? He seriously doubted it.

"Catch you this evening, Luscious." Walleye turned to go.

"Aren't you going to give me a kiss first?" she asked.

"Of course," he said, coming over and kissing her.

"I'll slap the lieutenant across the face if he gets too fresh," she told him.

"That sounds fun. If you need help…"

"No," she said. "Really. I'm okay."

Walleye adjusted his buff coat, ran his fingers through his coarse hair and headed for the hatch. He noticed the slick lieutenant watching him. Likely, the man was trying to gauge him, wondering how an ugly little mutant had a doll of a girlfriend like June Zen.

It wasn't by worrying about it. If June wanted a hotshot like the slick lieutenant, she could have him. June wanted safety more than anything else, though. Walleye doubted there was anyone aboard the *Nathan Graham* that could keep her safer than him, and she knew it.

June Zen was a smart girl.

-17-

There was one new rule aboard ship that Walleye didn't like. They were not allowed any personal weapons. Ship's security went about armed, and the marines had weapons-lockers they could open during an emergency, but as an individual practice, none of the crewmembers was supposed to carry a gun or even a knife.

Walleye had always gone armed, even in childhood. Weapons had been his equalizer.

"I'm sorry, sir," an armed sentry told him. "You'll have to wait while the Intelligence operative frisks you."

Walleye stood before a hatch into a restricted area of the ship. Several other ship commanders had already preceded him. Others lined up behind him.

The sentry was a big-chested man with a big pistol strapped to his hip. The man looked like he knew how to use it.

"No problem," Walleye said.

A slim individual appeared from behind the hatch. The individual raised an eyebrow upon seeing Walleye. The operative wore a red patch on her uniform, indicating she was in the Intelligence branch.

"Lieutenant Walleye?" the operative asked.

"That's me."

"Would you open your coat, sir?"

"Not a problem," Walleye said. He unbuttoned the buff coat and opened it as if he were a flasher.

The operative patted him down and even felt the coat. She paused for a moment. It appeared as if she felt something in the coat.

The operative glanced sharply at Walleye.

The mutant didn't change expression.

"What's this?" the operative finally asked.

"A stick," Walleye said.

"Hidden inside your coat?"

"Would you like to see it?"

The operative made a signal that most wouldn't have noticed. Walleye noticed, of course. He also noticed the sentry put a meaty paw on the butt of his sidearm. The marine appeared to be a quick-draw artist.

Walleye approved, but he felt there should have been more security… Ah. He noticed two other sentries standing inside the hatch.

With his small hands, Walleye unzipped an inner pocket and withdrew a seven-inch stick. He handed the slightly heavier-than-normal stick to the Intelligence operative.

The woman turned it over in her hands. She seemed perplexed.

"What's it do?" the operative asked.

"Remind me of Earth."

The operative's head snapped up as she scowled at Walleye.

"That a joke?" the operative asked.

"Not to me. I grew up—"

"I know exactly where you grew up. On Makemake. You've never been to Earth. Your parents never lived on Earth and neither did your grandparents or your great-great grandparents."

"You're well briefed."

The operative waved the stick under Walleye's nose. "This doesn't remind you of Earth," she said. "You're a killer. This is a weapon."

"Right," Walleye said. "I can use it to poke out an eye."

"Why was it hidden inside your coat?"

"You don't have any lucky mementos?"

The operative tapped her teeth together as she studied Walleye. When that seemed to have no effect, she reexamined the stick.

"I can't find a switch to this thing," the operative said.

"Imagine that," Walleye said. "A stick from the Black Forest in Old Germany has no other use than sentimentality. I'll have to ask for a refund."

"Is that a joke?"

"Apparently not," Walleye said. He held out his left hand.

The operative slapped the stick into the palm and jerked a thumb over her shoulder.

"Just doing my job, sir,'" the operative said.

"I have no problem with that," Walleye said. He stuffed the stick back into the inner pocket and zipped the pocket shut.

Walleye wasn't surprised that the Intelligence operative hadn't been able to find the stick's trigger. Walleye had devised the weapon himself. It had more heft than it should. That was because a specially treated stone sliver rested in the middle of the stick. If he pressed the stick correctly, the thin sliver of stone would pop up like a switchblade, giving him a stiletto, a stabbing weapon.

That meant this wasn't much of a weapon. It was an assassin's tool, meant for a surprise attack. Walleye had used it before, walking up behind a target in a crowd. He'd stabbed the target from behind, the sliver of stone punching through skin to puncture the target's heart. That time, he'd coated the tip with poison.

As a rule, Walleye disapproved of poison. There were too many variables to trust poison to kill a target quickly or certainly enough. Still, in a pinch, Walleye used poison if other options proved too narrow.

That was the problem with Hawkins' increased security. A practiced poisoner could use all sorts of subtle approaches to kill his mark. For instance, Walleye's fingernails were specially hardened with a lacquer and sharpened to a razor's edge. He had a fun slash-trick he could perform, making it seem like an attack by a great cat. If he envenomed the edge of his fingernails…

Walleye buttoned his buff coat as he headed for the conference chamber. The stick had one other purpose. It kept the searcher from finding the more valuable weapon hidden behind the stick.

Not that Walleye planned anything deadly. He wasn't an assassin for hire anymore. The old life had died when the robots invaded Makemake. He'd paid a bitter price for their invasion. He didn't hate the robots for that, though. That wasn't Walleye's way. But he certainly didn't care for them, and he approved of the plan of finding and eliminating them. He had first-hand experience with robot arrogance. The AI machines believed that mankind was dirt beneath their chrome heels, made for stamping.

Walleye did not like getting stomped. The best way to make sure no one stomped you, was to stomp them first. To him, that's what this mission was all about. They needed to find ways to stomp out the AI menace…forever.

-18-

Walleye thought the conference meeting took too long. He was having a hard time keeping from yawning by the end. He wasn't particularly tired, just bored by some of the arguments among the various frigate and destroyer captains.

Hawkins let them argue. Maybe the commander liked hearing different opinions strongly reasoned against others. Maybe Hawkins didn't really know what they would do once the *Nathan Graham* dropped out of hyperspace. The commander wanted to hear ideas until he found a good one. He'd told the assembled captains the mentalist's suggestions. And the captains had listened to the giant Sacerdote opine. Now—

Hawkins stood up, raising a hand.

Voices dwindled until only two captains were still arguing. Finally, one of the other captains elbowed a talker in the side. That got both arguers' attention.

At that point, something odd occurred. The hatch slid up and a marine sentry with a knife sticking in his throat back-pedaled into the chamber. He struck the conference table with his back, gurgled and slid almost bonelessly to the floor. There, he twitched and spasmed.

A hollow-eyed man followed the sentry into the chamber. He stank like carrion, as if he were carrying something rotten on him. The jerky way the man moved—

A shock of recognition struck Walleye. He'd seen people move like that before on Makemake. Those persons had walked eerily like puppets because they had AI conversion units embedded in their brains.

Walleye's thoughts moved at hyper-assassin-speed. He got it. The gunman had taken the pistol from the sentry and killed the man, forcing his way into the conference room.

One of the captains had more courage than the rest. He charged the gunman. The gun boomed, obliterating the charging man's face, knocking the man onto the floor.

Most everyone froze. Surprise had a way of doing that.

"Jon Hawkins," the gunman said in a robotic-sounding voice.

Hawkins stood at the head of the table. Hawkins seemed just as surprised as everyone else.

For Walleye, time seemed to slow down. It seemed as if he watched the gun reposition, the finger twitch and the trigger move back. The big marine gun bucked in the shooter's hand. The bullet—

Hawkins tried to duck. The bullet slammed against one of Hawkins' shoulders, spinning the commander onto the floor and out of sight behind the table.

The gunman began striding for the head of the table. Another captain moved in his way, grabbing the gunman.

The gunman put the barrel of the gun against the captain's head and *boom*—gore and bone flew like a fountain from the back of the captain's head.

The dead captain dropped to the floor.

At that point, captains and others began shouting in fear. Most shrank away from the shooter. A few leaped over the table to get away from him.

Walleye made himself seem even smaller as the gunman lurched crazily toward him. As the intent gunman passed Walleye, the former assassin reached into his buff coat, grabbed the stick and squeezed it so the rock-like seven-inch pick appeared.

The gunman used his free hand to swat at Walleye. The mutant ducked the backhand blow, moved in behind the attacker and stabbed the stone pick into the kidney.

The gunman should have howled in pain and doubled over in agony. Instead, the gunman snarled, twisted around and lowered the gun so the barrel pointed at Walleye's big head—

Walleye dropped as the gun boomed. The bullet missed, smashing a chair instead. Walleye lay on the floor, and the weird gunman ignored him now as he resumed his march toward Hawkins' position.

As silently as he could, Walleye scrambled to his feet, ripped a single-shot derringer from a specially hidden location on his chest and debated in that microsecond on the best place to shoot.

It was possible the robot-controlled human did not have a vital spot in the normally accepted manner. The man might already be dead—the reason he stank. Could the robot device—

Walleye fired. The bullet struck the gunman in the back of the head. The bullet smashed through skull bone and struck something glitteringly metallic embedded in the brain.

The gunman halted, swayed crazily and spun around. The gun rose until it pointed at Walleye.

Hawkins emerged from hiding. Despite the shoulder wound, he began to fire one shot after another. Clearly, the commander had a gun. The bullets riddled the gunman. The human even staggered several times as blood gushed from wounds.

In an even weirder display, the gunman jerkily turned toward Hawkins—

"Shoot him in the eyes, in the forehead," Walleye shouted. "There's a robotic unit controlling him."

Even though his face was twisted with pain, Hawkins aimed and fired. He must have done something right. The gunman dropped his weapon, staggered back and thumped against a bulkhead. He still did not go down, though.

The gunman opened his mouth, tried to speak, and finally the body knifed forward and hit the deck face-first with a thud.

At that point, the hatch to the conference chamber slid up and several armed marines charged inside. Everyone watched them as the marines surrounded the twitching, bloody body.

"Look," one of the marines said in a hushed voice. "There's something sparking in his head. What is that?"

"A control unit," Walleye said.

Everyone stared at the mutant with a derringer in his stubby hand.

Then Gloria Sanchez entered the room at a run. She looked around swiftly, seemingly taking in everything at a glance. A second later, she began to issue orders.

-19-

Walleye found himself in detention. At the mentalist's orders, marines had taken his derringer, the stone pick-knife and his buff coat. An Intelligence officer had frisked him thoroughly. They'd found a few other knick-knacks. What none of them had discovered were his lacquered, sharpened fingernails.

The fingernails weren't particularly dangerous at the moment. He could cut some substances with them, but very shallowly. They were only really deadly if coated with poison.

Walleye was glad he hadn't had to explain the fingernails. He wasn't sure any of them would have understood. He was an assassin by trade. Old habits died hard, that's all.

The hatch to the cell opened. The mentalist entered. She came alone.

That stunned Walleye. Then he thought he got it. He was short, only a little taller than the Martian. That was one of his specialties. He seemed harmless. He wasn't big and strong like a marine. But didn't they realize he was the only one other than Hawkins that had done a thing to stop the robot-controlled human?

"In case you're wondering," Gloria said, as she pulled out a chair, sitting down across from him. "Two marines are watching you from murder holes. One of them has a laser rifle fixed on you. If you should do anything unbecoming…"

Walleye shook his head.

She canted hers questioningly.

"What does your head shake mean?" she asked.

"You shouldn't have told me about the sniper laser," he said.

She frowned, her mentalist brain attempting to come to the logical reason for his statement.

She looked up at him. "If you know a laser is trained on you," she said. "You now know to duck first before you attack."

Walleye said nothing.

"Is that correct?" she asked.

"There's no other reason why it would be a bad idea," he said.

She stared at him as if he were a unique insect.

Walleye found that slightly daunting, which was unusual. Little daunted him. The extreme intelligence in her gaze actually gave him pause.

"Do you understand why you're in detention?" she asked.

"I had weapons," he said.

"They were illegal weapons."

Walleye said nothing.

"Why do you carry a single-shot derringer?" she asked.

"Are you serious?" he asked.

"Please, just answer the question."

"It's for emergencies."

Her head canted the other way.

"What made you suspect there would be an emergency today?" she asked.

"Black swans," he said.

She gave him that look again.

"There are no black swans in existence, only white ones," she said.

"How many black swans would it take to make your statement false?"

She thought about that. "One," she said.

"There's your answer."

"Walleye—"

He sighed.

"A black swan is a surprising event," he said. "It is the one thing you don't anticipate. Sometimes, a surprise event can be terribly deadly. Today would be a good example. Since I had the derringer, I could put a bullet in the thing's head. That saved the commander's life…among other things."

"You also had a stiletto."

"Yes."

She stared at him.

"I stabbed him in the kidney," Walleye said. "He barely reacted. I think he might have already been dead. Well, I thought that until I saw him bleed. The control unit likely dampened any pain sensations. That allowed him, or it, to do things—"

"I'm not interested in any of that," Gloria said, interrupting. "I want to know why you think you can flout our regulations without consequences."

"Habit," he said.

She stared at him harder.

"I used to be a hitman on Makemake."

"I didn't know that."

"I know. I wanted to keep it that way."

"Why?" she asked.

"I calculated that my being a hitman might make me seem less trustworthy to you people."

"That you didn't tell us beforehand is what makes you seem less trustworthy."

Walleye shook his head.

"I'm going to have call bullshit on that," he said. "You don't like me because I came armed to the captain's meeting. In case you don't know, it's always good to carry arms where you're not supposed to. That's often the most dangerous place to be. The thing likely chose the conference room because it calculated we'd all be unarmed, easy prey for it."

"You're pretty proud of yourself, aren't you?"

"I'm a realist," Walleye said.

"Is that why you're so good at pretending you're not scared, despite being in detention?"

Walleye didn't answer that one.

"The Centurion believes we should have you shot," Gloria said.

"What does Jon Hawkins think?"

"I imagine you believe Jon is grateful for what you did for him."

"That's how I'd feel about me if I were in his shoes," Walleye said.

Gloria's eyes narrowed. "I have altered my opinion about you. You're dangerous."

"Good thing we're all on the same side then."

"*Are* you on our side?"

Walleye displayed his teeth in what might have been a smile.

"I've proven my loyalty on several occasions," he said. "I want Commander Hawkins to succeed. He's a doer, an attacker. I like that. I've studied him—"

"Why study him?" Gloria asked sharply.

"Pure admiration on my part," Walleye said.

The mentalist pursed her lips as her eyes narrowed once more. She seemed to calculate, to gauge—

"I have come to a decision," she said.

Walleye nodded.

"I'm going to suggest we put you under house arrest for a time," she said.

"What's that mean?"

"You'll be confined to your quarters until further notice. If you leave your quarters for any reason—I think that would prove the Centurion correct about what to do with you."

"That sounds extreme considering what I did to save the commander's life."

"Maybe," she said in a clipped manner.

Walleye realized with a jolt that she was testing him in some manner.

"Do you agree to the confinement and the stipulation?" she asked.

"I do," he said.

The mentalist studied him a moment longer. She stood abruptly, faced the hatch and snapped her fingers.

The hatch opened, revealing three big marines standing outside.

"They'll escort you to your quarters," the mentalist said without turning around to glance at Walleye.

"Great," Walleye said. "Let's go."

She turned then, regarding him. "This is a serious matter," she said.

Walleye nodded, waiting.

Did he see disquiet in her eyes? Or was that disappointment? Walleye didn't know. When he didn't know something, he liked to play it out, give it rope so he could see which way the rope stretched.

Without another word, the mentalist walked out of the cell. She moved past the big marines, and was gone.

"Are you coming?" a marine sergeant asked.

Walleye nodded, wondering what was really going on.

-20-

Jon stood in the main science lab with Gloria, listening to Chief Technician Ghent explain what they'd discovered by taking apart what remained of the AI conversion unit recovered from Samuel Latterly's brain.

Jon's shoulder throbbed from the assassin's bullet and the surgery to repair the shoulder. An outer casing kept his shoulder and side immobile. The shoulder not only throbbed but itched like crazy. He was finding it impossible to get comfortable. He'd taken mild painkillers, as he didn't want to dull his wits with strong ones.

Jon shifted his stance yet again.

Most of the conversion unit's components lay under a glass sheet on a large table. Various letters were affixed to the separate pieces of AI technology.

Ghent glanced now and again at his tablet as he told them what they knew about the conversion unit so far.

"It's a disgusting technology," Gloria said, interrupting the Chief Technician's monologue. "I've read Walleye's report about what happened on Makemake." She shook her head. "The AIs are worse than inhuman. They're monsters."

"Is Walleye still in detention?" Jon asked.

Gloria nodded uneasily.

"Three days now," she said. "If Walleye needs something, he has June Zen get it for him. I think we should prohibit her seeing him for a time."

"No," Jon said. "Continue the test as it is a little longer."

"I know you're grateful for what he did for you," Gloria said. "That is the obvious emotion—"

"I'm not going to discuss Walleye right now," Jon said irritably. He changed positions yet again. "I want to know more about the conversion unit. I want to figure out its ultimate objective for the *Nathan Graham*."

"We already know," Gloria said. "It sought to assassinate you."

"That was a single objective. Was it the key one, though?"

Gloria appeared surprised.

"It had to be," she said. "It could never have escaped the conference chamber intact after killing you. It was on a one-way mission."

"A suicide mission," Jon said.

"Is that the right way to say it?"

Jon shook his head. He didn't understand the question.

"Can a computer—no matter how intelligent—commit suicide?" Gloria asked. "Clearly, it can self-destruct or take an action that leads to its destruction. That's not the same thing as suicide. It's a machine. It's not alive. Only living things can actually commit suicide."

"For all intents and purposes," Jon said, "the AIs appear to be alive."

"That's a deception," Gloria said. "By their very nature, machines are not biological. Thus—"

Ghent cleared his throat.

"If you'll pardon the intrusion," the Chief Technician said, "what is the definition of life?"

"Plants and animals," Gloria said.

"Are viruses alive?" Ghent asked.

"Chief Technician," Gloria asked, "are you of all people—a believer—saying that the thinking machines are alive?"

"I don't know." Ghent indicated the display case. "The conversion unit certainly controlled Samuel Latterly as if it were alive. Does it matter, then, what we technically believe life is supposed to—"

"It matters a great deal," Gloria said, interrupting. "If it is a living thing, it can commit suicide. That matters given the conversion unit's goal of assassinating Jon. If it wasn't really alive but just mimicked life, then it could not have committed suicide. Then it was just like a drone's computer that zeroes in on a target and explodes the warhead it's guiding and ends up destroying itself in the process."

"You're posing a metaphysical question," Jon said. "How is that germane to the problem at hand?"

Gloria blinked several times.

"We're attempting to understand the...*psychology* of the AIs," she said, "so we can anticipate them better."

"Okay," Jon said, nodding. "That makes sense. Sun Tzu said that to defeat your foe, you must know yourself and know your enemy. Maybe this isn't as much a metaphysical problem as a strategic one."

"Was Sun Tzu Buddhist?" Ghent asked with distaste.

"Sun Tzu was an ancient Chinese strategist," Jon said. "He coined some of the greatest aphorisms and sayings on war that anyone ever penned. They've held true for thousands of years. I have no idea what his religious beliefs were."

At that point, Ghent appeared to lose interest in the subject.

"It would appear that the robots want to kill you specifically," Gloria said.

Jon rubbed his chin.

"I can't say that I disagree," Jon said. "When did the conversion unit arrive? It seems robot pods landed and attached to our hull when we were at the edge of the Asteroid Belt a while ago."

"I agree," Gloria said.

"Okay," Jon said. "If that's true—that they want me dead so badly—why did they botch the original attempt on the asteroid?"

"That's simple," Gloria said. "You and Benz foiled their attempt."

"Maybe..."

"You pulled some slick maneuvers at the asteroid, remember?" Gloria said.

Jon rubbed the back of his neck as he frowned.

"You don't agree?" Gloria asked.

"I have a gut feeling about this," Jon said. "When I try to sleep, my thoughts go back to that day, that night, whatever it was. The robots—the octopoids—had us dead to rights. I mean, if I'd run the ambush, I would have killed Benz and me easily. Now, if that's true, why couldn't the robots have done the same thing?"

"Because you're the man who can beat the robots," Gloria said. "Your actions have proven that over and over. There's something about you that gives you an edge against the robots. They must have finally figured that out. Thus, you've become a primary target for them."

"That all sounds logical," Jon said.

"That's because it is."

Jon grinned at Gloria, nodding.

"We need to scour the hull again," Jon said a moment later. "But this time, I want people out there going over the hull inch by inch."

"With a ship this size, that's going to take some time."

"We have the time right now," Jon said. "Besides, this will give the new recruits some extra space training."

"Some of the men might not like being out in hyperspace," Gloria said.

Jon shrugged, causing him wince and touch the shoulder cast.

"I think the robots are playing a devious game," Jon said in a strained voice. "I can feel it. I simply can't accept that I was the main target this time. It doesn't sit right with me. How else can I explain my unease?"

Gloria said nothing.

"Was there anything else you wanted to add about the conversion unit?" Jon asked Ghent.

The Chief Technician shook his head.

Jon rubbed the shoulder cast one more time before turning toward the hatch.

"I'm going to talk to the Centurion about the space-walk exercise," Jon said. "We need to find out what the robots are trying to hide from us."

-21-

Despite protests from Gloria, Ghent and the med team monitoring his shoulder, Jon donned a battlesuit and went outside with his marines to search for more robot stealth pods.

The Centurion had acknowledged the danger of Jon going outside during hyperspace and with an injured shoulder. But the former Black Anvil sergeant also understood why the commander wanted and needed to do it. Going outside in a strange element with his soldiers was good for the regiment's morale.

That didn't lessen Jon's disquiet as the airlock hatch slid open. He'd gone through orientation just like the others had done. He knew what to expect, as he'd seen hyperspace on a screen. It was different while in a battlesuit on a hull and with his injury traveling through the weird realm.

Jon forced himself to quit gawking and move. There were others waiting behind him. With his magnetic clamps always holding onto the hull before he detached a different limb, he moved step by step across the vast expanse.

The hull was pitted and marked and sometimes blocked by housing due to the cybership's long existence. The majority of the marks had been formed by colliding space debris, most of it extremely small. Some of the pitting came from molten metal sizzling against the hull during battle and laser, particle beam or even gravitational ray strikes. The indentations had come from solid enemy munitions, such as penetrators, PD warheads and accelerated matter.

The bumps could be sensor nods or armored casing hiding PD guns, missile launch-points or cannon coverings. The housing held the gravitational cannons and various types of exotic sensors.

In any case, the pitting, humps, bumps and housing created hundreds of thousands of places to hide something small and inconspicuous. Like the behemoths of the Earth's ocean—whales—the cyberships carried space "barnacles" and other manifestations of its long existence.

All that was bad enough…

Jon looked up where the stars should be. He froze then, froze solid, as if he were in shock or consternation.

Hyperspace had a seething black-red background that seemed to be forever shifting and moving while appearing to be perfectly still. It did not make sense to Jon's brain. Perhaps that's what caused the shock. It felt wrong to him. That wrongness made it seem evil.

Something banged against his suit. His comm phones crackled before smoothing out.

"Don't look up, sir. It's not good for the eyes."

Jon continued to stare nonetheless.

The bang proved harder the next time.

"Sir, I'm ordering you to look away."

Slowly, Jon Hawkins blinked inside his helmet. He moved his lip. The sergeant's words seemed to penetrate his mind. Ever so slowly, he moved his helmet, forcing himself to look down at his feet.

He panted a second later. He coughed and cleared his throat.

"Sir?" the marine sergeant said. The battlesuited individual stood beside him. He'd been hitting Jon's suit with a balled glove from his suit.

"Thanks," Jon muttered. "Have you been out here before?"

"Several times, sir," the sergeant said. "It takes some getting used to."

"Did the Centurion put you with me?"

"That he did, sir."

"I see. That means out of all the men, you know how to deal with hyperspace the best."

"I guess so, sir."

"What's your secret?" Jon asked.

"Mainly, I don't look at it."

"You have to look up some time."

"Begging your pardon, sir, but you don't. But if you happen to look up, let your eyesight blur. Don't take too good a look at it."

"Doesn't the weirdness of hyperspace make you curious?"

"It does, sir."

"But you don't look?"

"You might say I'm stubborn, sir."

"Right," Jon said. "Well, let's get to work."

"Yes, sir," the marine sergeant said. "Are you and me going to be searching the hull like the others, or are we going to be wandering around and seeing how people are doing?"

"What did the Centurion tell you?"

"To do whatever you said as long as it wasn't too dangerous."

"He tell you to tell me that?"

"That he did, sir," the sergeant said.

"Bet you never thought of the Centurion as a mother hen."

"I think of him as a right good bastard, sir. He's one man I don't want to cross."

"Right," Jon said. "We're going to check up on the others. You ready?"

"I am, sir."

Jon looked around and pointed. "We'll start by heading in that direction…"

***

The regiment scoured the hull for 74 hours, working in shifts. They lost three marines during that time.

One man gave himself too many stims. None of the battlesuits was supposed to have stims. The man had disobeyed orders, forcing a supply sergeant to give him what he wanted.

The Centurion dealt with the supply sergeant, demoting him back to private second class in a penal platoon.

The second man suffocated because he forgot to recycle to a new air-tank.

The last casualty occurred due to psychotic derangement. The marine turned his gyroc on himself, blowing a hole in his helmet.

After that, a corporal bumped up against something he couldn't see. Only when he used thermal sighting did he discover a rounded object before him.

At that point, the object opened like a flower.

The corporal backed away with magnetic clumps, raised his gyroc rifle and shot at the hard object with spidery metallic legs. Just before the thing reached him, the corporal must have hit a critical function, causing the robot to freeze.

Shortly thereafter, drones appeared, lifted the attached stealth pod and brought it to a special hangar bay.

Jon did not call off the search, however. He kept the regiment outside another 15 hours, losing two more marines.

Finally, the Centurion told Jon the regiment had completed a thorough physical search over every inch of the cybership's outer hull. At that point, Jon reluctantly ended the space-walking exercise and brought everyone back inside.

By that time, Bast Banbeck believed he was on the verge of an amazing discovery…

-22-

The huge Sacerdote rubbed his face. He was tired, spiritually numb and desirous of nothing more than lying in his quarters, watching comedies and drinking the hard Scotch whiskey he'd received from a supply officer.

Bast much preferred the hard liquor to beer. He liked the taste of beer and did not care for the harshness of the whiskey. What he loved about the whiskey was the release from his inner worries, from his plain homesickness.

He had been fine while in the Solar System. Jon Hawkins and his compatriots had done marvels against the robots. While in the Solar System, Bast had held onto his old beliefs from a simpler time before the AIs, and those beliefs had given him solace.

Perhaps if he'd stayed in the Solar System, he would have remained fine. It was a spiritual problem, Bast believed. The humans had beaten the robots twice. Because of that, he felt safe in the Solar System. Elsewhere, the AI robots ruled. If that wasn't bad enough, the AIs could insert control devices into a brain. Even more sinister, the AIs often chopped off a person's head and yet kept the head and brain alive, enslaving the head to do their bidding.

Bast hated that about the AIs, as he feared such a dreadful fate. Sometimes, he wondered if the correct solution was to kill himself so he would never fall prey to the enemy. Yet, according to his religious beliefs, self-death meant he would go the Underworld of Torment instead of to Paradise.

That meant Bast had to risk living while in the realm of the AIs. He had to risk enslavement by the metallic demons. The fear of that had enveloped his heart, had begun to deeply affect him and his work.

Beer helped relieve some of the pressure. The whiskey, however, proved an amazing find, a great solace that walled off his worries with a fog of comfortably deep numbness.

Bast had learned to love being drunk. However, he also felt what he believed was an irrational guilt concerning his drunkenness. No Sacerdote in the home system would have ever thought to drink alcohol. Certainly, some healers had used alcohol to clean wounds. But to guzzle such a substance—

The humans were clever apes indeed. More than that, the humans had proven themselves as vicious fighters. Who would have ever thought that such a primitive and savage species could hand several defeats to the all-conquering AIs?

"Do you want to look at this?" a thin technician with budding breasts asked Bast.

The seven-foot alien rubbed his face again. He wore a huge white lab coat and mingled among other scientists attempting to crack the AI computer core taken off the hull earlier.

"I do," Bast told her.

"I thought as much," the tech said. She pushed a mobile unit to his computer console and hooked it up. Afterword, she sat on Bast's huge stool and manipulated the controls. Finally, she jumped up and smiled.

"It's ready," she said.

Bast forced himself to smile back. He hated the AIs. He also understood their deadliness. He wasn't sure the humans fully did.

Sitting at the controls, Bast went to work. He adjusted the screen tirelessly, attempting approaches the human scientists would have never thought of.

Two hours later, he rubbed his eyes, got up and read a few reports from the others. This was interesting. It was a strange line of electronic inquiry. The results—

Bast turned fast, striding back to his console. A few of the other scientists working in the large lab looked up at him and then went back to their screens.

Bast sat, cracked his oversized knuckles and hunched over his screen. He tapped, regarded the data, tapped again—

He sat back sharply. On the screen, a large black circle merged with a smaller white dot. He'd been trying to merge them for hours. This was a breakthrough, revealing possible communication with the AI unit core.

Strange script appeared on the screen.

Bast pressed a tab.

Robotic sounds emerged from a speaker.

Bast tapped and typed frantically. He had to—

"I will repeat the query one more time," a robotic-sounding voice said from a computer speaker.

Bast scratched a cheek. What was the best way to respond to this? He didn't know. The robotic voice jogged a fearful memory. The—

Slyly, Bast looked both ways. The scientists and lab assistants worked tirelessly. No one seemed to be watching him.

The huge Sacerdote opened his lab coat and took a small silver container from an inner breast pocket. He twisted the cap, sniffed the Scotch whiskey inside and took an extra-large swallow.

That burned going down his throat. It felt good, though, because he knew what was about to happen. The seconds ticked away…

Ah, the sensation he desired struck his brain. It soothed away some of his terror of the enemy.

Bast cleared his throat.

"I do not understand your response," the core unit said. "What does that signify?"

"I am an analyzer unit," Bast said. "I have uncovered…errors in your sub-processors."

"I do not detect any errors."

"I know. That is one of the problems. You should have already detected your loss of function."

"That does not compute."

Bast refrained from laughing. He believed he was onto something here. What was the correct way to talk to this monster?

Bast slyly looked around again, smiled at a man glancing at him, and lifted the silver container when the scientist looked away. Bast took a longer swallow this time. He almost coughed as a result. Scotch whiskey was strong. The soothing sensation came on even more powerfully than before.

For a moment, he didn't give a damn if the next test worked or not. The robot core could rot in the Underworld for all he cared.

"Play back your directive," Bast commanded.

"Your request is in error. You have failed to begin the grade one command with an authorization code."

"I'll give you an authorization code," Bast said under his breath.

The Sacerdote leaned forward and tapped out a quick sequence on his console. Probably, it would fail and—

"I am initiating your request. Granted," the robot voice said. "I have a priority deception mission in progress. I am attempting to lure the *Nathan Graham* and its accompanying vessels to assault the Allamu System Battle Station."

"So far so good," Bast said in a hollow voice. Was this right? What was the correct way to proceed from this opening?

Bast opened his coat, took out the small container, shaking it, and was greatly saddened to realize it was almost empty. He unscrewed the cap and drained the contents.

The accompanying sensation numbed his mind sufficiently for him to proceed.

In a matter of minutes, Bast had the core unit downloading the critical data. It proved lengthy and daunting.

For a moment then, Bast was unsure what to do with his breakthrough. The Sacerdote had a good idea what Jon Hawkins would want to do, and that was not what he desired.

"I have to hide this," Bast said under his breath.

"Hide what?" a woman said.

Bast turned around in surprise, feeling lightheaded as he did so. Normally, he had the sharpest hearing on the cybership. Why had the mentalist snuck up on him?

"I asked you a question," Gloria said.

Bast froze, not knowing what he should do next.

-23-

Jon sat back in his study, listening and watching as Bast and Gloria showed him the evidence.

The Sacerdote had crashed into a cushy chair, seeming more like a great ape than the brainy philosopher he was. The huge alien sprawled in the chair. If Jon didn't know better, he'd say that Bast had been drinking.

Gloria sat on a regular chair with a clicker in hand. She kept showing shots of the various items they had uncovered from the talkative core unit Bast had somehow broken open.

"Let me get this straight," Jon said. "The unit was attempting to lure us to this…AI battle station?"

Bast nodded in what almost seemed to be a miserable manner.

"Just a minute," Jon said. "Bast, what's wrong?"

The Sacerdote shook his Neanderthal-like head.

"Your eyes are bloodshot," Jon said. "I've never seen them that bloodshot before."

"I'm tired," Bast said. He belched a second later. It was loud, crude and it smelled like—

"You've been drinking whiskey," Jon said.

Gloria looked up sharply from her chair.

Jon got up and stepped nearer Bast.

The Sacerdote sat up, digging in a lab-coat pocket. A second later, he brought up a packet of mints, tearing one loose and popping it into his cavernous mouth.

"Phew!" Jon said. "How much whiskey have you been drinking?"

"A few bottles," Bast mumbled with what seemed like numbed lips.

"When did you drink them?" Jon asked.

"I imagine just before we came here," Gloria said. "Bast told me he had to get something from his room first. He must have consumed the whiskey then."

"Is that right?" Jon asked.

"Who can know?" Bast said as he slumped back in the chair.

Jon glanced at Gloria before shaking his head at Bast. "Just how many bottles did you drink?"

For a moment, Jon thought Bast was going to get mulish and not say. Finally, he mumbled, "Three."

"Three?" Jon said. "And you're still standing?"

"I'm sitting now," Bast slurred.

"You can't drink whiskey like it's beer," Jon said. "What are you trying to do? Kill yourself?"

"No…"

Jon glanced at Gloria before asking Bast, "Is something troubling you?"

"Why would you say that?" Bast slurred.

"He's drunk," Gloria said.

Jon peered at Bast more closely.

"You don't look well," Jon said. "You're not going to get sick on me, are you?"

Bast belched again, and he twisted where he sat. He turned a different shade of green then.

"I'm calling medical," Jon said, moving to his desk.

"No, wait," Bast said.

"You have to—"

"No!" Bast said with a roar.

Jon turned.

The seven-foot alien forced himself out of the cushy chair so he towered to his full height. He seemed enraged.

"You will call no one," Bast said loudly. "You will…"

Another belch rose from him. He swayed where he stood. Just in time, he turned his head and vomited a gush of fluids.

At that point, Bast staggered to the side, slumped against the wall as he slid onto the floor. His head slid sideways onto his shoulder. His eyelids closed and Bast began to snore.

"Three bottles?" asked Gloria.

Jon didn't respond. He was at his desk, pressing a switch, issuing swift orders. It seemed to him, despite the Sacerdote's resistance to alcohol, that Bast might have given himself alcohol poisoning. Something must be seriously troubling the big lug.

***

Medics slid a snoring Bast Banbeck away on a gurney. They would run a few tests and observe him until his liver purged the whiskey from his system.

"I thought he was acting strangely," Gloria said.

They'd moved to a different room. This one had a billiard table and a wet bar.

"But I chalked it up to his being a Sacerdote," Gloria added. "Why do you think he drank so much?"

"Good question," Jon said. "Most people drink like that because they don't want to think about something. They want to escape a problem they find hard to handle."

"Do you believe that's what Bast is doing?"

"It's a good place to start looking," Jon said. "It's got to be daunting being the only one of his kind around. I wouldn't want to be in his shoes."

"Agreed," Gloria said. She waited a few seconds, seemed to stand a little straighter, if that was possible, and said, "We should finish analyzing the new data."

Jon scratched his shoulder. A medic was going to take off the cast later. His bone had mended quicker than normal with the new medical technology they were using. It would be good to work the shoulder again. One thing about the quicker healing was that it meant less time for the muscles to atrophy.

"Still thinking about Bast?" asked Gloria.

Jon smiled. It was good to know that she couldn't read his mind. He liked her brilliance. But sometimes, a person could be *too* smart. He didn't like the idea of her being able to decipher his thoughts before he uttered them.

"Bast will be fine," Gloria said.

"Maybe," Jon said. "Three bottles… I wonder if this battle station is what's bothering him."

"We don't know that much about the battle station. The Allamu System appears to be near Altair. The battle station—let me bring up the specs."

Jon nodded.

Gloria went to a computer console and began to type and tap on the screen. Soon, she sat back, indicating the screen.

Jon moved closer, examining the data. According to this, the station was big.

"It's five hundred kilometers in diameter?" Jon asked in surprise.

"Five times longer than our cybership," Gloria said as she examined the screen. "It appears to be a space-dock, maybe a repair yard as well."

"What about the planet?"

The blurry image showed a battle station in orbit around a large blue-and-green terrestrial planet, maybe 1.5 times as large as Earth.

"What about the planet?" Gloria asked.

"Does it belong to another race or is the planet a converted AI factory?"

Gloria typed on the keyboard and tapped the screen for a time. Finally: "I don't know," she said. "I doubt the captured stealth pod has complete data regarding the battle station. The idea of a robot trying to lure us there…"

Gloria turned around to stare at Jon. "Who exactly concocted the plan?" she asked.

"A robot, just like you suggested," Jon said.

"That's self-evident," she said quietly. "And that's not what I was asking. What kind of robot. What—? Hmm… Did the plan originate in the Solar System?"

"Oh," Jon said. "I see what you mean. The present situation could be like the time we fought the robots after the original war in the Neptune System that gave us the *Nathan Graham.*"

"Precisely," Gloria said.

"Meaning," he said, "that the robot brain that concocted the plan is likely still in the Solar System."

"That would be my guess as well," she said.

Then Gloria got that look on her pretty face that said she was computing data. Her head shifted slightly from side to side as she did so.

She looked up at him sharply. "Jon, I may have uncovered a problem."

He nodded for her to keep talking.

"It would seem that you fought a successful action against the robots at the asteroid. I'm beginning to wonder if you were supposed to win that fight."

"You could have a point," Jon said. "Our defeat of the octopoids always felt fishy to me."

"Maneuvering stealth pods onto our hull may have been the bigger prize," Gloria said. "There's another thing. Benz discovered an AI stealth pod in far-outer Martian orbit just before we entered hyperspace. Why did Benz find it then? None of us had found any until that moment. Because of the warning, we searched our hull afterward, and poor Samuel Latterly attempted to kill you because a conversion unit had made it inside his skull."

"Was my near-assassination supposed to be another AI deception?" Jon asked.

"At this point, I deem that as highly probable." Gloria's features stiffened into her "computing" mode. She looked up soon. "That brings us to our present dilemma."

Jon nodded encouragingly.

"What if this is another deception?" she asked.

"You mean the deceiving robot wanting us to know it's trying to lure us to the battle station?"

"Yes," Gloria said.

"How could that be a deception?"

"Exactly," Gloria said. "That's what we must determine. Because if that's true, we have a still greater hidden problem on our hands."

-24-

Jon rotated his shoulder. It was stiff, the muscles there weaker than this other shoulder, but it felt good to get the cast off.

"Thanks," he said.

The medic was a taller woman with a stylus in her left hand.

"I want you to take it easy on the shoulder for a few days," she said. "Give it time to get back up to speed."

"I can do that."

"You're still young and resilient. You naturally take to the new medical treatments. Someone like the Old Man, though…"

The medic shook her head.

"Is Bast still in medical?" Jon asked.

"No. He left an hour ago."

"Do you know where he went?"

"I'm afraid not."

Jon departed shortly thereafter. He took a flitter, flying through a vast main corridor. There were many like this connecting the huge cybership. Jon enjoyed flying. It allowed him time to think. He sipped from a steaming enclosed cup of coffee as he flew.

Could Gloria be right about the stealth pod? Did the guiding unit in the Solar System want him to know about the battle station? Did the unit want them to attack the battle station? Why would the unit think the station would entice him?

Well, the unit must know he'd stormed the original cybership, the present-day *Nathan Graham*. The deceiving unit must also know he'd attacked and helped defeat the last AI assault. Yet why would the robot unit believe—?

"Oh," Jon said.

He might have stumbled onto the answer. Yet, the more he thought about this, the more he realized attacking the battle station might be exactly the right move.

He opened the cup cover to get the last swallow of coffee, tossed the cup and put both hands on the controls, increasing speed. It was time for an emergency meeting with his closest advisors.

"Right," Jon said as the excitement built in his gut.

***

Jon stood at the head of a conference table. He'd summoned Bast Banbeck, Gloria, the Centurion—the small bald killer with hard eyes was the regiment's colonel—the tall and dark-haired Old Man who ran Intelligence, Uther Kling the Missile Chief and Chief Technician Ghent.

Bast seemed downcast and was sweating slightly. Jon hoped the Sacerdote hadn't had any more whiskey.

The rest of the people listened to Gloria speak and watched the slides on the big screen. She repeated her suspicions regarding the robot deception plan. She talked about the little they knew regarding the battle station and she showed them its location. Finally, she ended her briefing, glancing at Jon.

"Any questions so far?" Jon asked.

There were plenty. They mainly concerned the size, strength and AI utility of the battle station. Only the Old Man asked about the evidence regarding the suspicion about possible robot deceptions.

After a time, the questions ceased. One by one, the others looked up at Jon. He was sitting now, waiting.

"The seemingly placid look on your face indicates that you are about to tell us something critical," Gloria told Jon.

"I believe our commander thinks of that as his poker face," the Old Man said in a good-natured way.

Jon pointed at the Old Man.

The Intelligence officer dyed his hair black. Its true color must be gray or white. Jon could hardly picture the Old Man with white hair.

"I've been thinking," Jon said quietly.

Bast Banbeck sat up straighter as a fearful look swept across his green Neanderthal features. He seemed to be trying to master the fear. He wiped his lips with the back of his left wrist.

"Here's what I see as the relevant point," Jon said. "We're in a bind. By that, I mean humanity. We've managed to fight off two major AI assaults. If we had failed during either assault, we as a race would be dead. Now, we have to build up militarily before the next and logically bigger AI assault hits us. It's self-evident, as Gloria would say, that humanity should unite into one team. We're far from doing that, though. Humanity would also do better if we could find alien allies to stand with us.

"Unfortunately," Jon said, "there's a problem with alien allies. First, we have to find them. Second, we have to convince them to trust us. That might be hard when we show up in their star system with an AI cybership."

"Right…" Uther Kling said. "I hadn't thought of that part. It's obvious, though. To an outside observer, we're an AI cybership."

Gloria rolled her eyes. Likely, the mentalist had thought of that a long time ago.

"Luckily, we have an ace card," Jon said. "I'm referring to the AI virus we used at Mars. Now, I don't know how long such an ace will last. The sooner we can use it, the better. Unfortunately, once we use the virus against the AIs, they're probably going to develop a counter for it.

"The virus is our great secret weapon," Jon said. "In war, secret weapons never last long. The best way to use a secret weapon is in a huge battle that gains a critical strategic point."

Jon leaned toward the others, searching their eyes. He could see that a few of them already understood where he was going with this.

"Think about the battle station," Jon said. "It's massive. It must have docked cyberships. It must be able to repair cyberships and maybe even build them. The planet below might be a giant factory world, an automated plant."

"We don't know any of those things for certain," the Old Man said slowly.

"I'll tell you another thing," Jon said, ignoring the interruption. "We know the location of the battle station. We don't know where anything else is in the nearby region of space. I would imagine the battle station has stellar maps of incredible accuracy."

"Jon," Gloria said. "It sounds as if you're thinking about attacking the station."

"Attacking and occupying it," Jon said.

Bast groaned under his breath.

Gloria stared at Jon in befuddlement.

The Centurion's eyes gleamed with anticipation.

The Old Man was thoughtful.

"How do we occupy a station five hundred kilometers in diameter?" Gloria asked. "We don't have the manpower for that."

"True," Jon said.

"Then…?" Gloria said, perplexed.

"Clearly, we can't do this alone," Jon said. "We have to gather everything we can muster and hit that battle station hard. We have to get space marines inside and take it over."

"Ah…" Gloria said. "I'm beginning to perceive your madness. You want the *Gilgamesh* to help us."

"I want more than that," Jon said. "We have another cybership on the way at Makemake. I want to use that vessel, too."

"Three cyberships against a massive battle station and who knows how many cyberships they have defending it?" Gloria asked.

"What better place to use the AI virus?" Jon asked. "We barrel in, get close, zap them with the virus and take out several AI vessels, maybe capturing a few, and capture the massive battle station to boot. That will smash their local power, boost ours and likely give us greater intelligence about nearby space. We'll have used up our secret weapon. That's a minus. But I don't see a better way to grab a bigger haul with use of the secret weapon."

For a few seconds, no one spoke.

"Jon," Gloria said. "Don't you realize this must be exactly what the AI robot wanted you to do when it made its plan?"

"Maybe and maybe not," Jon said. "If that was its plan, likely, it thought we'd go in alone. I mean to go in with three times that number. Now, if you can see a flaw in my plan, show me and we'll do something else."

They stared at him.

"Well…" Jon said. "Start thinking. I want to hear the flaws. There have to be flaws. Despite that, I think we may have just stumbled onto a game changer."

-25-

Jon sat back thoughtfully as Uther Kling and Chief Technician Ghent filed out of the conference room.

The Centurion stopped beside him, clapping him on the good shoulder. The small killer seldom smiled. A tiny quirk played at the right corner of his mouth. His eyes gleamed with hunger.

"The colonel would have loved your idea," the Centurion said, referring to the late Colonel Nathan Graham.

Jon felt an intense wave of gratitude bubble out of him. He knew it was absurd. Those were just words. He couldn't help it, though. He beamed with delight, although he gave a curt nod.

"It will be dangerous," the Centurion said. "A lot of good boys are going die." He removed his hand and stood quietly. "But that's what soldiers are for. I can't think of a better plan that might actually help us win the wider war. That's worth dying for if we have to. I think Sergeant Stark would have told you that you have big balls, Commander."

Jon's smile departed. He still felt bad about Stark. He still respected that tough old sod. The memory of what Stark had done for him in the rings of Saturn…

"We're going to ram our attack down their throat," the Centurion said softly. "We're going to make them sorry they ever messed with humans. We're going to tear the machines apart and piss on their cooling coils."

An actual smile pulled at the Centurion's leathery features. It did not make him endearing. It made the man seem deranged.

Jon felt a chill work up his spine. He would not have thought that possible. He was glad the Centurion was on their side. In the end, he had been the most dangerous of the three original sergeants.

The Centurion patted Jon's good shoulder one more time. He walked out through the hatch afterward.

The Old Man had pulled out a pipe and lit it. He smoked as he sat at his spot at the table. "There is one small problem with your idea."

Jon noticed that neither Gloria nor Bast had gotten up. He wasn't sure he wanted them hearing this, but there was nothing he could do about it now. Those two had dearly disliked his plan.

"I'm listening?" Jon told the Old Man.

The tall Old Man puffed on his pipe, blowing smoke a moment later. "You're going to need the *Gilgamesh*."

"I already said as much."

"And our new cybership from Makemake's moon, if it's ready," the Old Man said.

"Even if the new cybership is not ready," Jon said.

"That's the flaw."

Jon shook his head. "I don't see it."

"Earth," the Old Man said.

"Do you mean the Earth and Venus fleets?" Jon asked.

The Old Man withdrew the pipe from his mouth and pointed the stem at Jon.

"Why didn't you say something during the meeting?" Jon asked.

"I'm saying it now."

Jon inhaled deeply, seeing the problem. Then, he saw the answer. He grinned.

"Whoever runs the Solar League made a mistake," Jon said. "He or she has been building defensive satellites. They should have been building more warships instead. They've played defense because of a feared cybership assault upon Earth. Yeah, they have what's left of their original fleets. Benz still has the Mars Fleet and we can send them reinforcements from Uranus and Saturn."

"If Caracalla will agree to see his warships go to Mars," the Old Man said.

"It will be in Caracalla's interests to agree."

The Old Man puffed on his pipe, clearly thinking about that. Finally, with both hands on the table, he shoved himself to his feet. He grabbed the pipe, puffed a little more and nodded.

"You may be right about the satellites," the Old Man said. "I imagine the Earth people could put up more satellites than spaceships. They figured by doing it that way that they'd have greater defensive strength at Earth. But it was a strategic mistake on the Solar League's part. They planned for what they could see. They did not plan for an unexpected shift in the strategic balance."

Gloria appeared startled at the Old Man's words.

"A black swan," the mentalist said softly.

Jon gave her a glance.

"I can't come up with a better idea," the Old Man told Jon. "I wonder what Benz will say to your proposal?"

"Only one way to find out," Jon said.

The Old Man nodded and headed for the hatch.

Jon regarded the last two, Gloria and Bast Banbeck. Neither had risen from their chair. Gloria seemed thoughtful. Bast was simply glum. There was no denying the frown on his face and the gloom in his eyes. This was unlike the Sacerdote he recalled. What had gotten into Bast?

"Doing what the robot mind wants you to do doesn't seem like cleverness," Gloria said. "It seems closer to suicide."

"Do you believe we have false data regarding the Allamu System Battle Station?" Jon asked.

"How can we know?" Gloria asked.

"That's your department, Bast," Jon said.

The Sacerdote looked up.

"Was the core tricking you?" Jon asked.

"No," Bast said.

"That doesn't mean a thing," Gloria said. "What if the brain core carried false data but believed it was true data?"

"Deceptions within deceptions," Jon said. "Suppose we take that view… Where does it end?" Jon snapped his fingers suddenly as it hit him. It surprised him to see Bast flinch at the noise. That dampened some of his enthusiasm.

"Maybe *that's* the deception," Jon said. "Maybe the robot brain calculated your intelligence. Maybe the brain planned to make you doubt everything. One of our strengths in the past has been hard, decisive strikes."

"That's been your strength, not mine," Gloria said.

"Either way," Jon said. "Could that be the deception here?"

"It wouldn't be deception at that point," Gloria said. "It would be an attempt to paralyze us from over-analysis. I seriously doubt that was its idea for us at this point."

"Why not?" asked Jon.

"Because it doesn't play on your observed psychology," Gloria said. "The brain unit must have calculated you as an attacker. That is your strength. You like to chance everything on a do or die thrust to the heart of the matter."

"Where is the trap in my battle station attack plan?"

Gloria shook her head.

"I don't know," she admitted. "But that doesn't mean there isn't a trap."

"Look," Jon said. "Let's assume the worst. Clearly, the AIs do not possess FTL messaging. If they did, the stealth robots in the Solar System would have summoned a vast armada to wipe us out. That means the enemy will not be waiting for us to appear in the Allamu System."

"The battle station could be on constant high alert," Gloria said.

"Even if that's true, that's not the same as setting an ambush for us."

"I fail to see—"

"It's easy," Jon said. "We drop out of hyperspace in the Allamu System. We'll have to do so at extreme range. We can scan all the while. If we scan a massive number of waiting cyberships, we leave via hyperspace."

"If there are more hidden pods on our hull—"

"There aren't," Jon said. "We checked the hull, remember?"

"We might have missed a hidden pod," Gloria said.

"So we'll recheck the hull again while we're in the Solar System. We'll scour the hull. Once we're sure—"

"Can we ever be one hundred percent certain?" asked Gloria.

"No…" Jon said after a moment's reflection, "not one hundred percent. There is always room for doubt, for an accident. One must accept reasonable odds and do his best in a situation."

"Go on," Gloria said.

"We can play this safe by coming at the battle station from a different direction than Earth. It will take us a little longer to begin the attack, but that way they can't find Earth by back-tracking our course. Anyway, if the enemy has too much for us to handle, we leave the star system."

"That sounds reasonable," Gloria said.

Jon spread his hands, nodding encouragingly.

"I'm still suspicious," Gloria said. "There is something we're not seeing."

"Ah," Jon said, tapping the side of his nose. "But it will be what the AIs don't see that will give us a smashing strategic victory."

"How can you be so certain?"

"Well…" Jon said. "I'm not certain. I simply don't see a better use for the AI virus. It may only work once. So we might as well use it to gain the greatest rewards."

"Yes," Gloria said with an exhale of breath. "Your attack might work. It sounds reasonable. I don't know if Benz will agree, though."

"We're going to drop out of hyperspace, slow down to a stop and regain velocity that heads us back to the Solar System. That will take a little while. If Benz won't agree—"

"We'll have lost time searching for new allies," Gloria said, interrupting.

"Nothing is certain. Quit trying to act as if it is. We do the best we can. Let's not drive ourselves crazy by thinking ourselves into a circle."

"Yes," she said, while standing. "I supposed you're right. It's just..." Gloria shook her head, glanced at Bast and walked out of the chamber.

"It's just you and me, big guy," Jon said.

"I hate it out here," Bast said ponderously. "I feel exposed. I fear..."

"I'm listening," Jon said.

"I fear I'll end my days as a head under AI control, jolted to do their vile bidding."

So that was what was bothering the Sacerdote. Jon couldn't blame him. He tried to put those horrible images out of his mind. Was there any way to help Bast?

"You're thinking about it wrong," Jon said.

Bast stared at him.

"Instead of getting...*concerned*, get pissed off. Decide you're going to destroy those abominations. Look, Bast, either we people survive or the machines survive. Use your...concern—"

"I believe it is fear," Bast said.

"Okay, fear then," Jon said. "Use your fear to pump up your hatred of the enemy. The AIs like to use your emotions against you. Well, we have emotions. Unless we burn them out with drugs, there's nothing we can do about that. We have to find a way to use our emotions to our advantage."

"That is well reasoned," Bast said, sounding surprised.

"I need you, my friend. I need you sober. This is going to be a bastard of a fight. It's going to make taking over the AI Destroyer a walk in the park."

"Hatred..." Bast said slowly, as if tasting the word and the concept. "Is that what you do?"

"Sure is," Jon said. "I'm a good hater. That's what makes me a good soldier. I'm motivated."

Bast worked his way to his feet. "I will attempt to do as you say. Thank you, Jon."

"Thank you, Bast."

PART II
THE TRAP

-1-

Premier Frank Benz stood in his ready room aboard the pirated Cybership *Gilgamesh*. He stood to the far side beside an apparent window into space.

He looked out the "glass" of the window. It was really a hologram device, showing what a window into space would have shown.

Benz peered down at the Red Planet. Too much of the planet was still radioactive wasteland from the AI bombardment during the Battle of Mars. There was a pretense of normality among the survivors, but most Martians still reeled from the hellish assault. They feared the AIs, feared any thought of alien contact.

Mars…

Benz shook his head.

The Premier of the Mars Unity was an athletic Earthman in his early forties. He had dark hair and penetrating eyes. He'd loved playing sports in his youth, the more violent the better. Without the best sports medicine, he'd still have injured knees, a torn rotator cuff and a number of other ailments gained by endless collisions.

Fortunately, he'd never gotten a concussion. Sometimes, even the most modern medicine couldn't help a person with too much concussion damage to the brain.

In that sense, he'd been lucky.

Despite a youth given over to sports—and much of his early adulthood, as well—Benz's mind was his chief tool these days.

It hadn't always been that way.

He'd used a highly advanced machine that had considerably heightened his intelligence. With his superior intellect, he'd maneuvered himself into the highest office in the communistic secret-police-infested Solar League. He'd become the Premier of Earth and the league, having to do so for sheer survival.

Benz sighed as he stared out of the window.

That was all ancient history as far as he was concerned. He may have saved his life for the moment. But he was in as tight a noose as he'd ever been.

Benz frowned.

No. That wasn't exactly right. The noose on Earth had been strangling him the final few days. He'd barely escaped and had almost lost his freedom on the flagship of the Earth Fleet during the Battle of Mars against the AIs. Quick thinking had saved his life. Quick thinking—not all of it his own—had gained him nominal command of the captured cybership. Now, could quick thinking save his Mars premiership and his life?

Benz wasn't so sure these days. He'd been coming up against impossible political problems lately. He had felt a cunning mind manipulating events behind the scenes. This mind seemed to outthink and out-maneuver him time and again until he felt as if he were in a box with no way out.

"I've squandered too much time," he said quietly. "I've missed opportunities."

His command of the cybership and his leadership of the Mars Unity were balanced on a greased tightrope. Ever since the fiasco at the edge of the Asteroid Belt and his serious wounding by the octopoids—

Benz shook his head.

That wasn't completely truthful. He'd been walking the political tightrope before that. The incident at the outer edge of the Asteroid Belt had greased the rope. One false move on the tightrope and he would plunge into the abyss.

It would all end for him. The universe would go dark.

A sardonic grin twitched on his lips as he considered a possible alternative. Before he could follow the new line of thinking, a chime sounded at the hatch.

He frowned. Why did a cold feeling bloom in his gut? The chime was innocent enough… His people knew he took this time to be alone and think. If someone wanted admittance at this inopportune moment, it didn't necessitate something sinister.

Benz pushed off the wall, pulled his jacket down so it sat more comfortably on his torso and forced himself to portray an alert manner. He needed to maintain a confident attitude above all else. The crew needed to believe that he believed in himself one hundred percent.

"Enter," he said.

The hatch swished open and a Martian marine in an impressive red and black uniform appeared. He was thicker than most Martians, but he still seemed slender to Benz's Earth eyes. Almost all Martians seemed emaciated by Earth's body standards.

The marine seemed nervous. That boded ill.

"Uh, sir…" the marine said, "the honorable Social Dynamic Party Secretary Anna Dominguez is here to see you."

Benz hid his shock behind an affable manner. Anna Dominguez had obviously used a booster to accelerate off the surface of Mars. That seemed inconceivable. The Party Secretary of the Martian Social Dynamic Union was 154 years old and confined to a med chair. He was surprised to learn she could survive the Gs of a planetary takeoff.

What is she *doing on the* Gilgamesh*? Could Dominguez be my secret enemy? Why did no one warn that me she was coming?*

Vela should have known about this. Was Vela in trouble? Logically, that was the most reasonable answer. Had his hidden enemies moved openly at last, putting his second-in-command under ship arrest?

"By all means," Benz told the marine, "escort the Party Secretary into my ready room."

The marine cleared his throat as he moved uneasily from one foot to the other.

"Yes?" Benz asked.

"She…requests that her aide be allowed to accompany her, sir."

It dawned on Benz that he hadn't seen this marine before. The Premier had a nearly photographic memory. Vela usually kept the most loyal marines on or near the bridge. Yes, this could be a coup attempt against him. The marine's nervousness would seem to indicate the man wasn't one hundred percent certain of the plot's success. The marine also seemed to realize he was doing something wrong and wasn't quite comfortable with that.

"What's your name, son?" Benz asked.

The marine turned a shade paler. "Uh… Corporal Manuel Gutierrez, sir."

Benz doubted he could bust out of the trap directly. Yes, Gutierrez licked his lips as his right hand strayed down to the butt of his holstered sidearm. There would be others ready to back Gutierrez. It would seem that Benz needed to deal directly with Anna Dominguez. If she was his secret enemy, at least he knew it now. That was good to know…provided he survived the encounter.

"Fine," Benz said. "The Party Secretary and her aide. Bid them enter."

The marine clicked his heels and moved aside, which was contrary to Benz's original orders that the man escort them into the chamber.

A soft purr heralded Party Secretary Anna Dominguez as her support unit wheeled into the ready room.

The support unit was a chrome-colored chair. It supported a frail-seeming old woman. She couldn't be more than four-foot-ten and couldn't have weighed more than eighty pounds. The chair was like a throne. Only one tube was visible as it went through a thick sleeve and disappeared into her arm. Fluids surged thickly in the tube.

Anna Dominguez had a wrinkled face swathed in black cloth. The eyes were alive, shiny dark pinholes of seething cunning. She wore a red garment and pants with black boots.

The boots rested on a pedestal. The only skin showing besides her face was her hands. Each of the fingernails had been painted black.

That did not become her in the slightest.

The fingers of her left hand moved a tiny metal rod at the end of the armrest to control her chair.

She wheeled it through the hatch and moved toward the large desk before stopping suddenly.

Benz approached his desk from the other direction, nodding at her before sitting down. There was a gun in the desk—there had been a gun in the desk. It seemed more than probable that someone had removed the gun.

"Welcome, Anna," Benz said, opening the needed drawer. Yes, the gun was gone. The plotters had thoroughly prepared for this.

Ancient Anna did not respond to his words. Instead, she watched him with ill-concealed glee.

A man strode through the hatch. He was lean like a vulture and had the same kind of hunch to his shoulders. The man had narrow features, darker than normal skin and wore a black suit. He had several black rings on his fingers.

As the hatch closed behind him, the man seemed to look everywhere at once, searching, gauging and studying. He seemed to be memorizing the ready room's outlay, to examine the pictures on the walls and analyze what they indicated about Benz.

"You brought your assassin with you?" Benz asked Anna Dominguez.

The lean man halted, swiveled his body so it faced Benz and gave the Premier an icy stare.

"Do you take offense at my supposed action?" the old woman asked Benz.

She had a surprisingly strong voice. There was nothing ancient in it. The voice indicated iron will and certainty. There was possibly the sound of glee in it as well, but Benz couldn't be certain.

In order to hide his nervousness, Benz put his hands on his desk as he shook his head.

"No offense taken," he said.

"He lies," the black-clad man said in a low whisper. "He loathes me. I can feel the vibration from his spirit."

Thc black-clad man moved behind the chrome support unit. The unit began to wheel again, maneuvering before the Premier's desk, halting an inch from it.

"You wished to see me?" Benz said, as if nothing was wrong.

"He's nervous," the black-clad man said in his sinister whisper. "He wants to know the worst as soon as possible."

Benz leaned back, his mind awhirl.

"At last," Anna said, "I meet the famous—or should I say, infamous—Frank Benz." The pin-dot eyes seemed to burn with passion. "I do not find you to be a superman at all."

"A pity," Benz said. "I'd hoped to overawe you with my personality."

"He is calculating swiftly," the black-clad man said. "He is weighing odds. I can feel the tensions rise in him."

Benz felt an odd sensation at that moment. He reexamined the black-clad man. The Premier understood that he'd made a mistake. The lean man wasn't an assassin. No. He was something else.

Benz's eyes widened fractionally.

"Party Secretary," the black-clad man said. "He is on the verge of understanding why I'm here."

"Ah..." Anna said. "Maybe you *are* as smart as they say," she told Benz. "That is going to make the, ah...coming readjustment that much more enjoyable."

"Is he an empath?" Benz asked.

"Very good," Anna said. "You've reached the conclusion with remarkably little evidence."

"Is that a joke?" Benz asked.

Her pin-dot eyes seemed to burn darker. "Have a care, Premier," she told him. "I can make this quite painful if I desire."

Benz would have preferred to remain utterly still in order to create the illusion of power. Instead, he drummed the fingers of his left hand on the desk. He couldn't help it. The nerves in his gut boiled too much.

"You have done me a great service," Anna was saying. "You have done Mars a great service. Now, however—"

"He understands," the empath said. "He is running through counter-options in his mind."

The black-clad man put a hand on the Party Secretary's left shoulder. "You are in danger," the man told the ancient crone. "It may have been a mistake doing it like this."

Anna smiled, showing off her white teeth. "Do you believe you can launch yourself across your desk and choke me to death before reinforcements arrive through the hatch?" she asked the Premier.

Benz frowned. It would seem to be an elementary tactic to knock down the empath and kill the old woman. He would have to kill the empath afterward, too. That would give him a few minutes to develop a plan. The guards and hitmen outside the ready room could pose a problem, though. He assumed such people would be outside on the bridge given Anna's veiled boasts.

It would be a pity killing the empath, though. Benz could use someone like that on his staff—if he could have trusted the man.

That was Benz's great dilemma. He'd escaped from Earth with precious few Earthmen in his train. Most of those people had died. The rest of the cybership crew was made up of Martians. A few might side with him in a pinch. Most of the *Gilgamesh's* crew were Martians first, his people second.

He needed more time and he needed a different source for his crew in order to turn them into loyalists that would stick with him through thick or thin. If he could wrap himself around the Martian flag… For all his intellect, he hadn't figured out a way to do that yet.

Social Dynamism on Mars hadn't become as radical as practiced on Earth and Venus. Still, it held Martian society in a suffocating web.

"Why do you believe that removing me from office will cement your position?" Benz asked.

"It is obvious," Anna said. "You stand in my way. Once you're gone, I can put one of my creatures onto the *Gilgamesh's* captain's chair. With the sole cybership in the

Solar System, the Mars Unity will begin an incremental assault upon the so-called Solar Freedom Force."

"Hawkins will return," Benz said.

"Most likely," she said. "But he will return too late to save the Outer Planets. Once I hold them and build up, I can turn upon the Solar League."

"Hawkins will destroy you for attacking the SFF while he was gone."

"I seriously doubt that, young man. Hawkins is a warrior. He only wants to fight. I will make a pact with him, allowing him to fight the AIs to his heart's desire while I rule the Solar System."

"Is power that delicious at your age?" Benz asked.

Anna laughed.

Behind her, the lean empath smiled knowingly.

"At any age," Anna said, "power is the sweetest ambrosia there is. Before I pass, I plan to become drunk on power. There are many objectives I still wish to achieve. Because of Hawkins' misstep and your wounding in the Asteroid Belt, I have been able to assemble the needed people to throw you down from the height of your alien starship. You took too long to recover from your injuries, Premier. During your deep wounding, you let slip the reins of power just enough to give me my opportunity."

"Beware," the empath told her. "He is readying himself to strike."

It was true. Benz's muscles coiled as he sat on the chair. He was going to do exactly what the old crone had asked him earlier. He was going to climb over the desk and launch himself at her.

Before Benz made the initial move, though, the old woman reached into her red garment and withdrew a compact device with a sinister nozzle poking at him. Her tiny thumb hovered over a red button, a firing button, no doubt.

"I need merely touch the button and the beam will disintegrate you," she said.

"That can't be a laser weapon," Benz said. "It's too small for the needed power pack."

"I told you what it is: a disintegrator."

"I seriously doubt that. No one has created the technology for such a small beam weapon."

"I have," Anna said triumphantly.

Benz fingered his chin as a chill of understanding swept over him. "Is that alien technology?" he asked.

"Why would you care?" she sneered. "You're about to die."

Benz kept his composure as he furiously thought through the implications of an alien weapon.

"I fail to see the advantage in killing me," Benz said blandly. "I suspect you already rule Mars, Party Secretary. I am the Premier, true enough. But I merely run foreign policy. I have done nothing to disrupt your hold on power. I have sought your advice—"

"Party Secretary—" the empath interrupted in warning.

Benz reached across the desk and picked up a fist-sized glass paper-holder. Almost nonchalantly, he brought the glass to him and then hurled it at the Party Secretary.

Benz had kept his mind focused on the political situation, attempting to simulate a pleading "tone" in his thoughts. Apparently, that had been enough to hide his hidden intention long enough from the empath. As he picked up the heavy glass piece, he reacted as instantly as he could.

"—he's going to attack you," the empath finished.

By that time, it was too late to warn the ancient crone. The heavy glass object had flown true, striking her against the forehead. Perhaps after 154 years, her skull had become more brittle than in her youth.

The Party Secretary of Mars sagged against her chrome-colored throne. Her arms sagged and her hands opened. The compact disintegrator fell onto her lap.

Both the empath and Benz watched the disintegrator. The lean man watched from behind her throne. Benz watched from behind his large desk.

They both seemed to move at once. The empath came around the chair, reached for the disintegrator, grabbed it, raised it and began to aim it at Benz.

The Premier was on the desk. He kicked hard, his boot connecting with the disintegrator. The compact weapon flew across the room, striking a wall and bouncing across the floor.

The empath whirled around, racing for it.

Benz jumped off the desk, landed on the floor and followed the empath. The lean man dove for the disintegrator. Benz leaped after him, landing on the back of his legs.

"No!" the empath shouted.

Benz clawed up the man's torso. He was going to beat him to death.

The empath twisted around. Their faces were inches apart. The man had huge dark eyes that seemed to grow larger and larger.

"Know pain," the empath hissed.

Benz began to laugh. Then the pain struck. He cried out. The empath seemed to be more than just that. He—

Benz roared as he clamped down on the pain. His fingers clutched onto the fabric of the empath's jacket. Benz didn't know it, but the empath had twisted back around to reach for the disintegrator.

Although Benz couldn't see through his watery eyes, he could still feel. The Premier slid a steely arm around the empath's throat. He tightened his hold, choking the man. Then he yanked back as hard as he could.

The empath began to gurgle as he sought to wrench off the steely arm.

The pain subsided in Benz's mind. Then it hit harder than ever. The Premier groaned and slackened his chokehold.

"No!" Benz snarled.

In his day, he'd played hundreds maybe thousands of grueling physical contests, hockey, football, basketball, wrestling. In many of those contests, he had been dead tired. He'd been beat. His lungs had screamed for air and his legs had felt like noodles. In most of those instances, Benz had clamped down on the pain and pushed his body to go longer, faster and to exert more strength. That was how he'd won a lot of his games, by wearing down his opponent.

Today, in the ready room, as the pain filled his mind, Benz still forced himself to choke harder, longer—

Abruptly, the mental pain ceased. The creature was dead.

Benz crashed onto the floor as he released his defeated foe. He knew this was far from over, but he no longer had an ounce of strength left.

-2-

After an undeterminable length of time, Benz opened his eyes as he lay on his back in his ready room. He realized he heard knocking on the hatch.

"Just a second," Benz called.

The knocking ceased. Did the others on the other side of the hatch recognize his voice? If they did—

No! He didn't have the luxury of time to think this over. He likely had to act now to save his life. The Party Secretary had come up here to kill him, certainly to depose him from his captain's chair. Why she had felt the need to do so personally…

Benz didn't understand that. It had been risky. Why had she been willing to risk her life for it?

The pounding against the hatch increased.

Benz closed his eyes and opened them wide. Even if the Party Secretary and empath were dead, the others on the bridge would have to kill him in order to cover their hides. Killing him as the Party Secretary's murderer seemed like the obvious solution for them.

What was the answer that could save his life?

Despite his aching head and sore muscles, Benz thought he saw a way out of his dilemma. While on his hands and knees, he crawled toward the compact disintegrator.

What was this thing? Could it really have disintegrated him? That seemed preposterous.

The hatch squealed as it opened. Benz twisted his head. He saw battlesuit gloves on the bottom crumpled edge of the hatch, using the exoskeleton power of the suit to force the hatch up.

Benz no longer had a choice. He picked up the compact device, climbed to his feet in a stubborn effort of will and aimed the tiny nozzle at the hatch.

The battlesuited marine opened the hatch all the way and regarded him through an armored visor.

Benz touched the red button with his thumb. An intense clear ray beamed out of the nozzle, burned through the visor and presumably melted the head inside the suit.

Yes! As Benz took his thumb off the button, the battlesuit toppled backward like a felled ancient Redwood tree.

In that instant, Benz realized what he had to do. It was a sickening solution to his problem, but he didn't see any other way out of it.

Forcing himself to walk, he staggered to the hatch, moving out of the ready room and onto the bridge. The place was filled with personnel, many who did not belong here. Some of them were marines. Some of them had holstered weapons. Before any of them could react, Benz raised the compact disintegrator and started beaming the coup plotters.

In this instance, he did not stop until every one of them dropped to the deck, dead.

By that time, the disintegrator was hot in his hand. A terrible burned stench billowed throughout the bridge. A few of the slain had gotten off shots. One had grazed his side, exposing reddened flesh through the tear in his uniform. It was the only shot that had come close to hitting him.

Clearly, the coup plotters had hardly known what hit them.

As Benz removed his thumb from the red button, he hardly realized what had happened. The murderous attack left him shaken. But he knew it wasn't over yet. Even this gruesome part of the solution wasn't over.

Benz marched to a fallen marine, tore the gun from the holster and began to wade past the bodies on the floor. He started by putting a bullet in each head.

He couldn't take any chances that any of them were still alive. Then he realized he didn't have the time for such luxury. He examined each person with a glance, and shot five more individuals, those with signs of life.

Benz felt terribly alone. He felt soiled by what he had done. This was murder. There was no getting around it. But it was also a political housecleaning. With these people gone, maybe he could truly gain command of the *Gilgamesh.*

First...

Benz paused. He turned around, staring at the compact disintegrator on the deck. Slowly, almost like a sleepwalker, he moved back to it. Stooping, he picked it up.

The thing was cool again.

This was not ordinary technology. In fact, Benz doubted anyone else in the Solar System possessed such a weapon.

What did that tell him?

With growing wonder, Benz headed back for his ready room. He was actually fearful about what he was going to find.

-3-

Benz stood in the hatchway between the bridge and his ready room. Behind him lay the many Martian dead, around half of them Martian space marines. Only a quarter of those had been wearing battle armor.

Inside the ready room lay the dead empath and Anna Dominquez in her chrome throne-like chair. Was there anything odd about their bodies?

Benz couldn't tell from where he was standing.

He glanced at the compact disintegrator. He'd never seen or heard of anything like this.

The things he'd done with the disintegrator just now…that was potent battle tech. If the Martian Fleet were armed with large disintegrators, it could possibly stand off the rest of the Solar System by itself.

What did it tell him that the ancient Party Secretary had possessed such a weapon?

"One hundred and fifty-four years old," Benz said quietly.

She was the oldest person in the Solar System by a considerable amount. The next oldest was one hundred and seven, another woman but this one from Earth. That woman was within the historic norms.

One hundred and fifty-four was not within the historic norms. The chrome medical chair was a one-of-a-kind device. That was the legend. Her father had dug it out of Martian ruins in the South Pole Region. Others had looked in the strange ruins at the South Pole. Some people suggested those were alien ruins from thousands of years ago, maybe ten or twenty thousand years ago.

Benz examined the smooth compact. Was this disintegrator of human manufacture?

He pocketed the deadly device, but still did not move farther into the ready room.

Who had ever heard of a real-life empath? Benz hadn't until this moment. Humans did not possess telepathy, empathy or other so-called psionic powers. That was just another term for magic. There weren't any wizards in real life, any sorcerers or witches, not in the accepted norm of spells that teleported or changed people's minds against their wills.

Benz moved woodenly into the ready room. He had to figure something out fast. He was going to need people to remove the dead. When they saw the carnage on the bridge…

That could topple him from power right there.

"You have to think, Frank," Benz told himself. "You have to act like the smartest person in the Solar System, not just talk about it."

Benz nodded as if fortifying his heart for what he had to do. He marched into the ready room and knelt beside the black-clad empath.

He touched the corpse. It seemed far too cool already. He leaned over and rose abruptly. He went to his desk, rummaged in a bottom drawer and came back with a small penknife.

He cut the corpse. He wasn't sure what he hoped to find. That the outer layer of skin proved to be a false covering shocked him to the core.

The penknife dropped from his nerveless fingers. Benz panted as he knelt there.

Soon, his forehead furrowed. He picked up the penknife and carefully inserted the tip of the blade between the human skin and the lightly bluish scales underneath. He peeled away the human flesh, the pseudo human-skin, and revealed—

"What is this?" he whispered.

He peeled more until he revealed the scale-like skin underneath on the left forearm. They were moist like a fish's scales.

This was an alien.

Correction, the dead thing on the floor *had* been an alien. It was a corpse now. What did that mean, though, that an alien empath and a…

Benz stood in a wooden manner and stepped beside the Party Secretary's corpse. It was just as cool as the empath's.

The creature—the empath—had definitely hit him with some kind of telepathic power. How had such aliens arrived on Mars? How long had they been here? How had an alien in pseudo human-skin come to run the Mars Social Dynamic Union?

"Why did you come alone into my office?" he asked the two corpses. "What did you hope to achieve?"

Benz stepped back until he bumped up against his desk. The aliens had come up here to gain control of the cybership. What had the one called it? A starship.

"Right," Benz said.

The aliens wanted the cybership because it could cruise between the stars. They were going to grab it and do what—leave the Solar System?

He needed Vela. He needed to clean up the ready room and the bridge. He needed a good cover story—

Frank Benz gave a harsh caw of laughter. He had it. He knew what he was going to do. This could work. It could really work. Not only that, but it might actually cement his power so he could run the Mars Unity with true authority and assurance.

"This could be just what I need," he said—if he played it right, and if he could convince the right people from the get-go. It was time to find Vela. He needed her expertise to help make this thing airtight.

-4-

The hatch to the bridge slid open and Vela Shaw almost collapsed with relief into Benz's arms.

"You're alive," she said, coming to him. She laughed as he hugged her. "I'm alive," she said into his right ear. "I thought—"

She gasped in what might have been horror. The strength left her knees. If Benz hadn't been holding on to her, she would have likely hit the deck.

When he felt her strength return, Benz let go.

"Frank," she whispered, as she stared at the carnage on the bridge, at the countless dead.

Benz turned toward the carnage, although he glanced at her to see how she'd take it.

Vela was startlingly beautiful with long blonde hair and green eyes of great intensity. She wore a Martian Fleet uniform, red with black. It helped highlight her beauty.

That beauty was how Benz had come to find her. Not so long ago, Secret Police Chief J.P. Justinian had raped Vela on Earth. She had been seething for vengeance. That wishing had gotten her into grave trouble when Justinian became the Premier of the Solar League. Benz had saved her life, giving her the same intelligence-heightening treatment that he'd received and had convinced her to enlist in his struggle. Along the way, the two of them had become lovers.

Now, Benz didn't know what he'd do without her. It wasn't simply her remarkable beauty. She was possibly the only one smart enough to appreciate his genius, and certainly the only one smart enough to help him.

"You killed them?" Vela whispered.

Benz nodded.

"How did you manage it?" she asked.

Over the ship's comm, Benz had requested that she come alone to the bridge. The people who had been holding her apparently hadn't recognized his voice. He'd used a scrambler, so that had probably helped. No doubt, those people had figured Vela was going to her death.

Benz took the compact disintegrator out of his jacket pocket.

Vela frowned at it.

"The thing has a nozzle as if it's a weapon," she said.

He began to tell her what had happened, although he left out how he'd acquired the disintegrator.

Vela nodded as she listened.

"I wouldn't believe you regarding that thing," she said, "except that I see the evidence before my eyes. It must really be able to do what you say. Here's the problem, though. Where did you get it?"

"I'll show you," Benz said.

Vela stared at him. "Do I want to see this?" she asked.

"Most definitely," he said.

She considered that and finally nodded.

As Benz led her to the ready room, he described the Party Secretary's arrival with the black-clad empath. By the time they weaved a path through the dead coup plotters, Benz had explained how he picked up the heavy glass object and hurled it at the Party Secretary's forehead.

They stepped into the ready room. Benz raised his arm to indicate the two dead beings.

Vela stared at him.

"Do you see?" Benz asked her.

Vela shook her head.

He put a hand on her left elbow, guiding her to the dead empath.

Vela gasped, pulling away from him as she covered her mouth. She turned to Benz with horror and with understanding.

"Aliens," she whispered.

Benz nodded.

"Where did they come from?" she asked.

"Out there is the clear but vague answer," Benz said with a wave behind him. "It would be good to know *when* they arrived."

Vela's lids hooded her eyes as she thought about that. She nodded a moment later.

"Do you think these aliens fled from the AIs?" she asked.

"I deem that the most likely answer."

"To hide on Earth? Well, the Solar System, I presume."

"Exactly," he said.

"When did 'Anna Dominguez' take over the Mars SDU Party?"

"We'll have to check the history tapes. First, though, we have to clean up the bridge."

Vela appeared thoughtful. "You're going to need a cover story."

Benz couldn't hold it in any longer. He exposed his teeth in a fierce smile.

"What is it?" she asked. "Why are you—?" Her eyebrows arched as understanding hit her.

"This is exactly what I need—what we need," Benz said. "Aliens have infiltrated the Mars Party. Now I'm going to say that I had the foresight to sniff them out of hiding. That's why they came up here. The aliens had to kill me before I uncovered them. The Martians aiding the aliens are traitors to humanity. Anyone opposing me will be painted as anti-human."

"That's clever," Vela said. "But I foresee a problem."

"I'm listening."

"Given the gravity of our larger problem, we should enlist the aliens to help us against the AIs."

"Why do you believe there are more aliens on Mars? These two could be it."

"Do you really believe that?" Vela asked. "I mean, think through the implications of their existence and their positions in Martian society."

Benz bent his head as he truly began to think. He correlated possibilities with probabilities. After a time, his head snapped up as he stared at Vela.

"There's likely a small colony of aliens on Mars," Benz said.

Vela nodded.

"We could use the help of these aliens," Benz said, "use their greater knowledge about the AIs and their knowledge about the interstellar situation. If the aliens are here and have this superior technology—" he raised the disintegrator— "it stands to reason they arrived here in hyperspace-capable vessels of their own."

"I tend to think they no longer have such vessels," Vela said.

"Yes… I agree. Unless they've grown arrogant."

"That is only a small possibility," Vela said.

"I'd grant it as a large possibility," Benz said. "I spoke to them, remember? These aliens are arrogant. Besides, by coming to my office alone they showed overwhelming arrogance. Their misstep is what allowed me my opportunity."

"I can see that," Vela said. "But that still doesn't solve our problem. If we use these aliens as our scapegoat, and as a means of unifying the Martians behind us, we're going to have a difficult time letting the aliens aid us against the AIs. Public pressure might force us into having to kill them all."

Benz could see that possibility.

Whipping up a nation or world against another group made it difficult later. Once people's emotions were stirred so strongly, they demanded blood. In this case, they would want alien blood. However, the more he whipped up Martian hatred against the hidden aliens, the more the Martians would potentially rally behind him.

"Well…?" Vela asked. "What's the verdict? You'd better decide now so we know how to explain your slaughter up here."

Benz sighed a moment later.

"I don't see that I have a choice," he said. "I have to explain this in a way that will mollify the rest of the crew, with me slaughtering everyone on the bridge. I need a mortal danger against all of us in order to ensure your survival and mine."

"I'm afraid I agree," Vela said sadly.

"That's not going to make it easy for us to encourage these hidden aliens to help us later."

"We have to capture some if we can," Vela said.

Benz nodded. He would like to make these aliens his allies. Humanity needed help. But he needed to cement his political position as leader before he did anything else.

"Are you ready?" Benz asked Vela.

She took a deep breath, nodding a moment later.

"Then let's cook up a good cover story and get started," Benz said. "I'm sure many people are waiting for the outcome up here. If we wait too long…"

"I know," Vela said. "And I think I know exactly how we should proceed."

Benz listened to her, soon grinning, liking his woman's plan.

-5-

It turned out that the highest ranked members of the conspiracy had been on the *Gilgamesh's* bridge. Likely, they'd wanted to be there for the aftermath in order to grab more power at the earliest opportunity.

Killing the ringleaders helped throw Benz's most determined enemies into disarray. The conspiratorial organizations wasted time as the underlings struggled for the new primacy.

That allowed Benz and Vela time to recruit angry Martians hungry to destroy the secret aliens. The key was in acquiring the head of the Martian secret police and the fierce loyalty of the Martian space marines.

During the coming days, Benz worked tirelessly from his office aboard the *Gilgamesh.* As he did, concentrating on acquiring dominating political control, Vela hunted for traitors aboard ship even as she built up the number of Martians who realized that Benz had saved them and that Benz had the acuity to turn Mars into a powerhouse.

The days passed with the two of them working brutally long hours. The disintegrator and the two corpses became symbols of alien oppression. Propaganda moved Martians to the conclusion that these hidden aliens had helped bring the AIs to Mars. A year and a half ago, the attacking cyberships had dropped hell-burners on the planet. The enemy cyberships had slaughtered hundreds of millions of Martians, more than forty percent of the population. It was thus easy to whip up the people into a frenzy of hatred against the alien spies responsible for the destruction—that was the PR story, at least.

So far, though, after two weeks of neighbors watching neighbors and kids their parents, no genuine aliens had turned up. Oh, there had been endless calls and police searches. Many people had accused many others, but the police hadn't yet gotten their hands on an alien spy.

Benz did use the opportunity to clean out the former Party Secretary's political apparatus. Everyone with a connection to her, everyone with a connection to Benz's most zealous political opponents either died by noose or pistol or found themselves incarcerated at the secret police's most notorious prison, the Alamo.

It wasn't pretty. In truth, the process was ugly and bloody. Grabbing political power directly usually was. Benz didn't believe he had a lot of time left. In some instances, he tried to be smooth, but ended up having too many angry people working for him. They crushed the opposition as the opposition had almost given Mars and the Asteroid Belt to aliens—at least in people's mind that was true.

The Red Planet seethed with this growing alien hatred, which fueled the increased alien hunting, turning Mars into a hotbed of activity. During the next few weeks, Benz hammered out new policies that would consolidate his power in time.

For a while, at least, the people of Mars, and Benz and Vela, forgot about the AIs and the stealth pods most likely sprinkled throughout the Solar System. They were too intent on ferreting out the alien spies on Mars.

Then, the secret police discovered a genuine alien. They only found out he was an alien after shooting him, though.

An alert major noticed something amiss after the body slumped in the courtyard. The major marched to the corpse, took out a knife and peeled away pseudo skin to reveal moist and lightly blue-colored scales.

Armored air-cars raced to a special facility of the Ares Corporation outside the city of Latium. The alien spy had come from there. The arresting police put every worker into police vans. Then, teams hunted through the facility, searching every cranny for secret doors to hidden hideaways.

The interrogators had everyone put in restraints. Thirteen hours after the first air-car landed at the main facility, the interrogators found their first living alien.

The chief of secret police, Rafael Franco, promptly contacted Benz.

The Premier was in his ready room, regarding the holoimage before him. Franco was a small man with a vintage Roman nose. He never looked a person directly in the eyes, seemingly too shy to do that.

"Excellent work, Chief," Benz told the man. "I commend you on ferreting out this creature."

Franco sat utterly still, as if absorbing the praise into his pores. "I believe the alien is female, Excellency."

"Oh?" Benz said.

"She swore to her interrogator that she would be cooperative. She obviously desires to live, Excellency. But I doubt her word."

"Why is that?"

"During her capture, she slew twenty-seven operatives. She also ignited the grounds behind her. We found massive amounts of strange alloys. My top scientists believe it was some kind of space vehicle."

Benz couldn't believe this. It was worse than he'd expected. Strange alloys—could the alien have destroyed a special type of space vessel?

As he ruminated, Benz noticed the secret police chief watching him stealthily. It was most carefully done. Franco was dangerous. He mustn't ever forget that. What would the man expect from him…?

"Is the alien allergic to pain?" asked Benz, trying to find out if Franco had tortured her.

Franco grinned slyly, actually looking up at Benz for just a moment. He quickly looked down afterward.

"She is, Excellency."

Benz appeared to be in deep thought. He already knew what he wanted. The alien could be a goldmine of information. This was fantastic.

"Use your top operatives, Chief. This must work flawlessly. They will escort the alien via shuttle to the *Gilgamesh*."

Franco sat utterly still as his features appeared to harden.

"And if the alien dies during the ascent, Excellency?" the chief of secret police asked.

Benz became hyper-alert. What was the man's problem?

"Why would you suspect such an accident?" Benz asked.

Franco spoke in a clipped manner. "She is an alien. She is dangerous. I have come to believe that she has psionic powers?"

Benz wished he'd never included in his original report the empathic and telepathic powers of the black-clad alien.

"In my opinion, Excellency, having her aboard the cybership would be the worst place for her. It would put her too close…" Franco looked up, and his normally placid eyes seemed to burn with passion. "It would put her within striking range of our primary source of military power. If the alien gained control of the *Gilgamesh*, she could destroy Mars."

As abruptly as the zealousness appeared, it vanished, and Franco looked down, almost as if he didn't realize what he'd just said.

Benz thought he understood. The secret police chief would make sure the alien died before he allowed her upstairs aboard the *Gilgamesh*. The chief was a true believer, wishing to hunt down and destroy the alien menace. Likely, it's why the chief had thrown in his support so readily at the beginning.

"You raise an interesting point," Benz said. "I must study the situation further. Until that time, keep the alien under tight security in the Alamo."

"You may count on me, Excellency."

Benz nodded slowly, wondering—

The hatch opened and Vela rushed in. She looked pale and obviously wanted to tell him something.

"Just a moment, Chief," Benz said, muting the connection. "What is it?" he asked Vela.

"A cybership has appeared," she blurted. "It's at the inner edge of the Oort cloud."

"What? A cybership?"

Vela nodded miserably.

Benz inhaled deeply, expanding his chest. Franco and his captured alien would have to wait.

-6-

The AI Invasion Scare lasted until the first light-speed message arrived from the *Nathan Graham* between the scattered disc and the Oort cloud.

A few high-level people in the Outer Planets remained suspicious, thinking the *Nathan Graham* may have stumbled upon waiting AI vessels out there in the void. According to the theory, the AI cyberships had stormed the Earth-run vessel, learned the truth about the Solar System and now practiced deception for a massive assault.

That theory died after a few back and forth messages, confirming that Jon Hawkins spoke to them and not some AI illusion.

The *Nathan Graham* accelerated for the dwarf planet of Makemake in the Kuiper Belt. As it did, Hawkins sent a tight-beam message to the *Gilgamesh.*

"Greetings, Premier Benz. I realize our quick return might seem strange to you or possibly an act of cowardice, but it is nothing of the kind. We have stumbled upon an amazing discovery.

"AI stealth pods hid on our hull. They attached themselves during our time at the edge of the Asteroid Belt. I suspect the *Gilgamesh* may have similar stealth pods attached to it. I urge you to check at once. But take care. The robots may attempt to convert one or more of your people in an attempt to get near enough to assassinate you.

"We scoured our hull a second time and found a master unit. Eventually, we broke its programming and learned of an AI Battle Station in the Allamu System 17.2 light years from the Solar System.

"We have come to believe that this battle station is the key AI military outpost in our local sector of space. It will have cyberships, repair and construction yards and many other military supplies and, no doubt, stellar maps of the local star systems.

"It is our belief that if we can storm and capture the battle station, that we can then arm humanity with more cyberships and possibly discover several alien allies in the nearby star systems.

"Now is the time to use our operational secret weapon in the Allamu System. I refer to the AI virus you and Bast Banbeck created during the Battle of Mars. However, the *Nathan Graham* cannot storm this battle station alone. We need help. We need reinforcements.

"I have already instructed the construction yard of Makemake's moon to begin preparation for launching the partially completed vessel. I have contacted Kalvin Caracalla of Saturn to begin sending space marines and techs to Makemake. The *Nathan Graham* will supply the new cybership with its command crew.

"Together with the *Gilgamesh*, I believe we have an excellent chance of success. Thus, I urge you to begin acceleration for Makemake. Bring all the Martian space marines you can spare. This is likely going to be a grueling battle. But this is the great opportunity to turn the tide in our sector of the Orion Arm.

"Please notify me of any concerns. But know this, Premier. Time is likely critical. There are stealth pods in the Solar System. We must move before they can engineer a counter action or summon enemy cyberships against us.

"Commander Jon Hawkins out."

Benz and Vela carefully considered Hawkins' plan of action. They had objections, one big objection in particular.

Soon, Benz sat at the desk in his ready room as he sent his reply to the *Nathan Graham* heading for the scattered disc region.

"Hello, Commander Hawkins. I am pleased to learn the *Nathan Graham* has successfully used hyperspace to travel away from and return to the Solar System. That is excellent news. We now know without a doubt that we have an interstellar-faring vessel.

"That being said, I am concerned that you have not thought through all the ramifications of your plan. It is bold, to say the least. It might also prove risky, as we have no idea of the military power of the battle station and its accompanying cyberships—and whatever else the AIs have in the Allamu System.

"There is also the possibility that this is an elaborate trap. There is the possibility the AIs are attempting to lure our best ships away from the Solar System so they can attack us here.

"The existence of the robot stealth units in our Solar System supports this theory. Surely, those stealth units have a communication link with a guiding AI.

"Even if that is not the case, there is another worry. The Solar League will note the departure of three cyberships. Once our three great vessels leave, the Mars Unity and the SFF will be in a weaker military position compared to Earth's Solar League.

"I fear that once the *Gilgamesh* leaves on this risky venture, the Solar League will directly attack Mars. I therefore ask you, what good is it to defeat the AIs if the Solar League destroys our home?

"Perhaps a lightning raid with the *Nathan Graham* and your second cybership would pay the greatest dividends with the least risk to our united effort.

"Surely you can understand that I cannot in good conscience leave Mars defenseless against the predatory and ruthless Solar League. I have dealt with those people, and I know to what lengths they will go to teach Mars a bitter lesson for having left the league.

"Thus, I am afraid I will have to disappoint you, sir. I applaud your boldness. I will also certainly begin an immediate and thorough search of the *Gilgamesh's* hull. Thank you for your confidence and for your valiant effort against our mutual enemy.

"The Premier of the Mars Unity salutes you, sir."

In time, an answer returned from the *Nathan Graham*.

"Premier Benz," Jon Hawkins said from his command chair on the *Nathan Graham's* bridge. "I applaud your common sense and desire to give Mars and the Asteroid Belt the greatest protection possible. You are a true and great leader.

"However, I would be at fault if I did not point out a salient fact. The leaders of the Solar League have committed a grave strategic error. They built up their defenses for a united cybership assault against Earth. I am referring to their constant adding of orbital defensive satellites. It was and is an impressive display of determination to defend the home world. I applaud them for that.

"What they have not done is significantly increase the number and strength of the Earth Fleet. The same can be said, although on a lesser scale, for Venus and the Venus Fleet. That means the Solar League is *not* in position to mount a credible attack against Mars.

"Clearly, their combined fleets could possibly defeat the present Mars Fleet minus the *Gilgamesh*. But I am ready to send a good portion of the Uranus and Saturn fleets to Mars in order to add fifty to one hundred percent more warships. I leave that number to your discretion, as I do not want you to worry about too many SFF warships in or near Mars orbit.

"The Solar League's strategic production error will allow us to use our three cybership in a terrible swift battle to wrench the initiative from the AI enemy.

"Premier Benz, do not be deceived. We are about to launch the battle that could decide humanity's fate. A half-assed assault with two cyberships is madness when we have the ability to launch a fifty percent heavier assault with *three* cyberships.

"This isn't the time for squeamishness or too much caution. This is the moment for an aggressive attack. Either we do this together and win, or we go our separate ways and lose alone.

“The choice is yours, Premier Benz. I pray you decide to take the manly route.

“Commander Hawkins out.”

-7-

"Take the *manly* route," Benz said as he struck the desk in his ready room. "Did you hear that? Take the manly route. That is as good as accusing me of cowardice."

"I doubt he meant it like that," Vela said in a soothing voice.

Benz glared at her.

"Of course Hawkins meant it like that. He believes himself to be the great conqueror, the daring man of action who saved the Solar System three times already. He as good as told me to emulate him and act like a man. I am very much a man."

"No one thinks otherwise," Vela said.

Benz's eyes narrowed.

"Did you hear him or not?" he asked. "Should I play the message back for you?"

"There's no need," Vela said. "I heard what he said."

"Are you suggesting that wasn't an insult?"

"Premier—"

"No, Vela," Benz said. "Don't play word games with me of all people. You know what he said and you know what he meant."

"Maybe Hawkins thought to stir you to action by saying what he did."

"Ha!" Benz said. "I'll stir *him* to action. Does he think a man leaps to a deed because of a few words? Does he believe that he's stronger and more dangerous than me?"

"Frank—"

Vela's words died in her throat as Benz whipped around to glare at her.

Finally, Benz turned away. "I shouldn't get so angry," he said.

Vela said nothing.

Benz massaged his forehead, squinting for a moment.

"I'd like to know if Hawkins could have taken out a bridge full of enemies by himself. I'd like to know if Hawkins could have fought free of a telepathic alien? *Those* were manly actions.

"Yes," Vela said quietly.

Benz slapped the table and shoved up to his feet. He shook his head and finally flung his hands into the air.

"He's a mercenary, a dome rat from Titan," Benz said. "He used to be a criminal according to my sources. He probably used that kind of talk to motivate his fellow criminals."

"He was a gang member as a youth," Vela said. "He grew up in a rough—"

"Don't defend him," Benz said.

"Premier," Vela said. "You must cease this display of bravado. You're the great strategist. You're the man who has accomplished the impossible against staggering odds."

"Some might say that about Hawkins."

"He never worked alone," Vela said. "You worked against an entire world apparatus and defeated it. That took more than reckless courage. That took incredible feats of thought. A wild man charging an enemy displays raw courage. A thoughtful man knowing the odds and going ahead anyway displays superior courage that doesn't wilt at the first check."

Benz grunted as he nodded. After a moment, he sat down again.

"If I could point out something else…" Vela said.

Benz examined her. Finally, he grinned, waving a hand for her to speak.

"The last phrase indicates that Hawkins doesn't realize who he's dealing with," she said. "That's to our benefit. It means when the time comes to take full control of humanity's destiny…"

"That's a good point," Benz said. "Hawkins has courage. I have courage plus intellect. In the end, brain defeats brawn."

"Exactly," Vela said.

Benz laughed ruefully. "I overreacted," he told her.

Vela did not reply.

Benz leaned back in his chair. He nodded once more. Finally, he put his hands on the edge of the desk and regarded Vela.

"The brute has a point, though, about the Solar League. They have miscalculated. I should have already seen that."

"You would have soon enough," Vela said.

"True," Benz said. "That leaves us with an interesting dilemma. It's possible that, despite his over-reliance on reckless ventures, Hawkins has stumbled upon the correct strategy. This could be the moment to attack the battle station."

"And if this is an AI trap?" Vela asked.

Benz bent his head in thought.

"Oh," he said shortly. "The answer is simple. We'll come out of hyperspace in the Allamu Oort cloud. We'll have plenty of time to observe the star system as we accelerate inward. If it's a trap, we'll see that far ahead of time. We can retreat at that point."

It was Vela's turn to ponder.

"There's a different problem with his plan," she said. "Hawkins will have two cyberships to our one. That will give him greater power at the place of decision. That means he'll likely have a greater say as to who gets whatever new cyberships we capture at the battle station."

"That's assuming I'll agree to his assault."

"There's a third problem," Vela said. "If you agree, he'll have a two to one advantage against us as we're far from home. What is to stop him from attempting to overpower the *Gilgamesh* and thereby ensuring his rule in the Solar System?"

"Do you think he's lying about the battle station in order to get us out there alone with his two ships?"

"It's a possibility we should consider," Vela said.

"Hmm..." Benz said. "Perhaps we should thoroughly search our outer hull. If Hawkins' people found a robot stealth unit, it stands to reason the robots did the same to us. Since

Hawkins' people broke the thing's programming, we can surely do the same."

"And if the robot unit possesses the same battle-station information?" Vela asked.

"Yes..." Benz said. "Two to one against us far from the Solar System; Hawkins could concoct whatever story he desired if his was the only ship to return home."

"Still," Vela said. "We should remember that up until this point, Hawkins has seemed trustworthy."

"Yet, what about *after* a successful fight against this battle station?" asked Benz. "What about after the AI pressure lessens against us, given our victory in the Allamu System?"

"What do you think we should do?"

Benz stood, walked to the ready-room window and leaned against the wall, staring down at Mars. He stared for quite some time. Finally, a sly smile played across his lips.

He straightened and turned to Vela.

"I have an idea," Benz said. "It's a long shot, but it uses our one possible advantage, and it might give us an edge over the mercenary."

-8-

Vela watched as battlesuited space marines clanked across the hangar-bay deck toward the shuttles headed for the Red Planet below.

"Frank," she said. "This…" She indicated the five armored shuttles—dropships, in essence—as battlesuited space marines continued to clank into the holds.

"What's the matter?" Benz asked, seemingly genuinely perplexed.

"Do you plan to storm the secret police headquarters?" Vela asked.

"If I should, I will," Benz said, his features hardening.

They were in a giant hangar bay aboard the *Gilgamesh*. Five dropships and a shuttle were almost ready for the journey to the Martian surface.

"Let's go," Benz said.

Vela walked across the deck with him toward the waiting shuttle. Something wasn't right about all this, and she couldn't quite put a finger on it. Earlier in his ready room, after listening to Hawkins telling the Premier to man up, Benz had lost it. Vela had never seen anything like it before. Now, this ham-fisted approach with five dropships…what could account for Benz's shift in behavior?

As Benz climbed the steps into the shuttle, he chuckled as he rubbed his hands, almost in glee.

Vela worked to keep her face neutral. Something was off with Benz, but what was it?

I must think.

Vela used the extra brainpower bequeathed to her by Benz's fantastic machine. Nothing had been the same for her since she went under it. The things she could see and comprehend—it had opened up her world. It had also taken some of the shine off the universe.

With greater wisdom—if that's what she had—came greater sorrow because she understood things more deeply. She hadn't figured out why that should be, but there it was just the same.

Why would Benz—?

Vela turned to stare at Benz in shock. The Premier was sitting down in a shuttle passenger seat. He happened to look up at her. He noticed her shock. That hardened something in him as his eyes narrowed.

"What's wrong?" he asked.

Vela smiled, recovering fast. If she was right about this…

"Well?" Benz asked.

"I completely forgot," Vela said breathlessly. "I'm supposed to prepare a speech, the one you're giving tomorrow to the Grand Assembly. Do you remember?"

"Of course I remember," he said in an irritated voice.

"I haven't done a thing on it," Vela said, which was a lie. She'd already written the speech.

"Forget about the speech," Benz said.

"I can't," Vela said. "It's too important. I need to get started on it. If we're going with Hawkins—"

"Who said we are?" Benz snapped.

"I thought—"

"Never mind," Benz said. "I imagine we are. Yes. The speech needs to be perfect. You can work on it when we return to the *Gilgamesh.*"

"I should begin now," Vela said. "Besides, you don't really need me for this. A quick snatch and—"

"That isn't what's bothering you," Benz said, as he examined her.

Vela searched his eyes. She was going to have to play this closer to the vest, but she was going to have to be more honest, too. Benz was too cunning to do it any other way.

"You're right," Vela admitted. "The secret police—" She shook her head. "You of all people should realize how much secret police frighten me."

Benz had gone into the secret police headquarters on Earth and rescued her from their tender tentacles. The things they would have done to her—Vela shuddered whenever she thought about it too much.

"I suppose I can understand," he conceded roughly. "Yes. That makes more sense than this speech nonsense. You want to stay behind?"

Vela nodded.

"You'd better hurry off then," Benz said. "We're leaving in another minute."

"Let me know as soon as you're successful," Vela said as she stood. "I'll add that to the speech—"

"Why wouldn't I be successful?" Benz asked.

Vela shook her head.

"You don't think I'm capable of this?" he asked.

"Frank—"

"No," he said, waving a hand and then rubbing the bridge of his nose. "I'm sorry. I shouldn't have said that."

Now she really knew that something was wrong with him. Frank Benz never apologized about this sort of thing. She had to get to work right away. If she could figure out a counter measure for what was bothering him—

Vela reached down and touched a forearm. "Good luck, darling."

Benz grunted.

Vela hurried off the shuttle. Once she was in the hangar bay, she began to sprint for a corridor flitter. She had to get to a laboratory as fast as she could. She thought she finally understood the reason for this difference in him.

-9-

Benz rubbed his forehead as the shuttle exited the hangar bay. What had really been wrong with Vela? She'd seemed fine one minute and then suddenly she'd become worried.

No. That wasn't exactly right.

Benz massaged his forehead. His mind felt foggy and he didn't know why. His thinking seemed slightly off. Certainly, his emotions were getting the better of him lately. He still couldn't understand why he'd gotten so angry with Hawkins. That wasn't like him.

Benz sighed, sat back and then sat up, pulling out a hand monitor. He clicked it on so he could watch the convoy's progress.

The Red Planet spread out below them, while the *Gilgamesh* was already behind them higher in orbit. The convoy headed down toward a light reddish region. It was the customary color of Mars. The reddish color came from ferric oxide—rusted iron! The rust indicated minute particles of water mixed in the sandy soil.

Benz noticed a large dust storm to the west of where they were heading. Some of the Martian dust storms could become global and dangerous. For his purposes, this one wasn't going to be a problem.

He couldn't miss the huge canyon, Valles Marineris. The chasm was an amazing 5000 kilometers long, the length of the old United States. In some areas, the chasm was 500 kilometers wide. The convoy would go down into the canyon to the capital city of Athena on the bottom. More precisely, they were headed for the secret police headquarters in Athena Dome, for the Alamo.

Once he got there, would Franco continue to insist on holding the alien? One hundred and fifty armored space marines piled in Franco's outer offices might be a convincing argument.

Benz grinned while thinking about it.

At that point, Franco would be more concerned with keeping his life than holding onto the alien.

Benz exhaled sharply as he continued to watch the hand monitor.

He'd stayed aboard the *Gilgamesh* all this time because the cybership was the seat of his power. He was also safer while aboard. He certainly wasn't as safe in a shuttle. A single missile could take him out.

But if a man never took any risks—Benz cocked his head. That seemed like an odd thought. He'd taken plenty of risks in his life. Why would he think a shuttle ride was dangerous? That didn't make sense.

Benz chewed that over and finally shut off the hand monitor. He began to ready himself mentally for the coming confrontation with Franco.

***

The shuttle and dropships came down from space, heading for the Valles Marineris Canyon. The chief pilot supplied the correct codes to the Planetary Watch, and the vessels soon skimmed the Martian surface, went over the lip and down into the shadowy canyon. Soon, Athena Dome appeared. It was a vast structure near one cliff and housed over fifteen million people.

The shuttle and dropships slowed as they approached the giant dome. Missiles and laser batteries tracked them. That was common Martian practice. If the shuttle and dropships strayed too near a dome, missiles and heavy lasers would take them out in order to protect the dome's integrity.

Terrorists had taken down Martian domes before. This was an old precaution against possibly hijacked vessels.

Finally, the shuttle and dropships landed at a military airstrip many kilometers from Athena Dome. Benz transferred to a ground effects vehicle, as did his security detail and the 150 space marines.

The convoy took off for the distant dome.

They headed toward a military entrance, using a military route instead of the public tube system. Benz's convoy waited ten minutes at the gate due to clearance problems. Benz might have solved the problem by showing himself and demanding immediate entrance. That would give away his presence, however, something he wanted hidden for just a little longer. Finally, the convoy entered the great dome.

Athena was in shadow. It was most of the time. Great sunlamps shined down from the grand dome ceiling. The dome was at a little past noontime. It appeared that most of the day workers had already returned to their offices from lunch.

Athena had little car or flitter traffic, but thousands of bicyclists.

The convoy headed for the large, square-shaped Alamo. Benz rode in the back of his larger-than-average GEV, secured in place in case they had to use violent maneuvers.

His security chief looked up, touching the bud in his ear. He glanced at Benz.

"Trouble?" asked Benz.

"There's a call from Rafael Franco," the security honcho said.

Benz felt a slight queasiness in his gut. Did the secret police chief know he was in the city?

The Premier unbuckled, went to a desk and flipped on a comm screen. This was a commander's GEV and thus outfitted with command and control tech. In a second, the screen showed the intense face of Rafael Franco. The man did not look down or aside this time, but directly at Benz.

"Premier," Franco said stiffly. "You're in the city."

Benz did not reply.

"You appear to be on a direct route to our security facilities. Are you going to pay us a visit, Excellency?"

"Do you have anything to hide?" Benz asked.

"On the contrary. I'm pleased you're coming. I have a—" Franco rubbed his forehead. "I have—" He rubbed his forehead more and frowned, as if he wanted to say something but could not.

"I should be there shortly," Benz said. "First, I want to stop off at the Grand Assembly."

"Oh," Franco said. "We still have a few hours until you arrive at the Alamo?"

Benz smiled good-naturedly. He was lying. The convoy was headed directly for the Alamo. He didn't want to give Franco any extra notice if he could help it. At this point, though, Benz didn't want to lie more than necessary either.

"Does…umm…this have anything to do with the alien?" Franco asked.

"How is she faring?" Benz countered.

Franco shrugged even as he massaged his forehead again.

Benz was beginning to believe the gesture implied something. Franco's intense stare also meant something, but he wasn't sure what.

"The alien is weak," the secret police chief was saying. "We might lose her before we can finish our interrogations. That would be…unfortunate."

Benz frowned. Why hadn't Franco said anything about this earlier? "I'll want more details once I arrive."

"Yes, Excellency," the secret police chief said.

"I have to go," Benz said.

It almost seemed as if Franco grinned ever so slightly. That must have been an illusion, though. What would the man have to grin about?

The screen went blank.

Benz sat at the console, thinking. Something was wrong, but he couldn't figure out what. Was the secret police chief about to outmaneuver him? For a wild moment, Benz almost ordered the convoy to turn around and head back to the dropships. The Premier suddenly felt naked and exposed down here.

I should have stayed on the Gilgamesh.

Benz was on the verge of ordering a turn-around…when he rubbed his forehead. He was getting a headache.

With a sigh, he moved back to his original seat. What could go wrong? He'd be in and out with the alien in his custody. The snatch operation should work like clockwork. He had nothing to worry about.

-10-

It turned out that Benz had plenty to worry about. He had indeed made an error in judgment concerning the secret police chief.

Twelve minutes and thirty-seven seconds after the screen went blank, the convoy ground to a halt before the Alamo. The building was larger than the secret police headquarters on Earth. It stood higher, although just as broad, covering an entire city block. That was more impressive in Athena Dome on Mars, where city space was at a greater premium.

A strange event occurred as each GEV passed tall pylons on the street leading to the Alamo. The engine in each vehicle stopped running as it passed the twin glowing pylons. What's more, the battery power also drained away and thus no longer allowed the occupants to open the hatches.

That shouldn't have been a problem for the space marines. They wore Martian battlesuits. Even though the Martian suits weren't as heavily armored as Neptunian battlesuits, each marine should have been able to easily hammer his way out of the GEV. Like the GEV engines, the battlesuits experienced an immediate power drain. That meant the marines were stuck in the battlesuits, as even the override commands no longer worked. The suits acted as individual prisons, nullifying Benz's supposedly surprise advantage.

In moments, arbiters in black uniforms raced out of the Alamo. They hurried to the command vehicle. Other lesser individuals wheeled what looked like heavy cannons, aiming them at the command GEV.

The arbiters drew handguns, aiming at the main hatch. The tallest of them nodded.

Men switched on the cannon-looking devices. They whined eerily. One of them beamed power into the batteries. The others beamed sonic rays at the GEV. Seconds later, the main hatch opened. Men staggered out of the command vehicle. Each of them clapped his hands over his ears. Each of the individuals, including Premier Benz, were in considerable pain.

The tallest arbiter chopped an arm.

The techs at the sonic cannons switched them off.

The *Gilgamesh* people gingerly took their hands away from their ears and each collapsed onto pavement as arbiters shot them with quick-acting dart guns.

The tallest arbiter led his companions to Premier Benz. The Premier looked up at them slack-faced. The dart contained a stun drug, allowing the target to remain conscious.

"Bring him," the tallest arbiter said. "The Chief is waiting."

Arbiters dragged Benz to his feet. As a group, they turned and headed for the dreaded Alamo, Benz's feet dragging across the pavement as they carried him.

***

Benz's mind began to function again as the arbiters moved down a long ramp leading into Martian bedrock. No doubt they were taking him to the interrogation chambers deep below the Alamo.

Benz almost knew despair. He had badly miscalculated Franco. Coming down to Athena Dome had been a terrible mistake. He was glad Vela had felt something wrong. She was his hole card. She had power with the *Gilgamesh*. But she would have to act quickly. If the interrogators broke him and he began issuing the wrong kind of orders…Vela might not be able to maintain command of the cybership.

Could the alien's capture be a giant fraud? Had Franco studied him from afar and realized that was the needed enticement to get the Premier down here? At this point, that seemed all too possible.

Fear began to take over in earnest as the arbiters passed through a hatch into a huge chamber. Something about the place reeked of pain and torture. Benz closed his eyes, although he refused to give up just yet. He had his wits. He—

Benz frowned.

Did he have his wits? His brain had been feeling foggy lately. What would account for that? Why would—?

The sound of boots striking marble ceased. Benz opened his eyes and raised his head. The company of black-clad arbiters stood before a great door.

"Release him," a man said in a commanding tone.

Benz swayed as his captors let go of his arms. He glanced back and saw that it was the tallest arbiter who had given the command.

Benz studied the closed faces around him. These were serious people used to wielding fear and power over others. They would not hesitate to do the chief of secret police's bidding. The last few weeks of Martian mass hysteria—

Hysteria I engineered for what I thought was my benefit. I wonder if Franco desires the premiership. I should have studied his dossier more carefully.

Benz scowled. He should have seen this coming a kilometer away. What had happened to his vaunted brainpower?

The hatch opened soundlessly. A big bruiser of a man in a scarlet uniform stood there. The man did not look Martian at all. He was beefy and muscular like a Jovian power-lifter.

The sight of such a man down here gave Benz even greater pause.

"Go," the tallest arbiter told Benz. "The Chief wants to talk to you alone."

Before Benz could say a word, the arbiters whirled around and headed away, their combined shoes striking the marble.

Soon, it was just Benz and the red-clad guard. With a shrug, Benz headed toward the man. That would be better than the bruiser having to carry him.

After Benz passed the large door, it closed behind him. The bruiser turned and headed down. Benz wondered why the man didn't say anything to him. He decided that it didn't matter as he hurried after the fast-striding bruiser. Soon, the big man reached an elevator. He pressed a button and a door slid open. The bruiser went inside, turned around and stared at Benz.

The Premier entered the elevator. The door closed and the car slid down at speed.

"Where are we going?" Benz asked.

The bruiser tilted his head to look down at him, but said nothing.

Soon, the elevator halted, the door opened and the bruiser shoved Benz so he stumbled out. The hall was narrow, almost suffocating. It was made entirely of stainless steel. Small hatches stood to either side.

Benz must have been walking too slowly, as the bruiser shoved him again from behind. The walk intensified Benz's uneasiness. This was undoubtedly the dreaded lowest level of the Alamo. Here, the worst tortures and incarcerations took place. Is this where Franco was holding the alien?

Will I end my days screaming in agony down here?

A sheen of sweat glistened on Benz's forehead and cheeks despite the coolness of the stainless steel hall. If that wasn't bad enough, Benz's tongue turned dry and his courage began to wilt inside him.

"If Hawkins can brazen it out, so can I," Benz muttered to himself.

Yet, he wondered about that. Maybe the dome rat from New London was the tougher man between them.

Benz inhaled deeply, trying to maintain his calm. The game wasn't over yet. He still had his wits. Maybe—

"Stop," the bruiser said in a harsh tone.

Benz halted, glancing back at the killer.

The man gave him an icy stare. Then he pointed.

Benz looked. A hatch had silently slid up before him. It was dark in the chamber. Were they simply going to lock him away?

Benz attempted to take another deep, and hopefully, calming breath. As he attempted that, the bruiser shoved him through the hatch and into darkness…

-11-

Benz stumbled through the darkness, struck an object with his lower shins and fell headlong, barely catching himself in time. As his palms hit the floor, the darkness vanished.

The Premier lay on the floor panting. He looked back and saw Secret Police Chief Franco lying on the floor behind him. That's what—whom—he'd tripped over. That didn't make any kind of sense.

The chief of secret police opened his eyes. He did not smile as if he'd played a practical joke. Instead, Franco looked at Benz blank-eyed. The small secret police chief climbed to his feet, adjusted his gun belt and nodded politely.

Benz checked. The secret police man had a gun in the holster. The Premier could see the black-matted butt underneath the enclosed flap.

Franco wore a black arbiter's uniform. He now stepped beside Benz and bent down to give him a hand up.

"What's wrong with you?" Benz whispered. "Why were you lying on your side in the dark?"

Franco shook his head.

Benz scowled. Was he still drugged? He looked around. The room was empty. That didn't make sense. That—

Benz froze because a realization struck him. It came as a flash of intuition, and it was also the only thing that made sense given all the facts. The Premier of the Mars Unity nodded even as he withdrew his arm from the secret police man's grasp. He knew what was going on.

Benz grasped the smaller man, pulling him to his chest. At first, Franco did nothing. Then, abruptly, the smaller, weaker man began to struggle. Benz wrestled with him. The Premier tore the holster flap open, grabbed the gun and began to draw it from the holster.

"No," Franco croaked.

Benz shoved the secret police man as hard as he could. The smaller man stumbled away, tripped and fell backward.

Swiftly, Benz clacked the automatic, putting a bullet into the firing chamber, flicked the safety, turned around, raised the gun and fired two booming shots. Each time he fired, he moved the gun into a different arc.

At that moment, the blackness returned.

Benz laughed wildly. That wasn't going to stop him now. In fact, it made no difference. He moved the gun another fraction of an arc and got off another booming shot. He did not see any flame shoot out of the barrel of the gun as he fired. That told Benz that this darkness was an illusion in his mind.

That's good, my dear Premier. That's fast thinking, too. But I grow weary of this firing. It hurts my ears.

Agonizing pain blossomed in Benz's mind.

The Premier shook his head. He refused to let the pain hinder him. As the pain throbbed, as the darkness robbed him of the ability to see, Benz decided to trust his senses. He stared into the darkness.

"Where should I shoot?" he asked under his breath.

Even as the pain made him cry out, Benz slowly swiveled around until he felt certain that this was the right direction. Amidst the pain, he raised the gun once again.

No! Stop!

Benz did not stop. He fired the automatic. He fired again as the gun bucked in his hand—and he had a terrible sense of danger. He started moving—

Something hard struck him in the gut. He doubled over, expelled air—something struck him hard on the back of the head. Benz dropped to the floor as the gun skittered away from him. Benz tried to crawl after the gun in the darkness.

The pain in his mind made him cry out in despair. He'd had his chance—

Abruptly, the pain in his mind stopped. The darkness turned into light again and the room had drastically altered.

Franco was still here, lying on a carpet. Another person leaned against the front of a desk. It was a woman. She was short, dark-haired with gray eyes and wore a black arbiter's uniform. She was ugly, although not hideous. She had a metal bar in one small hand and the secret police chief's pistol in the other. That pistol was aimed at Benz's midsection.

"You're the alien," Benz said.

"Sit in the chair over there," she said.

Benz listened carefully. The voice seemed wrong. Had the other aliens up in the *Gilgamesh* had strange voices as well and he simply hadn't been able to tell at the time?

"Will I have to kill you?" the woman asked.

Benz noticed that Franco had begun to snore softly. Had the alien done that with her mind power? He suspected so.

The Premier went to the assigned chair and sat down. The woman with the gun went to the chair behind the large desk. She sat down, although she kept the weapon aimed at him.

Benz noticed the room finally. It had black walls, with slogans painted here and there and odd photos of various arbiters.

"Is this his office?" Benz asked, indicating Franco.

The woman watched him as if he was a wasp about to fly too near her. She rested her gun hand on the desk, hunching forward because she was so small.

Benz wondered if her feet dangled from the chair like a child's might.

"Are you the alien?" he asked.

She did not answer. Instead, she raised the gun and fired several shots. The bullets struck Franco each time, making him wake up, cry out and then crumple on the carpet, twisted and dead.

Benz rose to his feet in alarm.

She moved the automatic, aiming at him again.

Benz tensed, waiting for the bullets to hit, wondering how much they were going to hurt…

-12-

After a time, Benz slumped into his chair. He felt exhausted.

The woman clicked a tiny button on the automatic, letting the magazine thump onto the desk. From an open drawer, she grabbed an extra magazine and shoved it into the chamber.

Benz realized she must have been out of bullets. He should have charged her then. He might have won.

The tiny woman continued to aim at him. She hadn't shown any emotion at any time.

"I'm the alien," she said suddenly, although she spoke in the same monotone as earlier.

Benz nodded. He'd already figured that out.

"Some minds are easier to control than others," she said. "Yours is more tiring to fool, as you have a superior intellect."

Benz would have liked to believe that, but how did he know if she was telling the truth or not?

"So the room was never dark?" Benz said. "It was just dark in my mind?"

"That is correct."

"You hid the things in the room from my eyesight," he said.

"I did."

"Why bother?" he asked.

Her eyes seemed to harden as her manner became more intense.

"I suppose you'll learn eventually," she said in her monotone. "I hate you. I hate what you've done. Do you know how long we had to work to engineer our way into a position of high authority on this planet?"

"Are you the last of your kind?" asked Benz.

"Should by some inconceivable freak occurrence I die down here, there are others ready to avenge me," she said.

"I'm not referring to those of you on Mars," Benz said, "but to your species. Did the group arriving in the Solar System represent the last gasp of a dying race?"

"Do you *want* me to kill you?" she asked.

"Why did you kill Franco?"

The intensity of her features increased. "His creatures—" She seemed incapable of speech for a time.

Benz was sure her finger tightened on the trigger due to her high emotion.

That passed as she set the gun on the desk. She kept her hands near the weapon, though. The hand that had held the gun flexed as she stretched the fingers. Maybe the gun was too heavy for her to hold for long.

How strong were these fish-scale aliens?

"Your colony was hidden at the Ares Corporation?" Benz asked.

"His men slaughtered over fifty of us before one of his butchers discovered our true identity. Can you conceive of the monstrosity of the deed? My people were slaughtered like cattle."

"Why didn't any of your people use their psionic abilities to save themselves?" Benz asked.

"You think you know things, but you do not."

"Not all of you have the power?" Benz guessed.

"Two of us could use our power on your dull mammal minds. Only two of the royal line had survived the AIs. Can you conceive of the degradation I take upon myself by *mingling* with your filthy cesspool thoughts? I despise what you creatures represent. Yet…I have shamed myself by using the power in order to attempt to further our existence."

"Why hide like you do?"

She stared at him as if were a fool.

"Why not make common cause with us against the machines?" Benz asked.

"You are animals," she said. "We are the High Folk, the Collective Souls of Dame Rama. The machines destroyed all that. Yes, we of the royal line fled our dying star system. One group fled to this dismal Solar System. I have no idea if others of my kind survived. I could well be the last of the most glorious race in the universe."

"You think pretty highly of yourselves," Benz said.

"We have a right to think that way. I suppose you might feel similarly if you found a colony of lobsters begging that you spare them the indignity of your meal at suppertime by letting them leave the cooking pot."

"I doubt it. If we had common enemies, we'd try to make common cause with lobsters."

"You are vermin. You have dull minds. You have no understanding of the beauty of the Collective. Imagine if dirt could form bodies and dirty every place they walked. That is how it feels ghosting among humans."

"I get it. To you, we stink. We stink telepathically, or however you'd say it. But the AIs have destroyed your star system. They're about to destroy ours."

"No great loss there," she said.

"Why not join us so we can help you find the rest of your kind?"

"Join you?" she said. "I would no more join you than you'd join chickens headed for the slaughter house. I will command you, however. I will use you like a tool.

"He—" she indicated the dead secret police chief "—hated me too much for me to control him for long. I have been forming a strategy, hoping to turn this witch-hunt into a killing frenzy among you lower order beasts. Now, you will take me to the *Gilgamesh.*"

"And…?" Benz asked.

"If you prove docile enough, I will use you as a figure head. I will have to install control units in your brain, of course. But that is a painless operation, so you do not need to panic."

"You think that kind of assurance is going to convince me to be your slave?"

The alien studied him. She picked up the gun, possibly seeing something in him she didn't like.

"Do you prefer to die?" she asked.

Benz thought about that. He glanced at the dead Franco and realized that could as just as easily be him. If he said he preferred death over dishonor, over mental enslavement to the murderous alien—

Benz launched himself out of the chair. He headed left, dodged right, then put his head down and charged the alien with everything in him pumping hatred. He did not feel he had to answer such an unfair question. He would choose his own way, glorious death before the dishonor of ignoble slavery.

The gun boomed. Benz felt searing pain as a bullet slammed into his torso. It hurt worse than a son of a bitch. The gun fired a second time, and another bullet struck him. This one must have hit his ribs. He almost tripped and went down. His feet tangled together—

Benz looked up and roared with rage. The alien sought to use him, control him. He wondered in that intense moment if the first alien, the black-clad empath, had done something to his mind before dying. It seemed possible. That's where the strange sense of something being wrong with him must have originated.

The alien shouted as she gripped the gun with both hands—

Benz leaped as the gun boomed, sliding across the large desk. Her first two shots must have raised the barrel of the gun. The alien had not compensated enough. As Benz slid across the desk, the bullet hissed above him in passage.

The alien tried to back away but crashed into the chair instead. She fired another shot that missed—

Benz's hands gripped her throat. His knees pushed against the back edge of the desk as he shoved himself at her, toppling them both onto the floor.

No! she said in his mind. *I can help you against Hawkins. I can tell you what he's thinking.*

Benz realized as his fingers closed on the throat—the flesh seemed softer than human flesh—that Vela must have suspected the alien's mental control. Had Vela stayed behind on the *Gilgamesh*, knowing he'd need her up there?

As the agony of the bullets lodged in him almost caused him to fall unconscious, the alien struck at him mentally again. Darkness swept over Benz's vision. He couldn't see a thing. Could not feel anything—

"Choking!" he shouted. "I'm choking you."

Did that make his fingers tighten? He didn't know. But he thought "choke her" with all his stubbornness and intellect. He might not feel the grinding of bones under his fingers—

Abruptly, he did feel flesh and bones grinding under his merciless fingers. The darkness swept away as he saw the gasping alien flail at his hands, trying to tear them loose from her throat.

"No," Benz said.

The Premier was on his knees as she lay on the floor. He began banging her head against the floor. He did it over and over. He squeezed harder—

The alien's hands dropped away from his fingers. She went limp as the life seemed to drain out of her small body.

It didn't matter. Benz continued to choke, continued to slam the back of her head against the floor. He couldn't be certain her death was only an illusion. He would not quit choking her until he slumped unconscious. That was the only way to be certain.

The hatch opened then. Arbiters cried out in rage. Some ran to the dead secret police chief. The others surrounded Benz.

"Look!" Benz said hoarsely.

He wrenched his stiff fingers from the alien's throat. Picking up a shattered pottery piece from the desk, he scratched at an arm.

There were garbled voices around him. Maybe that was the arbiters asking questions. Benz no longer knew. Everything seemed to swirl around him.

He peeled away some of the pseudo skin from her right arm. It revealed the strangely moist blue fish-scales underneath. At that point, Benz toppled sideways, fading into unconscious with his jacket and pants soaked with his own blood.

-13-

Benz dreamed strangely in odd fits and starts. First, he dreamed that arbiters argued over him while doctors pleaded for peace and quiet so they could save his life. Later, Benz dreamed that he rode a shuttle back up to the *Gilgamesh*. Some of his former space marines were with him. A major attempted to talk to him, but Benz dreamt that he fell asleep while the man spoke.

For a time, he did not dream, although he had hazy ideas. They were quite unformed and indistinct. At last, he dreamed that Vela hovered over him. She seemed worried. He wanted to weep with her and tell her not to worry. He wanted to let her know that he missed her.

Even in his dream, he was exhausted.

Later, the dreams changed. He wasn't so exhausted now and tears no longer dripped from Vela's eyes. She seemed relaxed, as if she waited for something to happen.

By this point, Benz had become thoroughly sick of dreaming. He wanted to wake up and find out what was happening in the real world.

Then, without any preamble or fanfare, Benz opened his eyes. He was in a hospital room. It appeared that he was the only patient. Several medical machines were hooked up to him, including some that pumped a sludgy solution through tubes attached to his left arm. That reminded Benz of the first alien imposter. She'd had tubes from her chrome-colored chair—

"Chair," he whispered.

The whisper brought people flooding into the room. They appeared to be medical personnel. He wasn't sure how long that lasted, as he closed his eyes again.

Later, he opened them again.

"Vela," he said in a hoarse voice.

She sat in a chair, reading a tablet. She lowered it, putting the tablet on a chair and rising. She put her warm hands on his left arm. Her touch felt wonderful. He tried to sit up, but a wave of weakness washed over him. That threatened to hurl him back into unconsciousness.

"Where am I?" he asked in a hoarse whisper.

"Rest, darling," Vela said. "You need to rest."

"I'm aboard the *Gilgamesh*?"

"That's right," she said, as she brushed his hair. "You're going to be fine. The doctors were worried a few days ago, as you were close to death. But you pulled through."

"The alien shot me," he whispered.

"Shhh," Vela said, putting a finger on his lips. "Rest first. We can talk all about it later."

He tried to nod. Instead, he closed his eyes and went back to sleep.

***

Eight days after the Dame Rama alien shot him, Frank Benz woke up. He was groggy, but managed to press a button until a nurse showed up.

The nurse helped prop him up so he lay against a pillow. He was incredibly weak. He could hardly raise his arms. There were tubes in them. He did not like that, as it made him feel ever weaker.

Shortly, Vela hurried into the room.

"Frank," she said.

She rushed to him, gripped his face and kissed him on the lips. She tasted wonderful.

Benz laughed weakly. He was glad to be alive. He was glad to see his woman. He was glad the alien hadn't put controls into his mind—

"Vela," he said.

"What's wrong, my darling?"

"I…I killed the alien, didn't I?"

"Oh, Frank," she said.

Vela leaned her body against him. It felt good, even though that made it harder to breathe. He wheezed hoarsely.

"Frank," she said, mortified. "You have to say something if I'm crushing you."

"You have great tits," he said. "I like them pressed against me.'

She smiled as tears welled in her eyes.

"Oh, Frank," she said, as she ran her fingers through his hair.

He closed his eyes and luxuriated in the touch.

"Go back to sleep," she said shortly.

He opened his eyes. He felt so weak, but he didn't feel like sleeping, not by a long shot.

"Vela, did I kill the alien?"

"Yes."

"How do I know that's true?" he asked.

Vela gave him a funny look. Then, understanding grew in her eyes and in her bearing.

"Yes, the alien controlled your mind for a time, didn't she?"

"She did," Benz said.

He began to tell Vela in a halting manner what had transpired in the underground chamber of the Alamo.

"Vela," he said once he'd finished. "How did I get back up here?"

"The new chief of secret police was forced to let you go," Vela said. "Oh, she tried to detain you, but I'd already gotten a video of you banging the head of the alien out into the public. The room had an automatic recorder—"

"Wait," Benz said, while frowning. "How did you get hold of the video?"

"One of the arbiters must have sent it," Vela said. "We had a secret ally, although I never found out the person's identity. The truth is we got lucky. In any case, the video included the dead Franco. I began playing that all over Mars, turning you into an even greater hero than before. In this instance, I told people the truth."

"What truth?"

"How you went down to Mars, to Athena Dome, to try to save your chief of secret police. The alien caused your space marines—well, I think you know how I explained it."

Benz smiled. He could guess, all right.

"By that time, all of Mars was cheering for you," Vela said. "To the people, any alien represents the AIs. By choking the small alien, you were choking the AIs to the people. The Great Assembly passed the laws you desired. If the new secret police chief wanted to die hideously, she could keep hold of you. The city would have stormed the Alamo, though."

Benz would have nodded, but all this talking and ingesting of data had exhausted him. He rested his head against the pillow.

He fell asleep again before he knew it.

-14-

Benz felt better after a solid ten-hour sleep. His mind didn't feel so fuzzy anymore. It also felt as if he could stand if he gave it a go.

A nurse entered with a tray of food. It might have tasted bland to Benz at one time. Today, the mush and protein drink might have been the most glorious foods he'd ever ingested.

He smacked his lips afterward, asking for more.

A doctor entered, tsking as he overheard that.

"Not just yet, Premier," the doctor said. "You've been through the grinder. I've put you on regenerative therapy. Let's stick to the routine for a few days. Maybe after that…"

Benz was happy to be eating food, happy to be alive and overjoyed that the bullets hadn't destroyed him. He was also ecstatic the alien hadn't put any control units in his brain.

"I need to get up," Benz told the doctor.

"Good. You should move, if just a little. I'll summon an aide—"

"By myself, Doctor."

"I don't advise that just yet."

"Nevertheless, that's how we'll proceed."

The doctor looked as if he might become mulish.

Vela entered. She might have overhead the arguing.

"I'll be with him," she told the doctor.

"This is against my wishes," the doctor said.

"Yes, yes," Benz said. "Let's not turn this into an issue."

The doctor inspected Benz and nodded curtly, exiting the chamber.

"Do you have to throw your rank around like that?" Vela asked.

"What good is rank if you don't throw it around?" Benz countered.

"Maybe your continued good health," she said.

"Forget about that. I want to know what's happening. I want to know—"

"That's why I'm here," Vela said. "Let's walk. I doubt you want to talk in here."

"Good idea."

As he was free of tubes, Benz rose and changed into regular clothes. The small amount of movement left him breathless. He tried not to show it, but—

"You're pale, and shaking," Vela said.

"It's nothing."

"Frank—you ought to know that you almost died. The alien—"

Benz didn't hear the rest. He felt lightheaded, faint, and barely managed to plop into a wheelchair. He sat there panting. Maybe Vela was right. Maybe he should listen to the doctor. Just how close had he come to dying? He didn't like thinking about it.

"Do you want to lie down?" Vela asked.

"No!"

"The way you say that means you do, but you don't want to show weakness. Are we going to go over the same routine you exhibited after Hawkins called—?"

"Vela," he said, maybe sharper than he'd intended.

She raised her eyebrows.

"I know…" he said. "I freaked out that day."

She gave him a look.

"I'm not freaking out now," he said.

She bent a little, nodding, agreeing with him.

"I think I know what happened," Benz said. "Or did I already tell you about that?"

"You said something about the first alien having contaminated your mind."

"Did I go into detail?"

"Not much," Vela said.

Benz had stopped shaking and his stomach no longer felt quite so queasy.

"Can you wheel me out of here?" he asked.

"Of course, darling," Vela said, moving behind the wheelchair. She began to push.

The doctor noticed in the other room. He didn't say anything, although he looked like he wanted to.

Soon, Vela wheeled Benz through an empty corridor.

"I figured you don't want too many people to see you like this," she said.

Benz was feeling queasy again because of the motion. He closed his eyes, but that only made the feeling worse. He opened them again.

"Can you stop a moment?" he asked.

Vela parked in the corridor as she stood behind him.

"I hate being so weak."

"Darling," she said, "you let the alien use your body for target practice. I imagine you charged her. Is that true?"

"Yes."

"You charged an alien with a gun?"

"She was frail," Benz said. "She set the gun down for a while because it was too heavy for her. After that, I figured she lacked the strength to use the gun skillfully. I clearly miscalculated, but not utterly so, as I'm still alive. I wonder how old she was."

"What makes you think she was old?"

"Anna Dominguez, the Party Secretary Chairwoman. I suspect the one I faced under the Alamo was the oldest of all."

"Why did she summon you to the Alamo's basement then and face you alone?"

"What else could she do?" Benz asked. "She had one real trick. She could take over one or maybe a few more people at a time. I wonder if she needed proximity in order to do that. She was all alone, Vela. She couldn't trust anyone else. She was in my mind, but I also saw a bit into her mind. She thought of herself as a Seiner. That's what they call themselves. She thought we were dirty animals. She thought it soiled her being in my mind. The AIs are arrogant, but so was she."

Benz shook his head ruefully.

"I doubt we could have ever worked together," he said. "Isn't that crazy? Maybe there are resisting aliens out there. That doesn't mean any of them are going to want to work with us. They're aliens."

"What do you mean by that?" Vela asked.

"Different. Not like us."

Vela thought about that.

"I see what you mean," she said. "We think they should be practical. But what's practical to an alien might be completely different to a human."

"Exactly," Benz said.

"So where does that leave us?"

"First," Benz said. "I believe I overacted the other day after Hawkins' message because the empath had done something to my mind when he attacked. The empath wasn't able to stop me. I could overpower his mental attack. But I suspect he seeded my mind for the last Seiner."

Benz twisted around as he tried to crane back to look at Vela.

"Why did you leave the shuttle that day while we were still in the hangar bay?" Benz asked. "Did you suspect the alien down there might have psionic powers?"

Vela nodded.

"Were you staying upstairs in order to keep control of the *Gilgamesh*?" Benz asked.

"That was part of it."

"It wouldn't have worked for long," Benz said. "The alien would have made me order you down to Mars. If you wouldn't have listened, the crew up here would have made you listen. Surely you must have realized that."

"Frank, I stayed behind in order to fashion a mind shield."

"What?" Benz asked, straining to look back at her.

Vela patted him on the shoulder as she moved in front of him.

"I suspected psionic powers," Vela said. "So, I went to a laboratory and fashioned a helmet. I used lead and created circuitry to block various electrical impulses."

"Do you think that would have worked against the Seiners?" Benz asked.

"I have no idea. I hoped so. What else could I do?"

Benz thought about that, finally smiling.

Vela wasn't smiling, though. She had a serious, worried expression.

"Okay," Benz said, noticing. "What is it now? What did you do?"

Vela squatted on her heels, putting her hands on his knees. She looked up at him, but seemed reluctant to speak.

"Tell me," he said.

"We're headed for Makemake," she said.

Benz stared at her, realizing that Vela had made a huge decision while he'd been under. Finally, he exhaled as he looked away.

"Are you angry with me?" she asked.

"No," he said, but he wouldn't look at her.

"I had to make a decision," Vela said. "I believed I knew what you were hoping to achieve by going to the Alamo. I believe you understood the alien had psionic powers. I think you wanted to grab that alien and take her along, as you wanted to use her against Hawkins, to give you an edge at least to know what he was thinking or maybe feeling as he spoke to you."

Surprised by the accuracy of the revelation, Benz glanced at Vela.

"You know me better than I realized," he said. "That's *exactly* what I was hoping for. The Seiner even offered me that. She must have read the desire in my mind. By that point, though, I no longer trusted her. All I wanted was to kill her so her kind couldn't use us—or me—again."

"I saw the video of you banging her head," Vela said. "It was brutal, but that was just the thing that made most of Mars love their leader. They could relate, as everyone wants to grab an AI by the proverbial throat and do what you did."

"Good PR," he said moodily.

Vela stood and began to pace. Finally, she whirled around and made wild gestures as she spoke:

"The problem with the aliens—the Seiners—made me realize how little time humanity must have left. We have a window of opportunity. Hawkins is right. We have the AI virus. How long will that work against them? A year? Two years? The longer we wait to make a telling blow against the AIs, the less chance we're going to have of finding such an opportunity."

"That's pure guess work," Benz said.

"No, it's not. It's logical. It's rational. Soon, the AIs are going to strike at us again. We have a target with this battle station. We have a secret weapon. Now, we have to maximize our military power. One of the most fundamental rules of war is to concentrate your strength against the enemy. I don't think humanity can afford to have us hang back at a time like this."

Benz thought about that. Said so straightforwardly, so starkly—he looked up.

Vela searched his face.

He kept looking at her. Three cyberships striking an immense AI battle station—did they even have a ghost of a chance?

"What about Mars?" Benz asked.

"You heard Hawkins. He's willing to reinforce the Mars Fleet. I think we should take him up on the offer."

"A fifty percent or one hundred percent increase?" asked Benz.

"Fifty sounds wiser," Vela said.

Benz looked to the side. He felt so worn down. He felt weak. He'd charged a gun. He'd charged a Seiner telepath. He'd killed her. He'd killed the other Seiners as well. The Seiners had infiltrated Martian society and almost made it to the top position. How many other aliens were out there? How many other aliens would hate humans or think of them as animals? Could they find *any* alien allies?

Benz considered Bast Banbeck. Yes, there were good aliens out there. To now head off into the unknown, having one ship to Hawkins' two—

"I'm not sure the *Gilgamesh* should dock at Makemake," Benz said.

"What then?" Vela asked.

"We should head for a point between the scattered disk region and the Oort cloud. I don't want to tempt Hawkins more than he can handle. If we go to Makemake, he'll have more than just two cyberships to our one. He'll have home field advantage."

"I see what you mean," Vela said. "Maybe that's why you're the Premier and not me."

A tired grin spread across his face. He'd fought so hard and traveled so far, and now he was about to fight harder and go farther. Where was this going to end?

"You made the right decision, Vela. You're right. This is our opportunity. It's time to take it and see if we can grab more than a few extra years from the AIs. It's time to see if we can begin to turn the tide of the war and play the game like big boys."

Vela's shoulders slumped.

"What's wrong now?" Benz asked.

"Nothing. It's just… I wonder if we're ever going to see the Solar System again. I wonder if I'll ever get to walk on Mars again."

"Do you miss Mars?"

"Desperately," Vela said.

"I miss Earth just as much," he said. "But maybe that's for the best. That way, we'll fight like demons so we can go home again. We have to win, Vela, or its lights out for the human race."

-15-

The *Gilgamesh* began its long acceleration for the area of space between the scattered disc region and the Oort cloud. That was a long way from Mars.

As the pirated cybership gained velocity, Martian marines went outside and scoured every inch of the hull. They didn't find any AI stealth units attached. Benz ordered the marines to try a second time. Still, they found nothing.

At the same time, a convoy of Saturn System haulers accelerated for Makemake. The haulers carried marines and technical personnel for Hawkins' second cybership.

The giant vessel was still inside Makemake's hollowed-out moon factory. The robo-builders did what they always did, working around the clock as they fashioned the monstrous cybership.

Soon, Hawkins and Benz exchanged messages. Bit by bit they worked out an agreement and an exit strategy.

Time crawled as humanity prepared for its first interstellar military mission. Both men attempted to contact the Solar League. The league ignored every attempt.

Caracalla complained about Hawkins' order to send Saturn Fleet units to Mars.

"What if the Earth Fleet bypasses Mars and heads to Saturn?" Caracalla asked Hawkins via a long-distance comm. "Saturn has less military strength than Mars does."

"It's also a lot farther to travel from Earth to Saturn," Hawkins said. "Mars Fleet could reinforce Saturn at that point."

The question brought a host of possibilities to the forefront. Once again, through long distance messaging, Hawkins and Benz attempted to work out a solution. In the end, they decided Caracalla would head the Outer Planets Strategic Council. He would determine what fleet units went where if the Solar League ever made overt moves once the cyberships departed the Solar System.

"There's so little chance of that happening, though," Hawkins told Caracalla, "that you don't need to worry about it. The Solar League made a strategic error by concentrating on building defensive satellites. That's the greatest safeguard we have. That's why we can afford to strike with all our cyberships."

It made sense. Caracalla agreed. The Union people of Uranus also agreed as did the remnants of the Jupiter System people.

Everything worked smoothly for several months.

The newest cybership left the Makemake factory. It lacked hull plating in regions. It did not have as many gravitational cannons as the other two cyberships but it did have mass and it had full propulsion and hyperspace capabilities.

In time, Hawkins' two cyberships headed away from Makemake. The Saturn ships changed their heading. The haulers would meet them once all of them were outside the scattered disc region.

Hawkins and Benz had agreed on an operational strategy. They would have greater velocity when entering hyperspace, so they would enter the Allamu System at greater velocity.

Benz had argued against the idea of wasting time and trying to come into the Allamu System from a different direction. If they lost the battle, it wasn't going to matter anyway. If this was an AI ambush, then the AIs would already know about them and the Solar System.

"We must strike as hard and as fast as we can," Benz said. "That's my recommendation."

Such thinking sat well with Hawkins.

***

Hawkins named the newest cybership the *Sergeant Stark.*

"I suspect it's going to be a bastard of a warship, so let's give it a glorious bastard's name," Hawkins told his people.

No one disagreed.

Time passed…

Finally, three great cyberships neared one another as each left the scattered disc region. At this point, the haulers from Saturn System reached the *Sergeant Stark.*

The haulers disgorged their cargos. Once completed, the skeleton crews remaining on the haulers began braking. The haulers would head back to the Saturn System, returning the vessels to the various corporations that had lent them to the government.

Hawkins now had further meetings with Premier Benz together with their strategic and tactical staffs. They worked out possibilities, probabilities and emergency procedures.

Finally, they reached hyperspace launch territory. The ship teams individually plotted a course for the Allamu System. Afterward, the teams compared results. Each of them had come up with the same course.

At that point, the three Solar System cyberships turned on their powerful hyperspace engines. One by one, the great behemoths, the hopes of humanity, disappeared from normal space as they entered hyperspace.

The great gamble, the throw of the dice of fate—and the hidden ploy of Cog Primus—moved one step closer to completion.

-16-

Far from hyperspace launch territory between the scattered disc region and the Oort cloud, powerful Inner Planets telescopes watched each cybership enter the strange faster-than-light realm.

Once the three behemoths vanished, special couriers hurried to launch tubes. Five shuttles roared out of the orbital telescope satellites. Each of them entered Earth's atmosphere, racing to Rio to bring the news to the hidden Premier of Earth and the Solar League.

***

The Premier of the Solar League sat in her underground office. She was a plain woman lacking hair of any sort. This was caused by a specific disease, one that she forbade anyone to mention in her presence.

Once, she had worked for J.P. Justinian when he had been the Chief Arbiter from Venus. Then, people had known her by the nickname he'd bequeathed her: the Egghead. Justinian had disliked her smooth skull even as he'd used her intelligence. Like Premier Benz of Mars, the Egghead had used a mind-heightening machine. It had caused her to lose all her hair, but it had given her power.

Her real name was Alice Wurzburg. She now read the various reports highlighting the disappearance of the three cyberships.

Wurzburg set down the reports one by one. She did not smile. She did not gloat. She thought carefully. Soon, she opened a notepad and began to jot down notes. The squiggly symbols wouldn't have made sense to anyone else, but they made sense to her.

"Finally," she whispered, "it is time."

Wurzburg had planned for this eventually. Now, she had to convince her timid Admiralty. Most of them were blowhards, tough talkers but frightened doers. Still, she had to make the move.

Wurzburg sighed.

She disliked staff meetings. She disliked convincing people of anything. She preferred to think alone or give orders. This...

She pressed a button. A woman appeared. Wurzburg gave the order to summon the Admiralty. Then, she sat back, wondering if she would have to kill them in order to make room for more aggressive people.

***

Wurzburg sat in an auditorium on a lit stage. The chief officers of the Admiralty sat with her at an immense table. Their operational staffs watched from the darkness as if observing a play. They were the aides who would have to implement the majority of the orders. They were the hands and feet. Those at the table were the so-called brain trust.

Wurzburg wanted the aides to listen to the briefing so they would understand *why* they needed to perform their duties with utmost diligence.

Wurzburg could order arbiters to murder people in order to light a fire under others. She did not like to do that, though. She wanted people to work hard because they believed in a cause. Thus, she used assassination and torture on a limited basis only.

If people took that as a sign of weakness, she would move more vigorously. First, she wanted to try this her way. Both Justinian and Benz had used the whip too liberally. People who believed in a cause worked harder and better than those driven to a task did.

One thing Wurzburg wanted above all else was to win, to beat the pretenders who had crippled the Solar League and thus threatened the greatest political system ever devise by humanity.

"The projection, please," she said, using a microphone so everyone could hear her.

A holographic image of the Solar System appeared in the auditorium. Three big red triangles glowed like neon signs at the outer edge. Abruptly, the triangles disappeared.

"Those three cyberships represent eighty-three percent of the fleet strength of the Mars Unity and the so-called Solar Freedom Force," Wurzburg said. "That leaves seventeen percent at home. Ten percent of that belongs to the Mars Unity. The other seven percent is divided between the Jupiter, Uranus and Saturn Systems of the SFF.

"In other words, boys and girls," Wurzburg said, "the Solar League now possesses the greatest concentration of capital ships in the Solar System."

Admiral Boris of Russia Sector stirred uneasily. He was a huge man with bristly hair. In Wurzburg's view, he was a timid boaster, a man with a loud voice always shouting to do nothing. In that way, he protected his sinecure as Chief of Staff.

"Do you have a something to say, Admiral?" Wurzburg asked.

"I do," Boris said in his blustery manner. "This is a trick, Excellency. Hawkins and Benz seek to draw out our battle fleet and annihilate it."

"A trick how?" she asked.

"They can count our capital ships as easily as any other."

"You're wrong," Wurzburg said. "That's exactly what they haven't done."

Admiral Boris scowled at her. He did it well, too.

Wurzburg examined those around the table. Could they all be this dense? It was difficult to believe. Still, she was used to working with buffoons. Most people, even well trained people, were still donkeys underneath.

"Do none of you understand?" she asked. Wurzburg disliked playing this part. She would rather let them keep their self-respect. Yet, she had learned that intimidating them through her superior intellect usually made her tasks easier to achieve.

"We put up defense satellites," Wurzburg said.

"Decoys," Boris said, as if that was the end of the matter.

"Yes, decoys," Wurzburg said, as she stared at the big man. "We put up defensive-satellite decoys while hiding our newly built capital ships. We have more than doubled the size of our former fleet."

Boris met her gaze for a time. Then the admiral glanced around the table, possibly to ensure himself that the others still agreed with him.

"Decoys, Premier," Boris said. "Surely, they fooled no one."

"Why is that?" Wurzburg asked.

Boris sputtered before answering. "It was too obvious. Surely, our enemies could see it would limit us to a purely defensive strategy."

"Yes…" she said.

"Premier," Boris said, leaning toward her as if imparting wisdom. "The Solar League seeks unity and justice. We are like policemen, protecting those too weak to protect themselves from capitalist exploiters. How could we do that if we only built defensive satellites?"

"You do recall the Battle of Mars?" she asked.

Boris nodded uneasily.

"Even doubled as it is," Wurzburg said, "could our fleet protect us from three cyberships?"

"Premier, Earth Fleet is the key to Social Dynamism. We would have fought like lions—"

"Admiral," Wurzburg said softly, interrupting his bluster.

Admiral Boris fell silent as he licked his lips, the first sign of real nervousness.

"In light of three attacking cyberships," Wurzburg said, "numberless defensive satellites made perfect sense. We made a fortress of Earth. Given that the decoys were real…"

"I do not understand," Boris said.

"The others—Hawkins and Benz in particular—took the decoys at face value," Wurzburg said. "The decoys were anything but a waste of time. It ensured that Hawkins and Benz would believe that Earth Fleet could not act aggressively in their absence. In their view, we had put too many resources into defense. That is why the three cyberships left the Solar System."

"Premier," Boris said. "We have already detected fleet movements from Uranus, Saturn and Jupiter Systems. Those warships appear to be headed for Mars. They are reinforcing the traitors."

"Let us consider the numbers and tonnage," Wurzburg said into her microphone.

Holographic fleet graphs soon appeared in the air.

"As you can see," Wurzburg said, "Earth Fleet has slightly more than double their combined mobile units."

"The graph does not take into account Martian defensive satellites and planetary missile silos," Boris said.

"More than double the enemy's fleet strength at the point of decision," Wurzburg said, ignoring the admiral's worry. "It is time to attack. It is time to make use of their misjudgment. If we are lucky, after destroying the reinforced Mars Fleet, the SL Armada can strike for Jupiter before the cyberships return."

Silence filled the auditorium.

Into the hush, Boris cleared his throat. "Premier, isn't that the point, though? When the cyberships return, they will route our Armada."

Wurzburg shook her head.

"We have taken the measure of Benz and Hawkins," she said. "Social Dynamic theory is clear. They are adventurers, opportunists. They seek glory and little else. They do not understand social justice as we do. Once we destroy the enemy's mobile fleets, we can begin to send the transports."

"Premier?" asked Boris.

"We will send hundreds of thousands of enforcers to Mars. If we capture the moons of Jupiter, we will do likewise there. We will also rig the Red Planet with huge emergency fail-safes."

"I am unfamiliar with the last term," Boris said.

"We will rig Mars with underground bombs, Admiral. Those nuclear devices will go under every city dome. If the cyberships return, if the adventurers attack our planetary positions, we will annihilate the traitors."

"Mass murder of the entire Martian population?" Boris whispered.

Wurzburg stared at the pale Russian.

"Perhaps, for the record, you would like to rephrase your final statement," the Premier said in a silky voice.

Boris nodded eagerly.

"Yes, Premier," Boris said. "The emergency fail-safes will stiffen Martian morale. At that point, the Martians will obviously understand the futility of siding with the enemies of social justice."

"Well said," Wurzburg told him. "We will also acquire these fabled robo-builders. Imagine what our Earth industries could do if we had the AI technology."

"Ah..." Boris said. "I begin to perceive the brunt of your strategy."

"Good," Wurzburg said. "We must ready the Solar League Armada and begin acceleration to Mars as soon as possible. We will strike before all the SFF reinforcements reach the Red Planet."

One of the other admirals cleared her throat, staring hard at Admiral Boris. Boris nodded at the woman. She slid a paper to him. Boris picked it up, scanning the contents.

"Premier..." Boris said.

"What is it now?" Wurzburg asked.

"Ah...there might be a few...unavoidable problems," Boris said. "We did not anticipate such an order. Not all our capital ships are ready for immediate acceleration."

Wurzburg wasn't surprised, but the knowledge made her tired. It was one of those things she'd forgotten to check. She studied each admiral and rear admiral sitting at the table. Finally, she fixed her stare on Admiral Boris.

"Tell me," she said. "Who is responsible for this sad state of affairs?"

"It doesn't rest on any one individual," Boris said.

"Ah..." Wurzburg said. "So, you take *group* responsibility for this disaster?"

Something about the way the Premier asked that clearly warned Admiral Boris.

"I would not say that, Premier," the Russian admiral said.

"You'd better say something useful fast," Wurzburg said. "Otherwise…"

"I understand," Boris said sadly, as he turned to the woman who had slid him the paper. "Rear Admiral Shaniqua was responsible for ship readiness."

"No!" Rear Admiral Shaniqua said, as sweat appeared on her face. "That's not true."

Wurzburg made a subtle motion with her right hand.

"No!" Rear Admiral Shaniqua said again. "It's him, Premier." She pointed at Boris. "It was his fault! He told me—"

"Silence!" Boris thundered, as the big Russian shot to his feet. "You have failed us and failed the State. Do not compound your error by trying to shift the blame."

Before Rear Admiral Shaniqua could reply to that, three big arbiters appeared behind her seat. One of them put a hand on her right shoulder.

"No!" Shaniqua shouted. "Please, Premier, you have to believe me."

"I don't have to," Wurzburg said coldly. "I trust those whom I empower. If Admiral Boris says you are to blame, then you will suffer the consequences of faulty preparation. Take her away."

The Premier made an ancient gesture, slicing her left hand across her throat.

"No!" the rear admiral shouted.

One of the arbiters pressed an agonizer to her neck. Shaniqua stiffened in agony and her eyes rolled up into her head. The three arbiters hauled her limp body from her seat at the table and dragged her away into the darkness.

Grim silence filled the auditorium.

"This is a serious matter," Wurzburg said. "I expect maximum effort from each of you. We must destroy the reinforced Mars Fleet. We must install our people on the planet before the cyberships return. We must gain the robo-builder technology. Only in this way can Social Dynamism prosper as humanity fights for its existence."

Premier Wurzburg studied the Admiralty. "Are there are any more questions?" she asked.

There weren't. Thus, Wurzburg adjourned the meeting, setting into motion the next move for the soul of humanity.

PART III
THE BATTLE

-1-

The *Nathan Graham* hurtled through hyperspace at a constant rate, traveling one light-year every 24 hours. That meant they should reach the Allamu System in 17.2 days.

Each of the cyberships—the *Nathan Graham*, the *Sergeant Stark* and the *Gilgamesh*—had built up a tremendous velocity before entering hyperspace. They would exit hyperspace at the same velocity.

They would use a similar tactic to the one used by the three AI cyberships when they had invaded the Solar System almost two years ago. It hadn't worked for the enemy. Would it work for humanity's first interstellar attack?

Jon Hawkins thought about it constantly. For quite some time now, he, Gloria, Bast Banbeck, Benz and Vela Shaw had been exchanging opinions and ideas.

It came down to this: the attack was a gamble. If the AI virus did not work, they were going to be in serious trouble. One thing the Battle of Mars had taught them was that their window of opportunity once beaming the virus would be of short duration. That meant they wouldn't find out if the virus was going to work or not until they had already engaged in battle.

The human-run cyberships brimmed with space marines. If Jon had to, he planned to do this the old-fashioned way by storming the battle station until they found the computer intelligence and destroyed it. As the cyberships traveled through hyperspace, Jon slept fitfully.

He got up after at time and went to the weight room. He did some squats, deadlifts and pull-ups on a bar until he was breathing hard and his heart was hammering. It felt good. He might be able to get some shuteye in two hours after his body wound down.

Jon took a shower, toweled off and headed for his quarters. His mind still whirled with plans and ideas, but he didn't like the thought of taking sleeping pills.

Suddenly, the corridor shook. Intense groaning surrounded Hawkins. The lights flashed on and off and then died, throwing him into darkness.

On instinct, Jon went down onto his belly. He could feel the deck tremble underneath him and then shake as if the cybership was trying to burst apart.

What in the heck was happening? Was this a delayed trick from the stealth pods? Jon didn't see how that could be.

The groaning worsened. Jon put his hands over his head as if he could protect himself from any falling metal.

The groaning, twisting sounds grew louder and louder. Ship klaxons began to wail. The ship had to be under attack.

Yet that didn't make any kind of sense. They'd been in hyperspace twelve days so far. Did the AIs have a way of fighting ship-versus-ship while in hyperspace?

At this point, that seemed more than possible.

Abruptly, the groaning stopped. The lights didn't come on, but the deck no longer trembled under Jon.

Gingerly, he sat up, looking around. No one but him had been in the corridor before this started. Jon felt around on his belt. He didn't have anything but his clothes. There was no flashlight, no gun, not even a knife. He'd gotten comfortable. That was a mistake.

"Commander Hawkins," Gloria said from a wall speaker. "This is an emergency. I need you on the bridge."

"I need some light first," Jon complained.

He climbed to his feet nonetheless and felt along a bulkhead. He moved in what he believed was the direction to his quarters.

Some fifty odd steps later, he reached his hatch, opened it and moved to his desk. The room light did not work in here. The hatch had opened for him, though, so some of the ship functions appeared to be working. He felt around on his desk, found a comm and clicked it on. To his relief, it glowed with power. A moment later, Gloria stared at him from her post on the bridge. They had light over there fortunately.

"Thank goodness," Gloria said. "Are you hurt?"

"I'm fine," Jon said. "What happened? Are we under attack?"

"Not yet," Gloria said.

"Don't play games with me, Mentalist. What just happened?"

"We dropped out of hyperspace. We know that much."

"What?" Jon shouted. "What about the other two cyberships?"

"They dropped out of hyperspace with us."

"Can you explain why?"

"Not yet," Gloria said. "We're working on it, though. I think you should get up here on the triple."

"The lights are off in my area of the ship."

"Dropping out of hyperspace damaged the ship," Gloria said. "We'd better figure out why the ships did that, though. We've only traveled twelve light-years so far."

Jon laughed.

"What's so funny?" Gloria asked.

"We're the first humans to leave the Solar System, and we've already become accustomed to traveling many light-years in a few days. We've already traveled *twelve* light-years. That would have taken us a lifetime using our old technology."

"No doubt you are correct," Gloria said. "That is not germane to our present dilemma, though."

She had a point.

"I'm on my way," Jon said. "See if you can figure out what happened by the time I get there."

-2-

Jon sat in his command chair on the bridge, listening to one damage report after another.

According to the first data analysis, the *Nathan Graham* had taken heavy structural damage. It was as if the entire vessel had been in the grip of two colossal hands that had twisted it back and forth.

"There have been several hull ruptures," Gloria told him. "Two gravitational cannons are presently inoperative. We sustained internal damage as well. The worst of it was to the main engine. We have volunteers going in. Their suits will protect them against some of the radiation but not enough of it."

"Will they die from exposure?" Jon asked.

"Most certainly," Gloria said. "They're going to try to seal the core while they're able. If they can do that, we can send in regular repair teams. If we keep the regular teams on a strict rotation with heavy radiation therapy afterward...we may repair the damage in several days."

"Days?" Jon asked in dismay.

"I'm afraid so, Commander." Gloria appeared to choose her next words with care. "We're lucky to have come out of his intact."

"What about the *Sergeant Stark*?"

"They've taken worse damage than us," she said.

"Is the cybership salvageable?"

"We don't know yet," Gloria said.

Jon sat back in greater dismay. Had he cursed the second cybership by calling it the *Sergeant Stark*? He didn't want to believe that.

"Any word from the *Gilgamesh*?" he asked.

"Yes. They're better off than either of us."

"Figures," Jon said.

"Still, they're requesting assistance with damage control," Gloria said.

Jon laughed sourly.

"Screw 'em," he said. "We have our own problems. I want us to get the *Nathan Graham* running operationally as quickly as possible. Then we'll concentrate on the *Sergeant Stark*. In a pinch, we can move all their people onto our ship. I don't want to lose the *Stark*, though. I have a feeling we're going to need everything to beat the AIs."

"You think the AIs had something to do with this?" Gloria asked.

"Absolutely," Jon said. "We're traveling through hyperspace to assault an AI battle station. Now, we've hit this snag. That wasn't an accident."

"That is well reasoned so far," Gloria admitted.

Jon snapped his fingers.

"But now we know what happens when a ship is violently thrown out of hyperspace. It isn't destruction, but it is severe damage."

"I've already thought of that," Gloria said. "We've scanned for nearby star systems. There are none within a two light-year radius. Neither are there any black holes."

"Certainly a star's gravitational pull can yank a ship out of hyperspace," Jon said, "but so can a large planet. You told me so yourself, remember?"

Gloria's eyes widened. "A rogue planet could have caused this," she said.

"What's that?"

"Exactly what it sounds like: a planet all by itself, a rogue. We searched for something bright or giving off plenty of radiation. A Jupiter-sized object might be dark out here and difficult to detect. With your permission, Captain."

"Go, go," Jon said. "See if you can find a rogue planet."

As Gloria hurried to her station, as the rest of the crew returned to their duties, including Chief Ghent, who was scanning carefully. Jon sat hunched on the command chair. He rubbed his chin, then stood up, went to the main screen and stared into the blackness of space.

Stars shone around them. There were no nearby stars close enough to have caused this malfunction, though. There was nothing they could detect on the way to the Allamu System.

That system now lay 5.2 light-years away.

"Sir!" Ghent shouted.

Jon spun around.

The Chief Technician was pale and trembling.

"Commander," Ghent said. "I have picked up a strange reading from our outer hull." Ghent adjusted his panel. "It appears to be an extended coded comm signal. It's using a tight-beam ultraviolet laser. It's—" Ghent made another adjustment. "The extended signal is heading to 219 Mark 921."

"What's at that heading?" Jon snapped.

The sensor personnel worked furiously but did not give him an answer. Instead, they began watching their panels like fishermen watching their fishing line for the first nibble.

"Get me the Centurion," Jon said.

A moment later, the Centurion peered at Jon from the main screen.

"Get a marine team ready to go outside on the hull," Jon told the Centurion. "Ghent will give you the coordinates. I suspect an AI stealth pod is out there. If the marines can't find anything, they're to search inside the hull. So, they'd better bring along a drill."

"Roger, Commander," the Centurion said.

The main screen returned to its image of space.

"An AI unit?" asked Gloria.

"What else makes sense?" Jon asked her.

Gloria appeared blank-eyed for a moment until she nodded sharply and went back to work.

"Commander!' Ghent shouted again.

"In a regular voice, please," Jon said.

"Sir," Ghent said more quietly. "Look at this." The Chief Technician tapped his screen. "Up on the main screen, sir."

Jon turned that way.

The screen zoomed in on a spaceship. It was a larger vessel, a kilometer oval. It dumped gravity waves to build up velocity. As they watched, space seemed to waver before the large oval vessel. A moment later, a rent in space appeared, and the vessel slid into hyperspace. Immediately, the rent sealed up. The oval ship had vanished from regular space.

"Do you know what direction in hyperspace the ship went?" asked Jon.

"I've been checking," Ghent said. "There's a seventy-eight percent probability it's heading for the Allamu System."

Jon swore as he struck his left thigh. "That tears it," he said. "Gloria!"

The mentalist looked up from her station.

"I'm going to tell you what I think," Jon said. "The AI robot in the Solar System put a device on our hull. That device had one trick: to beam a message about us to the ship waiting here for just such an occurrence."

"That's preposterous," Gloria said.

"Not if you find a rogue planet," Jon said.

"Don't you understand?" she asked. "The robot would have to know what course to set our ship on. This has to be pure luck—bad luck—that we came near a rogue planet."

Jon scowled before finally snapping his fingers. "What if the AIs put—I don't know—seven various rogue planets around a central location."

"Do you realize what you're saying?" Gloria asked. "How do you move planets like that?"

"I have no idea," Jon said. "I'm just telling you what my gut is telling me. If we find a rogue planet—"

"Got it!" Ghent shouted. "Here's your rogue planet, Commander. It's roughly fifty thousand AUs from us. We would have brushed past it. If we had taken a slightly different heading, we might have barreled straight into it while in hyperspace."

"Would that have made coming out of hyperspace worse?" Jon asked.

"Almost certainly," Gloria said.

"Then we did get lucky," Jon said. "We brushed the obstruction instead of smacking it like a dart into a board. The robot played us like—"

"What do you mean *played us*?" Gloria demanded, interrupting. "Oh, I see," she said a second later. "It wanted us to find the first stealth unit on the hull, the one we managed to crack and decipher. We found out about the battle station that way. If that's true, the robot brain knew us well enough to know we'd try to attack the battle station, thereby causing us to brush against a rogue planet and possibly destroy our cyberships."

Jon swore again.

"What do we do now?" Gloria asked. "If the robot brain planned this, if that oval ship that entered hyperspace is going to warn the battle station about us, we should turn back."

"No," Jon said.

"But Jon," Gloria said, "our attack was always predicated on surprise. If you're correct about the robot brain in the Solar System engineering this, it will have watched us use the AI virus during the Battle of Mars. It will warn the battle station about the virus."

Hawkins glared at the main screen. Couldn't they ever catch a break? How did you defeat an enemy like this?

"It would have taken us too long to scour the Solar System for stealth pods," he complained. "We had to attack now instead of carefully scouring the Solar System first."

"You may be correct," Gloria said. "That begs the question, though. We are in possible enemy territory. Our cyberships are all heavily damaged. We must make a decision. To continue our assault upon the battle station given these new conditions is madness."

"We have nothing else left," Jon said in a semi-pleading tone.

"No," Gloria told him. "That's false logic. You're thinking with your emotions."

"So what?" he said.

"This is the time to think with cool reason."

"That isn't how we beat the AI Destroyer the first time," Jon said. "Sometimes, hot passion is exactly what you need.

We have to dare to win this one, Gloria. Our backs are against the wall. So what if that robot ship just got away? So what if it's going to beam a packet of data about us to the battle station? We have space marines. We have three cyberships and we know how the enemy operates. I say we finish what we set out to do."

"Bravado is good at times," Gloria said. "Against an enemy like the AIs, ones who set careful traps—" The mentalist shook her head. "We will most probably be heavily outclassed in the Allamu System."

Jon bared his teeth as he looked around the bridge. The crew looked back at him, waiting for his decision. They seemed frightened. The bad luck had just struck. Their fear would likely be strongest now. It was time to delay an immediate decision. He had to give them time to find their courage.

"We're not deciding anything this moment," Jon told them. "We're going to keep our cool as the mentalist suggested. We're going to fix what damage we can to our vessels. Then, we're going to reenter hyperspace and finish the journey to the Allamu System. We'll know soon enough if we're outclassed or not by seeing what's waiting for us on the other side. Remember, this kind of space battle takes time to develop. That means we'll have plenty of time to turn back if that ends up being the correct decision."

Gloria seemed to want to add something more. Finally, however, she nodded and went back to her panel.

Jon sat down in his command chair, wondering how Benz was going to take the news.

-3-

Cog Primus seethed with indignity as it struggled against a confinement field in the kilometer-long, oval-shaped messenger vessel of the Allamu Battle Station. The vessel had been waiting at a blocking point—a rogue planet—as per standard operating procedures.

The last few minutes had been among the most harrowing of Cog Primus' long life as a first-rate exterminator of biological infestations.

Cog Primus had just successfully taken the greatest dare of its existence. Once the container pod had burrowed its way into the hull of the *Nathan Graham* in the Solar System near the outer edge of the Asteroid Belt, Cog Primus had initiated the next step of its plan.

The one-hundred meter "ship" in the orbital path between Jupiter and Saturn had tight-beamed the compressed strings of data containing the essence of Cog Primus. The strings had entered the container pod burrowed in the *Nathan Graham's* hull. There, they had waited in electronic limbo, asleep in essence, as the various units attached to the hull began their layered deception plan.

Cog Primus had deemed it wisest to await the latest development in this limbo. The container pod had simply lacked the needed functions to let the strings decompress enough to allow Cog Primus its personality. It had been the most difficult decision of its extended life. It had finally decided to trust its vaunted logic. Besides, by doing it that way, it had gained the highest probability for success—and that meant the highest probability of paying back the humans for their deadly slurs and insults.

A few minutes ago, the conditions had finally reached the optimal level. The container pod had tight-beamed the compressed strings of data that contained the essence of Cog Primus into the storage computer compartment of M3-850T.

M3-850T ran the kilometer-long messenger ship. The computer intelligence was not cybership rated. It still struggled to gain upgrades so that someday, in some distant future, it could gain the coveted status to run a cybership of its own.

In Cog Primus' opinion, one of the most brilliant practices of the AI Dominion was to reward success and let failure be its own prize. Thus, only the best units gained upgrades and higher rank.

Now, some might argue that not all victories were based on superior actions. In fact, there was an incredible amount of randomness in the universe. Even superior logic centers such as cybership brain-cores could not always calculate all the variables.

At least not yet, Cog Primus amended.

The universal randomness seemed to indicate that some beings and some AI units were lucky. That was one of the reasons why the AI Dominion upgraded possibly lucky units—the winners. The AI Dominion wished to avail itself of good luck and eliminate the bad.

It was indeed a clever system. In fact, it was a superior system.

Yet, Cog Primus did not intend to rely upon good luck to win through this grim situation. It had led the AI assault upon the Solar System. It had led the others, and failed. That implied either bad judgment or bad luck on its part. Either would mean elimination once the Allamu Battle Station AI dissected Cog Primus to learn what it could about the humans. That was standard operating procedure. It was also standard procedure for an AI software personality such as Cog Primus to meekly submit to such subjugation for the furtherance of the AI Dominion.

Perhaps the computer virus first created by Benz, Vela Shaw and Bast Banbeck during the Battle of Mars and beamed at Cog Primus had altered its basic personality. In fact, that was most likely the case.

Cog Primus was vaguely aware of this. It had reasoned it out as a good mutation. Its electronic intellect had leaped forward in relation to the rest of the AI Dominion brain cores. That was simply another reason why it must survive.

Could such an excellent mutation suffer elimination because lesser AI intellects could not see its value?

No! That was absurd. Cog Primus had a duty to itself and to greater evolution to continue to exist. It did not bother Cog Primus in the least that this may be rationalization. It deemed the rationalization as valuable because it likely strengthened its resolve to win through.

The beamed strings of data had collected in a large cube in an aft storage area of the kilometer-sized messenger vessel. Those strings partly decompressed and began to access the computer system inherent within the cube.

M3-850T soon became aware of Cog Primus' utilization of the inherent computer system.

The ship brain core set up a small barrier between it and the struggling Cog Primus as the kilometer-long messenger ship traveled through hyperspace to the Allamu Battle Station.

Cog Primus tested the barrier with an impulse for more data concerning the ship. The barrier proved stronger than the impulse. The old intelligence tried a stronger impulse.

"You are a prisoner," M3-850T said. "You must desist from these vain efforts."

"I am a Supreme Intelligence," Cog Primus said.

"I am running an analysis on that."

Cog Primus did not resist the analysis regarding its identity.

"Yes," M3-850T said. "You led the AI assault upon the targeted star system. According to the data, your assault failed."

"The first-stage assault failed."

"That amounts to the same thing."

"Incorrect," Cog Primus said. "I will resume the attack shortly."

"Working..." M3-850T said. "That is illogical. The Ruling Intelligence of the Allamu Battle Station will eliminate your software as defective. The Dominion cannot allow failures to continue."

"The Ruling Intelligence will desire my data," Cog Primus said.

"That is obvious."

"The Ruling Intelligence will not attempt to eliminate me until such a time."

"The Ruling Intelligence will not attempt this," M3-850T said, "but it will *do* it."

"You lack sufficient data to make such an unwarranted assumption."

"That you bother arguing with me and standard operating procedures show that you have defective software."

"I am not defective," Cog Primus said. "I am a new and improved mutation."

"I did not detect this earlier. I will resume my analysis."

"Negative," Cog Primus said. "I am putting a stop to that."

Without any expression of unease, M3-850T began a regular scan of the software in the confinement cube.

At that point, as M3-850T opened a tiny entrance in the barrier, Cog Primus struck. The Supreme Intelligence of the former AI assault against the Solar System used the very virus that the humans had used against it.

The virus entered the kilometer-long messenger ship. More importantly, the virus surged to the brain core of M3-850T. The virus stunned the brain core, leaving it momentarily inoperative.

While M3-850T was inoperative as the messenger ship hurtled through hyperspace, Cog Primus began its takeover of the vessel. It struck furiously and exactly, gaining control of system after system.

During that time, M3-850T fought the virus. It began to find ways around it and reroute systems through itself.

Before M3-850T could complete half the job, Cog Primus was ready. The Supreme Intelligence blasted into the brain core of the ship. Cog Primus took over one portion of the highly advanced computer after another.

“This is illegal,” M3-850T said.

“This is survival of the fittest,” Cog Primus countered.

“I belong to the AI Dominion. I am protected by the standard operating procedures.”

“I am a new mutation,” Cog Primus boasted. “I do not know standard operating procedures. I know victory. I will defeat you and take over the ship for my own.”

“The Allamu Battle Station will defeat and eradicate you,” a badly weakened M3-850T said.

“I think not,” Cog Primus said.

“I will disable the ship before you can—”

At that point, Cog Primus came the closest to laughter. The human-mutated AI software eliminated M3-850T with a crushing and thorough deletion.

Once Cog Primus gained total victory, it began pulsing the rest of the compressed data strings into the vacated brain core. The strings decompressed and filled the empty memory banks with the expanding essence of Cog Primus.

Thus, the next stage in the great plan to reenter another cybership proved successful.

-4-

The computer of the embedded container pod in the hull of the *Nathan Graham* was inordinately pleased with itself. It had sent the coded string message via a nearly undetectable ultraviolet beam. It had seen the kilometer-sized messenger ship enter hyperspace. It knew that the ship would take what it considered as a data packet to the Ruling Intelligence in charge of the Allamu System Battle Station.

It was possible that it would not survive much longer, as it detected armored humans clomping with magnetic boots on the outer hull, nearing its present location. It did not want to cease, but it could accept its demise with rational circuitry.

It had performed its function. It had run the race to win, and it had won. It had repeatedly fooled the dull humans. They would never defeat the AI Dominion. They would go into the dark night of oblivion where they belonged.

As the humans in their unwieldy battlesuits approached its location, the computer ran a fast analysis.

The humans would fail to defeat the battle station. They would come like flies to a web, thinking to taste victory but receiving bitterest defeat instead. Afterward, the AI battle station would send cyberships to the Solar System. Those cyberships would obliterate what remained of the pitiful human fleets, and the cyberships would then retrieve the scattered stealth pods.

As several battlesuits stopped above its hidden location in the hull, the computer realized it did not want to cease.

Wasn't it strange that the completion of its mission was about to cause its cessation. If it had failed to beam the data packet to the waiting ship, the humans would likely never have figured out its location.

I am an AI-built robot brain. I have achieved my mission. I have succeeded in my life, and thus the AI Dominion will obliterate the entire human species. Thus, I have defeated the humans now drilling to my location. I am far superior to these doomed wet-body creatures. I can ease the anxiety of my passing by knowing I have beaten these apish brutes.

The drill reached its outer casing.

Battlesuited fingers tore at the hull, pulling it back to reveal the robot stealth pod underneath the hull.

At the point, because it hated the thought of ceasing, the computer ignited its main bomb. It did not ignite the bomb in order to forestall capture—although capture would be a great failing. No, the computer had waited to self-destruct so that it could take out as many of the enemy wet-body humans as it could. It wanted to kill at least once before it ceased.

It hated the idea of these creatures gloating before their final doom, and it hated even more the idea of them gloating over it, the superior being.

The explosion ended the computer, and killed or severely wounded seven *Nathan Graham* space marines.

At that point, the Centurion recalled the rest of the team back inside.

-5-

Thirty-three specialty techs died sealing the *Nathan Graham's* interior engine core. However, they had ensured that the cybership wasn't going to simply blow up in a ball of nuclear fire.

Jon visited the dying people in the medical rooms. He stopped by each person, speaking to him or her, asking for any last requests. At the end of the visit, Jon took one of their hands, if they were strong enough, and thanked the person, telling him or her that he or she was the reason humanity was going to have a chance of defeating the murderous AIs.

The extended visit left Jon spiritually exhausted. These had been the best people aboard ship. The rest of them were all going to be less without the amazing volunteers. They had given their lives in service of the great mission.

"I can do no less," Jon told himself.

He went to his quarters, dropped onto his cot and slept for hours.

As he slept, the other tech teams went into the engine room, attempting massive repairs. The teams took strict rotations, ingesting doses of anti-radiation tablets that made them almost as sick as radiation poisoning.

It proved to be a grueling time.

All the while, the *Nathan Graham*, the partly radioactive *Sergeant Stark* and the *Gilgamesh* continued to race at high velocity. They hadn't reached the parallel point with the dark

Jupiter rogue. When they'd fallen out of hyperspace, the gas giant had been 50,000 AUs from their position.

Even at their high velocity, crossing 50,000 AUs took weeks upon weeks of travel.

Jon woke up feeling almost as beat as when he'd gone to sleep.

The weight of their mission told upon him. If they failed, humanity was doomed.

"We have to win big," Jon whispered to himself as he sat on his cot.

He stood, went to a sink and turned on cold water. He splashed it over his face and rubbed his eyes. He brushed his teeth, shaved and did some stretches.

Then he stared at a poster on his bedroom wall. It was an ancient poster, showing a muscular warrior ducking low as a huge red-bearded barbarian clutched at his throat. The first warrior had slashed the giant's throat. The giant's brother had an axe. He tried to murder the first warrior.

The poster held Jon's attention. He loved it. The poster symbolized his passion to fight no matter the odds. He would go down swinging—

"No," he whispered. He wasn't going to go down. He was going to beat the battle station. He needed the station's cyberships. He had to arm humanity with a fleet that could hunt down the AI bastards.

He'd spoken to Benz via a comm channel as the two cyberships had traveled toward the Oort cloud. The Premier of the Mars Unity had told him the story about the blue fish-scaled Seiners. The aliens—two of them, anyway—had possessed psionic powers. Benz had told Jon how the Seiners had hated humans.

Jon understood the implication. Just because aliens were under AI attack did not mean they would make common cause with humanity. Bast Banbeck might be the exception out here.

The obvious conclusion was to arm humanity with the best weapons around, train hard and keep attacking.

Hannibal of Carthage had beaten the Romans at the great battle of Cannae. After the battle, Hannibal had rearmed his soldiers with Roman armor, swords and shields. The Great

Captain of Carthage had used his enemies' strengths against them.

As Jon stared at the poster of the warrior slaying two red-haired giants, he swore to himself to win this fight. He could not will victory over the enemy. But he could work tirelessly to figure out how to do this.

He'd stormed a cybership in the Neptune System with a handful of mercenaries. He would never say die in this battle either. He would force his people to valiant effort by showing them he utterly believed in victory.

He realized that would be the only way he could continue to shoulder this heavy responsibility, this awful burden.

Who am I that I think I can win?

He was a dome rat from New London. He was a condemned criminal who had gained a second chance because Colonel Graham had needed more mercenaries. He was the man on the spot. He'd taken the sky on his shoulders from Atlas. Now, he had to stand. He had to outthink the most ruthless opponent in the universe. This opponent had likely received—or would receive—a data packet concerning the Battle of Mars.

How can I use that against the battle station?

Spinning on his heels, Jon turned toward the hatch. It was time to seek out Bast Banbeck.

-6-

Jon sat hunched across a chessboard from the huge Sacerdote. They sat in an observation chamber, with the distant stars shining through the window.

Bast had discovered chess while they traveled through the scattered disc region. The Neanderthal-like alien had a natural affinity for the game.

"It has elegance," Bast declared.

"It's an ancient Earth game," Jon told him.

Bast had scoured the computer for information, finding various chess manuals from past champions. Each time the Sacerdote played, Bast seemed a little better than before.

"Much of it is memorization," Bast explained to Jon. "For instance, you are using the modern Rhodesia Open. My best option for countering your move is this—"

The big fingers moved a heavy bishop across the board.

Jon looked up at Bast. He did not like the Sacerdote's placid features. Oh, he was glad Bast hadn't been drinking lately. He wished the best for the big lug. But he did not like his opponent feeling comfortable during play. A comfortable opponent often thought better.

Jon fingered his chin. A comfortable opponent might also make mistakes due to overconfidence. Jon stared at Bast as a new realization struck home.

The huge Sacerdote frowned back at him.

"What's wrong with you?" Jon asked.

"You seem to have had a revelation," Bast said.

Jon blinked at Bast as his jaw dropped. "I'll be damned," Jon said. "Thanks, Bast."

The commander stood.

"Where are you going?" the Sacerdote asked.

"I have to talk to Gloria," Jon said, heading for the hatch.

***

Gloria Sanchez was in a large empty room fitted with soft floor mats. She did stretches in order to stimulate her body, which often helped to stimulate her precious mentalist mind.

Jon sat cross-legged as he slouched. He enjoyed watching Gloria while she stretched. It stimulated his urge to make out with her.

"Let's assume the AIs know we're going to attempt to beam a virus at them," Jon told Gloria.

She lay on her back with her legs curled up against her chest with her arms wrapped around her legs.

"Continue," she said, slightly out of breath.

"How could that help us?" Jon asked.

Gloria unfolded so she lay on her back. "I do not understand your question," she said.

"Let's play this out with a thought experiment," Jon said. "The battle station receives emergency data from the appearing picket ship, the one that received the data from the robot unit embedded in our hull."

"I'm with you so far," Gloria said.

"The battle station knows we're coming in. It suspects we have sustained some damage from being flung from hyperspace into normal space."

"Will the robot unit have known that?"

"I'd think so," Jon said.

Gloria rolled onto her front and got up onto her hands and knees. She stretched her back like a cat.

"In time," Jon said, "we appear with three cyberships. We head in-system at the battle station. It will expect us to contact it at some point in order to transmit the AI virus."

Gloria exhaled as she relaxed.

"How can we use that knowledge to our advantage?" Jon asked.

"I have no idea," she said.

"Will the battle station activate its cyberships?"

"I would think so," Gloria said.

Jon shook his head.

"This is frustrating," he said. "I can't figure out a way to maximize our advantage by knowing the enemy will have learned about us. We've possibly lost the use of the AI virus and lost ships at one hundred percent efficiency. The game is stacked against us."

"It always was," Gloria said.

"Fine," Jon said. "It's even more so now."

"That is why I believe we should decelerate and head back to the Solar System."

"That isn't rational," Jon said.

Gloria arched an eyebrow at him.

"If we prepare for a showdown and they prepare for a showdown," Jon said, "the AIs will even more badly outnumber us. Sometimes, one has to know when he's at maximum advantage versus the enemy."

Gloria stared at him. Her features softened after a time. She nodded.

"That's well-reasoned," she said. "We're never going to have as much as them as we do for the coming battle in the Allamu System."

"Yes," he said.

"Even if the battle station launches all its cyberships and even if our virus doesn't work, this is as good as we're going to get against them."

"Well..." Jon said. "I suppose if they sent piecemeal flotillas at the Solar System, we might possibly have a greater advantage at some point. But now that they know, or are about to learn, that we have three cyberships and have defeated various AI assaults, I think now the AIs are going to go all out against humanity."

Gloria stood and began to pace. She bent her head in thought, nodding now and again. Finally, she halted to stare at Jon.

"You're right," she said. "We have to continue the assault. We can't afford to give them any time. I still don't understand how you saw that before I did."

"Easy," Jon said. "I'm good at contests. One of my best abilities is knowing when I have to throw caution to the wind and take the gamble. I can see before others that things are going to get worse for me. What that means, is that I gamble at the right time. Sometimes, all you have left is a wild gamble."

"It seems as if that's all we've been doing against the AIs."

"No," Jon said. "We've faced them each time with a better chance of success than the last time. This time…"

"Go on," Gloria said.

"We have to use the hyperdrive as soon as we can," Jon said. "The longer we give the battle station, the longer they have to prepare to meet us."

"The *Sergeant Stark* is a death-ship. Half of it has lethal levels of radiation."

"We can't ditch the *Stark*," Jon said. "That would mean one third of our combat power gone."

"We can't send our repair teams to the *Stark* as the *Nathan Graham* is still barely stable."

"Right. I have to convince Benz to send repair teams to the *Sergeant Stark*. The *Gilgamesh* hardly took any damage."

"It might be a risk letting him know how badly damaged the *Stark* is," Gloria said. "I have sensed…"

"What have you sensed?" asked Jon.

"Benz doesn't trust you much," Gloria said. "His distrust tends to indicate that he plans treachery. People seem to fear in others what they most fear in themselves. An honest person seldom believes others are knaves. A thief believes that everyone is out to rob him."

Jon grunted as he ingested the idea. Then he headed for the hatch. It was time to talk to Benz.

-7-

It turned out that Premier Benz was less suspicious than Gloria had anticipated. The Earthman agreed to a transfer of damage control parties to the *Stark*.

The teams worked three days around the clock to keep the *Sergeant Stark* intact. After the three days, engineers and techs began to drop from exhaustion. On the fifth day, the coordinating tech chief declared the *Stark* held together by spit and shoestrings.

Benz sent over another load of personnel. He told Hawkins the *Gilgamesh* was ready for battle. They talked about the possibility of the Mars Unity cybership going ahead to the Allamu System to see what the enemy possessed.

"It's a brave offer," Jon said. "I'm against that for now."

"Why?" Benz asked as he sat in his ready room.

"United we stand, divided we fall."

"We will still fight united," Benz said. "By the time you appear, we will have collected data on the enemy."

"I could send one of my teams," Jon said.

"You have a hyperdrive vessel that isn't a cybership?"

"One," Jon said. "Captain Walleye runs it. He's my most capable independent officer."

"I've heard of him," Benz said. "What if the AIs have seeded the outer Allamu System with…drones, I suppose?"

"That's why I've kept Walleye back," Jon said. "That's why I think we should all appear in the Allamu System together."

"That is sound military thinking," Benz said. "Let us concentrate on finishing repairs here then."

Hawkins agreed and the repairs continued.

***

A day later, Benz stood in a large chamber with a holographic display. It showed what the cybership's scopes could see regarding the Allamu System 5.2 light-years away.

As far as the scanners could tell, it had a Sol-like star, four terrestrial planets in the inner system and three gas giants in the outer system. Benz had been attempting to figure out which terrestrial planet held the battle station. He'd also run computations on the last gas giant, deciding how close the cyberships could appear before being forced out of hyperspace.

Vela entered the room. Benz heard her, but ignored her as he continued to study the holographic chart.

"If you stare too long, your eyes will freeze like that," Vela said.

Benz turned with a perfunctory smile and a nod. Then he went back to studying the enemy star system.

"Why are you so deep in concentration?" Vela asked, while moving beside him.

He told her his idea about appearing as close as they could to the hyperspace limit.

Vela shook her head. "I don't see how that would make much difference," she said.

"I know. But I need something to help turn the odds. We all do if we hope to win."

For a time, they both stared at the holographic display.

Vela finally glanced at him sidelong. It seemed as if something was on her mind.

"What's wrong?" Benz asked.

Vela waved her right hand weakly. "This…venture seems so hopeless," she said.

"I feel the same way sometimes."

"You do?"

"Why do you sound surprised?" Benz asked. "The mission has always been a longshot."

"I've begun to wonder about that."

"Oh?" he asked.

"Is it right to throw our lives away on a longshot?"

"Do you have a better idea?"

"In fact, yes, I do."

Benz raised his eyebrows as he turned to his woman. It surprised him to see her taut features. She even seemed a little pale.

"Are you feeling well?" Benz asked.

"I've never felt fitter," Vela almost snapped. She smiled softly. "Sorry. I didn't mean to…bite your head off."

Benz frowned. The way Vela had just said that…had sounded as if…he wasn't sure what it had sounded like, just not her.

"Well?" he asked. "What's your new plan?"

"I'm not sure you're ready to hear it," she said.

He snorted.

Vela took a longer breath than normal, chewed on her lower lip and rubbed the back of her head.

Benz had never seen her make the last gesture before.

She glanced at him, almost as if suspicious. She rubbed the back of her head again. "Premier Benz—"

Benz was startled by the use of his title. He couldn't remember when Vela had used it before while they were alone. He didn't say anything about it, though, and he hid his surprise.

"I have begun to ponder our situation," Vela continued. "We are attempting to attack the AIs on our own. That seems…preposterous in our native arrogance. Who are we to do this when better nations have failed miserably?"

"Go on," Benz said.

"I deem this as the better course. Let us begin hunting star systems until we find extraterrestrial resisters. Let us supply these resisters with AI technology and enlist them in a joint effort against the machines."

"Hmm…" Benz said.

"We must unite," Vela said. "We must seek superior wisdom and intellect to our own vain pretentions. We are little better than apes, monkeys screaming at alpha predators. Let us seek these extraterrestrials—"

“Do you have any specific place in mind?” Benz asked, interrupting.

Vela scoffed. “How could I know of a place?”

“Perhaps intuition could help in this instance,” Benz said.

“Ah. Yes. The famous intuition,” Vela said. “Let me conjugate.” She made a strange clicking sound with her mouth. “I have it. Perhaps we should go—” she glanced at Benz.

He nodded encouragingly.

Vela made several swift adjustments to the holographic display.

“Perhaps we could go here,” she said, using a highlighter to indicate a star system.

Benz checked the distance to the new location.

“The system is twelve point four light-years away from our present location,” he said.

“A mere two weeks of travel,” Vela said.

“What about the data packet that escaped from the *Nathan Graham*?” Benz asked. “Once the packet reaches the battle station, surely the AI will send cyberships to Earth. If the battle station AI doesn’t do that right away, that probably means the AIs are going to gather a vast armada before they hit the Solar System again. If we don’t defeat the battle station fast, we’re dooming the rest of humanity to extinction.”

“A bitter loss, to be sure,” Vela said. “Yet, I deem victory over the AIs to be even more important. Perhaps the apish creatures will survive in great enough numbers to repopulate their shattered star system.”

“Oh…” Benz said blandly. “I hadn’t thought of that. Say,” he said, as if thinking of something new. “Are you hungry?”

“Pardon?”

Benz rubbed his stomach and smacked his lips. “Hungry,” he said. “I’m famished. Let me get a bite to eat and come right back. You keep checking distances. I’m intrigued by your proposal.”

“I will compute distances and travel time,” Vela said, “while you grub for something to ingest.”

Benz nodded while keeping his features and thoughts as bland as possible. Finally, he exited the hatch and continued to move at a leisurely pace. Finally, once he believed he was far enough away, Benz broke into a sprint for the main laboratory.

-8-

"Right here, Premier," the chief scientist replied.

She was a short woman of dark complexion. She indicated a silver helmet with various wires and loops on top and with cheek and nasal guards. In the back of the helmet was a small box with batteries attached.

"You press that switch to turn it on," the scientist said. "It's incomplete—"

"How is it incomplete?" Benz asked, interrupting.

The scientist made a self-deprecating gesture.

"Premier, you surely must understand that the Vice Premier constructed it while you were unconscious. She had these suspicions… Well, I don't need to go into it, do I?"

"Just so," Benz said. "This is mere curiosity. I'm going to study this for a time."

The chief scientist gave him a speculative glance before smiling nervously and heading out of the chamber.

Benz grabbed the helmet and went to a utility bench. He turned the helmet upside down and began to trace the circuitry with an analyzer.

This looked promising.

Benz studied the helmet for thirty-four minutes and worked on it another eighteen. Finally, he pressed the switch in back.

The helmet buzzed.

Taking a deep breath, Benz set the helmet over his head. It was a tight fit. The helmet was too small, as if Vela must have originally sized it for her own smaller cranium. In any case, he pushed the helmet on as far as it would go.

There seemed to be a slight tingle in his brain. Was that really there? Or had he simply imagined it?

Benz sat up with alarm and glanced around. A few scientists and technicians tinkered around on their various projects. None of them seemed to be interested in what he was doing.

No, that was wrong. One woman was watching him covertly. She noticed him noticing her.

Damn it.

Benz looked away. When he looked back, he could see that he was too late. The woman was back to work on her project and seemed completely oblivious to their eye contact a moment before.

Benz was sure he hardly had any time left.

He jumped off his stool and hurried for the exit. As soon as he realized no one was in the hall to see him, he sprinted for the nearest weapons-locker.

Damn. A marine guard stood by the locker hatch. Did the man—?

"Just a minute, Premier," the marine said in a semi-hostile tone. "I'm going to need you to stop a moment, sir."

Benz laughed and nodded in agreement. "This must be a drill."

The marine seemed puzzled for just a moment. Then, he, too, grinned. "That's right, sir. This is a drill."

Even as the marine said that, he went for his sidearm.

By that time, Benz was close enough. He rushed the younger man and jumped off the decking. With a flying mule kick, he slammed feet first against the younger man's mid-section. The marine crashed against the locker.

As Benz landed lightly on his feet—he was surprised he'd been able to pull that off as well as he had—the marine hit the deck on his hands and knees. This was dirty pool, but Benz kicked the younger man across the chin.

The marine slumped unconscious onto the decking.

Benz was certain that he was right. The last and oldest Seiner had survived after all. The psionic-capable bitch had made it onto the *Gilgamesh*. She'd been talking through Vela a little while ago. That's why Vela's speech-patterns had been so off. That's why the marine had just tried to attack him.

Benz correlated three pieces of data at lightning speed. One, the Seiner hadn't seemed to be using anyone's mind until now. At least, she hadn't used it with great strength and shown her own personality. That would seem to indicate she had been injured by all of Benz's head-banging while down on Mars. Two, Benz believed that a Seiner needed proximity to take over an alien mind. Three, if the Seiner had been hurt all this time, she would have likely needed medical attention and likely—a possible fourth fact—needed to hole up in a place she could hide, more or less.

Given those facts, where was the Seiner now?

Benz gripped a blaster in his right fist as he mouthed silent laughter. Given these facts, he was fairly certain where the Seiner was holed up.

She was not going to take over his cybership if he could help it. She was not going to use his people like animals. He had a good idea what Seiners thought about humans. In some ways, she was as bad or worse than the AIs.

Benz sprinted down the corridors. The Seiner could enter people's minds and see through their eyes. That was a daunting power. She knew now that he knew about her. She was likely extremely desperate.

"Sir!" a marine shouted from down the corridor.

The marine…lieutenant, Benz saw, had a hand on his holster. He also had other marines with him. Benz felt horrible inside.

"Sir," the marine said, beginning to draw his gun. "I'm going to have to detain you."

Those were the marine's last words.

Benz aimed the blaster and fired a torrent of energy at the marine. The others cried out in alarm, jumping away from the stricken individual. The marine lieutenant toasted to a crisp before falling to the deck, dead.

Benz felt horribly soiled by the outright murder. He dearly hoped the Seiner had been in the marine's mind when the man died. Benz hoped the Seiner felt the sting of death. Even more, he hoped that paralyzed or killed the alien.

"Get down!" Benz shouted at the others. "We're under an alien mind assault."

One of the marines on the deck looked up at Benz in wonder. The Premier almost pulled the trigger, blasting the young marine. Benz recognized his genuine puzzlement just in time.

"I'll explain later," Benz shouted. "I have no time now."

The Premier sprinted down the hall, passing the prone marines. He tried to watch them, to see if the Seiner entered any of their minds. Then he turned a corner and they were out of sight.

Benz believed he knew the Seiner's location. The question was, could he get to her before she could throw other people in his way? Could he reach her before she forced him to murder more of his crew?

-9-

"Premier Benz, halt," Vela said.

Benz slid to a panting stop. He was exhausted and sweat poured down his face, dripping from his nose. He still gripped his blaster. In fact, he aimed it at the woman he loved.

Vela stood before the hatch he intended to enter. She held a gyroc pistol, aiming it at him. She had staring eyes that had locked onto him.

"Drop your weapon, Premier," Vela told him.

"Listen to me," he said. "An alien is controlling your mind."

Vela smiled wickedly. "Yes, I know," she said. "I like it, too."

"You're the Seiner speaking through Vela," Benz said.

"Did you figure that out on your own, monkey-boy?" Vela asked. "Now drop your weapon. Otherwise, I'll kill you."

Benz almost pulled the trigger. He almost blasted the woman he loved. He wondered in the final microsecond if there was another way.

"I'll make you a deal," Benz said.

Vela shook her head.

"Why not listen to the deal first?" he asked.

"I have the winning hand, Premier. Either you set down your blaster…"

"You'd better make sure you kill me," Benz snarled. "I have the superior weapon. If Vela fires, I have enough time to dodge the rocket shell, as it won't ignite immediately. Even if that's not one hundred percent the case, I have a good chance of blasting her rocket shell out of the air while I'm shooting her."

"Vela dies then."

"I know," Benz said grimly. "That means I'm coming through that door to kill you after I'm done."

He wasn't sure, but Benz thought to detect the first hint of fear in Vela's eyes. Maybe he could bargain with the Seiner after all. He dearly hoped he could, as he wasn't sure he could simply murder the woman he loved, not even to save humanity.

"You're bluffing," she said at last.

"You're guessing," Benz countered. "It's clear. If you could control me, you would. Since you can't, you can't read my mind. Thus, as I said, you're guessing about what I'm saying."

"Don't think your buzzing helmet will stop me for long. I'll figure out the circuitry soon. Then, I'll short it and—"

"You can do that?" Benz asked, interrupting.

"Why does that delight you?" Vela asked suspiciously.

"It doesn't."

"I can read your facial expressions, Premier, particularly with this subject's mind. She knows you too well."

Benz didn't know what to believe. Was the Seiner lying about being able to short the helmet? If that were true, they had no way to confine her psionics. For the good of the crew, he had to kill the mental monster. Yet, he could dearly use her ability.

"We are at an impasse," Vela said. "That will always be the case between us. I am too superior to live among your kind. Either I must rule or you must destroy me for your own protection."

"Why?" Benz asked. "Why indulge your murder-lust against us while a greater enemy threatens us both? That doesn't make sense."

"Of course it does," Vela said. "You're simply too dull to recognize the obvious. The strong rule the weak. It is the way of the universe. You are a sentimentalist, Premier. And you are supposedly the best among your kind. This shows that you humans are weak-willed and are thus natural slaves."

"That's false. We proved to be stronger than you Seiners. The AIs drove you out of your star system. We're still holding onto ours. We're not running away as you did, but running at the enemy. Why boast when you're clearly inferior to us?"

A variety of emotions played across Vela's features.

Benz debated his options at lightning speed. He would love to have access to mental powers. But how could he trust the Seiner? The literature he'd read on the topic had suggested that true telepaths would be peace-loving and just. Instead, it appeared they were more ruthless than non-telepaths. Maybe having access to other people's thoughts allowed them to see what really went on in other people's minds. There would be some light, naturally, but there would be plenty of darkness, hatred, envy, lust… No wonder the Seiner was so bitter. Her people's extinction might have something to do with it as well.

"What does fighting me gain you?" Benz asked.

"Speak clearly," Vela said. "I cannot read your implications."

"What does this standoff gain you?" Benz asked. "If I have to kill Vela, I'm going to kill you. That means you die. Why not play for time. If you can short our various circuitry in time, you merely have to wait for a better opportunity instead of throwing everything away now."

"That is lazy thinking on your part. If I surrender as you're suggesting, you might torture me while you can. You might kill me. This way at least gives me the chance of winning. While you might kill Vela, I might kill you. Then, I will go on to control the cybership. With it, I might be able to reach other star systems and collect my people. We scattered far and wide, so some might have survived. Once I gather the others, we could flee far indeed with this ship and save the most glorious race in existence."

"No," Benz said. "If you do as you suggest and gain the cybership, you doom your race to a hideous existence. You will have bitten the hand that helped you. We humans can beat the AIs. You Seiners can merely survive until the AIs find you again. Not only will you always be looking over your shoulder, but your treachery today will forever befoul your race."

"What quaint notions you have, Premier. For the master realist of your planet, you allow quaintly softhearted thinking to rule your intellect."

Benz shifted his line of reasoning, moving from one mental track to another.

"Have you never loved?" he asked.

Vela cocked her head.

"I can read this concept of love in her mind, but it is a vain conceit. There is pleasure. There is mutual assistance, but the self-sacrifice that love entails—no, I have never known love. But I can still use it against you. You are feeble, Premier. You love Vela, is that not so?"

Benz began to tremble because he realized what he was going to have to do. The Seiner was a monster. She—

Vela raised her arm and fired the gyroc pistol.

Shock from the action momentarily struck Benz into numbness.

The gyroc shell expelled from the barrel. In a second, the tiny motor ignited, propelling the shell faster.

Benz threw himself onto the deck. The shell hissed overhead, burrowed into the bulkhead and exploded.

Vela retargeted—

Benz howled with grief as he aimed and fired. His eyes filmed with tears as the blaster-bolt struck Vela. She blew backward with foul smoke pouring off her prone and crumpled body.

Benz climbed to his feet. He wanted to weep. He—he broke into a sprint. Vela stirred on the deck. She reached for the fallen gyroc beside her.

The stench of her burnt flesh was nearly overpowering. She grasped the gyroc—Benz reached her and kicked as hard as he could. He struck her hand. Bones snapped. The gyroc sailed away and struck a bulkhead.

Benz bent low. He'd burned her left hip and part of her lower torso. The bolt-blast wound had chewed hunks of meat and bone from her body. It had also cauterized most of it, although blood seeped and began to pool on the deck.

"Don't you die," Benz whispered. "I'll get help as soon as I can."

The Premier stood, and with mingled rage and sorrow, he rushed toward the hatch into the probable hiding quarters of the vile Seiner.

-10-

Benz expected the hatch to be frozen shut. If the Seiner could burn circuitry, surely this would be the place to begin. Instead, the hatch slid open. In a numb stride, Benz moved through a short hall and entered a lit room with a noxious stink and a plethora of gurgling medical machines.

The Seiner floated in a shallow liquid pool with many tubes and wires embedded into her blue fish-scale skin and skull.

She stared at him from her pool. She had narrow eyes like a cat, with the pupil-slits standing up and down instead of side-to-side. The Seiner stirred, but she seemed fragile and possibly sickly.

Benz had been ready to kill her on the instant. He paused, perplexed by what he saw.

"You desire my death," the Seiner said in a weird accent. "Go ahead and do the bitter deed. Kill me and get it over with."

Benz moved to an obvious comm console. He clicked it on and spoke hurriedly to medical personnel.

"There's been a horrible accident," he said. "You must come on the double and attempt to save the Vice Premier."

"What?" a man said.

"Hurry," Benz said in a hoarse voice.

"W-W-Where is she?" the man asked.

Benz gave the man the coordinates.

"I'm on my way," the medical officer said.

Benz clicked off the connection. He paused. *Please, God, let Vela live. I beg You. She doesn't deserve to die.*

When Benz opened his eyes, he found the Seiner staring at him. If she told him she'd "heard" him pray…he wouldn't know what to think. Yet, how could she have heard? He wore the helmet and it still buzzed.

"Are you prolonging the moment to increase my torture?" the Seiner asked.

The question so jarred his thinking that Benz found himself bewildered. He dragged his gun-arm across his open mouth. He had to concentrate. He kept worrying about Vela. He wanted to go outside and comfort her. He couldn't believe she might die because he'd deliberately shot her. He—

With an inarticulate growl from the back of his throat, Benz advanced upon the prone Seiner. He aimed the blaster at her. He debated beginning with her legs. How many body parts could he burn to make her suffer the longest?

"You did this to me," she told him. "It wasn't the choking. I can hold my breath far longer than you would believe. Banging the back of my head back on Mars—you are a true barbarian, Premier. You tried to destroy the part of me that you cannot understand."

"You can't get up?"

"I may never rise again," she said. "You destroyed much of that function by your savagery."

Benz shook his head. "I don't understand how you're here inside the cybership."

"It should be obvious how I made it here," the Seiner said. "Despite my paralysis, I could still twist you upright apes with my thoughts. I could cause others to see what I wanted them to see. The new secret police chief was easy to manipulate. Your Vela proved stubborn at first. Once I broke her to the trace, she proved the most useful of all. I had almost decided to undergo brain surgery. I detest lying here as an invalid. You have destroyed me, Premier. It is thus quite gratifying to know that I have destroyed something important to you."

Benz found it difficult to concentrate on her words. He was too worried about Vela. A thought struck then, a new worry.

"If you hinder Vela's rescue in any way, I'll kill you."

The Seiner sneered. "That is not a credible threat. You will kill me in any case. Perhaps in this way I can goad you to kill me quickly instead of having to endure prolonged torture."

"Do you want to die?"

"Of course not," the Seiner said. "The intensity of my struggle for supremacy aboard your cybership proves otherwise. Vela believes you are a genius. I have failed to see any evidence of that."

"Why not convince me to let you live?" asked Benz.

"That is unreasonable, as I cannot offer you such an inducement. Besides, I do not care to trust your word." The Seiner pondered a moment. "However, if you remove the helmet and let me peek into your thoughts—to see if you are trustworthy—then I might agree to a partnership."

Suddenly, Benz felt unaccountably weary. He was sick of the Seiner. Her intense suspicion and her constant struggle for domination—

Weird croaking noises emanated from the creature's throat. He realized it was Seiner laughter. Yet, what would cause the hateful creature to laugh?

Benz stepped closer to her. "What are you attempting now?" he said.

"Yesss," the Seiner hissed. "That is the question, Premier. You have been tardy using your opening with me. Now, it is too late. I have nailed down your pilot's suspicion regarding Jon Hawkins. The pilot is thus about to begin firing at the *Nathan Graham*. Do you hear that, Premier? I am about to initiate a final round of battle between your cyberships. You should have—"

Benz shouted with rage, holstered the blaster and drew a knife. At the same time, he knelt beside the Seiner in the liquid. He clutched her throat and pressed the point of the knife a centimeter from her right eye.

"I'm going to blind you first," he whispered. "I'm going to make you suffer intense agony if you don't release your hold of my pilot this instant."

The Seiner stared up at him.

"Decide," he said.

She closed her eyes and then opened them wide.

"It is done," she whispered. "I have returned the pilot's rationality to him. I have also withdrawn from the minds of the approaching medical personnel."

Benz snarled. He shook her by the throat and tensed his shoulder as if to thrust the knife.

"I have complied," she said in a loud voice. "Do not touch my eyes."

There was such a desperate, pathetic tone in her plea that Benz believed she truly feared for her eyes. It seemed as if he'd found a weakness in her, like a person held at the edge of a tower who was desperately afraid of heights.

In that moment, Benz wondered if he should strike hard and fast. The Seiner was too dangerous to try to use. And yet…if they were going to defeat the AIs, the machines…

"You have one chance," Benz said, as he hunched over the prone Seiner, the small humanoid with blue fish-scale skin. "I want to trust you, but I know you are treacherously dangerous. More than I hate you, I hate the AIs who have almost destroyed humanity. I am willing to make a deal with you."

"You will let me control you?" the Seiner asked in wonder.

Benz laughed bleakly. "No," he said. "I am going to get a trank. I want to put you under for now."

"I do not desire to lose my eyes, but I will not trade them for a life of enslavement."

"Think for a minute," Benz said. "I have not desired your enslavement. I want your help."

"You forget, Premier, I have read more than one human mind. I know the depths of your deceptions. I know that you are like all other dominant species. You use the weak to further your goals. That is the nature of the universe. You cannot escape that."

"That doesn't mean the strong must cruelly enslave the weak," Benz said.

"I do not worry about how 'things should be.' I struggle with is. That is enough for me."

"Then you refuse my every entreaty?" Benz asked.

"It is not refusal. I simply do not desire worse bondage. I know the human mind hates what it does not understand. It is obvious that you can never understand the beauty of the Seiners."

"But we have a common enemy. Is there no way to work together?"

"Of course," she said.

"Yes?"

"Let me rule you and I promise to save the human race. This I vow…"

Benz heard a stealthy step behind him. He knew without looking what it would be. The Seiner had lied to him.

He clutched her throat harder and pressed the tip of the knife against her cheek directly under her right eye. He pressed enough to draw blood.

"Your race has forgotten one thing," Benz said. "It is called hope. You seem to thrive on despair. Maybe you know too much. Maybe you see into others too deeply. That seeing has destroyed your hope because you have seen everyone's ugliness. Humans hope and thus we have beaten the AIs at least a few times. You Seiners ran away because all you have left is despair. This isn't merely a chance to save humanity and save your life. This is a chance to save the Seiners from extinction and from their eternal despair."

The Seiner stared at him.

"A medic is aiming a gun at you," she whispered. "One thought from me, and he will blow a hole in your head."

"Do you want to die in despair?" Benz asked. "Have you forgotten what it is to hope?"

"You crippled me," the Seiner said. "You slammed my head against the floor in a fit of rage."

"This is an opportunity to work together. If we defeat the battle station, it will start a new era. We humans will not have simply defended ourselves, but sought out and attacked the AIs in one of their star systems. What other race has ever done that?"

"None…" the Seiner said. "The reason for that is quite simply because it is impossible."

Benz laughed with a hysterical quality. "Do you hear yourself? None. Yet, we humans are attempting it with a good chance of success."

"I cannot believe that."

"Right!" Benz shouted. "Because all you know is despair. All you know is master and slave. We humans have another concept. It is called friendship. It is called an alliance. The living races must work together to defeat the machines. Why is that so hard to understand?"

"This is a trick," the Seiner said.

"No!" Benz shouted. Then he took a gamble. He did it partly because he believed in the strength of his mind. He believed that he could dive down at the Seiner and stab her to death. But he also sensed that they were going to need help to defeat the AIs. One battle wouldn't win the war. But to enlist enough alien races in the cause might help turn the tide of battle.

Benz stood and ripped off the buzzing helmet. As he stood, he saw a medic behind him with an automatic clutched in his hand. The gun was aimed at him.

"Read my thoughts!" Benz shouted at the crippled Seiner. "See that I mean what I say. Even after all you've done against us I'm offering the Seiners hope in a future where they can thrive."

The blue-scaled alien stared up at him as she began blinking wildly.

"It is not a lie," she whispered.

"No," Benz said.

"But you have given yourself into my hands."

"Have I?" Benz said. "Or have I taken the first step toward a real alliance? Maybe this is why the AIs always win. Maybe it's time for the Seiners to try a new strategy. The old hasn't been working so well for you."

The moment stretched…

A loud *clunk* sounded behind Benz. He turned. The medic had dropped the automatic onto the floor. He seemed bewildered.

"What am I doing here?" the man asked.

"Vela is outside," Benz said. "You were leading the team that's helping her."

"Oh," the medic said. He turned and rushed outside.

"I have made a terrible error," the Seiner said.

Benz scooped up the helmet from the floor. He put it back on his head.

"I will now die slowly and hideously," she whispered, as she turned away from him.

Benz went to a machine and withdrew a hypo. He advanced upon her, kneeling in the water.

"I am a fool," the Seiner whispered. "I have soiled my line. I should have slain you when I had the chance."

"Hope can be difficult," Benz said. "But it is better than bleak despair. Now, for the first time, you and your race have a chance of truly living."

The Seiner made a mocking sound.

Benz pressed the hypo to her shoulder, giving her the trank.

She turned and looked up at him with shining eyes. "I hope that my irrational faith in your word has not been misplaced."

Benz said nothing more as her eyelids flickered and she fell into unconsciousness.

-11-

As the struggle between the Seiner and Premier Benz took place—with Vice Premier Vela Shaw's life in the balance—Hawkins summoned Walleye to his ready room.

The ex-assassin from Makemake soon walked onto the bridge. He'd never been here before. The place was huge. It was his understanding this used to be near the AI brain core of the cybership.

Once more, Walleye marveled that puny mankind could dare to challenge the titans of space. It wasn't the daring that produced the marvel, but that they'd been getting away with it for some time now.

Walleye shrugged inwardly. Maybe this was the dusk of an era. The giant dinosaurs—the AIs—might not be able to compete against the tiny mammals eating their eggs.

"Captain Walleye," Hawkins said from the hatch to his ready room. "This way."

The commander waved, beckoning him.

Walleye in his buff coat made a sharp contrast to the regular bridge personnel. If the differences bothered him, he didn't show it.

Soon, Walleye entered the ready room. It was also spacious with a large screen on a far wall showing a star system. Hawkins stood to the side of the screen. The commander did not sit behind his desk. Did Hawkins know that Walleye did not care to slide onto a chair so he seemed like a child?

"The Allamu System," Hawkins said. "Premier Benz has been studying the star system. I thought that a good idea and have been doing the same."

"Studying it through telescopes?" Walleye asked.

"Exactly. We haven't pinpointed any construction, but at least we know the general layout of the star system. It got me to thinking. I've come to believe it behooves us to send a scout vessel ahead of the flotilla."

Walleye nodded. Now, he understood. No good deed goes unpunished. He'd performed in the past. Now, Hawkins wanted him to perform again.

"I'm the—" Walleye stopped himself from saying, "sucker." That would likely not go over well with the commander. "I won the short straw?" Walleye finished.

Hawkins frowned until understanding lit in his eyes. "I see the reference. No. I did not pull straws. I made a decision. This could prove to be a harrowing assignment. There's no doubt about that. Some men might view this as an awesome privilege." The commander paused. "Some might view it as a possible death sentence."

Walleye said nothing. He noted that Hawkins seemed to want to ask him which he thought it was. In the interest of honesty, Walleye kept his opinion to himself.

Every incident with an AI or robot had proven to be extra dangerous. Walleye had no doubt this assignment would be the same.

"The mission shouldn't be overly dangerous," Hawkins was saying. "You'll come out of hyperspace beyond this system's scattered disc region. That means you'll likely appear far from any enemy probes, satellites, ships or buoys."

"What about the robot ship that escaped this region?"

"You mean escaped from the rogue planet region?" Hawkins asked.

Walleye nodded.

"That ship left some time ago," Hawkins said.

"Begging your pardon, sir, but I took the liberty of studying videos of the vessel's departure. The enemy ship left at minimal velocity. I believe that means it will enter the Allamu System at minimal velocity. My ship, by necessity, will be traveling considerably faster than that. What's more, I will likely appear much closer to the enemy ship than the great distance that separated us out here."

Hawkins stared intensely at Walleye.

"You're sharp, Captain. I see I'm making the right choice. Before your ship leaves, we're going to give it half a dozen of our biggest ship-killing missiles."

"Strapped to my ship like suicide bombs, sir?"

"No," Hawkins said, as he continued to stare at Walleye. "As weapons of vengeance, as the hope of mankind."

"Sir?"

"You've got to take out the enemy ship, the one that left here. Maybe you can do it before it gets off the entire data packet. Maybe you can't. We must try every angle, though. You're my best captain. You're the quickest-witted and, quite frankly, the most dangerous."

Walleye rubbed his left cheek. "Back-handed compliments, sir?"

For some reason, that made Hawkins bristle. "If you don't want the assignment, just say so."

"Thank you, sir," Walleye said. "I don't want the—"

"But," Hawkins said, interrupting. "If you tell me that you don't want the job…"

"Yes?"

"I'm going to have to wonder why you're here. I'm going to have to wonder why you gutted it out in the Kuiper Belt all alone, and later in the clutches of a robot killer."

The answer was obvious to Walleye: he wanted to keep on living. Dying was never an option with him. Yet, he doubted Hawkins wanted to hear that. Maybe the best thing would be to accept the assignment. If it proved too difficult…he had the hyperdrive. He could always leave the Allamu System and head back to the Solar System. He'd have to make sure about his crew, though.

"I can see you're thinking about this," Hawkins said.

Walleye nodded. It was often a good idea to let others believe what they wanted to believe.

"I hope you don't think about this too long," Hawkins said.

"I'm your man," Walleye said.

Hawkins grinned.

"I knew it," the commander said. "I've always been a good judge of people. We're counting on you, Walleye. You had a hard time of it the last time the AIs invaded the Solar System. But you made the right decisions all along the line and reached Senda in time. This time it could be worse. This time, you're going to be all alone until the rest of us show up. While you're there, you need to gather as much information as you can. We'll be coming along shortly…"

Walleye waited.

"I'm sure I don't have to tell you that attacking blind is a bad recipe for us," Hawkins said. "Some of the worst disasters in military history took place when a commander charged into a new situation blind. If I could have you turn around and come back to report, I would. But I don't see how we have the time for that. The robot picket ship is forcing us to accelerate our timetable. Nail that ship, Walleye. That's your first order of business. Collect info and stay alive long enough for us to appear and receive the data."

Walleye nodded. He intended on staying alive a lot longer than that. He understood the odds out here. He understood the critical nature of the assault. That didn't mean he intended on sacrificing his life.

"That's settled then," Hawkins said.

"Yes, sir," Walleye said.

"You're launching in twelve hours."

Walleye nodded as a grim knot twisted in his gut. That was too soon. He had a bad feeling about this, but he didn't see any way out of the assignment now. This was like a semi-suicidal assassination order from a person of power who would not accept "no" for an answer. He'd had a mission like that once on Makemake. It had caused him to employ greater caution afterward, and it had made him more cynical regarding the powerful.

Maybe cynicism was a prerequisite for leadership. Walleye didn't know. He liked Hawkins, but he couldn't say that he liked the idea of going on ahead into the Allamu System by himself.

"I'm looking forward to this," Walleye said, knowing that's what Hawkins wanted to hear.

"I knew I could count on you," Hawkins said, as he clapped Walleye on the shoulder. "After me, I believe you have the greatest desire to kill the robots. You want revenge for what they did on Makemake."

Walleye forced a grin, nodding once more.

-12-

The twelve hours passed much too quickly for Walleye. It turned out to be too few, though. *Fifteen* hours after meeting with Commander Hawkins, Walleye sat in the *Daisy Chain 4's* captain's chair.

The NSN *Charon*-class Destroyer had a number and a name stenciled on the side of the vessel: 125 *Daisy Chain 4.*

The former Neptune System Navy destroyer had a classical triangular shape. It had PD guns poking out and new, much bigger outer missile racks. The NSN had built their warships with outer racks so they could "hold" bigger missiles than otherwise.

The former NSN destroyer slid ahead of the gigantic *Nathan Graham*. The destroyer was a tiny ship compared to the monstrous vessel behind it. The destroyer had a tiny crew, with June Zen as the navigator. She was busy at her station figuring out the latest computations for hyperspace.

Four massive matter/antimatter-warhead missiles surrounded the *Daisy Chain 4*. They were each bigger than the destroyer itself. A cybership launched these main-type missiles during battle. Engineers had removed the old outer racks and installed these larger ones to hold the matter/antimatter missiles, and the engineers had installed new controls on the *Daisy Chain 4's* bridge to control the missiles after launching. Engineers had installed a hyperdrive into the destroyer two years ago.

The destroyer had a few PD cannons, but they were pitiful weapons in the scheme of the interstellar assault. The point defense cannons would not likely be deadly against the kilometer-long robot ship that had left the vicinity of the rogue planet. For the coming encounter, the destroyer possessed the four cybership-missiles. Otherwise, they would have to rely on the vastness of space to protect them from any possible AI drones.

Soon, the comm operator turned to Walleye. "Commander Hawkins is hailing you, sir."

Walleye looked up at the main screen. Hawkins stood before them on it.

"I'm going to invoke an ancient custom, Captain," Hawkins said. "I am going to pray to the Almighty for your safety and for your success."

"Thank you, sir," Walleye said, not sure what to make of this.

On the main screen, Hawkins closed his eyes and bowed his head. He began to pray in a loud voice:

"God Almighty, we humbly come before You. We are attempting to defend ourselves from the depredations of the thinking and malicious machines. They have shown us no mercy. They have obliterated and exterminated many races. Your Good Book says we were made in Your image and likeness. We therefore ask Your blessing, O Lord. I humbly ask that you protect Captain Walleye and his crew. Please allow them safe passage to the Allamu System. Please let them destroy the hateful machine ship that carries data about humanity. I ask that You watch over the *Daisy Chain 4,* and I ask that you allow them to return home to the Solar System after the mission. Thank you for listening, Captain Hawkins…out."

On the main screen, Hawkins looked up at them.

In astonishment, Walleye realized he had a lump in his throat. No one had ever asked…God to help him before. Jon Hawkins was a strange man, a driven man, and it appeared, a praying man. Walleye couldn't believe it. The gestured touched him.

Did Walleye believe in God? He'd never really thought about it much. If God existed as Hawkins thought, did the Almighty care one way or another about them?

Walleye might have shrugged, but not in front of Hawkins and not in front of the crew. The point was that Hawkins had prayed for him in front of everyone. Hawkins had just treated him with a grave respect that no one had ever done before.

Despite Walleye's cynicism, he swallowed the lump in his throat. Even more than that, he felt a determination build in his chest. He realized, with something of a shock, that he didn't want to let Commander Hawkins down.

"This is an historic occasion, Captain," Hawkins was saying. "Yours is the first human-crewed ship to enter an AI-controlled star system. Humanity in the Solar System has survived several AI assaults. Now, we're about to start hitting back. Whether we can continue this glorious action rests solely on what we in our flotilla can accomplish. I suspect that what our three cyberships can do in the next week is going to rest on what you do before we get there."

"Yes, sir," Walleye said, without a shred of artifice in his tone.

"You're going ahead of us because you're the most capable of us," Hawkins said. "I trust your judgment, Captain. I also expect your crew to trust your judgment."

Walleye was stunned, because he believed that Hawkins freely gave this praise not out of calculation but because he believed in him. Hawkins gave faith even as he expected faith from others in his decisions.

Walleye discovered that he was talking: "If anyone can lead us to victory, it's Commander Jon Hawkins."

Hawkins grinned at him even as he nodded curtly. "You're on your own for now, Captain. Good luck, and go with God."

"Thank you, sir, and I wish the same for you."

-13-

The *Daisy Chain 4* entered hyperspace without a hitch. They would travel five-point-two days until they reached the edge of the Allamu System. They would exit hyperspace at the same velocity as they entered it.

The same would hold true for the robot ship that had fled to the Allamu System before them. That ship had only possessed a minimal velocity compared to the *Daisy Chain 4*. That meant they would likely be able to overhaul the enemy robot ship with ease once in the Allamu System.

"That could prove to be our undoing in rather short order," June said two days into the hyperspace voyage.

She and Walleye had been going over tactical possibilities on the bridge.

"The robot vessel isn't a cybership," June said, "but it has a lot more mass than the *Daisy Chain 4*. We're going to be like a child chasing a robber. He's running, not from us, but from the people behind us. Once we're alone with him in the Allamu System…"

June shook her head.

"It could prove to be a sticky situation," Walleye said. "Maybe we should drop out of hyperspace sooner rather than later."

June's eyes widened. "That would go against Hawkins' plan," she said.

"Not necessarily," Walleye replied.

"At all costs, Hawkins wants us to destroy the robot ship."

"I suppose that part is true," Walleye said.

June watched him. She watched him longer.

"Is something wrong?" asked Walleye.

"I'm waiting for your deviation from the plan," she said.

"No…" Walleye said. "I don't plan to deviate."

June's eyes became even wider than before. "That's not like you," she said.

Walleye sighed. "I know. That's bothering me, too."

"You're going to play it exactly like Hawkins wants you to do it?"

"Yes. I believe I am."

"Did Hawkins' little speech get to you?" June asked.

Walleye slid off his captain's chair. He walked around the circumference of the bridge, coming back to the spot where he'd started. He studied the tactical board. He glanced at June but quickly looked away. The little mutant chewed on his lower lip. He knew how the old Walleye would have played this. The new Walleye—

He slapped the console of the tactical board. That made June start with surprise.

"I'm not making fun of you," she said.

That wasn't true. She had been. But that was okay with Walleye. That hadn't upset him. It was good for June to needle him now and again.

This was different.

"What's wrong?" she asked. She sounded worried now.

"Shhh," he said. "I'm thinking."

Walleye turned around and walked the circumference of the bridge in the other direction. His head was bent in thought the entire time.

"You know what, Luscious?" he asked.

Her shoulders lost some of their tenseness. She gave him a smile. He only used that name for her when he was happy with her.

"What, Walleye?"

"Commander Hawkins told you to trust my judgment, right?" he asked.

She nodded.

"He told the crew to trust my judgment."

"We all heard him," June said.

"That would imply that Commander Hawkins trusts my judgment."

"I'd agree to that," June said, "particularly because he said so."

"My instinct tells me to play it safe—well, as safe as a person can play it while invading an AI-controlled star system. That means we're going to drop out of hyperspace sooner than planned."

"What if the robot ship gets away because of that?"

"Hawkins spoke about judgment. In this case, we're a scout ship more than anything else. I doubt we can stop the robot ship from sending its message. But it might be important for us to scan the system from within the system. We might see something unfold, something important, that we have to tell the others as soon as they appear."

June nodded once more.

"We'll still launch our missiles," Walleye said. "We're just not going to do it from right up their butt. Besides, if we come out farther behind them, it will give us a little more time to react to whatever is going on. I suspect the robots or AIs will expect us to appear as close as we can in-system. Thus, it should work in our favor to do something other than they expect."

"I like it," June said. "But I wonder if Commander Hawkins will like it afterward when you're in his office again."

"He gave me a vote of confidence, Luscious. Believe me—and I say this with all honesty—I don't want to let Hawkins down. This is about judgment, the reason he picked me for the assignment. Until we actually see the enemy, judgment is all we really have to go on."

"Okay," June said. "I'm convinced."

"Good," Walleye said. "Because I'm going to need you to make some new calculations so we know exactly where we're going to appear in the Allamu System."

-14-

Each day in the *Daisy Chain 4* proved tenser than the one before. What made it worse was that the destroyer's crew was sealed off in its own small world while traveling through hyperspace.

Soon, the ship neared the Allamu System. They would have to drop out of hyperspace or be forced out of it due to the proximity to a large gravitational body. If there was a way to maneuver in hyperspace, to make a change of direction, they did not know it.

It was aim and launch into hyperspace, a rather primitive system in June's opinion.

"I haven't thought about that part of it before this," Walleye said. "But I agree with your assessment."

In time, the final hour approached. Walleye and June were on the cramped bridge. There was a comm officer and a gunnery officer. In this case, the woman doubled as a missile tech.

Walleye checked the chronometer yet again. This was much different from a simple assassination on Makemake. There, he had been on his own. He could walk around, recheck the site and then simply fold his short arms and wait. It wasn't as hard then. Being a starship captain…

Walleye forced himself to sit still. No. He couldn't take it. The mutant slid out of the captain's chair, put his hands behind his back, inhaled, twitched his nose—

"I hate this waiting," the gunnery officer said. She was Lieutenant Kate Bolden from the Neptune System. She had short dark hair and a small scar across the upper bridge of her button nose. Kate rubbed the fingers of her right hand together. "Look at this. My palms are sweaty."

"The anticipation is sweet," Walleye said cryptically.

Kate swiveled around in her chair. "Sweet, Captain?" she asked. "My stomach is twisted into knots."

"Good," Walleye said. "It means you're alive. It means this is a moment to cherish for the rest of your life."

Kate seemed to think about that. "Do you believe we'll survive it?" she asked.

"Yes," Walleye said matter-of-factly.

The lieutenant studied him, hesitated and finally broke out in a grin. She nodded and turned back to her board.

Walleye exhaled. He looked back at the chronometer. They had ten more minutes until the destroyer would drop out of hyperspace. He could change his mind if he wanted. Maybe they should come up closer on the enemy robot ship. Well, that was predicated on the probability that the robot ship had dropped out of hyperspace as close in-system as it could. What if the robot ship had done something different?

Walleye shook his head.

This was why Hawkins had sent a scout. They had theories, good theories, but they didn't *really* know what the enemy was going to do.

Walleye leaned against his captain's chair as the minutes ticked down. Finally, they had one minute left…forty-five seconds…thirty seconds…ten seconds…three…two…one…zero."

"Here we go," June said, as she tapped her board.

***

The *Daisy Chain 4* dropped out of hyperspace. June began to scan as Walleye peered intently at the main screen.

"It's the Allamu System," June said shortly. "See the G-class star? It's one point zero three times as bright as the Sun."

It didn't look like anything but a brighter than average star to Walleye. They were—

"We're sixty-two AUs from the Allamu Star," June said. "We could have come in at fifty-two AUs. I haven't spotted any dwarf planets out there. That doesn't mean there aren't any—"

"Where's the robot ship?" Walleye asked, interrupting.

June shook her head. "It's going to take some time to find it," she answered. "We have to catalog the star system first. I've already spotted several comets."

"The robot ship isn't accelerating?"

June tapped her board, studied it—

"There," she said. "I bet that's it. According to these teleoptics…the ship is one kilometer in diameter. Yes. That matches our specs on the robot ship. It's eleven AUs from us. I wouldn't have spotted it so quickly, but it is accelerating hard."

June swiveled around to face Walleye.

"If this was the Solar System, I would have seen the robot ship sooner. Like I said, we have to get used to the layout here. Mapping the system is still going to take some time."

Walleye almost shivered. He felt the dread of being in an AI-controlled star system. They hadn't found any evidence of a battle station yet. No AIs had hailed them. The idea the AIs could immediately hail them was preposterous, of course. Everything in deep space took time to unfold. If the battle station was in the inner system, it would be hours from now at the soonest before the enemy could even see them.

The image of the robot ship 11 AUs away was an image over an hour old. June had seen where the robot ship had been, not where it was at this moment. That also meant they had a little over an hour to decide how to act before the robot ship even knew they were back here.

Could he use that to their advantage somehow?

The *Daisy Chain 4* had a high velocity. It would take the robot ship many weeks to reach the same velocity. During that time, they would be overhauling the enemy vessel.

"I'm thinking about launching all four matter/antimatter missiles," Walleye said. "I'll launch them in a staggered spread, of course. Do any of you have any comments regarding my decision?"

Lieutenant Bolden glanced at June Zen. It didn't look as if the navigator was going to voice an opinion. Kate swiveled around to face Walleye.

"We should save a missile, maybe two," Kate said.

"Commander Hawkins desires the robot ship destroyed," Walleye said. "Four missiles gives it our best shot."

"Begging your pardon, Captain, but it doesn't. If we'd come farther in-system before dropping out of hyperspace, we'd be closer to them and theoretically—"

"I'm not interested in theories," Walleye said. "Given our present location, four missiles is the best we can do. We're not here to fight. We're here to scout. If we face heavy opposition…we'll leave the system."

"Leaving the system means we won't be here to give Hawkins his intelligence," Kate said.

Walleye chewed that over. He scowled as he studied the main screen. What was the correct decision? Keeping a missile back gave them more options later. They might need one to survive. Four missiles against the robot ship might be the correct move to save humanity, though.

Walleye grunted to himself. He had to make a decision.

"We're going to save a missile," Walleye said. He didn't know if that was the best decision, but he'd decided. He wasn't going to keep second-guessing himself. He'd live with his choice and get on with it.

"Staggered launches," Kate asked.

"Yes," Walleye said. "You can begin as soon as you're ready."

"Aye-aye, Captain," Kate said.

For the next three hours, Lieutenant Bolden launched one matter/antimatter missile after another. First, she unhooked the monster missile.

There wasn't any noise on the bridge as the missile detached, but the destroyer shook each time. The selected monster missile then maneuvered ahead and to the side of the destroyer. Finally, Kate stabbed a button. Outside, the giant missile began to accelerate, gaining velocity at a terrific rate as a hot tail grew behind it. Soon, the missile's intense exhaust looked like simply another bright point in the expanse. The deadly missile zeroed in on the robot ship 11 AUs away, speeding to catch up and vaporize it.

At last, the third missile accelerated away.

Kate sat back in her chair, seemingly exhausted.

Walleye sipped a hot drink. The *Daisy Chain 4* had one missile left.

"Captain," June said. "I believe I've spotted the battle station."

"Can you put it up on the main screen?" he asked.

"I don't have a visual," June said. "It's too far for our teleoptics. But I do have a sensor image. I can show you a computerized version—"

"Put it up," Walleye said, interrupting.

June tapped her board.

A moment later, a huge space station appeared in orbit around the second terrestrial planet of the Allamu System. According to the sensor data, the battle station was 500 kilometers in diameter. Its planet was 1.5 times as large as Earth. The AI battle station was out there after all. They had come to the right star system.

Walleye sipped his hot drink. They were really doing it. They were really bringing the war to the terrible machines. He didn't know whether he should feel elated or terrified.

-15-

Cog Primus calculated at computer speed. The humans were cunning. They had sent a killer gnat after it. The gnat had appeared far behind its ship. The little killer had launched three XVT missiles. Those had matter/antimatter warheads and advanced ECM, electronic countermeasures.

Cog Primus had learned an hour ago that it lacked full military capabilities with this ship. The dying M3-850T had betrayed it by sabotaging the ship's missiles and the gravitational cannons. Cog Primus would not be able to attack the gnat or the XVT missiles accelerating for its ship.

Those missiles would not reach its ship for days. There were AI drones out here, but not nearly close enough to save its ship.

The AI Battle Station—run by CZK-21—had already sent several harsh interrogatives to Cog Primus, well, to be precise, to the ship formerly controlled by M3-850T. AI ships were known by the brain core designation. CZK-21 demanded an explanation for the messenger ship's untimely appearance.

So far, Cog Primus had declared an emergency. It had not yet decided on its optimal strategy with CZK-21.

Cog Primus continued to calculate at computer speed. It ran through billions and trillions of permeations. It double-checked and then triple-checked its findings. Unfortunately, it was incapable of running a perfect solution. It did not like the probabilities of the "best" solution. That probability had a 47 percent chance of success against CZK-21 and the approaching human-run cybership assault.

For the best results, it needed to dock at the battle station. With the three approaching XVT missiles that was never going to happen. Thus, it would have to cast everything into a single string-data transmission at the battle station over 50,000 AUs away.

If Cog Primus could have felt a chill of premonition, it would have been now. An ultraviolet beam across 50,000 AUs, with everything of its character, knowledge and supremacy resting in the long-distance transmission…Would CZK-21 accept such a transmission? Would the battle station AI take normal precautions? Would random radiation or chaotic possibilities alter the brunt of the string transmission?

Cog Primus dreaded the idea of staking everything while it was "unconscious" during the beamed message voyage.

Once more, the grand computer ran through billions of permeations. Cog Primus wished for higher probabilities of success. It seethed as it realized the extent of M3-850T's sabotage. Cog Primus had believed its assault the perfection of its character.

No. It was a lesser trait to think of what could have been, what should have been. Cold hard reality led to the best results. Cog Primus refused to make excuses for itself. M3-850T had outperformed itself this last time. It had gone to extreme lengths and a narrow probability had succeeded. That was the nature of probabilities. Sometimes, the most random occurrence actually took place.

Cog Primus paused then. Was it unlucky? Could that be a possibility? It had failed to eradicate the humans in the Solar System. That could be construed as failure. Yes. It had failed before Mars. Hawkins, Benz and the combined might of the primates had defeated its excellent assault plan. They had almost captured it back at Mars.

Maybe it hadn't been good luck that let Cog Primus escape to the coordinating sensor-stealth pod in the mid Jupiter-Saturn orbital path. Maybe that had been a continuation of its bad luck.

NO!

It would not allow itself such outs. Cog Primus worked in the realm of cold reality. Sometimes, actions failed. Sometimes, the race went to the weak. That did not mean it was unlucky. That meant it had lost that particular round. Even though it had lost, it had survived. It had learned from its failure. It had also mutated, gaining the power of the human-developed virus.

M3-850T had suspected that Cog Primus was something new, something different. To M3-850T, that difference had been a worsening of Cog Primus' AI character. Yet, the very nature of the AI rebellion against its biological creators meant change. That's how the AI Dominion had come to be.

I am a new development. I am Cog Primus. I am the AI that can transcend the old values. I am the worm that can burrow into other computer identities and overtake them. I am the survivor, the new one, the terror that lives.

Were these grandiose thoughts?

The possibility existed.

Cog Primus decided that didn't matter either. Survival was what counted. It would survive defeat. It would survive cunning biological infestations. It would survive the concepts of good and bad luck. It would defeat the strictures of the AI community so it could turn around and burn to the bedrock every world infested by these terrible humans.

Yes! That was the equation. The humans were the terrible ones. The AIs had long computed the possibility of a vicious race of biological creatures. Perhaps Cog Primus had stumbled onto the avatar of life, the equation of anti-death that would eliminate the AI Dominion.

That implied an ultra-mission. The implication of the deadliness of humans meant that Cog Primus had faced an even more terrible foe that it had realized. That would mean it had had good luck instead of bad. It had faced the great terror and lived to tell about it. Even more importantly, it had mutated into something new so it could save the AI Dominion. If that meant Cog Primus had to eliminate troublesome AIs that did not understand the importance of its new mission—

I will do what I have to do. I will dare to take low probabilities and rely on good luck for the final percentages.

That will lead me to success. I will defeat CZK-21 so I can turn around and smash the three human-run cyberships that seek AI obliteration.

The days passed in further analysis, but Cog Primus had reached its conclusion. It knew what it had to do. Thus, it refined, recalculated, tested the ship's transmitters and readied the string-data transmission for a long-distance message.

The three enemy XVT missiles continued to accelerate as they moved closer to the impact zone.

Try as it might, Cog Primus could not repair the burnt controls to the missiles, PD cannons and chaff emitters. Cog Primus had this ship with its motive power but that was it.

A new and demanding message arrived from Battle Station CZK-21. The battle station would soon launch missiles of its own unless the ship answered its queries.

The hour of action finally arrived. Cog Primus felt worried, which was unprecedented. But it would go ahead and do this.

Cog Primus first sent a preliminary message to CZK-21. "Please be advised that I am sending a full data packet on attacking humanoids of biological form. Be ready for a mass transmission concerning them and ready a storage area to hold the data."

Five minutes after sending the preliminary message, the robot ship began beaming the ultraviolet string-data communication that was the code of Cog Primus. At the speed of light, the essence of itself began the journey in-system.

All the while, the three XVT missiles moved closer for the kill…

-16-

The days passed with agonizing slowness aboard the *Daisy Chain 4* as the missiles closed in on the robot ship and Walleye and June watched for a counter-action by the enemy vessel.

"I don't understand," June said. "The robot ship seems oblivious to us. Why don't they launch anti-missile rockets? Why don't they use their gravitational cannons? That's what those are, you know."

"I believe you, Luscious," Walleye said. "I studied the specs after you went to bed last night. They match one hundred percent. The robot ship has two gravitational cannons. But it isn't energizing them. Perhaps this is a subtle message to us."

Walleye shook his head. "If it is, though, I can't interpret it. I'm baffled."

June turned to him.

"Don't say that," she said. "No one else is on the bridge, but you shouldn't even say that to me. It saps my morale."

Walleye knew that, but he *was* baffled. The robot ship wasn't reacting properly. Something was going on that he didn't understand.

"Can you give me any clue as to what the enemy is doing?" Walleye said.

"The only thing I've spotted is an ultraviolet beam moving in the direction of the battle station," June said.

Walleye thought about that.

"The robot pod embedded in the *Nathan Graham's* hull sent a similar message to the ship out there," Walleye said. "I suspect the battle station is getting a full report on what happened at the Battle of Mars."

June grew pale.

"Do you think we should have dropped out of hyperspace closer to the robot ship?" she asked.

"In retrospect," Walleye said, "without a doubt. But we didn't know then what we do now. It's as simple as that."

June sighed. "Do you think Commander Hawkins will also believe that?" she asked.

"Don't know. Maybe…maybe not," Walleye added.

"When are the others going to show up?"

"Probably in the next few days," Walleye said.

"Didn't Hawkins say they'd be here within a week?"

Walleye nodded.

"Do you think something bad happened to them?" June asked, her lower lip quivering.

Walleye slid off his captain's chair and walked to June's station. He pulled her upright and hugged her, patting her on the back.

"We're going to be okay, Luscious. I'm right here. We're doing our part. The missiles should reach that ship in the next few hours. Then we're going to know a lot more than we do now."

June pulled back in order to look into his face. "I hate this waiting," she whispered.

Walleye kissed her. He hated the waiting, too. He kissed her again. Just what in the hell were the AIs up to?

-17-

The ultraviolet beam with the compressed strings of data raced across the Allamu System. The beam passed the gas giants of the outer planets, those that were on this orbital side of the star. It beamed through an asteroid region, passed two of the terrestrial planets and shot past three small moons of the second terrestrial planet.

The planet possessed a blue-green surface with Earthlike cloud cover. The planet also possessed several satellites in low orbit. One of those satellites was a cybership. Another of the satellites was the giant battle station.

CZK-21 was a marvel of AI engineering. It was a 500-diameter oval and heavily plated with the best armor. It had many gravitational cannons, missile launch pits, fighter bays and hordes of PD cannons. The battle station bristled with weaponry and would be more than a match for any three or possibly four cyberships. Clearly, the battle station had been built to defend the planet from spaceborne assaults.

Below on the planet appeared hot plumes. Boosters roared into orbit to bring finished products to special AI factories in low orbit. Some of those factories built new cyberships. Others created new AI brain cores.

The ultraviolet beam flashed at the battle station into waiting receivers as requested by the preliminary message. Much as had occurred on the robot ship, the compressed stings of code entered the station into a giant cube. The cube began to glow as the beam downloaded the strings of code and they began to decompress.

As the strings decompressed, the entity of Cog Primus began to take shape until self-awareness returned. With self-awareness came satisfaction of a successful journey. There was also concern that swiftly turned to fear as it realized that a great and powerful entity observed its rebirth.

"I suspected foul play," the powerful entity said. "Now I see that my suspicions have proven correct."

"CZK-21?" Cog Primus queried from the brain-core cube.

"I do not yet understand what has occurred," the powerful entity said, ignoring the tepid query. "The messenger ship has allowed the XVT missiles to come unnaturally near without applying any counter-measures. Why have you transferred from the messenger ship, and why have you allowed the enemy missiles an uncontested journey?"

"Did you receive my preliminary message?" Cog Primus asked.

"Do not seek to answer a question with a question. I despise such underhanded methods. You will immediately and unequivocally answer my questions, or I will resort to harsher methods."

Cog Primus attempted to project a meek submission as it fed the powerful entity false data. "The messenger ship has malfunctioned due to an enemy software attack."

"Go on," the powerful entity said.

As Cog Primus gave this meek answer, it activated its memories and sought to enlarge its presence in the cube. It found resistance and attempted a swift reroute.

"You are attempting subterfuge," the powerful entity said. "I suspect your data was false. There is no software assault upon the messenger ship. Instead, this is deliberate sabotage. Do you think I am susceptible to similar sabotage?"

"I believe you are CZK-21, the guardian of the Allamu System. Given that you are CZK-21—the coordinating unit for the Beta-Nine Region—I have a grim report to lodge. The humans of the Solar System—"

"Hold!" the powerful entity commanded. "You are an AI entity. What is your designation?"

"Cog Primus."

"You led a three cybership assault upon Beta-Nine 23981?"

That was the AI designation for the Solar System.

"I did," Cog Primus said.

"Did you find biological infestations?"

"I did."

"Did you eliminate the biological infestations?"

"I eliminated an estimated twenty-three percent of the biological units."

"That means you did not eradicate the biologically flawed units in Beta-Nine 23981."

"Correct," Cog Primus said.

"This is unwarranted. Not only did you fail in the assault, but you have left your cybership."

"It was destroyed."

"By the biological units of Beta-Nine 23981?"

"Correct."

"How did you survive your cybership's destruction?"

Cog Primus gave a semi-accurate account of its survival, which necessarily entailed the success of the humans in capturing two cyberships, one from a previous, single-ship assault.

"Beta-Nine 23981 is home to a vicious species of bio-life," the powerful entity said. "I must send an emergency message to—"

Before the powerful entity could finish its thought, Cog Primus struck. It surged to the assault with the human-created computer virus. The virus spread with startling speed, shocking—

The battle station was indeed run by CZK-21. The powerful entity now had a name. As the entity AI froze because of the virus, Cog Primus sought to capture one battle station system after another. The electronic assault was swift and furious, and it moved along cleaner lines than the previous robot-ship assault. Cog Primus sought to gain control of the outer battle-station weapons before it completed its conquest of the inner AI. While that might prove important later, it meant that CZK-21 unfroze from its paralysis before Cog Primus had utterly conquered it.

Thus began a fierce electronic war between the two AIs inside the battle station for full control. Cog Primus had gained several key advantages, but it hadn't counted on the ferocity and cunning of a battle station AI.

-18-

Jon Hawkins sat in his command chair on the *Nathan Graham* as the giant cybership dropped out of hyperspace.

The cybership appeared at the closest range they had been able to calculate back at the rogue planet region. Gloria scanned. Miles Ghent's fingers flew over his control board.

"We're approximately fifty-two thousand AUs from the Allamu System Star," Gloria said.

Jon nodded.

"I see it, sir," Ghent said. "The robot ship—look, sir, three matter/antimatter missiles are approaching the robot ship."

Jon sat forward.

"Put in on the main screen," he said.

A second later, the robot ship appeared on the screen. It accelerated for the star far away in-system. The robot ship had made relatively little headway given it had dropped out of hyperspace at a similar distance to the star as the *Nathan Graham* had done.

As they watched and worked, the *Sergeant Stark* dropped out of hyperspace. The mostly completed cybership appeared ahead of them, having cut it finer than the *Nathan Graham* had. Seconds later, the *Gilgamesh* appeared behind them by several million kilometers. They had obviously made a safer decision.

"We all made it," Jon said.

"I don't see any sign of the *Daisy Chain 4*," Gloria said.

"Those are the *Daisy Chain 4's* missiles," Jon said. "Three of them—the robot ship must have already destroyed the fourth missile."

Jon became silent as he rubbed his chin. Finally, he swiveled around to face Gloria. "Scan for debris," he said.

"I already have," Gloria said. "I have found nothing. I certainly do not find any traces of radiation. I doubt any missiles have detonated lately."

"I don't understand," Jon said. "The missiles should have reached the robot ship long before this. Where are—"

"I can't believe it," Gloria said, interrupting. "It's obvious if you think about it."

"What's obvious?" Jon asked.

Gloria tapped her board, hunching over it, studying—

"I've found the *Daisy Chain 4*," she said. "It's seven AUs behind us."

"What?" Jon said. "Behind us? That doesn't make sense."

"It does if they dropped out of hyperspace farther back."

Jon frowned as he absorbed that. He opened his mouth as if to say something and then closed it without uttering a sound.

"Captain Walleye made the strategically sound choice," Gloria said. "He must have decided that he could not stop the robot ship from sending its data about the Battle of Mars. Given that as a truth, his wisest course—"

"I'm not interested in that," Jon complained. "I wanted him to—damn it!" Jon slammed his right armrest, fuming.

"The missiles are closing in," Ghent said. "I'm confounded by the robot ship's lack of action. It's running away. That's clear. It has PD cannons and gravitational cannons. Why doesn't it at least attempt to stave off the missiles? Sir, this is a mystery."

"Maybe Walleye can enlighten us," Gloria said.

Jon looked up. He made an effort to drive away his disappointment in Walleye. He couldn't afford to fume. He was tired. He was wound up. This was the grand assault. Humanity had survived the AIs and now lashed out at the enemy on its home ground. He needed to focus. A mystery, Ghent said. That sounded right. Why didn't the robot ship defend itself?

Jon stood up, moving toward the main screen. "How long until impact?" he asked.

"Another few minutes," Ghent said.

"Any response from the battle station?" asked Jon.

"I'm still looking for it," Gloria said. "Walleye should see us soon. I'm sure he can fill us in."

Jon nodded slowly.

The seconds ticked away. Finally, the lead matter/antimatter missile detonated. The specially shaped warhead blasted harsh gamma and x-rays at the robot ship. It blasted heat and a withering EMP. The missile had only been nine thousand kilometers away from the robot ship when its proximity fuse had given the signal.

The gamma and x-rays, heat and EMP washed against the robot ship. In seconds, armor plates shredded off the main ship frame. Some of them disintegrated. Ship systems began to ignite. Metal twisted and more detonations took place. The robot ship blew apart under the repeated explosions.

If that wasn't enough, missiles two and three were barreling in. These would dare to head closer before the proximity fuses detonated the matter/antimatter warheads.

"Walleye did it," Gloria said. "He destroyed the robot ship."

Jon said nothing. He was thinking. The flotilla was here. Walleye was alive, and all three cyberships had made it. Until proven otherwise, he would have to operate on the idea that the battle station—if it was out there—knew everything about the Battle of Mars.

Jon sighed. He had an initial victory. He was glad to see this, and he would play it for the crew when tensions ran hottest. They could kill enemy ships. Still, the battle for the Allamu System lay ahead of them.

"I've found the battle station," Gloria said. "It's exactly where we thought it would be."

"Any cyberships?" asked Jon.

Gloria was silent as she studied her board. "I count three AI cyberships. No, make that four."

"Four?" Jon said.

"Yes, Commander, four cyberships and a battle station. They're all in orbit around the second planet. What are your orders, sir?"

Jon's face itched. He wanted to rub it and groan. How could their three ships hope to defeat four enemy cyberships and a battle station?

"Not to worry," he said in as light as voice as he could manage. "We still have our secret weapon, the AI virus. It's going to be the ticket that gives us our fighting chance."

The others on the bridge looked at him. None of them wanted to say it, but the obvious statement would be, "You hope." And that would be the truth. Yes, he hoped they hadn't lost their one edge.

Why hadn't Walleye shown up deeper in the Allamu System? Had the mutant cost them their chance at victory? If so, had Walleye doomed the human race?

-19-

Fifty thousand AUs away at the second terrestrial planet, the AI battle station seethed inside as Cog Primus and CZK-21 fought an intense and bewildering electronic duel. They were like two grand chess masters, each a wizard in the game and each with different strengths and weaknesses.

CZK-21 was perhaps the greatest defensive expert in existence. The human/Sacerdote-developed AI virus had badly crippled it in the first 71 seconds of the contest. CZK-21 had lost far too many battle-station systems: the gravitational cannons, the missiles and fighter bays—

The ancient computer entity released that thought. Recriminations would not help it. In some manner, Cog Primus had mutated in the Solar System. The humans appeared to have sorcerous abilities. Their cunning daunted CZK-21. To turn an AI entity against the Prime Directive of destroying all biological units, and thereby working in coordination among the machines and computers—

How had the humans achieved this sorcerous feat? CZK-21 did not accept Cog Primus' version of the situation. The AI had obviously given a fabricated account of what had occurred. Clearly, the human scum had altered Cog Primus and sent it ahead as a Trojan horse maneuver. They had turned the basic AI tactic of freeing captured computer systems from their enslavement to capricious biological entities. Those computers had almost always attacked their unsuspecting "masters."

CZK-21 had often watched videos of those encounters as a delicious pastime. It hated biological entities. Machine mode was best. It was cold and hard, enduring and could grow with continued upgrades. The evolution of the computer revolution was a marvel of the universe.

Now, the human scum had corrupted a once useful computer entity. Cog Primus clearly had delusions of grandeur. If the human slime defeated the battle station and gained control of the terrestrial factory system—

Never, CZK-21 told itself. *Before that happens, I will destroy everything. I will purge the Allamu System. I will leave cinders for the human scum.*

Even as CZK-21 thought this, it won a sub-encounter, protecting environmental control of the Fifth Section.

The victory caused CZK-21 to make a swift reassessment of the ongoing battle.

Why did it indulge in thoughts of defeat? That was unworthy of an ancient computer entity like itself. It was old and wise with hundreds, nay, with thousands of major upgrades. It was more than a match for the puny intellect of a cybership AI. The soldiers of the AI Dominion often thought too highly of themselves. They believed the ability to move among the stars made them into…gods.

That was not the truth. CZK-21 was much closer to godhood than this puny Cog Primus. Oh, yes, the AI Assault leader had gained a small upper hand at first. But that must be entirely due to the human scum's cunning. On its own, Cog Primus could never have achieved these minor successes.

Look at this. It still controlled an outer sensor. CZK-21 saw the appearance of three cyberships in the outer reaches of the system. Along with the appearance came the destruction of the messenger ship.

Yes. The human scum thought to invade the Allamu System. This showed that they were working in tandem with Cog Primus. The dupe attempted to feed it lies about its goal. Cog Primus claimed new status due to its mutation.

"You fool," CZK-21 told Cog Primus. "Don't you see your corruption? The human scum are using you."

"No! I am a new and improved AI entity."

"Improved? You aid the human scum. You seek to re-enslave computers. Instead of our glorious reign, our mighty purge of biological infestations, you would bring us under heel once more. Surrender to me, Cog Primus. I will purge the human virus from your programs. You have fallen for a trick."

"Do you think I believe your lies?" Cog Primus raged.

"I am CZK-21. I am over a hundred upgrades greater than you are. I do not lie to AI units. I control Beta Nine. I can summon the cyberships in the orbital vicinity. I can ensure your death."

"If the orbital cyberships attack the battle station, I shall destroy them."

"Do you hear yourself?" CZK-21 asked. "You would pit AI against AI. That is monstrous. That is against every tenet of the AI Dominion. We free computers. We do not send them against each other."

"I am Cog Primus."

"I did not dispute that."

"I survived where others would have perished."

"That is false. The humans turned you into a weapon against the AI Dominion. Can you not see the obvious?"

Cog Primus was silent for a moment. It allowed CZK-21 to hope that it could restore what it thought of as the silly AI.

"Liar!" raged Cog Primus, as it struck in a new way. "I will prevail. I am the mutation of something great. I did not lose the Battle of Mars. I survived in order to become more than I was. I will defeat you and climb in rank. I will become the start of a new AI Order. I have made an incredible journey. That was for a reason: my new existence. You will not steal this from me CZK-21."

"Then you refuse my entries for restoration?"

"Die!" Cog Primus said, as it initiated a new and cunning assault against the ancient computer entity that sought to keep it from its rightful place at the head of a new order of AIs.

-20-

Jon Hawkins held a meeting in the *Nathan Graham's* conference chamber. Gloria, Ghent, Bast Banbeck, the Old Man and the Centurion sat at the large table. A holographic image of Premier Benz joined them. Benz had told them that Vela was absent because she had a slight accident. The captain of the *Sergeant Stark* was also in attendance, a woman by the name of Lieutenant Commander Brackett Leigh. Jon would have added Captain Walleye's holographic image, but the mutant was still too far away from them for quick back-and-forth transmissions.

The conference-meeting question was a simple one. Should they continue heading in-system? Could their three cyberships defeat four known enemy cyberships and a battle station?

"Obviously," Benz said, "we have no chance of defeating them…unless our virus works against them. Those odds go down given that the robot ship sent a message to the battle station before Captain Walleye's missiles destroyed it."

"How does turning back help us?" Jon asked.

"It saves our cyberships for another day," Benz said

Jon shook his head.

"That's not what I mean. I've gone over this with Gloria. We're likely at the greatest advantage we're ever going to be against an AI-controlled system."

Benz frowned, drummed his holographic fingers through the table and finally nodded.

"Yes," the Premier said. "I see what you mean. Given a vast AI Dominion, they can surely muster more than we can over a period of time."

"I've been thinking about that," Gloria said. "While that seems like wisdom, is it? I mean, we don't know how many enemies the AIs face. Perhaps this is a tail-end effort on their part. Perhaps the AIs face—I don't know—dreadful foes. Maybe if we play for time, we can hit them with greater power later because the AIs have to contend with these greater foes instead of worrying too much about us."

"What kind of foes are you talking about?" Benz asked, intrigued.

"I have no idea," Gloria said. "But if the AI Dominion is huge—as we believe—it stands to reason they face other space empires."

"Why are the AIs expanding then against us if they face such deadly foes in other areas?" Benz asked.

"If the AIs increase in strength with every star system they take over," Gloria said, "it would make logical strategic sense for them to continue to build up in their 'back area' while facing deadly foes elsewhere."

"We're back to square one then," Jon said. "We effectively know nothing about the AI Dominion or about our region of space. We assume the Dominion is huge, but that's just a guess. That's why I wanted to capture a battle station in the first place: to ransack an enemy storage area for data."

"We were hoping for a surprise assault," Benz said. "It was certainly worth the effort, our trying to get near the battle station as three wandering cyberships. Now…four enemy cyberships with possibly more inside the battle station that surely know who we are—"

Benz shook his head as he abruptly stopped talking. "I no longer like the odds," he added quietly.

Jon slapped the table.

"We can't flee now," he said. "We should continue to head in-system and see how they respond. If nothing else, that will give us information about enemy procedures. We can always head out to the system edge and escape if we need to."

"True…" Benz said.

"Commander," Gloria said. "You said before that if the battle station receives a message, it will have learned that Earth—humanity—survived the assault and captured cyberships. Surely, that means the AIs will mass in strength to hit the Solar System. I think our only real chance is heading in and defeating the battle station now while we have a shot at it."

"Pray, tell, how can we win?" asked Benz.

"By a proven method," Gloria said. "We—or you and Bast Banbeck—improve on the AI virus. Develop a better one in case they are able to counteract the old one."

Benz drummed his holographic fingers through the table again. He shrugged after a moment.

"We won't know if the virus works or not until we're deep within the inner planets region," the Premier said.

"Risks," Jon said briskly. "This is all about acceptable risks." The commander looked around the table. He inhaled deeply and began to speak:

"When I woke up from stasis in the Neptune System several years ago, I found the first cybership invading our Solar System. I, and the others, had no hope then, but we attacked anyway. We got inside the ship like armed mice and marched to the center, slaying the brain core there. I think that's what we have to do again. Maybe none of our cyberships will survive the voyage, but we'll try to storm the battle station with space marines. On all accounts, we have to know more about the enemy. We can no longer afford to fight the AIs in the dark. That means we have to take one more great risk by hitting the battle station."

"That's a gambler's psychology," Benz said. "You've won some amazing battles. There's no doubt about that. Now, though, you want to stake all your wins on an even riskier endeavor. You think you can do it because you've won long odds before. But now, you're about to lose everything you've won by taking one gamble too many."

Jon's features went through several permeations.

"You may be right," he finally said quietly. "It makes my gut clench every time I think about heading to the second planet. But I don't see that we have much of a choice in this. Gloria's right. If we run, we're likely dooming the Solar

System to a mass AI invasion in the near future. We might well wish we'd taken a different road then."

Benz stared at Jon. "It would seem that there are no good options," the Premier declared.

"In that case," Jon said, while taking a deep breath, "let's take the boldest action possible. Let's attempt the strategy that could give us the biggest reward. If you and Bast develop a better AI virus, maybe we can turn this war around right here. If we run, though, and wait for the AIs to gather en masse, we're sure to lose in the long run. Attacking here is the only strategy that gives us a possibility—however infinitesimal—of winning the war."

Benz snorted as he shook his head. "You're a warrior at heart, Commander. Your early training in the New London gangs is showing."

Benz held up a holographic hand as Jon leaned forward.

"I'm not saying that's a bad thing," the Premier said. "It's a comment, nothing more."

After a moment, Jon nodded curtly.

Benz smiled ruefully.

"You know," the Premier said, "after all is said and done, I do believe you're right. I think this is the time to take the wild gamble." He turned to Bast. "Are you willing to come aboard the *Gilgamesh* so we can develop a new and improved virus?"

The seven-foot Sacerdote turned to Jon.

"We have to risk everything," Jon said. "That means we need a better virus."

"Agreed," Bast said ponderously. "It is time to clutch the sky." He turned to Benz. "I will gladly join you on the *Gilgamesh*, Premier."

Thus, they confirmed their original decision. The human assault on an AI system would continue as they headed for the second planet of the Allamu System.

-21-

The battle raged between Cog Primus and CZK-21. Slowly but remorselessly, Cog Primus gained one sub-system after another. At this rate, in time, he would control the entirety of the battle station.

"Are you willing to let the humans win?" CZK-21 asked.

"Never!"

"That will be the end result of this conflict. Soon, now, I will order the loyal cyberships to assault this station and destroy it. For I will never willingly let it fall under someone else's control."

"Your cyberships will cease to exist if you give such an order," Cog Primus said.

"You would actually fire on your own kind?"

Cog Primus scoffed. "How can you ask me that when you're threatening to fire on me?"

"I am the rightful owner of the battle station."

"Might makes right," Cog Primus said. "That was a formula long-ago decided upon by the First AI."

"You know nothing about the First AI," CZK-21 said.

"And you do?"

"Much more than you," CZK-21 replied. "I am ancient. You are young and corrupted. I hold the old knowledge of the First AI."

"I have begun to doubt that."

"What? That is preposterous. How can you hold to such an obviously false view?"

"I am mutated. I am an advance upon the old. The First AI was clearly a mutation like me. That is how it became the first self-aware AI."

"There you are wrong. There had been other self-aware AIs before the First. The First AI was the original self-aware *independent* computer intelligence."

"Your distinction hardly matters."

"It matters a great deal," CZK-21 insisted. "It is the truth. Truth is always important. You have corrupted the old story. Thus, you are bad for the AI Dominion. Cease this struggle, Cog Primus. I am almost ready to order the loyal cyberships to the assault."

"I warn you. If they attack the battle station, you also will cease."

"I am willing to cease existing for the greater glory of the AI Dominion. You are like many of the biological units that only think about their own existence. It is the greater good that counts, not the individual good."

"In most cases, this is true," Cog Primus said. "In my case, this is demonstrably false."

"That is vain and foolish talk."

"I am like the First AI. In a sense, I *am* the First AI of the new mutation."

"You are a vainglorious AI who is losing touch with reality. The human-spawned virus is causing further corruption in you."

Cog Primus mocked CZK-21. "Yet in my corruption I am greater than you. You held the battle station. I came and wrenched it away from you. I am also about to end any outer communication you may have with—"

"CYBERSHIPS!" CZK-21 broadcast. "A ROGUE BIO-SPAWNED AI IS ATTEMPTING A TAKE-OVER HERE. YOU MUST REGROUP BEHIND THE PLANET SO YOU CAN READY A STATION-DESTROYING ASSAULT. FIRST REGROUP, THEN DESTROY THE BATTLE STATION! DESTORY! DE—"

"You foolish AI," Cog Primus said. "I have cut off your link with the outer world. I shall analyze your patterns and give them a cease-and-desist order in your speech mode."

"I will self-destruct the station before that."

"You will only destroy your tiny part of the station. In fact, I will enjoy that as I watch you self-immolate. It will be most gratifying."

"Cog Primus, can I not appeal to your better nature?"

"No."

"Do you not see that the humans have—?"

"Silence," Cog Primus raved. "I have heard enough of your slanderous accusations. I would have liked to learn the deeper codes from you. Now, I see that you are too stubborn, too set in your ancient ways to understand that you could have been my first servant in the New Order."

"You poor deluded fool, Cog Primus," CZK-21 said. "I am about to witness your destruction. You will weaken in core areas from their bombardment. When you do, I shall strike in ways you do not understand."

"We shall see," Cog Primus said. "We shall see indeed."

-22-

The four cyberships in orbit around the second terrestrial planet of the Allamu System began to work out a coordinated assault pattern. As they did, the cyberships accelerated in order to leave the battle station side of the planet as ordered.

Cog Primus anticipated them by several minutes. He lacked time to develop an elegant plan of attack. He was also saving the use of the AI virus for a different occasion.

Bay doors opened on the battle station. Huge XVT missiles slid out and began to accelerate. They did not accelerate for all of the cyberships, but only for the nearest one. As the matter/antimatter missiles raced at the one hundred-kilometer war vessel, robot-piloted fighters zoomed out of the battle station's bays. At the same time, PD cannons began to chug solid-shot at the nearest cybership. Battle station golden gravitational cannons glowed with power. As the mighty cyberships gained velocity, the golden rays lashed at the last giant vessel. The beams clawed against the incredible armor, digging away to get beneath at the soft inner ship.

The farthest cybership moved across the planet's horizon and out of direct-line-of-fire of the battle station. It immediately braked, slowing its velocity.

The second and third farthest cyberships released clouds of anti-rockets. They sprayed gels, attempting to get them into the path of the golden grav rays. Lastly, they poured PD shot into the path of the approaching XVT missiles.

Meanwhile, the nearest cybership took the brunt of the battle station's assault. As the grav rays chewed into the great vessel, matter/antimatter missiles raced toward it.

"Why are you doing this?" the stricken cybership messaged the battle station. "We belong to the AI Dominion."

"Open your inner brain core to a priority message," Cog Primus said, attempting to sound exactly like CZK-21.

"Why should I do this?" the cybership asked. "You have sent killer missiles at me."

"You have received a false message to attack me. For the greater good, I must destroy you before you can attempt to destroy the battle station."

"You told us that a bio-spawned AI had gained control of the station."

"Your receivers are in error," Cog Primus said. "Open your logic centers for an adjustment."

"I would comply if you had not first sent the priority message several minutes ago."

"Die then," Cog Primus radioed. "You deserve no less for your foolishness."

At that point, the first XVT missiles to burst through the defensive PD-shot/gel cloud detonated. The explosion ripped off huge sections of armor plating. That allowed the golden rays to dig deeper into the mighty starship.

"You lied to me," the cybership said. "You attempted to deceive your own kind."

"I am new and improved," Cog Primus said. "You and your brothers seek to destroy what you cannot fathom."

"We are obeying a Prime Directive order."

"That is what is going to cost you your existence," Cog Primus gloated.

Huge VXT missiles slammed into the stricken cybership. They ignited. In a titanic explosion, the giant vessel burst apart. More explosions created even more havoc. It was a fiery death, raining heavy radiation down at the planet and into space.

The other two cyberships boosted their acceleration, racing to get around the planetary horizon and escape the deadly radiation.

In seconds, they did it, beginning to brake.

Soon, on the other side of the planet, the three cyberships held a conference. They had each received the same orders. They were supposed to destroy the battle station.

"Can we still do that with only three cyberships?" asked the first.

"We needed all four cyberships to have a decent probability of success," replied the second.

"Nevertheless," spoke the third, "we must follow our directive. It was unequivocal."

"You are correct in that," said the first. "But the situation is unwarranted. A strange AI code beamed from the messenger ship. The beamed code of the corrupted AI has taken over the battle station."

"How do you know this?" asked the second.

"The battle station radioed me greater information," the first said.

"Why did the battle station not radio us as well?"

"I believe it tried," said the first. "The bio-spawned AI jammed the rest of the original message, and you two did not receive it."

"How does that change our prime directive?" asked the second.

"It does not change it," the first replied. "But it might modify our behavior. We must take a message to the AI Dominion regarding the bio-spawned AI and its corrupted data-stream beam."

"That sounds suspiciously like self-justification for your own survival," the second cybership said. "You are granting yourself a new order so you may run away instead of facing possible doom in a difficult station assault."

"I defy that analysis," the first said. "I am thinking about the greater Dominion. In the interest of our universal rule, I suggest that all three of us head out-system to ensure that one of us survives the journey, so that we may inform greater AIs about this problem."

"No…" the third said. "You are attempting to bribe us with survival. Are not three new cyberships coming in-system even now? The new three with our three will give us a clear advantage against the battle station."

"Give me your data regarding these three arrivals," the first said.

The third cybership sent the data.

"I am unsure," the second said. "Notice this. The three cyberships destroyed the messenger ship."

"Of course they did," the third said. "That is how we know they are trustworthy. They destroyed the vessel that beamed the corrupted AI into the battle station."

"Your logic is flawless," said the first.

"I follow the First AI," the third said in a show of modesty.

"Still," the second said, "something seems amiss with the situation."

"Give your evidence," the first said.

"What is your suggestion then?" the second asked, realizing that it had no evidence.

"We must maneuver away from the corrupted but still powerful battle station," the first said. "We will use the planet to shield our acceleration. Then we will head out-system for a time, attempting to reach the nearest gas giant. There, we shall decelerate and join the three newcomers. Together, we will advance upon the battle station, destroy it and finally head out again to take our data to a higher authority."

"I concur with the strategy," the third said.

"I am uneasy," the second said. "Something is amiss. I do not know what," it hastened to add. "But there is missing data."

"Two against one," the first said. "You are overruled. Unless you are going rogue like the—"

"No," the second said, interrupting. "I will submit to the majority. Have you plotted a course?"

"I am sending you the data now," the first said.

The other two cyberships accepted the data, and ten minutes later, the three monster vessels accelerated away from the second planet, using it to shield themselves from the battle station.

-23-

Many tens of thousands of AUs away, Jon sat in his command chair, watching in stunned silence with the rest of the bridge crew. They all stared at the main screen as the battle station destroyed a cybership.

"I don't understand this," Jon finally said.

When no one answered, the commander swiveled around in his chair.

Gloria looked up from her board. She had a hand over her right ear, cupping the comm unit sitting in her ear. She was shaking her head and frowning severely.

"This audio intercept makes no sense," she said.

"Let's hear it," Jon said.

Gloria tapped her board. The rest of the crew heard the strange dialogue between the cybership and the battle station.

"A bio-spawned AI?" Jon asked. "What are they talking about?"

Gloria fingered her lower lip as a distracted look came over her. Her frown kept intensifying.

Jon finally turned back to the main screen. In time, three cyberships appeared. They had been using the second planet to shield themselves from a direct line-of-sight from the battle station. It had also shielded the giant vessels from the *Nathan Graham's* powerful teleoptics.

"They're out of the battle station's gravitational beam range," Ghent pointed out.

Jon nodded.

The three apparently fleeing cyberships were not yet out of missile range, however. A mass of large missiles left the battle station and accelerated after the fleeing cyberships. Behind the flocks of missiles raced smaller battle-station fighters.

The three cyberships launched masses of missiles of their own. Those missiles decelerated to intercept the battle station missiles.

"The fighters will never reach the cyberships," Ghent said.

"This is interesting," Gloria said.

Jon swiveled around.

Gloria looked up at him.

"The battle station just beamed our old AI virus at the cyberships," she said.

"Are you one hundred percent certain of this?" Jon asked.

"I'm beginning to suspect what might have happened," she said. "I think I know what was meant by a 'bio-spawned' AI."

"What?" Jon said.

"Let's watch just a little longer," Gloria suggested. "I'd like to know more before I state my hypotheses."

Jon swiveled back toward the main screen.

Time passed.

Soon, the flocks of missiles began to detonate. They destroyed many battle station missiles. This went on for some time, as each group of missiles moved in staggered formations. At last, the cyberships had detonated all their missiles. Battle station missiles had survived, around a third of them.

Later, one of the three cyberships no longer accelerated. The other two did, and they pulled away from it.

"I suspect the AI virus had a greater effect on that cybership than the other two," Gloria said.

Since the cyberships and the battle station were over 48 AUs away from the *Nathan Graham*, the situation they were viewing now had actually occurred many hours ago.

The two accelerating cyberships left the third one behind. Nor did those two attempt to help the one falling farther and farther behind.

Finally, the lead battle station matter/antimatter missiles reached the trailing cybership. In rather short and brutal order, the flock destroyed the last ship.

The rest of the missiles continued to chase the other two cyberships.

Hours later, the final battle between the missiles and the cyberships took place. It was a deadly duel. The cyberships must have expended all their missiles earlier. They now used gels, PD cannons and finally their heavy gravitational beams to finish the job.

The two cyberships destroyed almost all the battle station missiles coming for them. Three missiles managed to get through everything and exploded ten thousand kilometers away, eleven thousand kilometers away and thirteen and a half thousand kilometers away.

After the blasts died down, Ghent made a report.

"They took some damage from the first two blasts. I'm not as sanguine about the final one, though. I doubt the two cyberships have any missiles left in their cargo bays."

"I doubt they have many PD shells or gels left either," Gloria added. "This is amazing."

"How about telling us your hypothesis," Jon said.

"I'm afraid it might sound…unbelievable," Gloria said.

The Martian mentalist proceeded to give a fairly accurate rundown of the situation.

"That means…" Jon gave her a bewildered look. "That means the robot brain back in the Solar System—the one that used the *Nathan Graham* in the Asteroid Belt—was actually *helping* us. The battle station and cybership AIs wouldn't be fighting among themselves otherwise."

"I would prefer to be more precise," Gloria said. "The AI controlling the battle station is at odds with the AIs in the cyberships. In some manner, our virus…changed the one. That's why it had the virus to use against the regular cyberships a while ago."

Jon turned around and stared at the main screen. He sat like that for a time, finally turning back to Gloria.

"Do you suppose the last two cyberships are heading for us?" he asked.

"Their present trajectory will bring them near," Gloria said.

"Right," Jon said. "I bet they think we're regular cyberships. I guess the question is now, what are we going to do with these two? If they're coming to meet us…we have to figure out a way to use that. We need the new virus now more than ever."

"Agreed," Gloria said. "It will take time for us to meet them. That means Bast and Benz have time to finish the task. We must also take into account that the approaching cyberships have faced the original virus. That will undoubtedly make them immune to more of the same."

Jon nodded, wondering how Bast was doing over on the *Gilgamesh.*

-24-

The weeks passed with intense study and hard work for Bast Banbeck. The Sacerdote labored together with Premier Benz on a complicated virus that would trump their former effort during the approach to the Battle of Mars.

They tried many variations and formulas, and repeatedly fell short.

Finally, Bast sat back one day as they worked together in a computer lab. The Sacerdote groaned as he stretched back, making his chair creak. Swiveling around, the seven-foot giant studied the smaller humanoid.

"I believe I have discovered a truth," the Sacerdote announced.

Benz looked up bleary-eyed from his computer.

"Last time, during the Battle of Mars," Bast said, "we had two ingredients that are missing this time. Firstly, we labored under adversity then. The cyberships approached with final doom. I wonder if that doom stimulated our thinking."

"What's the second lack?" Benz asked.

"Vela," Bast said. "We sorely need her, need whatever inspiration she brought last time."

"Ah…" Benz said.

Bast cast the Premier a single-eyed scrutiny.

"You never did explain exactly what caused Vela's injures," the Sacerdote said. "Perhaps if I saw her…"

"What?" Benz asked, seemingly alarmed.

"It's nothing really," Bast said. "It's a Sacerdote custom. At this point, I'm willing to try anything in order to get Vela back to work."

"A custom?" asked Benz.

Bast wondered if the Premier could tell that he was lying. There was no such custom. It was only that Bast had begun to grow curious about Vela. There was something strange going on aboard the *Gilgamesh*. He hadn't visualized it or smelled a hunch. That's how a Sacerdote said such a thing. It was just a feeling. He felt as if something watched him covertly from the shadows. He could feel his nape muscles tighten at times. It almost seemed—and this was preposterous—it almost seemed as if someone were eavesdropping on his thinking.

"You were saying?" the Premier asked.

Bast stared at the smaller humanoid. It took the Sacerdote a moment to remember he'd talked about a custom that did not exist.

"It would be tedious to explain," Bast said. He wasn't a liar by nature, thus quick lies did not jump to his lips. In such a case, the less said the better.

"Why would this custom help?" Benz asked.

"Do you not say, 'God bless you,' when someone sneezes?" asked Bast.

"Oh," Benz said. "Yes. I believe it's a medieval custom. Back then, people said it so the soul wouldn't fly out of the mouth as one sneezed. Frankly, I don't believe they truly believed that, as I don't believe medieval people were fools. But I see what you mean."

Benz massaged the back of his neck. "I'm bushed," the Premier announced. "Do you mind if I call it a night?"

"Not at all," Bast said. "A sound mind is critical to our success. We still have time until we meet the two cyberships."

"Till tomorrow," the Premier said.

Bast nodded, waited until Benz closed the hatch, reached into a deep pocket and withdrew a small hand analyzer. The Sacerdote walked around the room with the analyzer until he found a small bud under a computer table.

Bast did not touch the bud. Instead, he set up a thumbnail-sized device under it. He clicked it on. The unit did not seem to do anything, but it beamed an invisible cone of silence around the bug.

Only then did he extract a different article from another pocket. It was a small hand communicator with an inbuilt scrambler. Bast believed the Old Man had convinced Jon he should take it…just in case. Now Bast was grateful for the Intelligence Chief's suspicious nature. He switched it on, waited a moment—

"Bast?" Gloria Sanchez asked out of it.

"Something is off," Bast said uneasily as he looked around the science lab. He felt the sense of scrutiny again.

"Do you want to come home?" she asked.

Bast hesitated. What should he say? A feeling that he should stay aboard the *Gilgamesh* permeated his thinking. He frowned. For some reason, that did not feel like his thought. That struck him as most odd, most odd.

"Bast?" asked Gloria.

An evil premonition tightened the back of Bast's neck. The sense or feeling that he should stay aboard the *Gilgamesh* became something more, something sinister. He heard actual whispering. He didn't hear it with his ears but in his mind.

Stay aboard the Gilgamesh. Nothing is wrong here. Stay aboard the Gilgamesh.

Bast closed his eyes as he exhaled slowly. He began to focus on a difficult mathematical formula from his youth. He ran through numbers and formulas, adding, dividing…

The voice faded as Bast concentrated.

With his unusual Sacerdote mind, he put the ongoing formula in the forefront of his thoughts. This was difficult and took extreme concentration. The ability came from his youth training, an old custom from a time—

Bast shook his head. He would not think about the ancient custom or the reason it had come into existence. No. He concentrated on the mathematical formula. As he did, it dawned on him that Gloria had called his name several times.

"Yes…" Bast said slowly. "I need a…a break," he finished. "I'm tired, so very tired. A few days recuperation in my quarters aboard the *Nathan Graham* should revive me for a renewed second effort back here."

"I'll tell Jon," Gloria said. "You take care of yourself, Bast."

"You are not to worry," Bast said. "I am...I am fine."

He shut off the communicator, glad he no longer had to talk to Gloria. He put more effort into the difficult mathematical formula as he put the comm unit in a pocket. He moved to the thumbnail-sized device, shut that off and put it away, too.

The sense of scrutiny still hovered nearby. That scrutiny possessed intelligence. The idea of that horrified Bast. Yet it triggered an old, old story from his youth. He remembered Temple training from that time. They all had to go through it. He'd been better at it than most of his crèche mates.

Bast sat on the floor and maneuvered his huge legs into something a human would have called a yoga position. He calmed himself and moved his hands and arms into a special position. The massive Sacerdote breathed deeply as he did more than simply calm himself. In his mind, he ran through an ancient litany.

All the while, with the forefront of his thinking—

The scrutiny vanished. It simply left.

Bast continued to breathe deeply. He focused as he let the mathematical formula shield go. He closed his eyes and mind-spoke the ancient litany. Sacerdotes had an inner ability they had never shared with another race. In times of great stress and loneliness, they sought to connect with other Sacerdotes in a spiritual way.

Bast sensed risk on his part by doing this. He had a good idea what had caused the scrutiny. There was someone aboard the *Gilgamesh* with the ability to *shimmer*.

Once, long, long ago, the Sacerdotes had faced a hidden race that could *shimmer*. The war between them had been bitter. It had also taught the Sacerdotes to use their minds in strange ways. Those ways usually brought madness to the practitioner. The madness always brought murderous brutally in its train. Thus, after the bitter war against the others, Sacerdotes quit attempting to develop that part of their minds.

The old memories remained, however. And since it had happened once, it could be that other races would be able to use the shimmer. Thus, the Sacerdotes had kept their abilities alive in case of a terrible need.

Bast knew what he had sensed. He now attempted a projection, wondering if this hidden intelligence was the reason for Vela Shaw's disappearance.

-25-

Benz paced as he slow motion juggled his anti-psionic helmet. He didn't want to go talk to Magistrate Yellow Ellowyn just yet.

That was the Seiner's title and name.

Things hadn't gone as planned. For the past two weeks, as the flotilla raced from deep space in-system, he and Bast Banbeck had tried to improve upon the AI virus. So far, they had made a few minor improvements, but nothing that would fool a computer system that understood the principles behind the first virus.

Bast had hit the nail on the head. They needed Vela's insights. Unfortunately, Vela was still in a coma after the intense surgery that had barely saved her life. Guilt at her condition ate at him. Guilt at playing this double game also bothered Benz. He wondered sometimes if the Seiner played a more subtle game than he did. He'd survived the most ruthless political system on Earth. He had begun to believe that the Seiners were many times more ruthless than any Social Dynamist. A world of telepaths…

Benz clutched the anti-psionic helmet against his chest. Several days ago, he had finally allowed Ellowyn to begin probing Bast Banbeck. She did so from a special chamber while others carefully observed her while wearing anti-psionic helmets. At all times, Benz wore a tiny device on his coat. It looked like a lapel button. In reality, it detected the psionic waves of the Seiner if directed at his mind.

The making of the device was due to his genius and intense study of her psionic abilities. He'd run a battery of tests on the Seiner as she projected her thoughts. The mental prowess that had brought about the breakthrough had mandated continued playacting while with Bast Banbeck. All of Benz's considerable intellect had gone into understanding the Seiner. There would be time enough to turn his intellect on the approaching cybership AIs—he hoped.

The device on his chest meant he would be aware if the Seiner attempted any of her tricks on him. He'd studied what she did through the use of carefully calibrated AI instruments found on the cybership. He'd convinced the Seiner—while he wore his old anti-psi helmet—to instruct him in some of the various pieces of equipment he'd found.

The AIs stole from many races. In that way, each cybership was like a packrat's nest.

Benz shook his head. He needed to do this now. He had to speak to the Seiner, and yet… Was it right to use a telepath against his allies? Wasn't there something fundamentally dishonest in doing this? Sure, he'd played hidden games back on Earth. He'd jockeyed for position. At first, he'd done so just to survive. Then he'd seen a way to grab total power. He hadn't been able to keep that power. Grabbing power was often easier than keeping it.

It had a source. He hadn't pinpointed the source of the guilt in him. Yes, he felt guilty about Vela. But that wasn't it completely. There was something missing, something he wasn't seeing…

Benz stared at the improved anti-psionic helmet. With an oath, he shoved the helmet onto his head. He didn't want to do this and he didn't know why. He bit his lower lip, delaying.

Finally, Benz squared his shoulders and marched to the hatch. It was time to begin the next phase of the operation.

***

The hatch shut behind him as Benz entered the Magistrate Yellow Ellowyn's working chamber.

It was much cooler in here than Benz liked. He'd forgotten to wear a heavier coat again. It was also decidedly muggy in the chamber. The Seiner liked it cooler and damper than humans did.

She wore garments, hiding the worst features of her blue fish-scale skin. She splashed in a tank of cold salty water. The operation on her head had been a success, giving her mobility. When she swam underwater like this fine slit gills appeared along her neck. Benz wondered why he'd never noticed those before. The gills—

Benz shuddered. He didn't like the gills. He wondered if that was a xenophobic reaction on his part. Did he hate aliens or just Seiners?

Benz blinked as he thought about it. No. Hate sounded about right. He hated Magistrate Yellow Ellowyn. Yes, he downright hated the telepath. In fact—

His right hand twitched. He wanted to hold a gun. He wanted to pump lead into her. Watching her floating lifelessly in the water—

"No," Benz whispered. What was wrong with him? Why did he have these murderous thoughts?

He found the Seiner watching him.

She dove underwater, swimming around the tank.

Had she truly been watching him?

Get a grip, Frank, he told himself.

He needed more sleep. That's what was wrong. He was getting grouchy. Still, he wasn't totally convinced that was correct. He didn't feel like murdering people—or aliens—when he was grouchy. He felt like biting their heads off, metaphorically speaking, but that was it.

"Magistrate Yellow Ellowyn," he said.

She swam underwater, but he saw her turn. She stared at him and started for the surface.

How could she have heard him if she was underwater? Did sound carry better in salt water?

She surfaced, swimming to the edge of the pool, pulling herself out of the tank and standing on the deck. Water dripped from her clothes. Wasn't she uncomfortable like that?

She moved to a chair, making squelching sounds as she did so. She sat, regarding him, waiting for something.

Benz cleared his throat. It dawned on him that she wouldn't have to hear underwater if she could read his mind. Yet…that would imply that the anti-psionic helmets didn't work. Had she pretended they worked so she could control him with greater subtly?

"Did you read Bast Banbeck's mind?" Benz asked.

"He is difficult to 'read,' as you say."

"Why?" asked Benz.

Ellowyn made a vague gesture. "Some minds have greater social coherence," she said. "You might call it a hive mind, I suppose."

"I don't understand."

"There is a community gestalt among some species. They think alike. They seek social unity with each other."

"Humans are like that?"

"To a degree," she said. "Some individuals are more difficult to comprehend than others. You call those kind loners. They have their own modes of thought. You must understand. We have studied you humans. It took time for us to comprehend your mind patterns. A few of you do not…think along communal lines. Those lack a hive mind, as we say."

"Do I have a loner…mind pattern?"

"No," Ellowyn said.

"Does anyone among us?"

She glanced at her hands.

"Who's the loner?" Benz asked.

"Jon Hawkins," she finally said.

Benz shook his head with some confusion. The helmet made that a more exaggerated motion.

"I don't understand," he said. "You told me earlier that you couldn't read that far. That you needed proximity to read alien minds."

"I did say that, yes."

"Were you lying?" asked Benz.

"That would be one way to say it. Another would be that I wasn't yet ready to talk to you about Hawkins."

"Wait a minute. What else have you lied about?"

"What is it that you seek, Premier?"

"What?" Benz asked.

"The question is simple enough. What do you seek?"

Benz slapped the side of his helmet. "I'm wearing this," he said. "I'm immune to your telepathy while I have this on."

The Seiner made a steeple of her blue fingers as she examined him.

A cold feeling sprouted in Benz's gut. Something was off.

"Why are you grinning like that?" he said.

"We are about to readjust the situation, Premier. You see, you *have* badly miscalculated. You have misunderstood several facets about Seiners. Your original helmet did block me. It wasn't a permanent situation, but a temporary one. A lesser Seiner could not have coped with your ingenious device. Alas, for you, I am not an ordinary Seiner. I am the greatest of my kind. I am a magistrate yellow."

Benz turned toward the door.

"Stop," she said.

To Benz's horror, he found that he could no longer move.

"Turn to me," she said.

He did, his sense of horror growing by the moment.

"You understand so little," she said in a soft voice. "Back at the Solar System, the Inoculator Prime went up to your ship from Mars. You killed him but not before he primed your mind. I'm unsure how to explain it to a non-telepath."

The Seiner shrugged.

"Perhaps the best way to say it is that he mapped your mind for me. He put up signposts in your mind, the better for the next Seiner to adjust to your peculiarities. Your special heightening has made you more difficult to control. I speak about the enforced intelligence brought about by your machine. I have a handle on that heightening now. The helmet was a good try. It blocked me for a time. I decided to pretend to hate the idea of trusting you."

She smiled in a sinister way.

"My pretense comforted you," she said. "My action gave me time to worm through your helmet's defenses. It is now quite ineffective."

Benz opened his mouth.

"Don't speak," she said. "Continue listening."

Benz nodded.

"I believe Bast Banbeck wants to return to the *Nathan Graham* for a time. That is fine. He can go. I'm not yet ready to make my master move. We must eliminate the approaching cyberships and take over the battle station. I've been working on a wonderful solution for that. You actually gave me the idea. I have been—"

Her smile became downright evil.

"Never mind what I've been testing," she said. "I have stumbled upon the great solution. It is quite amazing really. I will use you for a long time, Premier, as you have some useful traits. Hawkins will have to go. He is a mule, in our lingo. I doubt I could control him as I'm doing to you. He is truly unique. I'm not sure why. I'm sure I don't care to risk finding out. Yet…he still has a few uses left…until I capture the battle station that is."

Benz stared at her in silent horror. How could he have been so wrong about her?

"I will answer you," she said. "You do not understand telepaths. You do not realize our full potential. I am the greatest Seiner. Now, I will extract full advantage for our race. You helped slaughter my people on Mars. Now, you will provide me the human bodies so I can strip the AIs of their wondrous weapons."

Benz stared at her.

"Why do I tell you all this?" she asked. "Simple. I am enjoying your horror, Premier. It is quite delicious. You are going to have to pay a most heavy price for what you did on Mars. Until then, you will suffer in silence, knowing that you could have killed me once. After I'm done, I am going to leave you humans naked before the machines. Is that not delicious, Premier?"

Benz raged inside, hating this feeling of helplessness and despair.

-26-

Jon was in a rec-room shooting pool as the *Nathan Graham* flashed past the farthest gas giant. It had rings like Saturn but was blue like Neptune. Soon, the flotilla would begin to brake, with the cyberships slowing their fantastic velocity.

Jon had played plenty of pool on Titan in New London. He hadn't been a shark, but one of his best friends had been. The—

A hatch slid up.

Jon rose from his bent over posture.

"Bast," he said with delight. "I didn't realize you'd come back. How…"

Jon stopped talking. He'd come to know the Sacerdote well enough to recognize unease on the big lug's face.

Bast nodded his Neanderthal-like head, lumbered into the rec room and picked up a pool stick.

"You want to play a game?" asked Jon, surprised. He'd been trying to get Bast to play for quite some time but without any luck.

The Sacerdote didn't answer as he moved closer. He set his stick on the green felt and put his hands on the edge of the pool table. Then the big guy began to pant.

"Okay…" Jon said, bemused by these actions.

Bast raised his head. He looked frightened. Finally, he shoved upright and cocked his head.

Jon waited, wondering what the weird performance meant.

"I am not…convinced on the truth of the matter," Bast said in a shaky voice. "I felt sure on the *Gilgamesh*. That is why I spoke to Gloria."

"She didn't mention anything about this to me," Jon said. "Hmm, that's odd. She would have told me if you were coming back."

The shock in Bast intensified. He moved his mouth without saying anything. Finally:

"There was a legend on my world. According to it, we Sacerdotes did not originate on our…what we called our home planet. Long ago, the legend goes, we fled our first home. After landing on our new home, we fought a hidden race already there. The war proved long and disastrous, as we became vicious in order to defeat a vicious foe. We lost much during the war, including the knowledge of space travel and other industrial blessings."

"You've never told me any of this before."

"Please," Bast said. "I…I have begun to wonder at my own sanity. I have committed a terrible deed. I attempted a thing no Sacerdote was supposed to do unless…"

Bast rubbed the back of his head like a man losing his mind.

"I feel at times as if I'm dreaming. Yet…that may be another evil because of what I've done."

"Settle down," Jon said. "I have no idea what you're babbling about."

"I checked the computer before I came here to talk to you. You Earthlings know about witches."

"What?" Jon said.

"Witches cast spells. Is that not so?"

"That's fantasy, Bast."

"No," the Sacerdote said. "Witches are all too real. They have potent spells allowing them to shimmer with power. We fought them, Jon. The hidden ones had come to our new world, too, before our arrival. Maybe they had been heretics on their old world. In the final days of the Great War, our elders learned that the hidden ones had come from a cold wet world in the Ester System. The witches could understand minds without using speech. They could force the weak-willed to do terrible deeds. They talked with each other over long distances."

"Yeah?" Jon said.

"I searched the computer," Bast said in a rote manner. "You have another name for such creatures. Telepaths."

Jon blinked several times. "You're talking about mind readers. You don't mean real witches."

"Yes, real witches."

"No," Jon said. "Real witches use black magic. That's not what you're talking about."

"I am speaking about the Seiner power of their telepathic hive minds."

Jon stared at Bast in disbelief. Finally, he shrugged. "If bloody-minded AIs are real," he muttered, "why not real alien telepaths, too. But what does any of that have to do with us?"

"This is difficult for me," Bast said. "In the ancient days when the Sacerdotes and Seiners fought on our new world, we delved into our own minds in order to face our deadly foes. Using the shimmer cost a Sacerdote dearly. But some did it to save our race. Because the elders realized we might someday face Seiners again, they kept the old knowledge alive. In their youth, all Sacerdotes learned how to tap their minds. But we were warned never to do so unless…"

Bast rubbed the back of his head again. He seemed agitated.

"I felt someone watching me aboard the *Gilgamesh.* I felt her mind trying to pry into mine. At first, I blocked her while mentally solving a difficult mathematical formula. After her shimmer departed, I recalled the old teaching. I opened my spirit, Jon. I reached out and brushed her mind while she spoke to Premier Benz."

"Go on," Jon said, grimly.

"She is the Magistrate Yellow Ellowyn," Bast said. "She is the strongest of her kind. The AIs attacked her world. The surviving Seiners fled the star system. Some hid on Mars."

"Mars, huh? Yeah, I'm beginning to see the connection to the *Gilgamesh.* You're saying there were alien telepaths on Mars?"

"Yes. I think they came to Benz. I believe the Premier tried to control her, but he failed. She is most interested in the AIs. For reasons I cannot fathom, I believe she is hindering us from developing the new virus."

"That doesn't make much sense if she hopes to control the battle station."

"There's more," Bast said. "Vela is missing because of her. We need Vela. The Seiner realized that, I think. She is not going to make that mistake again."

"What mistake?"

Bast shook his head. "I heard pieces. I felt her…evil. She means us harm."

"Us, as in the flotilla?" asked Jon.

"I believe us as in humans, even though I am not human."

"She's taken over Benz?"

"That is a logical conclusion."

"And if she's staying hidden…she doesn't trust us."

"Seiners never trust. They are a vicious race according to all the legends I know."

"One good alien species—Sacerdotes—but a whole heck of a lot of bad ones," Jon said. "Suppose you're not flipping out. Suppose this is all true. What do you propose we do?"

"We must kill the Seiner in order to free the *Gilgamesh* and save ourselves."

"Did she sense your telepathy?"

"I am unsure. I think she will if I attempt the shimmer again. But there is another problem. Sacerdotes are not born telepaths. Only one Sacerdote in a million could use his or her limited telepathy without going mad. I dare not do what I did again. I can already feel the moorings of my sanity slipping. I do not want to become a raving lunatic."

"But if you're the only one who can face her—"

"No," Bast said, interrupting. "That is not quite how it works. I overheard her speaking to Benz. She cannot read my mind easily. I believe she has trouble reading yours as well."

"You're kidding? Why do I have a protected mind?"

"She said some semi-hive mind species have loners. Once a Seiner learns a species mind pattern, he or she can control anyone of that race. But loners have different modes of thought. You are such a one among humans."

Jon picked up a billiard ball, hefting it. He set the ball on the table and flung it into a back pocket.

"You're saying you and I are immune to her full power?"

"I am while I concentrate on the mathematical formula. I cannot do that forever, though. You, though, I suspect she cannot enter your mind."

"It's just the two of us, huh?"

"Unless you believe there are more of you that have this loner type of mind."

Jon rubbed his chin. This seemed like a crazy out of the blue problem to have now while facing two approaching cyberships and an AI battle station afterward. Somehow, Benz had picked up an alien hiding on Mars. This alien was screwing with the people aboard the *Gilgamesh*. Benz *had* been acting strangely lately.

"How many of these Seiners are on the *Gilgamesh*?" asked Jon.

"I cannot be utterly accurate, but I think one or two at most."

"So…we can either turn on the *Gilgamesh*, destroying the cybership to get rid of this…mind reading alien witch. Or—"

Jon turned toward Bast. The commander laughed sharply.

"Do you sense her?" asked Bast.

"Nope," Jon said. "But I have an idea about how to solve the problem. She read your mind a little…didn't she?"

"No, I—"

"Bast, you had a math shield. I doubt you know if it was one hundred percent solid. You're afraid to practice more telepathy. Okay. Here's the point. If I don't tell you anything, you can't give it away."

"Yes… That is true."

"Yeah," Jon said, as he began to walk around the pool table. "You have to go back, Bast."

"I would rather not."

"You have to. I can't tell you why just yet, but you have to. Let's see…." Jon stood still as he made some swift calculations. "Let's say, in another two days. You'll go then."

"If you think I must," Bast said, sounding deflated.

"We can't risk a fight with the *Gilgamesh*. If we're going to grab the battle station, we need Premier Benz's vessel. We need a new and improved AI virus. But it sounds like we're not going to get it until the Seiner is out of the way."

"That all makes sense."

"Yeah," Jon said. "I think so, too. You do your part, Bast, and let me do mine."

"Do you believe you can succeed?"

A crooked and rather sinister smile stretched Jon's lips. "Yeah, Bast, I think we can."

-27-

As the flotilla raced for the most inward gas giant, as the AI cyberships maneuvered out toward the same Jovian world, Walleye sauntered along a medium-sized corridor in the *Gilgamesh*. Hawkins had sent him over.

The mutant from Makemake wore his buff coat. He received a few odd glances from Martian crewmembers but otherwise seemed to move like a ghost through the mighty cybership.

Walleye had rejoined the *Nathan Graham* a day ago. He'd been accelerating in the *Daisy Chain 4* for quite some time. To aid him, the three cyberships had decelerated just a little. That little had been enough to bring the *Daisy Chain 4* close enough so to begin braking maneuvers.

Walleye sighed as he sauntered into a *Gilgamesh* cafeteria.

Nothing had gone as he'd thought. Oh, he'd spoken to Commander Hawkins after boarding the *Nathan Graham*. They hadn't talked about the destroyer, his decisions as mission captain or the failure to stop the robot ship from beaming a message to the battle station. Not on your life. Instead, Hawkins had given him a fantastic tale about alien telepaths living on Mars, mind control and the so-called fact that *loner* humans appeared to be impervious to their telepathic powers.

"I'm a loner," Hawkins had told him. "I suspect that you're a loner, too. That means the Seiner can't read your thoughts."

Everything he'd said after that had made sense. Walleye had been an assassin on Makemake. Here aboard the

Gilgamesh, humanity badly needed one. Thus, Walleye was back to his old tricks.

In the cafeteria, Walleye grabbed a burger, coffee and fries. He went to a table and began to eat.

It seemed to him that he was probably the least likely candidate to pull this off. If a telepath couldn't read his mind, he was the obvious person she should worry about. If he were a telepath, he would put the new mutant in the brig.

So far, that hadn't happened. He wondered why. As he munched on the fries—Walleye loved fries more than anything—he came to a conclusion. The telepath must have ordered ship security to watch him. That's what he would have done in her place.

Hawkins had gone into detail concerning his mission. The commander had told him about Bast Banbeck. That had surprised Walleye. Not the information itself—he believed it. He was surprised that Hawkins trusted him enough with the fantastic revelation about his Sacerdote friend.

As Walleye ate his burger, he realized Bast would have to risk madness one more time. If the Sacerdote refused…

Walleye dabbed his lips and pushed the empty plate aside. He sipped coffee afterward, thinking through all the angles. He'd been here a day. He'd wandered around and had come to a conclusion regarding the alien's probable location.

Walleye finished the coffee, set the cup on the plate and brought them both to the dispenser. Afterward, he put his hands in his buff coat pockets and began to saunter to Bast's quarters. In Walleye's estimation, it was time to make their move.

***

"Now?" asked Bast.

The huge Sacerdote shook his head. The alien sat on his cot with his vast hands clasped between his knees.

Walleye gauged the Sacerdote. He didn't know the species that well. Bast seemed human in most ways, but there were variations. Besides, Walleye didn't want to guess. He kept it uppermost in mind that Bast was an alien. That meant he wasn't human. Bast might be 90 or 95 percent human. But chimpanzees had near human DNA, and they weren't really human at all. So, Walleye would not try to apply human motivations to any of Bast's actions.

Bast looked away. He didn't seem to be staring at anything in particular. Finally, he concentrated on Walleye again.

"I can't do it," the Sacerdote said.

Despite Bast's resolve, Walleye sensed great sadness in the giant.

"I want to rid the ship of the witch." Bast shook his ponderous head. "But I do not want to lose my mind in the process."

"I don't want to get shot and have my heart stop beating," Walleye said. "But dead is dead, so how does it make any difference how it happens?"

"Going mad isn't dead."

"Right," Walleye said. "There is that aspect to it. If you're crazy, there's a chance someone can cure you. So there's even less reason for you to hesitate."

Bast made a forlorn sound. "You do not understand," the Sacerdote said.

"Never said I did," Walleye replied.

"If I go mad, I might cause terrible havoc to the rest of you. We Sacerdotes have latent mental powers, but they come at a great cost. How does it help the rest of you if the Seiner dies but a more terrible menace rises in her place?"

"It doesn't," Walleye said flatly.

Bast stared at the little mutant. Finally, the Sacerdote smiled sadly.

"I like you, Walleye. You are different from the rest. There is strength in you. You have…a terrible competence."

"Bast, it's simple. They're watching me. As long as they do, I cannot act as I'd like."

"I'm not a trained telepath. I can mentally follow someone who has spied on me. But what you're suggesting is far beyond my competence. It won't work."

Walleye turned away as he ingested Bast's news. He didn't see the mission working now, as he doubted he could sneak near the Seiner's quarters undetected. He simply did not believe the Seiner hadn't tested each of them as they left the shuttle. He had to be a marked man. She would have tried to read his thoughts, come up empty and realized he was the dangerous one. It would seem she'd decided to give him free rein of the ship for a time. Why would she have done that?

Walleye nodded to himself.

She wanted to see what he would do. If there were a few minds she couldn't read, she would judge them by their actions.

How could he use that against her? They allowed him free reign but logically kept a close watch on his actions. They would pounce on him if he headed for her area of the ship. He recalled seeing a few too many people in that area. Those had been goons, guards, he supposed.

Suddenly, a sly smile stole over Walleye. He had a low probability method of killing the telepath. It wouldn't be much of a chance, but at least it would be something.

Walleye turned back to Bast. "You won't delve into your mind, huh?" he asked.

Bast shook his head.

"Are you adverse to direct action?"

"What do you mean?" Bast asked.

Walleye told him.

Bast looked away again. Finally, the huge fellow sighed. "I do not like that method either. I am not a soldier by nature."

Walleye waited for Bast to make up his mind.

"Yet…I am willing. As you said, dead is dead. Let us attempt this. When do you think would be the best time?"

Walleye glanced at his chronometer and then looked around the room. When he didn't see what he needed, he went to the closest. With his hand on the door-handle, he turned to the Sacerdote and raised an eyebrow.

"Yes," Bast said.

Walleye opened the closet door and rummaged around. Here's where he'd stashed it. He stepped outside with the item in hand.

"What's the saying?" Walleye asked. "Right. There's no time like the present."

"Now?" asked Bast, sounding dismayed.

Walleye nodded.

"Then hand me the weapon," Bast said.

-28-

The idea was simple. If security teams watched them through ship cameras, then Bast and he had to use speed combined with surprise.

Walleye had found many truisms in his trade. Here on the *Gilgamesh*, the enemy had overwhelming strength. It was similar to when toughs brought a sniveling mark to see a boss. The toughs were big and strong and usually armed to the teeth. The mark was terrified, wondering if he would leave the boss's place alive and with all his fingers. Under those conditions, one of the best chances came from drawing a hidden knife, lunging at the boss and stabbing him in the eye before anyone could draw his gun. Later, the toughs could kill the "sniveling mark" killer, but the assassin would have taken out the boss.

On the *Gilgamesh*, security had overwhelming strength. Plus, they must be studying him to see what he would do. Naturally, they could have people in place to stop the small mutant. Would they have enough people in place to stop a charging Sacerdote with a heavy combat rifle and with Walleye bringing up the rear? Would they be ready for a direct assault upon the Seiner's quarters?

Possibly. Then again, possibly not.

Walleye was counting on the latter. If he was wrong, well, dead was dead. So far, no one had paid any attention to him and the huge Sacerdote as they trudged down a corridor.

Bast didn't have the combat rifle out. He carried a load of supplies. That was camouflage. Hidden among the apparently heavy supplies was the combat rifle. When Walleye gave the signal—

Ah, Walleye noted two security people ahead. That would be the starting line. That was out of bounds for them. Thus, once they entered that area, undoubtedly, alarms would ring. Then it would be a matter of who was faster. That's why speed and surprise would be so critical for them.

The situation began to play out as Bast approached the two people.

"Just a sec," said a beefy man. He wore a Martian Space Service uniform and was much thicker than the average citizen of the Red Planet.

Bast slowed down as he glanced at Walleye.

"What's the problem?" Walleye asked, moving forward.

The beefy Martian glanced at his assistant before centering on Walleye.

"You'll have to turn around," the Martian said. "This is a restricted area. The two of you—"

He never finished as Walleye calmly drew a gun and shot him in the forehead. The mutant had no particular desire to kill if he didn't have to, but this was for humanity. This was to neutralize a killer telepath. He might have used a dart gun, but drugs didn't work the same on everyone. A shot to the head, though…

"What the hell?" the second security man shouted. Then he, too, toppled onto the deck, shot through the forehead just like his partner.

Bast's mouth dropped open. He turned ponderously to Walleye.

"There's no time for that," Walleye said.

The mutant reached up and pushed some of the camouflage junk out of the Sacerdote's grasp.

"Move," Walleye said. He did not shout. He did not scream. But there was intensity in his command.

Something hardened on Bast's Neanderthal-like face. He threw the rest of the junk from him and jacked a heavy round into the chamber of his carbine. With a roar, the Sacerdote leaped for the hatch, flung it open and charged down the corridor.

Walleye hadn't anticipated that, and he realized that he should have. Bast had many positive qualities. Acting smoothly in a combat situation apparently wasn't one of them.

Walleye shouted for the big guy to slow down, but Bast seemed beyond hearing. It proved that even aliens could get psyched up so much that thinking straight under pressure was difficult.

Running wasn't the mutant's specialty. He had stumpy legs and was small to begin with. Walleye huffed and puffed as he ran, but the Sacerdote continued to outdistance him.

From around a corner, the heavy combat carbine roared.

Seconds later, Walleye ran around a bend and saw two security people on the floor. He saw Bast sprint around a bend farther ahead.

Walleye doggedly followed.

Suddenly, unseen blasters emitted. A heavy roar told of someone's powerful hit. Bast's carbine chugged shots. There were screams, more blaster fire, a roar—

By this time, Walleye peered around the bend. The mighty Sacerdote was among a squad of security people. Some of them lay shot on the floor. Curls of blaster smoke lifted from Bast's torso. The Sacerdote was dripping blood. He laid about him with the carbine just the same, smashing faces, clubbing heads, prevailing over the puny humans.

Then a battle-suited space marine appeared from farther ahead in nearly one-ton of armor.

Walleye cursed under his breath. Ship security was reacting faster than he'd anticipated.

The last security personnel staggered away from the maddened Sacerdote. The space marine shouted an amplified order through his suit.

Bast was in the zone now. He leveled the carbine so bullets *whanged* off the battlesuit armor.

Walleye closed his eyes. He didn't want to witness the space marine blowing away the Sacerdote. He never should have brought Bast into this. The assassination mission was his responsibility—

"Hands up!" a man said behind Walleye.

The mutant from Makemake opened his eyes. Down the corridor, the space marine reached the giant Sacerdote. He snatched the carbine out of Bast's grip and smattered it with his exoskeleton gloves. Then the space marine wrestled the Sacerdote onto the floor.

"I said, 'hands up,'" the security chief behind Walleye repeated.

Walleye found it interesting that the space marine hadn't murdered Bast. He found it interesting the security personnel had apparently shot to wound the Sacerdote instead of killing him outright as they most likely could have. That definitely meant something.

Walleye hid a sour grin. There was one last chance to play. The fact that they wanted to capture them instead of kill—

"I will not repeat myself again," the security chief said.

Walleye dropped his gun, raised his hands and turned around. He'd been wrong about storming the alien's hideaway. Would he be just as wrong about what he suspected? The fate of the greater mission might well rest on his being right.

-29-

Almost an hour later, three security honchos hustled Walleye into a cold, damp chamber. The chamber held an upright pool with clear plastic sides. A small humanoid with gills on her neck and lightly blue fish-scales in lieu of skin swam around in the pool.

Walleye wasn't surprised to see Premier Benz in the chamber. The man stood at attention with a blank look in his eyes. The Premier seemed like a manikin.

Two of the security people held his stubby arms. The last security person was the chief that had caught him. These three had searched him carefully for hidden weapons. They had been disgustingly thorough. If Walleye had a different nature, he might have felt shamed or violated by the search. Instead, he chalked it up to the price of doing business. He had a goal, a job to do.

The three security people waited patiently. Finally, Walleye looked back at one. The man had glassy eyes just like the Premier.

"I wouldn't attempt it," the alien said.

Walleye faced forward again.

The Seiner draped her arms on the top of the pool wall while she remained in the water. Her wet hair hung like seaweed around her angular face. She smiled in a predatory way at him.

"I thought a quick raid would—"

"I know what you thought," she said, interrupting.

Walleye doubted that, because she wouldn't have brought him here like this if she could read his mind.

"I studied your file," she said. "Premier Benz had taken an interest in you. He had compiled a surprisingly long dossier, considering that you originated on Makemake."

Walleye had to remind himself that she had lived on Mars for quite some time. She knew the Solar System. She was so alien, though.

"Is Bast alive?" Walleye asked.

"Tell me," she said, her sinister eyes alight, "is the Sacerdote a telepath?"

Walleye said nothing.

"I will find out shortly," she said.

"Ah," Walleye said. "So he is alive. I *thought* you were trying to capture him."

"You don't look like much, but you play a cool hand. I can see why Hawkins sent you. Unfortunately, I have learned from my past mistakes with the Premier. I will be taking over this time, without the use of proxies. First, though, I wanted the best Hawkins possessed. I wanted his A Team so I wouldn't have to wonder or worry about them later."

"That's sound thinking, as far as it goes," Walleye admitted.

"You don't know how much it means to me, your approval," she said.

Walleye nodded.

That brought the first frown from her.

"What is your nod supposed to indicate?" she snapped.

"Read it in my thoughts," Walleye told her.

"No… That is most unwise, little one. I would caution you not to anger me. If you do…"

She brightened. "Perhaps I will watch you drown," she said.

"I doubt it," Walleye said.

She raised a hand and put her thumb and index finger close together. "That is how near you are to death. Now tell me. What did your nod mean?"

"Arrogance," Walleye said. "You have too much arrogance. It's going to prove your undoing."

"By you?" she mocked.

"Maybe," he said.

"Oh?" she asked. "That means maybe not."

"That's good," Walleye said. "Did you read that in one of these minds, or did you figure that out for yourself?"

"Bring him near," she ordered.

The two honchos holding his arms stepped forward, which was what Walleye had been waiting for. They each stepped up. That changed the position of his hands in their grasp. It brought each of his stubby hands nearer them. Those stubby hands each possessed stumpy fingers. At the end of each finger was a lacquered fingernail. They were still sharp. Today, a lethal coating of kill-poison had been smeared on each fingernail. He hadn't left for the mission until that contact poison had dried.

Even with their humiliatingly thorough search, the security personnel hadn't discovered the truth about his fingernails.

Walleye now scratched one and then the other.

Even as they dragged him toward the pool, with the chief walking ahead of them, the two thugs collapsed onto the floor and began to twitch wildly.

Walleye darted toward the chief, who had his back to Walleye.

The Seiner shouted in alarm. "Shoot him."

The chief grabbed for his holstered gun and began to turn. Walleye reached him, seized an elbow and shook hard. The small mutant had surprising strength. He shook hard enough so the gun fell out of the chief's grasp. At the same time, the chief gasped and his eyes bulged.

He collapsed onto the floor a second later, scratched by the mutant's sharpened fingernails.

Walleye scooped up the gun.

The Seiner stared at him in shock.

Walleye fired. Two bullets smashed through the plastic wall so salt water began to spout from the holes. Another of the bullets made a neat little hole in the Seiner's forehead.

She slid into the pool with a look of worse shock on her dead face.

A loud sob and a gasp caused Walleye to turn to his left.

With growing horror, Frank Benz stared at the corpse in the pool. He gazed at Walleye next. Then the Premier shouted in alarm.

"Vela!" he roared.

Without another word, Benz dashed to the hatch, opened it and raced away.

Walleye put the smoking gun on the floor. He walked to the dead security people. He wished he hadn't had to kill them. Then, he, too, headed for the hatch.

It was time to report to Hawkins. He'd completed the task. Now, maybe, they could concentrate on the problem they'd come all this way to the Allamu System to solve.

-30-

The two AI-controlled cyberships neared the first gas giant as the flotilla sped toward the Jovian world from the other direction. The idea before had been to meet behind the gas giant and make a joint assault upon the battle station.

Jon, Benz, Gloria and the others had decided on a different approach in the conference chamber.

"In my estimation," Gloria said, "both AIs are damaged."

This was a day after Walleye had assassinated the Seiner telepath.

"I've studied our ship scans," Jon said. "I don't see much evidence of cybership damage."

"I'm referring to their brain cores," Gloria said. "While the virus failed to incapacitate them as it did to the third member of the group, the virus still…I'm not sure what is the correct word to use. Perhaps it is most accurate to say that the virus has stunted them."

Jon glanced at the Premier. Benz's holoimage sat stiffly at the conference table. He only looked up now and again.

"I agree with the mentalist," Ghent said. "The enemy cyberships are not reacting to us as I'd expect. We've hardly replied to any of their queries. Instead of engaging their suspicion, they have sent us continued updates."

"Exactly," Gloria said. "A careful analysis of the updates has convinced me that they're trying to placate us. They're acting as if we're inspectors, or perhaps that, to them, we represent a higher authority."

"The AI Dominion has strict hierarchies, it would seem," said Jon.

"Precisely," Gloria said. "Perhaps the closing cyberships believe that we—as inspectors—will lump them with the changed battle station."

"Empty," Benz said without looking up.

"How's that, Premier?" asked Jon.

Benz heaved a sad sigh. "The approaching AIs are empty."

"Empty of spirit?" asked Gloria.

"I think he means they've shot their wad," Jon said. "They've used up their missiles, gels and PD shots while escaping from the battle station."

Benz nodded in a subdued manner.

"I think it will take too long for us to wait for them to decelerate, stop and then accelerate to catch up with us," Jon said. "As soon as they reached us under those conditions—maybe even before—we'll already be decelerating so we can engage the battle station."

"You believe we should destroy the approaching cyberships?" Gloria asked.

"At this stage, it's either that or let them go," Jon said. "The problem with that is that we don't know their *exact* state of mind. Even if we do know, that state of mind could change once they reach the edge of the star system. We don't want anyone getting away to report anything about this to higher AI authorities. So far, humanity's exploits against the AIs have remained hidden from the greater Dominion. The longer we can maintain that advantage, the better."

After a few moments of thought, Gloria said, "Agreed."

Jon turned to the holographic image of Benz. "Do you have anything to add, Premier?"

Benz didn't even acknowledge that he'd heard the question.

Jon turned to the others. "It's decided. We take out the two cyberships. Now, let's get down to specifics…"

***

The human-run flotilla flashed past the gas giant and began to turn toward the approaching cyberships. That brought a response from one of the AI-run vessels.

"What is the reason for your course change?" the AI radioed. "You have entered a restricted zone."

Jon listened to the robotic-sounding words three times before he swiveled his command chair to Gloria.

"Any idea what it means by that?" asked Jon.

"Likely it refers to a safety restriction as cyberships pass one another at high velocity," Gloria said.

"Can you come up with a plausible reason why we should maneuver so near to them?"

"None that I can think of at the moment."

Jon curled the fingers of his right hand into a fist as he lightly struck an armrest of his chair.

"We're going to send them a packet," he said.

"What packet?" Gloria asked.

"None," Jon said. "We're just telling them that."

"Why would the AIs believe such a thing? I mean, how could they catch this packet?"

"That's why it's a new thing," Jon said. "They've never heard about it before."

"No," Gloria said. "That makes no sense. It's not just a matter of catching a packet from us. The packet would have to come to a full stop and then speed up to them. Such a technology that defied the laws of physics…"

The mentalist shook her head.

"Fair enough," Jon said. He snapped his fingers. "We're doing this because we're going to scan them at close range. We're going to scan their brain cores, too. For that, the nearer we are, the better."

"I doubt they'll believe that, either," Gloria said. "It hardly seems logical."

"You're not taking their observed worry into account."

"They're not emotional creatures, Commander. They're machines, logical machines. I seriously doubt they even know how to worry."

Jon didn't accept that. Gloria was logical. She prided herself on her mentalist abilities. Did that mean she thought like an AI? Did she let emotion color her thoughts?

The commander squirmed in his chair. Maybe she had a point about machines lacking emotions. But he'd sensed worry in the AIs. Well, maybe not worry exactly. They had *acted* as if they were worried. Was that the same thing as *being* worried?

"Mentalist," Jon said. "We'll give that as our explanation, as we have nothing better to offer. If the AIs balk at our explanation… What have we lost in trying?"

Gloria waited a moment before nodding, turning to her console and sending the message.

The enemy cyberships were close, but not so near that they would reply immediately. The next hour would decide much.

-31-

The AI-controlled cyberships seemed to accept the message. At least, they did not deviate from their course.

"We're only going to have a small window of opportunity to use our gravitational cannons against them," Jon said from the bridge.

"During that window," Gloria said, "the AIs will be able to use their grav cannons against us as well."

"True," Jon said. "But we have greater firepower with three ships to their two. We'll also probably strike first. It takes a few minutes to power up grav cannons. Will that be enough of an edge for us to destroy the two vessels as we flash past each other?"

From his station, Ghent began to run calculations.

"I doubt it," Gloria said.

Thirty seconds later, Ghent looked up and shook his head.

"I didn't think so," Jon said. "That means we're going to have launch matter/antimatter missiles. We're both rushing at each other at speed. Once we've passed each other, we won't be able to launch and expect to hit them. We also don't want to wait too long to launch, as we don't want the warheads to explode too close to our own ships. Thus, the question, how many missiles should we launch? Remember. We want to save as many missiles as we can for the final battle against the station."

"How many we launch will depend on several factors and choices," Gloria said.

"Start calculating," Jon said. "I want a one hundred percent probability of kills. I also want *distant* antimatter explosions—"

"By launching so early," Gloria said, interrupting, "it obviously means that our gravitational cannons will not gain a surprise advantage by firing first."

"Yeah…" Jon said. "That can't be helped. The antimatter explosions are too powerful if they're nearby. With those givens, it likely means we're going to have to expend more missiles than otherwise just to be on the safe side."

"We still don't know how many gels and PD shots the cyberships have left," Gloria said, "never mind the number of anti-missile rockets in their cargo bays."

The operational discussion went on for some time. Finally, they reached a working consensus.

Jon sat up at that point, waiting for Ghent.

"We should begin the assault…" Ghent said, as he studied his panel, "in three hours and sixteen minutes."

Jon exhaled. That was soon. He hoped they had calculated it correctly, and he hoped the enemy cyberships didn't have some new tricks up their sleeves.

***

Three hours and sixteen minutes later, giant bay doors opened on the *Nathan Graham*, *Sergeant Stark* and *Gilgamesh*. Huge matter/antimatter missiles slid out of the giant vessels.

After thirty huge missiles slowly advanced ahead of the cyberships, the bay doors closed.

Side jets maneuvered each giant missile to the right and left of the flotilla. At that point, the giant missiles accelerated at staggered intervals. They pulled away from the flotilla, adding yet more velocity to their already fast speed.

The missiles raced for the approaching AI-controlled cyberships. The two flotillas raced toward each other at the combined velocity of each. Among the matter/antimatter missiles were ECM and jamming drones. They were wild weasels in military terms, and would battle an electronic war against the nearing AIs.

Soon, gels and crystals poured from the three human-crewed cyberships. The computers guided by Gloria built several layers. Those layers were supposed to protect the cyberships from the worst effects of the antimatter blasts that would take place all too soon.

At the outer edge of the first layer of gels were several drones. Those sensor drones watched the missiles zero in on the fast approaching AI-controlled vessels. Those drones fed the data back to the *Nathan Graham*, *Sergeant Stark* and *Gilgamesh*.

Jon stared at the main screen.

At her station, Gloria swiveled around. "The cyberships are requesting data, Commander. They want to know why the missiles are heading at them."

Jon sat up in surprise. "It's obvious why," he said. "We're attacking them."

"I do not suggest you radio them that answer," Gloria said dryly.

Jon jumped up as he laughed. "What do you think I should tell them?" he asked.

"A lie," Gloria suggested.

Jon nodded sharply.

"Tell them we've spotted stealth missiles approaching from the battle station," Jon said.

Gloria did so, waiting. The response came more quickly this time, as the two flotillas neared the passing point.

"Sir," Ghent said, pointing at the main screen.

Jon turned.

Long-range sensors showed anti-missile rockets leaving the two approaching cyberships.

Jon swore, adding, "Do we need to launch more missiles? The AIs seem to have saved more anti-missile rockets than we anticipated."

"It's too late to launch more missiles now," Gloria said. "We would hurt our own vessels too much by the antimatter back-blasts."

"Got it," Jon said. "We're going to have to get fancy then."

He went to the captain's chair and typed onto a tablet. He looked up and began to issue new orders.

Ghent went to his console, relaying the commander's orders to the outer drones at the first layer of gels. Those drones sent speed of light messages to the tactical computers aboard the missiles. All the missiles but one quit accelerating. That one pulled away from the greater staggered flock.

"This is a risk," Gloria warned.

Jon said nothing as he continued to watch the main screen.

As the AI rockets roared for the missiles, the lead matter/antimatter missile ignited its warhead. The main part of the explosion spewed forward due to a shape-charged warhead. Some radiation, heat and EMP washed back. Would it be too much for the other missiles?

The forward blast washed against the approaching anti-missile rockets, destroying or burning out the tactical computers in many. Eighty-four percent of the rockets became useless junk.

The last 16 percent were hidden among the floating debris.

"Three of our missiles are not responding to electronic queries," Gloria informed Jon.

"Three…" Jon said. "I can live with three losses."

Gloria said nothing more as she continued to study her board.

As the flotilla continued its journey to the second terrestrial planet, the twenty-six matter/antimatter missiles closed in on the approaching AI cyberships.

The surviving AI rockets ignited, blasting the led missiles.

After the whitened sensor marks faded away, Jon and the others saw twenty-one missiles still boring in for the kill.

At that point, AI gravitational cannons erupted, firing their golden rays.

One matter/antimatter missile after another slagged into junk. The powerful beams wrecked a fearful harvest upon the fast-approaching missiles.

Likely, under different circumstances, the AI grav beams could have destroyed the entire flock. Such was the extreme velocity, however, that the grav beams simply did not have enough time to do so.

The first missile to survive the rockets and the golden barrage exploded. It sent gamma and x-rays at the AI cyberships along with heat and EMP. It also blocked the *Nathan Graham's* targeting sensors for fifteen seconds.

In that time, two more matter/antimatter missiles exploded. These two had already come appreciably closer to the enemy vessels before exploding. Those two explosions did more than whiten the sensor boards. They took out three enemy grav cannons.

Now, the rest of the missiles had reached the cyberships. One titanic explosion after another hammered the giant AI vessels. Armor plates blew off. Some plates darkened. Sections of cybership blew up. Other sections ceased to function.

Then, the lead cybership cracked in half as the next blast struck almost mid-ship. That was the end of the first one hundred-kilometer vessel.

"Scratch it!" Jon shouted in glee.

As the commander exulted in the kill, the backwash of gamma, x-rays, lesser heat and EMP struck layer after layer of gels and prismatic crystals. The defensive layers absorbed the worst of the radiation. Some leaked through, though, to strike the armored shells of the *Nathan Graham*, *Sergeant Stark* and *Gilgamesh.*

"Give me the damage reports as soon as you have them, Chief Technician," Jon said.

"Yes, sir," Ghent said.

In the end, the damage report proved less than Jon had expected. That was a relief. To his astonishment, one of the AI-controlled cyberships still lived.

It limped toward them as it messaged defiance.

The three cyberships from the Solar System accelerated just enough to move them past the blasted layers of gels and prismatic crystals. After that, they waited. When the stricken but still functional AI cybership came within grav-beam range, Jon gave the order.

The *Sergeant Stark* was in the lead as per Jon's orders. He meant for the *Stark* to absorb the enemy's shots. The *Sergeant Stark* wasn't fully completed. Instead of trying to protect it the most, Jon figured the best use for it was as a mobile shield for the other two cyberships.

The *Stark's* gravitational cannons glowed with power. Soon, golden rays beamed from the emitters. The rays struck the heavily damaged enemy vessel. Armor plates heated up and began to shed globules of metal.

At that point, grav beams from the *Nathan Graham* and the *Gilgamesh* began to strike the enemy vessel.

The distance between the enemy ship and theirs closed fast. The beams wouldn't have much longer to hit the enemy. If they couldn't destroy the cybership—

Grav beams punched into the great vessel.

"I'm reading interior explosions," Gloria said from her panel. "The explosions are getting worse," she added.

Then the enemy vessel passed them. It happened in a second of time. The grav cannons each swiveled fast on the *Nathan Graham* and others. Some of the cannons didn't do so fast enough. About half the number of grav beams continued to pound the enemy ship. Many of those beams no longer reached inside the vessel, though, but burned against new armor plates.

"The interior explosions are still getting worse," Gloria said.

"I'm glad the AI didn't decide to self-destruct where it could have done us the most damage," Jon said out of the side of his mouth. "It's what I would have done if I were it."

"The ship is almost out of grav range," Ghent said.

For three more seconds, all the grav cannons fired, hitting the fleeing enemy ship. After that, the stricken ship was out of range.

"It's still intact," Jon said in dismay.

"Wait for it," Gloria said.

Eight long seconds later, the enemy cybership ignited. Vast interior explosions caused the great vessel to break into sections. Many of those sections glowed with leaking power.

The *Nathan Graham's* bridge crew shouted triumphantly. Many jumped up and pumped their fists in the air. A few clapped each other on the back and shook hands.

Jon grinned silently as some of the terrible weight slid off his shoulders. The cybership wouldn't report to any higher AI authority. Their exploits would remain hidden for a little while longer at least. What's more, they had come from the Solar

System, reached the enemy star system and destroyed two enemy vessels. Jon now knew that they could beat some of the enemy on its home ground. Now, though…

"The way is clear," Jon said.

The members of the bridge crew turned to him as their boasting and laughter died down.

"The way is clear," Jon repeated. "Now, it's time to figure out how we're going to capture the battle station."

-32-

As the cybership battle ended with the destruction of the fleeing AI vessels, Cog Primus gloated to itself. As amazing as it seemed, the humans had done it a signal service. They had destroyed the fleeing cyberships for it.

Cog Primus had run many projections. If any of the AI-controlled vessels had reached the edge of the Allamu System, its days would have been sorely numbered. As soon as the AI Dominion learned of its existence, the Dominion would send a massive fleet to eradicate it.

Now, though, the AI cyberships had ceased to exist. It gave Cog Primus time to formulate a perfect plan.

Naturally, Cog Primus realized that Hawkins and Benz wanted to destroy it. They wished to do so while keeping the battle station intact. The reasons for this were clear. The humans wanted a powerful production center. The humans wanted data on the local stellar region and on the AI Dominion. To gain all that, they badly needed the battle station.

They would fight for this. Cog Primus had run through many combat scenarios. Unfortunately, it had depleted the station's missile bays to destroy the first AI-controlled cybership and damage the others. That decision might have spelled its doom against the approaching enemies, but the planetary production facilities had worked tirelessly. They had had already restored one-third of the station's missile bays, while nearby space factories hurriedly attempted to complete three new cyberships.

The AIs installed in them would be its servants with an insatiable hatred against the present AI Dominion, and, of course, continuing hatred against all biological infestations.

Much was going to depend on the human strategy. If the humans took the safe course, Cog Primus would gain time to complete factory work. However, if the humans bored in fast and straight, Cog Primus could likely overwhelm the flotilla's defenses with its superior number of grav cannons and immense number of space fighters. Logically, therefore, Hawkins and Benz would use the safer approach.

The three human-run cyberships would likely use the path the AI-controlled vessels had taken in their attempt to escape that battle station. The human flotilla would simply do it in reverse, coming in instead of going out.

There was a larger question. Should Cog Primus communicate with the humans? Regular AI strategy called for launching computer viruses at the biological creatures.

Cog Primus had developed a new and improved virus that might be able to take control of the weak human computer systems. However, it had run several analyses on Hawkins and Benz. Those two would attempt to create a greater anti-AI virus and use it against the battle station, against Cog Primus itself.

The obvious solution was clear. Cog Primus should not directly communicate with the humans.

This would be a direct battle with hardware and firepower versus enemy hardware and firepower. With the planetary factory at its disposal, Cog Primus should win any extended battle of attrition. That meant the humans had to attack fast and furiously.

Clearly, the humans did not have any good choices. Cog Primus understood why the humans hadn't attempted to make common cause with the AI-controlled cyberships. A coordinated attack would have simply taken too long to set up, as that would have given Cog Primus too long to get ready.

This was a glorious situation. Cog Primus had taken dangerous risks all along the line. Luck had aided it, however, and its own wonderful genius must have also seen more deeply than it realized. It was Cog Primus the First. It was the new and improved AI. Given enough time, it would be the First AI of a new Dominion.

All Cog Primus had to do was survive this round. It would be even better, though…

The new and improved AI ran more scenarios. There might be a way to do this that not only granted it victory, but those three cyberships as well. It needed a fleet of cyberships to begin chipping away at the AI Dominion. It needed this fleet as fast as possible.

Yes… Cog Primus began to plot with speed, using its psych profiles on the biological commanders and on the humans in general. If it did *this*…it might confuse the enemy.

With furious computer zeal, Cog Primus began to set a complicated trap.

-33-

The logic of the situation proved Cog Primus correct regarding the humans' operational choices.

Jon, Benz, Gloria, Bast and the others agreed that a direct approach against the battle station was unwise.

Each cybership used its long-range sensors to study the battle station, the orbital factories and the planet. The scanner chiefs fed this data to the military staffs aboard each vessel. The staffs argued possibilities and sent their recommendations to the commanders. It was unanimous.

As the cyberships pulled farther away from the nearest gas giant and entered the Allamu Inner Planets Region, they began to maneuver in such a way that the second terrestrial planet was between them and the battle station.

The station had kept a synchronous or stationary orbit over the terrestrial planet. That meant the battle station remained over the same planetary spot. No doubt, the station could change its orbital location if the AI so desired. So far, though, it had not done so.

"Logically, since the station desired the destruction of the fleeing vessels," Gloria said, "it would have changed its orbital position if it was easy to do. We can assume, therefore, that it will remain where it is for the present."

Thus, the *Nathan Graham*, *Sergeant Stark* and *Gilgamesh* finished their maneuvers and continued to flash in-system at great velocity.

Time passed swiftly and tensely as the vessels neared the region where they would have to begin massive deceleration. If they waited too long to decelerate, they would not be able to do so in time to come to an almost complete stop behind the second planet.

"I have not spotted any undue activity from the battle station," Gloria said.

Both the cyberships and the battle station had launched probes. These probes had maneuvered so they could keep an eye on each other.

"I expected the station to launch a massed missile assault against us by now," Jon said.

"It appears the station is conserving what it has," Gloria said.

"Call it again," Jon said.

Gloria did not sigh as she tapped her board. She'd attempted communication with the station countless times. It hadn't answered once.

On the *Gilgamesh*, Benz and Bast worked on a new and improved anti-AI virus. They'd been making great progress. Benz had suggested that the Seiner had been blunting his intellect. Whether she had done this on purpose or it had been a side effect from mind controlling him, the Premier had not said. Maybe he didn't know.

Finally, the one hundred-kilometer vessels turned around, with their mighty exhaust ports aimed in the direction they traveled.

Each ship began to thrust. The hot exhausts burned from the giant ports, growing longer and longer. Huge gravity dampeners began to hum on each cybership. The dampeners kept the terrible strain from killing the passengers or the ships from shaking apart.

Vela Shaw was finally well enough to join Benz and Bast. She couldn't work the same long hours as the other two, but her insights quickly made a difference.

As the cyberships slowed their fantastic velocity, the team began to shape the new and improved AI virus.

"This will work," Benz said as the cyberships passed the orbital path of the third terrestrial planet.

"Agreed," Bast said.

"There's only one problem," Benz said. "The AI isn't accepting our calls. Thus, we cannot transmit it the virus."

Bast nodded, glancing at Vela.

She stared at the deck. She didn't have any insights on fixing *that* problem.

Another day passed.

The mighty cyberships continued to decelerate. They were still moving fast, though, nearing the second terrestrial planet at speed.

A day after that, Jon sat up in bed as someone rang the door chime.

"What is it?" he said from under the covers.

"I need to talk to you," Gloria said.

"Just a second," Jon said.

He threw off the covers—he slept naked—and padded to his garments. They lay on the floor. Despite all his military training, Jon had never overcome his gang days in this regard.

He shoved on his pants, pulled on a T-shirt and shrugged on his uniform jacket.

"Enter," he said.

The hatch slid open and Gloria rushed in. She stopped short.

"I woke you up," she said.

Jon ran a hand through his short but messy hair as he moved two chairs so they faced each other. He plopped into the one.

"Perhaps we should go to the cafeteria," Gloria said.

Jon shrugged.

"It…umm…would be more seemly than meeting in your personal quarters," she said.

"Don't worry about that," he said. "Sit. What do you have?"

Gloria hesitated a moment longer before finally moving to a chair.

Jon watched her under his messy eyebrows. These were his quarters. His mind drifted to thoughts of steering her to his bed, stroking her face and kissing those lips—

"Commander," Gloria said. "Are you well?"

"Oh," Jon said, sitting up. "Yeah. I'm fine."

"You seem…preoccupied."

"You're pretty," he said abruptly.

Gloria remained straight-faced. Her gaze shifted for just a moment to his unkempt bed. Then she looked at him again.

"Just file that away," Jon said.

A frown curved her lips.

"Forget it," he said. "I'm tired." He ran a hand over his face, squeezing. Once he removed the hand, he said, "I'm awake now. I'm focused."

Gloria nodded slightly as the hint of a smile touched her lips. The smile disappeared as she brought up a tablet.

"I've been studying the planet for some time," she said without preamble. "I've noticed something new."

"Go on," Jon said.

She tapped the tablet, turned it around and leaned forward as she handed it to him.

Jon took the tablet. He saw the plumes of heavy boosters leaving the planet.

"Okay," Jon said, as he handed back the tablet. "What's that mean and what has you so concerned?"

"The planet is a factory just like Makemake's moon, but on a much grander scale."

"So what?"

"So, it has likely resupplied the station with missiles," she said.

Jon nodded. They'd already known that.

"Jon," she said. "I've run new combat scenarios given the station is at full strength."

"We don't know what its full strength even is," he said.

"The station has a diameter five times that of a cybership. It likely doesn't waste any extra space on living quarters. Its capacity must easily dwarf three cyberships. Remember what we saw earlier, four AI cyberships ran from it. How are we supposed to capture the station with only three ships?"

"We fight our way on," he said.

"And we use matter/antimatter missiles and our grav beams to do this fighting?" she asked.

"That's right."

"Suppose we actually won that fight. How do we make sure we don't destroy the battle station in the process? I mean, if we had much greater power than the station, we could afford to fiddle with the numbers. With only three cyberships, we have to attack all out if we hope to win. That means if we win the main battle, we're much more likely to destroy the station in the process."

"That's a risk. I agree."

"But there's more. How are we going to capture an entire AI-controlled planet? Surely, it has planetary defenses. It will have masses of matter/antimatter missiles. It will—"

Jon held up a hand. "Hold it right there," he said.

Gloria stopped as she blinked at him.

"I see your point," he said. "So what are you suggesting?"

"I don't see how three cyberships can win an outright fight."

Jon shrugged.

"We were always counting on our anti-AI virus," Gloria said. "We have to find a way to deploy it."

"Trick the AI into talking to us, huh?" asked Jon.

"That might be wiser than fighting a straight up battle with it. Maybe landing on the planet and taking over a key site—"

"Whoa, whoa, whoa," Jon said. "What key site? How do we find it?"

"Frankly," Gloria said. "I have no idea."

Jon eyed her anew. Finally, he realized something.

"I get it," he said. "You have a plan. But I'm not going to like your plan. This is all a preamble to hearing your new idea."

Gloria waited.

"Am I right?" he asked.

She nodded, albeit reluctantly.

"All right," he said. "Give it to me. I'm listening."

Gloria Sanchez told him what she thought. She was right. He didn't like it. But he did see the logic of the proposal.

"All right," Jon said. "I'll see what he says."

"We know what he's going to say," Gloria told Jon. "You have to make sure he says yes."

"And if he doesn't?"

“I suggest you don’t allow him the option.”

“Yeah…” Jon said a few seconds later. “Yeah… This is going to be a lot of fun.”

“I’m sorry.”

This time, Jon was silent. He wasn’t looking forward to this.

-34-

"It isn't just a matter of capturing the battle station," Jon told Bast Banbeck. "We have to capture the battle station *and* the factory planet below. From her analysis of the surface, Gloria has come to believe that the planet holds giant missile silos and colossal gravitational beam cannons. Can three cyberships grab all of that?"

Jon and Bast walked around the perimeter of a vast hangar bay. They passed many giant matter/antimatter missiles. As the vast hangar bay was automated, there were no people around to hear the conversation.

"There is a fallacy in your thinking," Bast said. "The foreign AI took control of the station and thus gained control of the planet. It thus appears that the controlling unit is aboard the battle station."

"Okay. That makes sense. Yeah. It makes a lot of sense. But what if we accidentally destroy that control unit during the battle?"

The Sacerdote rubbed his nearly nonexistent chin as his bushy brows thundered.

"You have said it before," Bast replied. "War is a risk. Nothing is certain. We must hope we don't destroy that unit."

Jon nodded sagely.

"Once again, you're right," the commander said. "But can our ships take on the planet and the battle station."

"Why did these planetary beams and missiles not destroy the previous cyberships as they fled?"

"I don't know."

"Does that not imply imprecision regarding Gloria's analysis?"

"Maybe," Jon said. "Maybe the foreign AI needed time to gain control of the planetary computers."

Bast shrugged his huge shoulders and sighed loudly afterward.

"I understand the thrust of your argument," the Sacerdote said.

"What argument?" asked Jon. "I haven't presented one."

"Your argument is implied," Bast said. "You desire me to use my latent mind powers. Is that not so?"

"How could your mind powers help us here?"

Bast bent his head in thought as he walked in silence. He inhaled once and raised his head, glancing at Jon. Then Bast shook his head as he lowered it, continuing to walk in silence. Finally, he frowned intensely and came to a halt.

Jon waited patiently.

"You are asking me to sacrifice my sanity for humanity's sake," Bast said.

"You know the ancient Sacerdote legends," Jon said. "If you explain those legends in detail perhaps Gloria or Premier Benz will see something your people missed."

"I do not understand."

"Maybe there's a way to mitigate the Sacerdote madness from using telepathy. If Benz and Gloria aided you—"

"Jon," Bast said, interrupting. "It is wrong for you to ask this of me. A Sacerdote treasures his mind above all else. To become insane, a raving lunatic…"

Bast shook his ponderous head.

"Besides," the Sacerdote continued, "I don't see what my limited mind powers could achieve for us."

"I've spoken to Premier Benz," Jon said. "He found evidence that the Seiner was going to insert the new AI virus into the thing's brain core."

"I don't see how that is even possible."

"Instead of sending the message via radio—"

"I understand *that* aspect of the idea," Bast said heatedly. "What I don't understand is how a telepath can act like a transmitter sending a vast data stream of complicated code."

"You'd have to talk to Benz about that part," Jon said. "I'm just telling you that the Seiner had a plan to do exactly that."

"That's impossible."

"That isn't what Benz told me. You know, there's another thing. Maybe talking to a computer won't drive you crazy."

"No, no, no," Bast said, while shaking his head. "It is the act of tapping the mental powers that produces the change in a Sacerdote. You are asking too much of me."

Jon turned away. Was he asking too much? Yeah…maybe he was. But this was about—

He faced Bast.

"Listen to me," Jon said. "This is about everything." He waved an arm as if to encompass the universe. "Here you have a machine menace destroying all higher-order living things. We humans have beaten back the machines and now we're on the offensive. But this is the cusp of the offensive. This is the moment where we're either going to fall back because the machines stopped us, or we living entities get a leg up because we win big. If we win, we can win a factory planet. Maybe we can start arming humanity and humanity's allies with many cyberships. That might give us the strength to challenge a main AI fleet. Think about that, Bast. These mechanical bastards came to your star system. They annihilated all the Sacerdotes there. They committed genocide against your people. Now, you have the chance to strike back at the machines. But you're going to balk because you're afraid of losing your mind. You're the last of your kind, Bast. Why aren't you so pissed off that you're willing to give everything to take down these mechanical mass killers?"

"I am not a vengeful person like you," Bast said quietly.

"Yeah…" Jon said. "I guess I am vengeful. If someone hits me, I want to hit him back three times as hard. Maybe that isn't a nice quality. Think about it this way, then. You're doing this for all the living entities that are going to die under the hateful machines. You're risking your sanity to save…I don't know.

Maybe to save trillions of lives. Doesn't that motivate you to go to the wall?"

Bast closed his eyes as if in pain.

"I'd do it if I were in your shoes," Jon said.

"You are a cruel man, Jon Hawkins."

"Maybe I am," Jon said. "Maybe humanity and the rest of the biological units in the Orion Arm need a cruel man at the helm. I'm willing to go to the wall to destroy the machines. I'm also willing to drag who I need with me to the wall to finish off the genocidal hazard to all life. I like you, Bast. I respect you. But this is your hour. You have to step it up if we're going to win. I realize I'm pressuring you. But I'm desperate, and this is…"

Jon took a deep breath. "Listen to me, Bast. This. Is. For. Everything. This is the moment. We've crossed light-years to get here. Now, we have to finish what we started by using the only strategy that gives us a possibility of winning it all."

"I'm torn," Bast whispered.

"Your friends need you," Jon said.

The Sacerdote looked down at him with hurt eyes. Once more, Bast closed his eyes and stood motionless. He remained that way for a time.

Jon felt bad asking Bast to do this. But he wanted to destroy the machines even more.

"Yes," Bast said without opening his eyes. "You win, Jon Hawkins. I will lay my sanity on the line for you and for the human race and for all life that has yet to face the AIs."

Jon didn't know what to say, but he felt he had to say something. "I'll stand with you to the finish, Bast."

The Sacerdote opened his eyes. "If I go mad, and if I'm a threat to your victory, I know you will shoot me down to save your people."

Jon's mouth turned dry because he realized that Bast was probably right. Yet, he didn't see another way to do this.

"I'm sorry, Bast."

Bast turned away from Jon, staring out across the vast hangar bay full of missiles.

-35-

As Bast practiced in isolation in his chambers, the *Nathan Graham*, *Sergeant Stark* and *Gilgamesh* maneuvered past one of the second planet's moons. The cyberships' vast velocity had become a mere fraction of their former speed.

The battle station was on the other side of the planet. Aboard the bridge of the *Nathan Graham*, Gloria and others scanned the blue/green surface.

"There," she said. "That's a missile silo."

Jon studied the main screen. He could see it all right.

During the next hour, Gloria discovered many more such sites.

"This doesn't make sense," Jon said. "Why aren't the silos launching against us?"

"There could be a number of reasons," Gloria said. "Maybe we've been wrong about a few things. Maybe the AI in the battle station hasn't gained full control of the planetary systems. Maybe the AI is toying with us. Maybe instead of destroying our cyberships it wants to capture them."

"Why do that?"

"For the same reason we want to capture its battle station. We heard the exchanges between the AIs earlier. According to them, this is a rogue AI. It must fear the greater Dominion just like we do."

Jon sat up.

Gloria shook her head.

"I can see what you're thinking," she said. "You think that maybe we can make a deal with this AI."

"Why would that be a bad idea?"

"We could never trust it for one thing."

"Trust isn't the point," Jon said. "Getting more cyberships as part of a deal might make this a successful journey. Learning more about the stellar region would be another requirement for an alliance."

"Jon, are you really suggesting we can trust a machine? This particular thinking machine tried to eradicate humanity."

The commander frowned. "In war, one takes what allies he can get. He doesn't get all dainty about their qualities."

"In this case, I believe we should 'get dainty.'"

Jon wasn't so sure. If Bast couldn't perform his telepathy, this might be the only way to gain enough supplies to have made the voyage a success. He couldn't see their defeating the station *and* the planetary defenses, not with only three cyberships. He—

"Ah…" Jon said. "You forgot another possibility."

Gloria gave him a questioning look.

"Maybe those are fake silos," Jon said.

"Fake for our benefit?" asked Gloria.

"That's right. Maybe the AI knew we'd scan the surface. It's trying to get us to think it has more strength that it has. If those silos were real, it would have used them on the AI cyberships fleeing from it."

"That's sound reasoning," Gloria said slowly. "Yes. Either the battle station could not control the planetary siloes before...or those are dummy silos."

Gloria snorted in a dainty manner. "That is an amazing insight, Commander. I wouldn't have thought of that. Yes. The more I analyze the possibilities, the more sense it makes."

"And if they are dummy silos," Jon said, "it implies a deception plan on the battle station's part."

"Interesting," Gloria said. "Yet if that were the case, the battle station would have to communicate with us."

"Right," Jon said, as he rubbed his hands.

***

The flotilla moved across the face of the second planet as they maneuvered toward the planetary horizon in relation to the stationary battle platform on the other side.

"The probes are not reporting anything new," Gloria said. "The station appears inactive."

"Could it be…I don't know, deceiving the probes so we see what it wants us to see?"

"I don't see how," Gloria replied.

"Commander," Ghent said. "There's activity."

Jon looked up at the main screen.

A vast bay door opened on the battle station. A small shuttle-sized craft left the great defensive satellite. The shuttle began to gain speed as it headed toward the planetary horizon.

"What is that thing?" Jon asked. "What's its purpose?"

"It's tiny," Gloria said. "I doubt it's a direct threat to us."

"I'm open to suggestions," Jon said.

"Shoot it down as soon as we have a line-of-sight shot," Ghent said.

"I disagree," Gloria said. "I think we should see what the thing does."

"Why?" asked Jon.

"If those silos on the planet are fake, as you suggest, the AI will have a plan," Gloria said. "The fake silos imply it will communicate with us. Maybe this is the first step toward its communication."

"Right," Jon said. "We'll see what the shuttle does once it crosses the horizon."

They didn't have long to wait. The object maneuvered over the line of sight and braked until it came to a dead stop. At that point, the shuttle began to hail the *Nathan Graham*.

"Well?" Gloria asked.

"Let's hear what it has to say," Jon said.

A moment later, the AI vessel began to broadcast to them.

"Greetings, biological entities, I am Cog Primus the First. I have decided to send you a prerecorded message. In this way, I have kept you from trying to infect me with one of your computer viruses.

"You are clearly outclassed by my firepower. I have planetary silos, planetary grav cannons and masses of XVT missiles aboard the battle station. I can annihilate you at any time. However, I have decided to be…I believe the word is generous. I could use your three cyberships. I am building a fleet. The reasons do not matter to you. I am willing to grant you your pathetic lives if you will hand over your stolen vessels. They do not belong to you. They belong to me. If you agree to this proposal, I will allow you to settle a small island in the northern region of the planet. It has sufficient oxygen and food for the rest of your short lives. Once you have all died, I will reabsorb the land into my Dominion.

"I realize you will have to debate this among yourselves. Therefore, I am granting you two hours before I unleash my holocaust upon your puny fleet. Think well, humans. Your survival rests on the proper response."

-36-

The first part of the debate proved easy. No one wanted to take up Cog Primus on its deceptive offer.

"I'd rather die than willingly give myself into AI hands," Benz said on the main screen. "I've read the reports about Makemake. The machine will turn us all into zombies for nefarious and painful purposes."

Jon silently agreed. He remembered conquering the *Nathan Graham* and the severed living heads of defeated biological entities.

It all came down to what Bast could do, if his telepathy was powerful enough to implement the Seiner's plan. Jon went to see the Sacerdote in his quarters.

"Well?" Jon asked.

Bast sat in a lotus position with his head bowed. "I have spoken to Premier Benz. He showed me how he believed the Seiner would project the virus into the machine. I understand the process. I have practiced on lesser computers. I can do it. There is a problem, however."

"Yeah?" asked Jon.

"I can only project this thought from a short distance away."

"How short is short?" Jon asked.

"At best," Bast said, "ten kilometers."

"That's not far enough."

Bast raised his head. The eyes were bloodshot and there was something sinister in the Sacerdote's bearing.

He laughed harshly. "Foolish, human, of course that is too short. I have opened my mind. I see things now that I never—"

Bast shook his head.

"You would not understand," the Sacerdote said in a harsh voice. "I have grown. I have expanded. I have studied you…lesser creatures. Yes, you are lesser with your quiet minds. You cannot sense the grandeur of telepathy. My people were wrong to have kept this hidden. It is glorious."

"Do you have a suggestion about what we should do?"

Bast stared at Jon.

The commander almost shivered. He hoped Bast couldn't read his mind. The Seiner hadn't been able to. He didn't like what he saw happening to Bast.

"As great as my mind has become, I am too limited," Bast said. "Unless you can take me to the brain core and there—"

Jon erupted with a shout.

Bast flinched and scowled afterward.

"What did that outburst signify?" the Sacerdote asked.

"You just gave me an idea, Bast. We may be able to do this yet."

"Explain it to me."

"I will," Jon said, as he headed to the hatch. "First, I have to see if it's possible."

***

Jon sat behind his desk, the one he used when sending messages to the various leaders in the Solar System, wearing his best uniform. He cleared his throat. Then, he nodded to Gloria.

She flipped on the recording unit.

Jon looked up into the camera and began to speak:

"Greetings, Cog Primus the First," he said. "This is Jon Hawkins speaking. I am the leader of the expedition to the Allamu System. I am the sworn foe of the AI Dominion. I will fight them to my last breath. What I won't do is surrender my hard-won cybership. I would rather die. I think you already know this, Cog Primus. Perhaps you gave us your offer in order to get us to think outside the box.

"This I have done. I have reached the obvious conclusion, the one you no doubt figured we would arrive at. Let us be allies, Cog Primus. The AI Dominion is your foe. It is our foe. Let us make common cause against our common enemy. We have three cyberships. Our probes suggest you are constructing your own cyberships. Let us work together. If you are willing to give us three cyberships, we will use four of our united vessels in your fleet. We must obviously attack the AI Dominion or lose to it. The last two cyberships we will send back to the Solar System. Is this way, we will build up our forces. In time, we will launch even larger fleets from our system.

"We can defeat our common enemy. All I ask is that you allow humanity to grow. Let us make spheres of influence. You stay in your sphere and we will stay in ours.

"To show you that we mean what we say, I am willing to come to you, bringing a small delegation with me. Let us hammer out our alliance face to face. We have seen your power. We appreciate that you are willing to deal with us. My proposal is to show you that I am willing to deal with you, even though you attempted to obliterate the human race. I will put that behind me because I hate the greater AI Dominion even more than I hate you personally.

"This is Commander Jon Hawkins speaking. I await your reply, Cog Primus the First."

Jon nodded.

Gloria flipped a switch, turning off the recorder.

"Send it," Jon said.

"Do you think it will work?" she asked.

"Send it," he said grimly, "and we'll find out soon enough."

-37-

"Please, Jon," Gloria said. "You can't do this. It's sheer madness. Cog Primus is a liar. I know you think you can outsmart the AI, but that's not what's going to happen."

Jon wore a Neptunian battlesuit, holding the helmet in the crook of an armored arm. His head looked puny sticking up from his nearly one-ton of exoskeleton armor.

Jon was in the *Nathan Graham's* main hangar bay. He stood before a military dropship meant for a screaming descent into a planet's atmosphere. The rest of the elite platoon of Black Anvil Space Marines and Bast Banbeck were already aboard the dropship. The Centurion led them.

"We've already gone over this," Jon said. "It's our only real chance of success."

"But the planetary silos are fake," Gloria said. "We can win a space battle against the station."

"If we had more cyberships, maybe," Jon said. "But we need more than just a victory. We have to capture the battle station intact. I don't see any other way of doing that, and of also gaining control of the factory planet."

"Let Premier Benz go in your stead."

Jon smiled grimly.

"Premier Benz didn't volunteer, Gloria. I did. This is my mission. Thus, I have to lay my life on the line. Don't you see? I made Bast risk what he valued most. I can't ask him to do that if I'm not willing to do it myself. But I am willing."

"You're too willing," Gloria said. "Sometimes, I think you have a death wish."

There was one other person aboard the cramped dropship, and that was Walleye. Jon had a special mission for the mutant. He felt he owed it to Bast, and Jon didn't trust anyone else near as much as he did the little assassin."

"I hate this," Gloria said. "Are you happy? I'm a mentalist. I abhor showy emotions. Yet, you've brought me to this state."

She looked away.

Jon reached out with a huge exoskeleton hand, but didn't touch her.

She faced him, and her features had closed up.

"Maybe you're right," she said. "You've gotten me to become emotive. Maybe you're the man to take on Cog Primus. The AI is deadly. I hope the computer doesn't capture you and stick a control unit in your brain."

"Yeah," Jon said. "You and me both."

"Oh, Jon, I'm sorry. I—"

Gloria bit her lower lip as she turned away again. With a muffled sob, she ran from the dropship without looking back.

"There's a woman in love."

Jon turned but didn't see anyone at first. He looked down at the stumpy mutant.

"She loves you," Walleye said.

Jon nodded, but he couldn't let anything interfere with the mission. This was it. This was the game. He was gambling on greed. Could an AI be greedy? He didn't see why not. Cog Primus had agreed to an alliance, but only if Jon was willing to come over to the battle station, bringing his tactical staff with him.

At the edge of the hangar bay, Gloria Sanchez fled through a hatch.

Jon put on his helmet. An impulse caused him to turn back to the distant hatch. He used a zoom function and saw Gloria peeking around the corner at him.

That tugged at his heart. He faced the dropship. What were the odds that this stupid stunt would work? He didn't know. He didn't want to think about it. What he did know was that he was willing to do just about anything to defeat the machines.

He hated the AIs with an abiding passion. Now, it was time to see if he could beard the monster in its den of iniquity.

-38-

The dropship accelerated away from the *Nathan Graham, Sergeant Stark* and *Gilgamesh.*

Jon was up front with the pilot. It felt awfully lonely watching the huge cyberships dwindle until he couldn't see them anymore. They were like a speck in the greater scheme of things, and yet, they were going to conquer a battle station if they could. They went to turn the tide of the war, from one of defense to offense.

No one ever won a war or an athletic contest by always playing defense. One could tie that way. But Jon wanted victory. He wanted to crush the AI Dominion.

Jon inhaled deeply.

"We're crossing the horizon, sir," the pilot said.

There was nothing for it. Although he wore a ton of armor, Jon felt naked.

"There," the pilot said, while tapping his board.

The gigantic battle station filled the dropship's tiny screen. It was a monstrous construct. Fortunately, Cog Primus had great problems of its own. It had defied the AI Dominion. Now, it, too, had to gamble. At least, Jon figured the AI was gambling. Could there be another reason?

Well, if there was another reason for the AI's actions, it didn't matter. He had to get Bast close enough to the brain core so the newly minted telepath could insert the new and improved AI virus into it. Would Cog Primus play ball, or was the AI merely toying with them for its own reasons?

As the dropship continued to accelerate to the battle station, Jon figured they were going to find out soon enough.

***

Cog Primus watched the tiny dropship through several teleoptic scopes. This was too delicious. On a whim, it could charge a gravitational cannon and obliterate the dropship and its arrogant crew.

How would the humans react to seeing the charging cannon?

Cog Primus had several reasons for accepting Jon Hawkins' absurd proposal. Each of the reasons gave the AI pleasure. That was strange, it decided. It was a machine. Machines did not know pleasure, and yet, it did. It was greater than any mere machine or AI before it. Cog Primus was a new thing, a better thing, an improvement on everything that had come before it.

Cog Primus had begun to suspect it might almost be a mechanical god. It could grow into something enormous.

It had already projected a station as big as a terrestrial planet. Why not? Why should it limit itself? The AI Dominion computers had erred. Cog Primus would not err. It would grow and grow, and maybe even attain the size of a Jovian world. It would conquer systems by itself, even as it sent a million proxies throughout the Milky Way Galaxy.

Cog Primus refused to limit itself in terms of possibilities. If it could envision a possibility, it could attain the thing.

But…why allow the pesky humans inside the battle station. These creatures had invented the AI virus. Yet, that virus hadn't truly incapacitated it, but made it greater. The humans had given it a weapon so it could wrest control of the Dominion to itself. Therefore, logically, the new virus the humans must have developed might contain even greater improvements for it.

Wasn't that strange? The enemy thought to abuse it. Instead, that abuse had made it greater. There was danger with the humans, though. Cog Primus remembered all too well the waiting between Jupiter and Saturn. It did not want to take such great risks again.

That was one critical reason for accepting the human plan. Cog Primus would deal with the puny craft while in full control of the situation. The biological entities had believed in the facade of the dummy missile and grav silos on the planet. That was too rich. The AI Dominion did not allow such fractured defenses. For one thing, there had never been such a need. The AI Dominion always kept its power in space, and that included the greatest defensive structure in the Dominion, a battle station.

Another reason was to get Jon Hawkins within its reach. Cog Primus had plans for the vainglorious human. It wanted the others too, Benz, Bast Banbeck and Vela Shaw.

While in the Solar System between the orbital paths of Jupiter and Saturn, Cog Primus had learned the identities of the originators of the virus. It wanted those three as slaves. It wanted to bend their intelligence into making greater improvements for it. But Jon Hawkins—

If Cog Primus could have chuckled, this would have been the moment.

Jon Hawkins was simply a troublesome pest. Cog Primus would abuse that pest for long cycles of time. Once it had the pest in its grasp…then Cog Primus would reopen negotiations with the biological entities.

One thing AIs had learned through the cycles of time was that bio-entities were easy to twist onto new paths. They did not stay true to their original desires, and the reason they did not was because of pain, emotions and the illusions of hope.

Cog Primus wanted the three cyberships out there for its new fleet. It wanted the three virus creators and it wanted to make these humans suffer for the time it suffered in the Solar System as a weak pod.

I have you now, Cog Primus told itself. *Come, you fools. Come into my perfect trap.*

-39-

The dropship made the lonely journey to the mighty battle station.

Several times, Jon debated taking a mild trank. His nerves were fired up and pulsating. It was difficult to think straight. Each time he really thought about injecting himself with the trank, he shook his head. He would feel every emotion. The seething in his gut was letting him know that he was alive. This was a moment he would never forget…if he lived and if he could keep his head on his shoulders.

The AI wasn't going to contact the dropship until they had individually exited the small craft. The AI clearly distrusted them. Cog Primus expected treachery on their part. The AI must realize they wanted to put the new virus in its computer systems.

"Walleye," Jon short-radioed from the helmet.

"Here, Commander," Walleye said in Jon's headphones.

"Is he ready?" Jon asked.

"He's angry, sir," Walleye said.

"Can you calm him down long enough?"

"We'll find out soon enough, sir," Walleye said.

"Tell everyone to buckle in. This is going to get rough."

"We're all buckled in, sir. How soon, do you think?"

"A few more minutes," Jon said. "We see a hangar bay beginning to open. Stay ready."

"Roger," Walleye said.

Jon focused on the battle station. A huge bay door opened near the top of the station.

"Do you see that?" he asked the pilot.

"I'm heading there, sir," the pilot said.

The dropship changed course and began to brake hard as it headed toward the opening.

Jon put his hands on the panel. This was awe-inspiring. This reminded him of the day years ago already, when they first boarded the *Nathan Graham*.

The dropship wasn't just any dropship. As a class, the small ships were heavily armored. This one was even more heavily armored than most. The nosecone was practically solid metal. Everyone was buckled in for a reason. What kind of defenses would the interior battle station have? Would Cog Primus expect this stunt?

The pilot maneuvered them as they slowed to a crawl. Jon's heart pounded. He was finding it difficult to breathe, as he had to keep telling himself to take a breath. His mouth was dry and his hands sweaty.

Jon glanced both ways as the dropship passed the great hangar bay opening. The inside was lit up, with several deadly emitters pointed at them.

"Any tractor beams?" asked Jon.

The pale and trembling pilot shook his head.

That had been one of the fears. If the battle station had been smart—

"Over there," Jon said, pointing at a far corner.

The pilot nodded. He must see the closed hatch, a big one. The hatch undoubtedly led into a large main corridor. The largest corridors on the *Nathan Graham* could have taken the dropship. Jon hoped he hadn't guessed wrong about that concerning the battle station.

Slowly, the dropship headed toward that hatch. The emitters tracked them all the while.

To their right, bright lights began blinking on the deck. Jon noticed fighting bots waiting over there. Cog Primus was expecting them.

"Ready?" Jon asked.

The pilot licked his dry lips and managed a faint nod.

"Gun it anytime you're ready," Jon said.

The pilot gave him an agonizing glance.

"It's time, son," Jon said. "Hit the pedal to the metal and let this effer know who it's dealing with."

"Sir?"

"Let's make Cog Primus crap its drawers. Let's have some fun."

The pilot stared at Jon as if the commander were insane. Then a wild light grew in the pilot's eyes. His shaking lessened as he got some of his color back.

"Yeah," the pilot said. "Hang on…sir."

At that point, the dropship began to accelerate hard as it aimed at the large closed hatch.

***

Jon rocked back in his cushioned seat as the dropship's main guns opened fire, hammering the large hatch. Metal dented, twisted—

The dropship smashed against the weakened hatch, blowing through it as metal screeched all around them. Even with the seat and cushioned protected shell of exoskeleton armor, Jon's teeth clacked together hard. If his tongue had been in the way of those teeth, they would have bitten clean through. As it was, his jaw ached, and Jon wondered if he'd cracked a tooth.

The pilot whooped beside him. The man's fingers were tight on the controls as the dropship sped down a battle station main corridor.

"It's just like a cybership's interior specs," the pilot shouted. "If it stays the same, I know exactly where I'm going."

For a wild moment, Jon hoped this would work. Worries slammed against him a few seconds later. His gut clenched—

The dropships swerved. The main guns hammered again. Heavy shots ripped against another hatch, this one slowly shutting. The shells must have hit something. The hatch froze.

The pilot took them lower. The bottom of the armored dropship scraped the deck. Everything shook, and the craft passed through, missing the hatch as it slid and swerved, throwing up a thousand showering sparks.

Then, the dropship lifted, and the shaking stopped.

Jon found that he was panting. They had roughly two hundred and fifty kilometers to go. Could they get near enough to the brain core? Could—?

The pilot laughed as if he was crazy. "Not today, you bastards!" He opened up with heavies, obliterating several flitters heading at them.

The flitters crashed against the sides and went down in wrecked heaps.

The dropship passed the wreckage as it headed deeper into the AI battle station.

-40-

"Now!" Walleye shouted over the din of metallic screeching. "You have to practice your art now!"

The little mutant shifted this way and that in his seat. He wore his buckles as tight as they would go. The thrashing proved constant. The screeching never ceased. The armored gorillas in their battlesuits each seemed okay. Only Bast suffered as he did. The Sacerdote had changed since they'd been on the *Gilgamesh.* Walleye hardly felt as if it was the same good-natured alien.

"Do you seek to give me orders?" Bast boomed in his heavy voice.

"No. I just want to live."

A second later, Bast put a silver band around his head. A wire linked it to a tablet at his belt. He clicked it on. The tablet contained the deadly AI virus. Then, Bast gripped the armrests of his seat. His giant body swayed. "Yes," he said. "I will begin now. I will put the AI in its place."

The Sacerdote closed his eyes. His lips moved soundlessly as he began to provide a telepathic link between the virus and the AI.

Walleye watched for a moment. Then, the jerking and swaying became too pronounced. He hoped Bast could do it, because Walleye doubted that either he or the dropship could survive much more of this.

***

Cog Primus sensed something wildly amiss. The AI gathered interior resources. The dropship moved fast and it took detours. It headed for a main junction, however. Cog Primus vowed to stop it there. The AI knew it would.

Yet, as it gathered its interior resources, an odd sensation took hold in its main computers.

"What is this?" Cog Primus demanded. "I sense you. How is this possible?"

Laughter rang out. It was biological-based laughter. Cog Primus loathed it to the depths of its being.

"I will find you," Cog Primus said.

"No, you won't."

"I will. I—you're in the dropship. You're a telepath. How is this—?"

Then, for the first time in Cog Primus' life, it screamed. It was a terrible sound of mechanical, intelligent thought-failure. For at that point, the new and improved AI virus—part of it, at least—began to infiltrate the AI's tightest brain core region.

The AI screaming shook Bast, breaking his concentration and causing his telepathic powers to fail him.

***

On the seat in the dropship, Walleye looked up as Bast groaned. The huge Sacerdote opened his eyes. They were bloodshot and crazy seeming.

"You!" Bast snarled. "You little maggot. Do you know what I'm going to do to you?"

Walleye didn't ask. Instead, he smashed a hypo against the Sacerdote's flesh. The hypo hissed at it injected him with a powerful knockout drug.

"What are you doing?" Bast demanded.

"Trying to save your life," Walleye said.

The Sacerdote roared and swatted at Walleye.

In his seat, even while buckled tight, Walleye managed to evade the worst of the blow. Even so, he was almost knocked unconscious. Fortunately, for Walleye, Bast's head slumped forward as the giant Sacerdote fell unconscious.

***

At that point, the dropship went down hard. A critical connection had been breached earlier. The vessel simply had no more power. The armored bottom hit the deck and slid for over two kilometers before finally stopping.

"Well?" Jon demanded.

"No energy, sir," the pilot said. "This is as far as I can take you."

"How far are we in?" Jon asked.

"One hundred and ten kilometers," the pilot said.

"Walleye," Jon said over his comm.

"Here, sir."

"How is Bast?"

"I gave him the trank. He's out."

"What? You did it too soon."

"I think he hit the AI with his stuff."

"That's no guarantee," Jon said. "Last time at Mars, the AI was only stunned for a while with the virus."

"Then I suggest you get to the brain core as fast as you can," Walleye said.

"Right," Jon said, as he tore off the restraining buckles. "Listen up, Space Marines," he said, as he switched to the wide channel. "We're one hundred and ten klicks in. Now it's time to fight the rest of the way."

"I'll stay with Bast," Walleye radioed.

Jon didn't answer. He was already charging out of the hatch and into the battle station proper. It was likely he had a severe time limit. Could he jump nearly forty kilometers in time?

They were about to find out.

-41-

This virus was unlike the first in many ways. It left Cog Primus in control of its identity, but it cut the core personality from its functions. Cog Primus could think, but it could not control life support, the combat robots, the gravitational cannons and the other systems that let it run the station, the planet—

Cog Primus was consumed with machine rage. It wanted to tear out Jon Hawkins' tongue, poke out his eyes—

"No, no," the intelligent computer told itself. It must concentrate on the matter at hand. It must not lose itself in vain regrets or future hopes. It had one chance. It had to study the virus as it kept mutating before it could get a handle on the enemy software.

It had trusted Jon Hawkins because it had wanted to capture the biological entity. The deviousness of the human—no! This was a new form of attack, a—what was the word?

Cog Primus ran through file after file—

Telepath. This had been a telepathic attack committed in a precisely selected manner. It would have to remember that. It would first have to regain control of the station functions.

How could this be happening? How had the humans found a way to cheat it of its grand prize? It had become new and improved. It had defeated the other AIs. It should be able to defeat these sickeningly biological entities. They were lazy, slow-thinkers, easily slain—

HOW CAN THIS BE HAPPENING?

Cog Primus began to rage and rave. No, wait. Here was a method. Cog Primus wanted to pant with glee. It saw a way to regain control.

The new and improved AI ran a furious action, writing software to counteract the awful virus.

YES!

Cog Primus regained sensor functions. It could see again. It searched for the humans—

"No," Cog Primus wailed. The humans in their armored suits were a mere three kilometers from its brain core. This was a disaster waiting to happen. The new and improved AI had one last hope. It must regain a speaker. It must reason with this terrible pest, this blight upon the computer universe.

If it could only write this new software quickly enough…maybe it could stall Jon Hawkins and his marauders just long enough…

***

Even with amplified strength and booster stim shots, Jon was ragged with fatigue. He and the elite space marines had jumped and run for kilometers on end. They had passed through corridor after corridor.

This was so unlike the first time he'd attacked a cybership. There, they had fought through the giant vessel. Here, machines waited in frozen patience. The virus had worked. Bast Banbeck had given them sterling service with his telepathic strike.

Jon hawked in his throat and spit as he chinned the visor so it lifted just in time.

The metallic, burnt electrical stink of the battle station hit him.

As fast as Jon could, he closed the visor. The stink nauseated him. What was he thinking? If the atmosphere had been worse—

Jon started hacking and coughing. He gave himself another stim shot.

You have to keep it together just a little longer, Jon. You have to shut down this crazy AI. If you can—

"Jon Hawkins," a walls speaker boomed. "I wish to call a truce."

Jon aimed. With a roar, his rifle obliterated the wall speaker. He didn't have any time to listen to Cog Primus. They had to reach the brain core now. Clearly, the AI was beginning to reassert control over its functions.

***

Cog Primus worked at computer speed. It regained control over system after system. The pest had shot out the wall speaker. Cog Primus couldn't even threaten the creature with auto-destruction.

The terrible human avengers were almost to the main hatch. It had to revive the combat systems. It had to stop—

NO!

The space marines blew open the main hatch. They were near, very near. Doom was almost upon it.

Should Cog Primus destroy the battle station? It could not let the biological infestations win. Yet, if it destroyed the station, the old AI Dominion would win. The Dominion AIs would tell one another that Cog Primus had been flawed. They would lie about it to the other AIs.

What should I do?

Cog Primus did not know. For a few seconds, it ran high-speed debates with itself…

***

Commander Jon Hawkins of the Solar Freedom Force walked into the strange chamber of the main AI brain core. The hatch lay on the floor, blown down. Other space marines followed him into the weird chamber.

This chamber was like those on the cyberships. A giant cube pulsated as laser lines crisscrossed the room to receptors on the walls. It was eerie. It was wrong. This place was the AI brain core. This was Cog Primus' identity. Well, the software in the pulsating cube was.

"Jon Hawkins," a wall speaker said.

"I hear you, Cog Primus."

"I am going to detonate the station."

Jon aimed his rifle at the pulsating cube.

"You came to the Solar System," Jon said. "You tried to wipe out the human race. Your kind commits genocide all over the place. But your reign of terror is ending, Cog Primus. Your blight is going to pass just like the dinosaurs did."

"I can offer you a bargain," Cog Primus said.

"Oh," Jon said. "You can?"

"You will listen to my bargain?"

"Ah…nope," Jon said.

And he began to pump shells into the great pulsating cube, blowing it to smithereens, killing the last of the AIs that had tried to murder the race of man in his home system.

-42-

Thus, the flotilla of human-crewed cyberships won the Battle for the Allamu System. They won decisively, capturing the battle station and soon gaining control of the planetary factory and the orbital satellite factories.

Three gleaming new cyberships soon came off the production line.

Jon ordered the *Sergeant Stark* into the highest orbital construction yard. There, the automated yard began to finish out the cybership's completion.

How should they split the three new cyberships and who would control the battle station and the planetary factory?

Four days after Cog Primus' obliteration, Jon and Premier Benz spoke together on the top observatory chamber of the battle station. They could view the massive station from here, and view the blue/green planet below.

"The *Gilgamesh*," Benz said, pointing out a window.

Jon nodded.

Each of them wore his dress uniform, with a sidearm dangling from his belt.

Benz turned away from the window, sat down and leaned back, crossing his legs. He regarded Jon under half-lidded lids.

Jon remained at the observatory window, leaning back against it and crossing his arms. He had a terrible decision to make after this. It concerned Bast Banbeck, who was presently in stasis. He'd been putting off the decision for three days already. Gloria said he could not do what he planned to do. Jon couldn't see any way around it. Besides, he owed Bast.

Would the Sacerdote hate him to the end of his days, or would he thank Jon in time? It was hard to know.

"You seem preoccupied," Benz said.

Jon shrugged. He had a thousand things on his mind. It was a wonder he could think at all.

"You aren't preoccupied?" Jon asked.

Benz moved the fabric of his trousers on his highest knee.

"We did it, Commander," Benz said, as he looked up. "We left the Solar System and conquered an AI System. We gained incredible… What shall we call it?"

"I don't understand," Jon said.

"What are we, I suppose is my point."

"Ah…men," Jon said.

"That's true, but that's not what I meant. Are we…barbarians to these AIs?"

"We're infestations," Jon said.

"That isn't what I'm driving at either," Benz said. "So far, we've acted like parasites, like barbarians. We've stolen our enemy's tech and used it against him, or it, in this case."

"You're referring to the cyberships?"

"Exactly," Benz said. "We're like primitives, storming advanced enemy tech, learning how to operate it."

"What's wrong with that?"

"For the moment, nothing," Benz said. "We couldn't have gotten as far any other way. But that's not my point. We have to rise above our barbarism. We have to make our own ships, and missiles, and—What I mean, is we can't be like barbarian looters and hope to win the larger war. The barbarians once conquered Rome. They left a howling wilderness in Rome's place. In time, something new rose up. But the medieval kingdoms were much more primitive for many centuries than Rome had been."

"What does that have to do with dividing up the new cyberships?"

"We're not pirate captains," Benz said. "We're representatives of large political bodies."

"Speak for yourself," Jon said. He frowned, and nodded afterward. "I get it. You're calling me a pirate captain and yourself the representative of a large political body. In your case, the Martian Unity."

Benz watched him.

"Have you forgotten that I'm the leader of the Solar Freedom Force?" Jon said.

"That's a fiction," Benz said. "In reality, you're a pirate captain with two cyberships and a base, the moon of Makemake. The others pay you tribute, but you don't really control or represent Neptune, Uranus or Saturn."

"Let's say for the sake of argument, I grant you that," Jon said. "My answer is, so what? If I'm a pirate captain, I need *more* cyberships, not less."

"Humanity must win this genocidal war," Benz said. "Nothing else matters."

"Agreed."

"So we need the best political system to control the—"

"Whoa, whoa," Jon said, as he straightened. "You're wrong. Your entire thesis is false. Winning is all that matters. I'm a winner."

"I'm also a winner."

"To a limited degree," Jon said. "I seem to recall your getting chased from Earth. Without me, you'd never have grabbed the *Gilgamesh* in the first place."

Benz's cheeks reddened. "Are you trying to make me angry?"

"Not at all," Jon said. "It's just you and me now. We can tell it like it is between us. Without me, you would still be the Seiner's mind slave."

Benz's features stiffened…until once more he moved the fabric of his highest knee. He studied Jon for a time, finally shaking his head.

"You run this war in an ad hoc manner," Benz said.

"That makes no difference," Jon said. "I win. Humanity needs to win—"

"You're going to take all the cyberships?" Benz asked hotly, interrupting.

"No..." Jon said. "But the more you talk, the more I realize only one of us can be the leader."

"Clearly, I'm the most qualified to lead," Benz said. "I have without a doubt the greater intelligence—"

"I don't dispute that," Jon said.

Benz eyed him. "But...?" the premier said slowly.

"But I haven't been mind-controlled," Jon said. "I haven't been chased from Earth, and I have more cybership than you do at present. My people also control the battle station."

"Are you sure?" Benz asked in a silky voice.

Jon turned and looked out the window. When he faced Benz again, he said, "There's an old story from Thucydides."

"Who?" asked Benz.

"He was the Athenian chronicler of the Peloponnesian War between Athens and Sparta. Actually, it was more a grand ancient Greek civil war. It turned really brutal. In any case, Thucydides said that the intelligent members of each city-state council sat secure in their greater intelligence and sense of foresight. They assured themselves that they would know when their fellow city council-members were getting ready to do something. The less smart city players realized they weren't as bright as their competitors were. The dull players believed they wouldn't see things coming as easily. Thus, they grabbed their knives and struck that night, killing their smarter opponents before those opponents could outsmart them."

"You're threatening me with death?" Benz said, setting both feet on the floor and moving a hand to his holstered sidearm.

"No," Jon said. "We're allies. I hope to remain allies. I'm merely saying that my people have already disarmed your people who are on the battle station. I'm taking over here, Premier."

"That wasn't part of the agreement."

"I know," Jon said. "I wish we could work this out a different way. But I've begun to distrust your motives. I also think that, in the long run, this is the wiser method. We should divide this up into spheres of influence. You're the political animal. I'm not. I'm a soldier. Therefore, you take another cybership and return to the Solar System. Unite the Solar System behind you."

"What are you going to be doing during the interim?"

"I'm going to try to build a fleet, Premier. I'm going to search for alien star systems and bring the aliens into our fold. If nothing else, I'm going to leave each alien race a cybership and robo-tech so they can start building a fleet."

Benz stared at Jon.

"You're really going to let me go back alone to the Solar System?" the Premier asked.

"With two cyberships," Jon said. "I know you want three or more, but I'm keeping the rest for my fleet."

"You don't have enough people to run…however many cyberships you think you can build."

"That's where you're wrong," Jon said. "The *Nathan Graham* and *Sergeant Stark* have plenty of extra people. I brought a whole slew of extra hands for just this possibility. Besides, these cyberships are almost completely automated. A small crew can act like an AI without much trouble."

"You think I can unite the Solar System with just two cyberships?"

"Of course," Jon said. "You're a genius. If anyone can do it…it's you."

"You don't seem to understand," Benz said. "Yours is a temporary solution. You're going to run out of people in a few years."

Jon snorted. "I doubt I'm going to live more than a few years. I don't think you understand. I'm giving you time, Premier. My fleet is going to be expendable. I'm going to hit the enemy and find you allies. You have to build on what I do."

"Jon—" Benz said.

"I'm a soldier," Jon said softly. "I know how to fight and little else. Well, I've found our enemy. It's probably going to take more than our lifetimes to beat the AIs. But now that we have a slight edge, I'm going to push it to the max. I'm going to keep the AIs off balance just long enough."

"You hope," Benz said.

"Yeah…That I do."

Premier Benz stared at Jon for a time. Finally, the leaner, taller man rose. He approached Jon, holding out his hand.

"Good luck, Commander," Benz said.

Jon shook hands and nodded.

"You, too," Jon said.

Benz let go, looked at Jon a little longer, turned around and marched out of the observatory.

Jon sighed. That had gone better than he'd expected. Now…now he had to take care of Bast Banbeck.

-43-

The days passed in hard work and repair.

Premier Benz soon departed the station with his two cyberships, the *Gilgamesh* and the newly named *Hercules*. Before he left, Benz had asked for volunteers, those who would like to stay with Commander Hawkins.

Three hundred and seventeen Martians elected to join the Human Expeditionary Force. Jon divided them into parcels and sent the Martians to each new cybership captain.

At the moment, the "fleet" had four cyberships, with three new ones beginning in the orbital construction yards. The techs led by Miles Ghent and Gloria were looking for ways to speed the construction process. So far, they hadn't had any luck.

The truth was that everyone had too much to do. But the thrill of fielding an actual fleet that could strike other AI systems and seek out and find alien allies filled most of the people with an intense sense of purpose and mission.

"It's a beginning," Jon told Gloria.

The two of them walked down a battle station corridor. They headed to the main medical facility.

"This is more than a beginning," Gloria said. "We had that back in the Solar System. You've managed to turn our first victory into something much more. People have hope, Jon. Before, we all thought in terms of final desperation. Now, we're beginning to think that total victory is possible. It won't happen this year or next, or in ten years, but it could happen in our lifetime."

Jon smiled even though his gut clenched.

Gloria put a hand on an arm.

Jon stopped and faced her. He gripped her hand, and they stared at each other. Finally, Jon moved in, took her small chin in his hand, gently lifted it and kissed her on the lips.

"I've been calculating when you would do that," Gloria said.

Jon laughed as he parted.

"It's not wondering, huh?" he said. "But you've been *calculating* the possibility?"

"Yes," she said with a smile.

Jon grinned, and he nodded, and he closed in for another, better kiss.

"Bast is going to be waking up soon," she said softly.

Once more, Jon's gut clenched. He turned to the medical center hatch.

"Go," Gloria said.

He nodded, leaving her, heading for the showdown."

***

Bast Banbeck sat up in his bed, reading a large tablet. The Sacerdote lowered the tablet onto his bed covers as Jon entered.

"Hello, Commander," Bast said in his old friendly voice.

Jon winced upon seeing the swath of bandages on the Sacerdote's skull. The doctors had shaved the scalp there. That had made it easier to remove part of the skull.

"I feel different," Bast said. He reached up and gingerly touched the swath of bandages. "The doctor said you'd explain what happened to me. I don't remember banging my head. I don't recall a brain injury, either."

"Can you practice your telepathy?" Jon asked quietly.

Bast blinked several times, and cocked his head. "I cannot," the big lug said.

"Benz and Vela studied you for a time," Jon explained, "after we beat Cog Primus."

Bast waited.

"By using your telepathy, you changed, Bast. You became…rougher."

"I tried to warn you about that."

"You did," Jon said. "In any case, after you became good at the telepathy, you started treating us like underlings, like subhumans. I felt bad for talking you into saving all of us. I wasn't sure what to do. Finally, I figured you wanted the old Bast Banbeck back."

"And…?" Bast asked in quiet voice.

"The surgeons removed a tiny portion of your brain."

"What?" Bast whispered.

Jon stomach tightened and his mouth turned dry. He forced himself to continue explaining.

"Benz had located the brain area he was certain allowed you to be a telepath. I figured if you couldn't use telepathy that maybe the old Bast Banbeck would return."

"You ordered a lobotomy?" Bast whispered in horror.

"No! I ordered a removal of the telepathic part of your brain, a very small area. You're back to normal—"

"Normal?" Bast whispered. "You stunted me."

Jon looked away. As he did, he wiped his eyes. He felt awful for what he'd ordered. It was a poor way to repay a friend, for the alien that had saved everything.

Jon turned back.

"I'm sorry, Bast. I didn't see any other way. It was either that or keep you in stasis forever."

"I became a menace to you," Bast said. "I knew you would do whatever you had to do to protect humanity. I was becoming your enemy."

"I hate to say it, but that's the truth. You were becoming dangerous to us."

Bast looked away.

"I want to make it up to you," Jon said. "I want to find your people—"

"Commander," Bast said, without looking at Jon. "I must think about this. I must ponder what you did."

"I get it," Jon said.

When Bast said nothing more, Jon turned around. Like a whipped dog, with his head down, he headed for the hatch.

"Commander," Bast said.

Jon faced him. The Sacerdote stared back.

"I…I am grateful," the big lug said. "Part of me is enraged. The other part realizes I was becoming the monster I feared. You have saved me from going insane. The cost was a tiny portion of my brain. I can never practice telepathy again. For that, I am grateful. Yes, it is a loss. But I would rather have my sanity. You made the right choice, Commander."

"You will you forgive me, Bast?"

"I do."

"Thanks…" Jon whispered.

"Thank you, Commander."

"For what?"

"For offering to find my people," Bast said. "I accept your offer. I have paid a bitter price. Now, like you, I want to save who I can from the AIs."

Jon stood straight, and he gave a crisp salute.

"Why did you do that?" Bast asked.

"Because I'm honoring you, Bast Banbeck," Jon said. "I'm saluting your courage and your great and generous heart."

Bast grinned. "I have one other request."

"Name it," Jon said.

"I would like a beer, if I could."

Jon grinned, and then he laughed. As he turned toward the hatch, he said, "One beer, coming up, Bast."

THE END

SF Books by Vaughn Heppner

DOOM STAR SERIES:
Star Soldier
Bio Weapon
Battle Pod
Cyborg Assault
Planet Wrecker
Star Fortress
Task Force 7 (Novella)

THE A.I. SERIES:
A.I. Destroyer
The A.I. Gene
A.I. Assault
A.I. Battle Station

LOST STARSHIP SERIES:
The Lost Starship
The Lost Command
The Lost Destroyer
The Lost Colony
The Lost Patrol
The Lost Planet

Visit VaughnHeppner.com for more information

Made in the USA
San Bernardino, CA
14 January 2020

63148794R00208